DISPUTED PASSAGE

Disputed Passage

by

LLOYD C. DOUGLAS

P. F. Collier & Son Corporation

PUBLISHERS · NEW YORK

WITH SINCERE APPRECIATION OF HER
CONSTANT ENCOURAGEMENT AND VALUED
COUNSEL THIS NOVEL IS DEDICATED
TO MY WIFE

Have you learned lessons only of those who admired you, and were tender with you, and stood aside for you?

Have you not learned great lessons from those who braced themselves against you, and disputed the passage with you?

WALT WHITMAN

Chapter I

It was two o'clock in the afternoon of the last Thursday in September, opening day of the fall semester.

The weather was unseasonably sultry, and the air in Doctor Milton (Tubby) Forrester's lecture-arena lay as inert and stale as the cadavers in the grim old anatomical laboratory adjoining.

But if the atmosphere of the dingy little theater was not refreshingly tonic it was emotionally tense. Whatever it lacked in sweetness it made up in stress; for Anatomy, under the brilliant but irascible Forrester, was reputed to be the stiffest course in the entire four-year curriculum.

Hopeful of being credited at the outset with the flimsy virtue of punctuality, the exceptionally large class of new medical students — one hundred and thirty-three; all men, this year, but eight — had assembled with the nervous promptness of first-time voyagers boarding a ship.

As for the personnel of the class, less than half were newly graduated from the main body of the State University only a mile distant. The rest of them had recently received their degrees — Bachelor of Arts or Bachelor of Science — in colleges of various rating, scattered all the way from the Alleghenies to the Coast. A few of the more gregarious imports had nodded and exchanged casual civilities in the Registrar's quarters, earlier in the day; but everyone felt himself a stranger in this unfamiliar setting; even the men who had been living for a quadrennium within a ten minutes' walk of the Medical College campus.

But no matter from how near or far they had come, there wasn't a person present this afternoon, in Tubby Forrester's amphitheater, who had not heard the dismaying legends of his impatience, his arrogance, his bad temper, his noisy tantrums. And yet it was largely on account of Tubby that most of them had decided to study medicine here. Tubby was mean as the devil, but he knew his stuff. Not only was he an anatomist of high distinction but a recognized authority on neurological surgery. His office walls were covered with impressive certificates of kudos bestowed by medical schools and renowned scientific societies, tributes embossed on vellum in four languages.

In not many medical colleges did the novice have access to such talented supervision in his early adventures with Anatomy. Tubby maintained that if a man had a natural flair for the subject his gift would show up promptly. He was ever on the alert for budding genius in this field. To his colleagues on the faculty he had confided that he was on a still hunt for potential anatomists who had the makings of neurological surgeons.

The ordinary, run-of-the-mine medical matriculate did not pause to reflect that he might be better off in a school where mediocrity was treated with more patience. The big thing was to earn a diploma bearing Tubby's distinguished autograph. Even a very small and useless spoon achieved some dignity if the word 'Sterling' was stamped on its handle.

But it could not be said that any of the ungifted had been deceived into the error of casting his lot with this great man. Tubby made no bones about the fact that he was interested only in the upper tenth. His attitude toward the large majority of his students was contemptuous and contemptible. His savage sarcasms stung them until their very souls were afire with hate and their eyes burned with defenseless fury. Hundreds of practicing physicians — ranging in age from thirty-five to fifty, and in locale from the Lakes to the Gulf and from Sea to Sea — were proud to be able to say that they had their Anatomy under Forrester, but they invariably added that Tubby was a brute, and many with better memories for the indignities they had suffered at his hands referred to him in terms much more unpleasant than that.

This afternoon, with ample time and a suitable environment for morbid meditation, the new class sat in the steeply ascending semi-circular rows of creaking seats, resting their forearms on the battered desks, scowling at their fidgeting fingers or absently thrumming the corners of their virgin notebooks. Occasionally they lifted an apprehensive glance toward the door leading from Tubby's office. The early Christian martyrs waiting in the arena for the lions' cage to open may have had at least the consolation that their impending discomfort would be brief. There would be four years of Tubby Forrester.

Tradition held that the first session with this erratic bully was guaranteed to be a highly interesting entertainment, provided you were not of the dozen or more who would be singled out, stood up on their feet, and given a chance to make or break themselves irrevocably in a preliminary skirmish where it was dangerous to be witty and a disaster to be dull.

Customarily he opened his address by referring to this meeting as 'The Acquaintance Hour' — a phrase that was expected to fetch a sardonic chuckle, for it was with such verbal lollipops that the University churches and the 'Y' angled for new student patronage. Irreverent as Satan, Tubby loved to toy derisively with these ingratiating clichés of organized altruism. But by the end of 'The Acquaintance Hour' all the subtlety of his mockeries would have been abandoned, and you would have had a taste of the real thing you had let yourself in for when you signed up for Anatomy under Forrester.

'If you have to be petted and patted,' he would growl, 'join the Glad-handers' Club, or the Back-slappers, or the Well-wishers. If you find that your system demands more sugar, there are plenty of institutions in this locality where you may have it for much less than the asking. They will teach you how to be as friendly as a wet dog. Tea will be served, songs will be sung, charades will be played. If you want your boots licked, they will do it for you. But don't expect any of that nonsense here! This edifice has been dedicated to Science. Here we strive to be precise in our research; honest in our nomenclature. If you are a jackass you will have to go elsewhere to be deceived into the belief that you are a zebra.'

* * * * * * * *

He was entering now from his office. Ten minutes overdue, he marched with jerky-gaited pomposity to the waist-high table that served as his desk. This table, mounted on large rubber-tired casters and topped with a two-inch marble slab, was six feet three in length by three feet wide; and you didn't have to be a medical student to guess what use was made of it when it wasn't acting as Tubby's lectern.

The class brought itself to rigid attention as the steely eyes comprehensively surveyed the well-filled theater. There was no need of building up any dramatic suspense here, but Tubby coolly looked the crowd over for a long moment while with both hands he rhythmically tugged at the platinum watch-chain spread across his ample abdomen, a disquieting gesture that suggested the whetting of a carving-knife.

'Dear Christian Friends,' he began, clipping his words. A general grin testified that Tubby was measuring up to the picture of him that everyone had conceived. 'This,' said the attitude of the class, 'is the fellow. No doubt of that. Hard-boiled, all right. A nine-minute egg.'

'It is indeed a pleasure,' railed Tubby, 'to welcome so goodly a number to our Acquaintance Hour. Among those who have preceded you through these charming halls, to take up the arduous activities of the most ancient profession — save one — some may have told you that in this snug little theater, and the more commodious workshop adjacent, we are just one happy family, loving one another all the day long.' He paused to let this mockery soak in and collect its wages in knowing sniffs and dry chuckles. His penetrating gaze raked the rows, tier by tier; a darting glance that dared you to withhold your tribute to his mordant wit. His attitude was that of a peeved sergeant inspecting a squad with the hope of discovering a loose button.

The pause was alarmingly lengthened. Midway of the top row, Tubby's sweeping search rested for an instant, carried on to the end of the row, returned to the middle, and concentrated upon a face that was quite unaware of the inquisition. There was a dead silence, but the inattentive one had failed to notice the ominous break in Tubby's address, apparently unaware that he was under fire.

Presently the sour flippancies were resumed, but they lacked their previous finesse. Tubby was not intentionally pulling his punches but they hadn't the old steam back of them. Again and again his gaze shot truculently to the center of the top row where it had met that impassive profile. It was a lean, strong, determined face, the features clean-cut as an image on a coin, and as immobile. The lips were in repose but not compressed: they did not denote animosity or disapproval. Had they been primly puckered into an evidence of hostility, Tubby would have been better satisfied. He would give the offended beggar another wallop; give him something to be sore about. But these lips were not registering distaste; not registering anything but unconcern. The deep-set eyes which Tubby had tried vainly to command were vaguely exploring a far corner of the neglected room where a soot-smudged wall met a discolored ceiling. It was obvious that the insufferable fellow either wasn't listening at all or felt that what he was hearing did not rate his respectful attention.

Tubby's speech, stridently satirical, scrambled on through the deep mud with heavy boots. Every man in the class — but one — sensed that an impious hand had been laid upon the halter of the professor's goat, but nobody's curiosity was urgent enough to risk a craning of the neck. The instinct of self-preservation was very active here, today.

The corrosive ironies continued for a few minutes, but Tubby was tiring of this mood. His tone and tempo changed abruptly. He patted his damp brow with a large white handkerchief, smiled briefly, endeavored to be playful, repeated — as if it were original — the old joke about specialization. 'If you must specialize,' he said, 'go in for Dermatology, for your patients will never get well and they will never die and they will never get you up at night.' And everybody laughed at this but one man, the obnoxious chap in the top row who — if he had heard a word of this ancient wheeze — was probably saying to himself that it would be impolite to laugh at a joke so weighted with infirmity. Damn the bounder! Tubby couldn't remember ever having been so befuddled. Again he came to a full stop, changed his gears, lowered his tone, became sincere. He talked of the doctor's life in unexpected phrases of forthright honesty. Properly viewed, he said, earnestly, it was not an occupation but a vocation, a life-commitment rather than a livelihood, an obsession rather than a profession.

'You will quickly classify yourselves into the categories where — by native gift and intention — you properly belong. You will do that in the course of your first year. According to our statistics, fifteen per cent of you are so dull and lazy that you will be fired — for the sake of the College, the public, and yourselves. Fifty per cent of you will make passing grades and receive degrees and diplomas. What you lack in talent and skill you may compensate with a pleasant bedside manner. Relying more upon sentimentality than scientific knowlege you may possibly earn twice as much by the administration of sympathy and aspirin as your contemporaries who may be twice as well informed.

'These two groups will account for sixty-five per cent of you. A quarter of the class will turn out to be better than average students; better than average doctors. You will do your work as well as you can, according to the light that is in you, and you will deserve credit for this fidelity.

'Of the remaining ten per cent — the top ten per cent — it is conceivable that there might develop something quite promising. Don't bank on it — but it might happen.

'I do not know, today, who you are — you of this interesting ten per cent. Perhaps you, yourselves, do not know. I venture a word with you at this time. This counsel is not intended for sluggards, trimmers, time-servers, or potential quacks; nor is it meant for the merely competent, however honest and industrious they may be. I am speaking now to the candidates for rating in the top tenth.'

He glanced up, rather negligently, toward the upper tier, and found himself looking squarely into a pair of ice-blue eyes that might easily have been related to his own. He drew a dry smile, and went on.

'And it is to be hoped,' added Tubby — as an afterthought in defining his restricted audience — 'it is to be hoped that no apathetic day-dreamer, who may have sat here in a coma until now, will too optimistically identify himself as a divinely ordained member of this privileged minority.'

It was very quiet. The class felt that Tubby had paid off somebody for inattention. The mystery concerning the professor's serious disconcertment was now cleared up. Everybody hoped the affair was a closed incident. The constraint had been annoying.

'You of the top tenth,' continued Tubby, 'will very soon become aware of your rating. You will not have to wait until you see your grades at the close of the semester.

'One of the most frequent mistakes made, in classroom admonitions, is the teacher's fatuous promise to his disciples that diligent application is a guarantee of the student's success. It goes without saying, of course, that the student who does his work to the best of his ability has more to show for the time he has spent in school than the sluggard. But the persons who comprise the upper tenth of the class must have much more to offer than mere diligence, however praiseworthy is their honest industry.

'There is a homely adage, customarily quoted with a

smile, which discourages any attempt to make a silk purse out of a sow's ear. This is far from funny. It is tragic. In the course of my experience here, I have been an unwilling auditor of classroom work sincerely performed by young men and women who had no natural gifts for this undertaking. Perhaps they might have succeeded brilliantly in some other quest: I do not know. But — no matter how hard they worked — they had no chance of achieving distinction. They were biologically ineligible. It was not their fault; it was their misfortune.

'In a much smaller number of cases, we have had students who gave early promise of future success, but lacked the courage to invest themselves whole-heartedly in their work. They were good for the hundred-yard dash, but they hadn't the wind required to do a mile; much less a marathon.

'Now it might be supposed that my next statement should extol the happy combination of brains and diligence; and these are, indeed, a promising pair of success-factors. But the upper tenth needs something more. The price of diligence is self-discipline. Concentration upon your work necessarily demands a resolute avoidance of time-wasting and distracting frivolity. You are quite aware of that. And it is a mere platitude to say that if you wish to get anywhere in preparing for this profession, you must give yourself utterly to your job.

'But that is not all. Self-discipline, in the opinion of the moralist, is always worth what it costs. And perhaps there is something to be said in favor of the martyr who, by living a sacrificial, self-controlled life, earns credits negotiable in some other, better world beyond the sky. I am not an authority on that subject. But self-discipline, practiced for the purpose of leaving one free to do one's chosen work, fails of its performance if one pursues it at the cost of very much fretting and conscious effort.

'Naturally, there will be occasional days when the collar will gall you. No matter how well you have yourself in hand, there will be times when the animal that is in you clamors for its rights. But if you find yourself in a continuous running fight with your appetites — to the extent that your mind is constantly disturbed — your sacrifices will not justify their expense.

'This leads me to say that the self-discipline of the upper ten per cent must be — for the most part — effortless and automatic. And it may become so, very quickly, if the claims of your vocation loom larger than the urgency of your physical desires. When the job becomes important enough to warrant your membership in the fortunate ten per cent, the outside distractions will not worry you.'

Tubby's voice had lowered to a conversational tone. It was almost as if he were having a heart-to-heart with a single individual in the privacy of a confidential interview. The class sat poised, deeply attentive. The silence would have been broken by a pin-drop. The cognitive little eyes drifted to the upper row of the amphitheater. The blondish young athlete who had ruined 'The Acquaintance Hour' was leaning far forward in his seat, with his elbows on his knees and his fists supporting a firm chin. His eyes were intent, his lips compressed. Tubby frowned, and continued.

'Out of this top tenth of the class, almost anything is likely to emerge. One never knows what may come forth from this exclusive group. Sometimes we run along for years, in this Medical College, without observing the rise of a student who promises to make an important contribution. Once in a blue moon, the upper tenth delivers to Medical Science an explorer, a discoverer, a trail-blazer.'

Tubby's next sentence sent a thrill through the closely integrated audience. You could feel it bang at your heart and magnetize your spine. You not only felt it yourself, but you knew that everybody else — to a degree — was experiencing this sensation.

'Is there anyone here,' asked Tubby, impressively, 'who will tell us — some day — what we want to know about cancer? . . . Will one of you — some day — give us a prophylaxis for infantile paralysis? The two important gentlemen who are to perform these feats are — if I may venture the prediction — already born. May I be still more hopeful and hazard the guess that they are already of age? It may be that they are experienced scientists, now on the eve of their discoveries. It may be that they are students in some medical school.' Tubby paused. The class sat transfixed, welded into one solid chunk. 'These two men,' declared Tubby, in a tone so low as to be barely audible — 'these two men may be in this room — *now!*'

He suddenly booted them out of their hypnosis. He tugged out his watch, shuffled his thick sheaf of registration papers, shifted his stance to the end of the autopsy table. His face lighted a little with a smile that suggested he was going to be funny again. The class straightened its back and drew a long breath, the first long one it had felt the need of for some time. Nobody looked at his neighbor. Nobody wanted anyone else to know how deeply he had been stirred. Tubby had gone at it again in another mood.

'And now,' he was saying, 'to all of you — regardless of your various ratings, regardless of what you are or may become, I charge you that the study and practice of medicine and surgery is a scientific pursuit to be approached with much the same attitude as you might undertake a post-graduate course in Geology. Keep your emotions out of it, and give your brains a chance. The less sentiment you apply to this enterprise, the better will be your workmanship. I have often thought of suggesting to my peers,' extemporized Tubby, 'that at least one year's internship should be spent in a veterinary hospital where the young medical student might pursue his work without the emotional interference of the patient's family.'

This, thought the weary class, was very good indeed. Tubby gave them all a chance to laugh merrily. Even the face in the upper tier broke into a grin. But it was far, far too late for this young Rip Van Winkle to wake up and take an interest. It wouldn't do him very much good now. Tubby sniffed and went on.

'Your present attitude should be that of a researchist seeking exact facts about the construction of the human

body. Unquestionably there is a place where it is in order
to consider Shakespeare's apostrophe — "What a piece of
work is man! how noble in reason! how infinite in
faculty! in form and moving, how express and admirable!"
But that place is not the anatomical laboratory. If you are
wise, my Christian Friends, you will leave all that to the
poets and parsons. It's their job; not yours. Your business
is to study man as a badly made contraption in need of
repair. Whether the human animal committed a blunder
when — in the course of his evolution — he resolved to
stand on his hind legs and face the world in an upright
position, is a question I should not presume to discuss in
all its phases. Personally, I am just as well satisfied not
to be walking on all fours. But when this animal tipped his
viscera from horizontal to perpendicular he incurred a
flock of disabilities. They begin to show up as soon as he
learns to walk.

'You want to keep it in mind,' declared Tubby, seriously,
'that orthodox theology is exactly wrong in its explanation
of man's woes. It wasn't Adam's fall that caused the
trouble: it was his rise. A dog may become so sycophantic
that he will sit up, now and then, for a moment, just to
flatter his master by imitation; but he has sense enough
not to do it very often or for very long. According to the
Bible, Eve was sentenced to bear her young in pain because she plucked an apple from a tree, in disobedience to
a divine command. Had she been content to munch the
apples that had fallen on the ground, she could have borne
her cubs without risk and without help.

'All this places you in an indefensible position as a
student. Your whole training is for the purpose of fitting
you to promote the cause of civilization. And the more
civilization we achieve, the poorer we are, physically.
Civilization has given us many benefits, no doubt; it has
also developed habits that have produced defective teeth,
defective eyes, ears, noses, bronchia. We still have a few of
the old glands that were of earlier value; now a menace.
May I repeat — you are to study man as a poorly made

machine that can't even support its own weight for very long at a time, in testimony whereof you are all sitting down to ease your freight at age twenty-three. By the time you're sixty-three, solicitous relatives will be following you about with a chair. You will still have a few years to spend here, perhaps. During the course of your career you may have become wise, noble, renowned. You will also have had your tonsils removed, and your appendix; perchance a kidney. You will be wearing artificial teeth and glasses and maybe a gadget to aid your hearing. . . . I want you to go into the anatomical laboratory with the understanding that a great many of the things you find out are not as they ought to be. The vital organs were originally intended to function in another position. Forget all this prattle about man being made in the image of God. If it's true, it's no credit to him. Anybody who wants to believe in that sort of thing had better keep out of the dissecting room.

'But — and this should cheer your hearts — while this anatomical laboratory, to which you are shortly to be introduced, is no place to look for fragrance or faith or fairy-stories, it is at least honest, which can't be said of legislative halls or art galleries or cathedrals. You are here in quest of truth. Once a fact is amply attested you are to accept it, no matter how ugly it is; no matter how much you wish it wasn't so; no matter how violently it collides with what you have previously thought and would still prefer to think. And don't make the mistake of imagining that the testimony is all in, and on file. Many a scientist, six feet underground, would suffer all the agonies of the supposedly damned if he could come forth today and read some of his own dogmatic remarks, long since reduced to utter nonsense by new findings. Remember that until a theory has been disproved — no matter how fantastic it may appear in the light of our current knowledge — it should be accorded the respect due to a proposition that might be proved — sometime.'

Tubby closed this sentence in an impressive tone that

signified he had said about everything. He looked up, and consulted the face that had annoyed him. The eyes were wide with interest. They were intensely aware and deeply thoughtful. Tubby didn't care what they thought. He disliked them. The fellow needed a trimming. Tossing open a huge portfolio of papers on the autopsy table, the professor — with a flash-back to the earlier mood of studied mockery — drawled, 'Now — with your patient indulgence, we will call the roll. On this occasion you will stand when your name is spoken, so that I may identify you, and also that you — for purpose of acquaintance — may identify one another. . . .

'John Wesley Beaven. . . . Kindly arise, John Wesley, wherever you are, and let the congregation see you.'

There was a stir in the top row. Amused faces, at all angles, turned in that direction. Seats squeaked and shoes scraped. Everybody was eager to see how a stranger might react to this kind of teasing.

A tall, handsome, Viking sort of fellow had risen and stood waiting whatever discourtesies the Medical College had to offer at the hands of its witty anatomist. Tubby's little eyes gleamed with satisfaction. He moistened his lips with the tip of his tongue while he deliberated the best technique of punishment for the bounder who had given him such a bad hour. Painstakingly polishing his pince-nez, he consulted the carbon copy of Beaven's registration form.

'I observe, John Wesley, that the first college you attended — where you spent your freshman and sophomore years — is a righteous little institution engaged chiefly in the manufacture and disbursement of Methodist preachers. That fact, coupled with your name, leads me to suspect that you have come to us from a pious home. We will endeavor to be on our guard against the use of any objectionable language in your presence.' Tubby waited for snickers, but apparently the class was hopeful of seeing a sentiment develop in favor of the mercy which almost any one of them might need before the hour was over.

'Thank you, sir,' responded Beaven, respectfully. The class smiled wanly. It was evident that Tubby's effort to enlist scorn for the six-foot, one-hundred-and-ninety pound newcomer as a tenderly nourished plant had not been an entire success. He would dig a little deeper.

'I assume, John Wesley, that you have thought a great deal about souls. There's a standing prize here for any dissection that reveals the former presence of a soul — or any need of a soul to operate the complicated machinery of the human body. Perhaps you might like to go in for it.'

'Perhaps,' said Beaven, unruffled. 'How much is it, sir?'

Tubby wasn't quite ready with a reply to that, and the class laughed merrily, hoping that Beaven's counter-query would be accepted in fun.

'I think we can safely sign the check, Mr. Beaven, and let you fill in your own figures.... Now — as a son of the true faith, you doubtless believe in the resurrection of the body. Do you feel that it is very good cricket for you to put your so-called God to the inconvenience of reassembling the bodies you expect to hack into bits in our charnel-house?'

Beaven drew a boyishly unaffected smile that spread over the room like a contagion.

'The final mobilization isn't my job, sir,' he replied. 'I suppose that whoever is in charge of it will just have to take them the way he finds them.'

The class enjoyed this very much, and shifted amused glances back to the pit.

'Doubtless,' said Tubby, dryly. 'Perhaps if you had taken time to formulate a more clever reply you would have observed that if God could create them, he should have no trouble re-creating them.'

'Thank you, sir,' agreed John Wesley. The class grinned again, but a bit apprehensively. This good-looking beggar had better mind his step, for Tubby was getting sore.

'But you do believe, do you not, Mr. — er' — Tubby leaned over his papers to recover the name — 'Beaven, that on the last day the trumpet shall sound and the dead shall be raised incorruptible?'

'Well, sir,' answered Beaven, after a little delay, 'one must be open-minded. The theory is rather fantastic, but — it hasn't been disproved yet.'

This brought a general ripple of friendly — albeit somewhat nervous — laughter. They all rejoiced in Beaven's courage, though something warned them that it was sheer foolhardiness. Tubby pretended to smile with tight lips.

'I can see, Brother Beaven, that you believe it. That should be of great assistance to you in your anatomical research. There will be occasions, on warm days, when you may find comfort in the thought that — eventually — bodies do become incorruptible.'

The class thought this mildly witty, and chuckled a little. Thus encouraged, Tubby regained all of the old arrogance, fixed a scornful gaze on his victim, and proceeded with the flogging.

'When you write home to your pastor, I presume you will inform him that you have fallen into a hell-hole of atheism.'

Young Beaven accepted this good-humoredly.

'He wouldn't be surprised.'

'Nor care?' pressed Tubby.

'Probably not.'

'Not interested in protecting the true faith?' Tubby's widened eyes simulated outraged piety.

'Well — not interested in any discussion of Theology that came from a Professor of Anatomy.'

The class gasped involuntarily. The fellow was committing suicide.

Tubby lowered his head until his jowls overlapped his collar. His little eyes were metallic.

'I suppose you are inferring that a Professor of Anatomy isn't qualified to think or talk about anything else but pickled corpses.'

There was a little pause before Beaven replied, very respectfully, very humbly, 'I was not inferring anything, sir.'

Without an instant's delay, Tubby leaped into this trap.

'Oh! Well! Now!' he barked. 'Now we are getting somewhere! You would like to take that back, eh? Very prudent of you.'

'Perhaps you misunderstood me, sir,' said Beaven, carefully picking his words. 'I was not inferring. I was implying. I imply. You infer. Is that not correct, sir?'

So, now, Beaven had finally disposed of himself. If all the reports about Tubby as a grudge-carrier were even approximately true, Beaven would never live long enough to be forgiven for this unnecessary insult.

'Thank you, Brother Beaven,' commented Tubby, with mock deference. 'Perhaps you would do better if you stuck to your Rhetoric. You may find Anatomy difficult. We shall see. You may sit down now, please.'

He hooked on his glasses with nervous fingers, and fussed with his papers. The class scowled. The next name was called perfunctorily amid much restlessness. Everybody, including Tubby, seemed eager to be done with it. On a couple of occasions there was a brief but futile effort to introduce some mild pleasantry, but the response was feeble and barely polite.

'That is all,' said Tubby, gruffly.

He gathered up his papers, thrust them untidily into the big portfolio, and stalked stiffly out of the room. Nobody moved until the office-door had slammed. Then a surly sibilant escaped, like jets of steam, in various quarters of the room; perhaps an involuntary hiss, perhaps the symbol of a rough epithet. Tubby Forrester had got off on the wrong foot with his new class of medics. From his behavior it was evident that no one was more aware of it than himself.

They slowly came to their feet, hitched up their trousers, clattered down the steps, and funneled through the hall-door, mostly avoiding one another's eyes. Every face recorded dissatisfaction. Anatomy was going to be tough. Tubby, at his best, was mean as dirt. Now he had special reasons for being testy and relentless. He would probably try to save his face by punishing the whole outfit.

Nobody — not even the men who had sat adjacent to him — felicitated Beaven on his audacity. Two or three, for sheer humanity's sake, grinned amiably, and one chap winked at him, a wooden wink copied from the dummy on the knee of a ventriloquist. But almost everyone was intent upon his own departure. There was an unexpressed but perceptible sentiment to the effect that Beaven was partly to blame for this unhappy situation. Tubby had had it coming to him, no doubt; but Beaven would have done better to swallow his nasty medicine without any attempt at retaliation. His replies to Tubby's impudence were clever enough, but the class seemed to feel that Beaven would have been much more clever if he had kept his mouth shut.

And Jack Beaven himself now shared this belief. He felt suddenly outcast. For years he had been looking forward with keen interest to his medical course. Part of the pleasure he would derive from his associations with other young fellows intent upon the same work. Now he had made things difficult for himself — and them. He had made a bad start. He was sorry.

In the lower corridor, two girls stood talking; possibly waiting for another. Jack identified them as members of the class. The pretty brunette he remembered specially because she had stirred a bit of welcome entertainment at the roll-call. Tubby had called the name, 'W. Gillette,' adding, 'And if the "W" should happen to stand for "William," we may anticipate some skillful deductions at his hands.' Then this girl had risen, and everybody was amused. And she had carried it off very well, too; hadn't seemed a bit embarrassed.

'The "W,"' observed Tubby, when the ripple of laughter had subsided, 'probably stands for something else.' He was still glum, but trying hard to be amiable.

'My name is Winifred, Doctor Forrester,' she had replied easily.

'Are you intending to put "W. Gillette, M.D." on your office-door?' asked Tubby.

Everybody was very quiet. W. Gillette was not hard to look at, and she had all the poise in the world. Indeed, if she had had any more poise it might easily have been mistaken for brass.

'I haven't decided, sir. Perhaps you will advise me, when the time comes.'

This had brought forth a little patter of discreet applause during which Miss Gillette had resumed her seat. There was no further comment from Tubby, who apparently felt that the enlivening episode had come to a satisfactory conclusion. The fragile smile, with which he had regarded this incident, quickly faded.

The Gillette girl was going to be popular. Jack glanced at her and the less physically opulent Miss Reeves as he reached the bottom of the stairs, and they gave him a comradely grin. He did not pause to speak. There wasn't much to be said. He felt that they would be better served if they did not too conspicuously espouse his cause.

After he had passed through the outer door into the mellow September sunshine, he heard his name spoken, and a patter of heels. He paused to find the girl at his elbow. She was smiling, and her dimples were very attractive.

'Please don't give it another thought,' she said, in the tone of a long-time friend. 'He'll forget all about it by tomorrow. Everybody is with you.'

'Thanks,' said Jack, warmly. 'Did I look like a lost dog?'

'Just a little. But — I suppose we're all going to feel that way until we get acquainted. . . . Good-bye,' she said, with her lips rather than her voice. Winifred flashed him another smile of loyalty, and turned to rejoin the Reeves person who had overtaken them.

'Good-bye,' said Jack, 'and thanks, again.'

The friendly overture momentarily brightened his spirits. It also perplexed him slightly. Perhaps the Gillette girl's audacity was prompted by an impulsive wish to cheer him up. She had indicated that she, too, was lonesome. Was that a bid for some social attention? Maybe not.

At least she was entitled to the benefit of the doubt. He hoped he hadn't seemed to lack appreciation of her cordiality. He rather wished he had been a little more gracious. Mightn't he have said, 'I'll be seeing you' — or something like that — instead of an unadorned 'Good-bye'?

Tubby's stirring remarks about self-discipline, as an imperative of success in the medical profession, had made an impression. Jack had not contemplated any personal resolutions; had been so sore over Tubby's insolence, and the wrangle they had had, that the thought of acting on the brute's advice — or even of considering it seriously — was distasteful. He realized, now, that Tubby's stern counsel on this subject had gripped him. The first evidence of it was the indifference he had manifested toward the girl. At the moment he could not define his reason for failing to do his part toward the promotion of their acquaintance. Tubby's command was at the bottom of it. Tubby had laid down the simple but savage rules for the governance of 'the top ten per cent.' Not only were they to practice a severe self-discipline, but were to commit themselves to it with such devotion that presently it wouldn't hurt, any more. It would become automatic.

There might be an element of truth in this. Perhaps old Tubby knew. He was a bachelor, reputed to be a glutton for work; probably had himself bridled and saddled; drove himself with spurs and a curb-bit. The earnestness — the solemnity — with which he had talked about self-discipline couldn't have been a mere theory with him. He had laid it on to the potential top ten per cent of the new class as if he were extending them monastic vows.

The appeal was quite thrilling. Perhaps it was worth an honest trial. And if you were going to experiment with it, a good time and place to begin was now and here. The longer you postponed it, the less likely you would be to make the adventure. Jack walked briskly to the street, sensing a curious state of maturity suddenly arrived at. He wished someone else than Tubby had provided the idea. It was an odd sensation to be so deeply moved by a

motive that had been growled at you, a recommendation
that had been thrust at you — by a man you had good
reasons to despise.

* * * * * * * *

At the next corner, a big fellow waited, grinned, extended
a hand; said his name was Wollason.

'You know mine,' drawled Jack, with a rather bitter
smile. 'Tubby kicked it around a-plenty.' They shook
hands from the same height and fell into step.

'You sure trimmed our sassy little Pekinese down to the
hide,' laughed Wollason. 'But he can still chew the
pants right off o' you.'

Jack nodded, and said he supposed so. Then his steps
slowed and he quizzically inspected his new friend's face.

'I say, Wollason, don't we know each other? Aren't you
Tony Wollason?'

'Sure! I was just waiting to see if you would remember.
I had a little advantage of you. While Tubby was reciting
your college background, and making fun of your school,
I was looking you over.'

'It's all coming back now,' said Jack. 'You were at left
half for Ashburn when I was playing right end with Milford.
Sophomores, weren't we?'

'Nineteen,' assisted Tony. 'The next year I went to
Lawrence, and — you went to Evanston; didn't you? ...
That last game of the season was a pretty fast one, wasn't
it?'

'You and I ought to know,' said Jack. 'We nearly got
put in the dog-house for mixing it in the open field. Boy! —
what a shiner you gave me!'

'Yeah — they would have put us out of the game, all
right, if the alumni hadn't protested. It was about the
only interesting feature of the day — as I recall it — and
the old boys were appreciative. By the way, they never
fixed my nose as good as it was before.'

Jack looked at the nose appraisingly.

'I'll repair it for you, one of these days, just for practice.'

'Like hell you will. You've done that nose all the damage I'm going to take off of you. Where are you living, Jack? I haven't found a room yet. Just got in this morning from Chicago. Sat up all night. Saving expenses. I still eat — but not to excess.'

'You might like it where I am,' suggested Jack. 'Rooming-house of long standing. Medics. Smells like it, too. But clean enough. Hard-bitten old lady named Doyle. She had one room left at noon.'

'How are the beds?'

'Mine isn't too bad.'

'How many lodgers per bathroom?'

'You'll be Number Six, I think. How many bathrooms are you accustomed to?'

'Anybody in the house taking piano lessons?'

'No piano. No saxophone. No small boy.'

'No beautiful daughter, pining for friendship?'

'No daughter, no friendship,' pursued Jack. 'No towels, no soap; and, this morning, no hot water. They're fixing the heater. Want to come and look? It's only four blocks from here.'

Tony nodded, and at a leisurely pace they proceeded up Hill Street.

'It's none of my business,' said Tony, 'but what the devil were you trying to do to yourself today? Don't you know that old Tubby can make things mighty rough for you? They say he has the memory of an elephant when it comes to paying off old scores.'

Jack pleaded guilty with a self-reproachful frown and a shake of the head.

'You're quite right, Tony. I was a dreadful ass. Haven't any excuse to offer. Tumbled into it by accident.' He hesitated for a moment, and then went on in a tone of confidence. 'It's only ten days ago that I was called home by the death of my mother. She was a fine example of the old school, in thought and behavior; uncompromisingly orthodox. I didn't share her opinions but I respected them for what they meant to her. Today, when Tubby was taking the old traditions for a ride, his smart-alecky manner annoyed me. Under any other circumstances, maybe I might have thought he was witty. I knew I ought to be chortling over his sour jokes, but I couldn't.'

Tony interposed with a brief proffer of sympathy, and said it was a pity that old Tubby hadn't known the facts in the case.

'I suppose that's what made him mad at me, in the first place,' continued Jack. 'And then, when he began taking me for a ride, I bristled up. I'm sorry, now; but he was so damned insolent.'

'How do you suppose he gets away with that stuff?' growled Tony.

'Because he's a genius.'

Tony shot a quick glance of inquiry, not sure whether this comment was ironical. Jack's face was honest.

'I mean it, Tony. Tubby's the real goods. He's a genius. Maybe that is the way you can spot a genius. They're all more or less goofy, unstable, conceited, overbearing ——'

'Oh — you're thinking about the temperamental artists,' interrupted Tony. 'Everybody expects that of the musicians and painters and such-like sissies — the sensitive boys and gals who have to go out and throw up when they see a couple of colors that don't match. But Tubby's a scientist.'

'All the same: scientists have had their weak moments, too. It's human nature. Even Koch and Pasteur were pretty cocky after so much fuss had been made over them. Remember? And Bigelow's fame in surgery didn't prevent him from being mean to his subordinates. Tubby can't help it. You see ——'

Tony snorted his scorn and hoped Jack wasn't putting Tubby Forrester into the same bracket with Koch and Pasteur.

'Why not?' countered Jack. 'It's an acknowledged fact that Forrester is one of the most distinguished neurologists of our time. Ask anybody!... And — that isn't quite all, Tony. Didn't you find yourself getting quite a kick out

of the sentence or two that Tubby fired off — the only
really sincere moment in the whole speech — about self-
discipline as the price of success in science?'

Tony chuckled, rather grimly, and said he guessed old
Tubby was too damn' mean to be approached with any
temptations to be frivolous.

'It would be easy enough for that bird,' he added.
'Nobody would ever ask Tubby to go out on a binge.'

'Maybe not — now,' agreed Jack. 'But something tells
me that Tubby has pursued this program of hard work and
no play — all his life. And he's scouting for candidates
who might be eligible to — to ——'

'Yeah — to take the veil,' sneered Tony. 'Well — not
me! I'll do my work as well as I can, but I certainly don't
intend to be a hermit.'

Jack's rejoinder was so tardy that Tony added, 'And I
can't picture you in that role, either.'

'No,' replied Jack, absently, 'of course not.'

'Got to have a little fun — as you go along.'

'Certainly.' Jack's tone was moody, preoccupied. He
made a little gesture toward the ugly brown house on the
right. 'There,' he said, 'it is — such as it is.'

Tony regarded the battered old box with a grin, and
remarked that if anybody should decide to renounce the
pleasures of the world in behalf of a big idea, this might be
an ideal place to locate.

'I wish you good luck with Tubby,' he said, as they
turned in toward the house. 'If you can't get along with
him, you may want to take his advice, and specialize in
English. The little lesson you gave him was a screamer.'

'I shouldn't have done it. It hurt him. I was hitting
him below the belt, when I reflected on his scholarship.
Nobody should attack him at that point. It might slow
him up.'

Tony sniffed.

'Why the hell should you care — if he was slowed up?'

'Because' — Jack's eyes suddenly grew steely — 'I
want Tubby to be at his best. He has a brilliant mind —

and I want to know what's in it. I want him to pour it out by the bucketful. . . .'

'Sounds as if you were planning to be a greasy grind.'

'I hope it wasn't a priggish remark. I didn't intend it so. But — if a man is going in for medicine, at all, he'd better go in deep; hadn't he? Not much point to one's preparing to be a mere hand-holder and crooner. If you're going in for a scientific career, you'd better be a scientist; hadn't you? If it costs something, you'd better arrange to pay it; shouldn't you? Tubby's right — at that point.'

'You'd better look out,' chuckled Tony. 'First thing you know, you'll be developing into another Tubby; starry bright and mean as hell. See here — I believe you really admire this little pipsqueak!'

'I admire his mind.'

'Maybe you should let him know that, pretty soon. And he'll forgive you.'

'I'd see myself doing that!' growled Jack.

'No — I'm afraid you don't like him.'

'Personally — I hate him.'

Chapter II

It was late afternoon, the twenty-fourth of December. All day the sky had been heavily overcast and for the past two hours the snow had been tumbling down in big wet flakes that gave no promise of remaining to provide sport.

The street-lights in the down-town business district had come on at three. Motor-cars churned and slithered and spun their chains in the brown slush as they backed away from curbs. Littered shops wearied of their own disorder and drooping sales-girls candidly yawned while mumbling praises of their tousled merchandise.

All of the students who could manage it had left three days ago for the holiday recess. Only a few of the University buildings on the main campus showed lights. The professors were helping their wives decorate small trees with baubles and tinsel; performing the rite with dignity and precision, and saving the tissue-paper.

Out in the Medical College zone the streets were almost deserted. There was a light in the Bursar's office in the Administration Building, and in the anatomical laboratory on the top floor of Lister Hall; but the rest of the institution had gone out of business.

Three of Mrs. Doyle's roomers had stayed on. Bugs Cartmell was remaining because he had recently acquired a new stepfather and didn't want to go home; Tony Wollason, because he lived in Wyoming and couldn't afford to go home; Jack Beaven, because he had no home to go to.

The widow Doyle, tall, gaunt, and grim, who had housed

five student generations of medics and spoke their patter with amazing fluency, was just back from having a chiropractic adjustment for the relief of her sciatica. She sat placidly rocking in the bay-window of her small living-room, chewing gum and perusing the current issue of her favorite magazine, *Astrology*. Christmas had never disturbed her routine. If parents of small children wanted to turn their houses upsidedown for a week, and litter their rooms with pine-needles, all well and good; but Mrs. Doyle saw no reason for the nuisance and expense of holiday decorations at her house. It had not been her policy to coddle her tenants. Some landladies of her acquaintance went out of their way to be nice to their students, and a precious lot of thanks they got for it. They would prime their pens on your rugs, wipe their razors on your towels, and polish their shoes with your curtains, no matter how much you pampered them. Mrs. Doyle was about as maternal as an incubator.

The house was quiet, dimly lighted, and chilly. Tony, having slept most of the day, had gone down town to a movie. Bugs had received by express a bottle of bootleg whisky from his elder brother in New York, craftily packed in a box marked 'storage battery.' Having generously planned to share the gift with his fellow-lodgers upon their return, he decided to sample it and make sure it would be good for them. One couldn't be too careful, these days. Confident of its quality, Bugs now observed that his feet were damp. Exchanging the shoes for his well-worn moccasins, he padded down to the kitchen where he hoarsely requested a pitcher of hot water, a handful of sugar cubes, and the loan of the nutmeg shaker.

Mrs. Doyle, who had not served as his chambermaid for two and a third years without learning something about his habits, remarked that his cold must have come on very suddenly. Sniffing him diagnostically as he stood by her side waiting for the kettle to boil she added, 'But I don't suppose you'll need a doctor.' Then she grinned almost archly, as to say that while it was certainly none of her business if he wanted to indulge himself a little — seeing it was Christmas 'n' all — he needn't imagine he was putting anything over. Bugs receipted the meaningful smirk with a rather rakish smile. No, he wouldn't need a doctor, he said; didn't believe in doctors, anyway; if he got too sick he would send for a faith-healer. Retiring to his untidy room on the third floor he had presently gone to bed, contentedly jingled, with a copy of *Arrowsmith*, a new novel which was said to deal with the medical profession. Some day, he reflected, he would write one himself. Nobody would like it, but it would be the truth.

Beaven had asked permission to work in the anatomical laboratory during the Christmas vacation. There was nothing unusual about the request except that first-year students were not in the habit of applying for such permits, which were mostly issued to seniors doing research on their graduation theses. Ordinarily, one asked Tubby's consent. But Jack wasn't seeking favors of Tubby, so he had put his request through the Dean's office, a procedure strictly in order, and the permission had been formally granted. Doubtless Tubby's O.K. had been secured, but Jack had spared himself the necessity of a personal interview.

The relation between the two had been a source of considerable amusement and conjecture. The earlier fear that Tubby, exasperated over his humiliation, might punish the whole class for Beaven's impudence, had been promptly relieved. He was impatient, exacting, sarcastic; but no worse than his reputation for ungraciousness.

The battle between the professor and his unlucky disciple continued unabated. Sometimes the class was much annoyed. But the animosity had its droll moments, too. From the first day, Tubby made it a point to badger Beaven about his religious upbringing and the piety he had imputed to him, invariably addressing him in the classroom with honeyed phrases implying that he was likely to be offended if not handled tenderly. Had Jack been a member of some monastic order, appearing in gown and cowl, tonsured and barefooted, he couldn't have been treated with more deference. At times, Tubby's mockery was so labored as to be very tiresome. On these occasions, Beaven's replies took no account of the mood in which the questions had been asked. Once in a while, Jack would play up to the role assigned him, and the dialogue had large possibilities, but before they were done with it, Tubby would be peevish. One day when the discussion related to the various phenomena of the endocrine glands, and much talk was made of physical functions speeded or retarded by mental states — the supernormal strength of the frenzied, the curious achievement of 'second wind' by track athletes, etc. — Tubby had spoken of the adrenalin suddenly poured into the blood stream of men on the battle-field, as a prophylaxis against hemorrhage, and raised the question whether the glands might — in an emergency — provide immunity against disease.

'Brother Beaven,' said Tubby, 'when Saint Francis kissed the leper, do you think his piety may have accounted for the fact — if it is a fact — that he did not contract the disease himself?'

'Yes, sir,' replied Jack, soberly. 'In the brotherhood to which I belong we frequently kiss lepers.'

The class thought this was going to be a lot of fun, and gave rapt attention to the combatants, all eyes bright with expectation.

'And you find that it does you no damage?' queried Tubby.

'Not to us, sir. It is our method of administering euthanasia.'

Everybody laughed and felt that Beaven had scored a point. Tubby didn't like it. For a moment it seemed that he was about to carry on with the serious discussion of his theme. Then he decided to put Beaven on the spot.

'That brings up an interesting question,' he said, severely. 'You seem to speak favorably of euthanasia. Are there any circumstances under which a doctor might seem justified by giving his patient a painless death?'

The class sobered. It looked as if Tubby was trying to

back his victim into a corner where any attempt at persiflage might be easily misinterpreted.

'It is against the law,' Jack replied.

'Is that the reason you would not do it?'

'It is a good enough reason.'

'Then you are never going to kill anybody when you
are a doctor?'

'Very likely, sir; but not intentionally.'

'Your murders will all be accidental?'

'Yes, sir — that is, all of them that I commit in a
strictly professional capacity.'

Tubby grunted, and resumed his lecture where he had
left off. It was clear to everybody, including himself, that
the interlude hadn't been a very dignified performance;
nor had he succeeded in making Beaven appear ridiculous.

One method of hectoring, which Tubby had practiced
freely during the early days of the semester, had been
abandoned. He had a trick of organizing the questions he
put to Beaven in such a manner that they admitted of
but one reply; questions so elementary that a high-school
student with a sketchy knowledge of Physiology would
have been considered a dolt if he had muffed them. But
it was to be noticed that Tubby had discontinued this
tactic. After the first couple of weeks, the class having
had time to turn in some assigned anatomical drawings,
Tubby left off treating Beaven as if he were a numbskull.
Quite to the contrary, he now began the habit of singling
him out when the question was exceptionally difficult.
On these occasions, Tubby was sour but civil. It would
grow very quiet in the classroom. Everybody would
expect — and hope — that Tubby, upon receiving a correct
reply to a hard question, might be decent enough to
express his commendation. But he would merely nod briefly
and proceed with the quiz.

'I can't see what he thinks he's going to gain,' the
comely Gillette remarked, one day, when they happened
to find themselves paired in the straggling procession that
ambled down the walk to the street. 'He knows you're

the best student in the class, and admits it by the sort
of questions he asks you. Why does he keep on trying to
poke fun at you?'

'He doesn't like me,' said Jack.

'Well — he certainly has got a nerve!' complained
Winifred, sympathetically.

Jack grinned and reminded her that Tubby was a nerve
specialist. He felt silly over Winifred's solicitude.

'It's a funny thing,' she continued, 'how he seems to
spend more time at your table in the lab than with anyone
else. I often wonder: does he go over there just to annoy
you and find fault? One day I saw him snarling at you,
and then he picked up your notebook and pinched on his
cute little lorgnette and scowled at your drawing for a
long time, and then scribbled something on it, and almost
threw it at you. And then stalked away, mad as a wet
hen.'

Jack shook his head.

'It wasn't quite that bad,' he said. 'Tubby was just
making a little suggestion; something he hadn't mentioned
in class. It spoiled my drawing, so I had it to do over;
but it was a very interesting ——' To Winifred's surprise,
Jack suddenly interrupted himself to say, 'Hold out your
hand. Spread out your fingers. Bend back the little one.
Stretch it out. Now bend back the next one. Notice the
difference. See how much more freedom you have with
the little finger?'

Winifred obeyed him, critically surveying her hand.
It was a very shapely hand, she was pleased to note, and
she hoped he might think so. Perhaps he would say something to that effect, when the impromptu lesson was over.
But he didn't.

'That's because,' he went on, as unmoved by the beauty
of her hand as he might have been if it belonged to a
cadaver, 'there's a different tendon structure serving the
little finger; not very much, but enough difference to be
noticed; slightly different caliber of nerve-fiber, too. That's
what Tubby was calling my attention to.'

'Mighty small matter to be making such a big fuss about,' she grumbled, loyally.

'Maybe — but it's these small matters that have made Tubby a great anatomist.'

Winifred pouted in his behalf, firming a very pretty mouth.

'So you still think he's great,' she said, 'after the rotten way he has treated you.'

'Of course,' declared Jack. 'Tubby's attitude toward me has nothing to do with his ability as a scientist.'

She regarded him with wide, perplexed eyes, almost as if they were total strangers, and did not reply for a long moment.

'I'm almost afraid of you,' she said, at length. 'I believe you're as cold-blooded as Tubby is. You two pretend to hate each other, but you don't; not really. I'll bet you're as nearly alike as identical twins. I think I know now why Tubby comes to your table and growls at you. He knows you've got something.'

'Pish!' said Jack.

'And I know something else,' Winifred went on, impressively. 'Yesterday he ordered your table to be pushed over on the north side, next to a window. And I said to Millicent Reeves, "I'll bet Tubby has put him over there, by that draughty window, so he will be cold and uncomfortable."'

Jack laughed.

'Maybe you're right,' he said. 'It is chilly over there.'

Winifred lifted a hand in contradiction.

'Ah, no, Brother Beaven. He put you over there so you would have the advantage of that north light.'

'Nonsense! I'm the last fellow in the world that Tubby would befriend. See here — he doesn't show any partiality. Hasn't he given you a square deal?'

'Sure! And he didn't scribble anything on my paper about that what-you-may-call-it tendon in the fingers.'

'Extensor,' supplied Jack. '*Extensor digiti quinti proprius,* for short.'

'Wow!' said Winifred, wincing. 'What a pretty mouthful! Do you try to remember all that stuff? I'm sure I don't.'

Jack frowned down upon her like an elder brother.

'You'd better,' he said. 'There will be an examination, some day. Tubby may be negligent about his parlor manners, but he wants everybody to know the Latin names for things.'

At the corner their steps lagged. Winifred drew a sigh and remarked that all work and no play might make Jack a dull boy. She looked him straight in the eyes as she said it, and his heart missed a beat. He had a fleeting notion to do something about it.

'Good-bye,' she said, caressing the word provocatively.

'Good-bye,' said Jack.

He sensed a sudden glow of well-being as he pursued his way down the street with lengthened stride and squared shoulders. It hadn't occurred to him why the damned old beast had moved him into that draughty corner. The girl had guessed the reason. Tubby wanted to give him a chance to do his best. Tubby hated him like hell, but was on his side when it came to the pursuit of their common task. Tubby deserved a spanking, but he was a great scientist. Jack laughed; laughed aloud; and then suddenly remembered that to laugh aloud — by oneself — was a sign of madness. For the moment, he had forgotten all about Winifred.

A few days later — it was nearly six o'clock — Jack was conscious of someone at his elbow. He had been working since four on a piece of independent research on the structure of the left subclavian vein. Tubby had remarked, seemingly rather more to himself than the class, 'The left subclavian vein: well — do your best. And when you have done your best, you will still have much to learn. I recommend your diligent study of it.' Jack had taken the hint and had stayed after the usual laboratory hours to do a painstaking dissection.

'Hello,' he said, absently. 'You still here?'

'My last drawing bounced back on me,' muttered Winifred. 'He told me to do it over. And now everybody's gone, and this place is dreadfully spooky. I've got the jitters.'

'Don't be silly,' said Jack, comfortingly. 'These people are harmless. Some of them were public nuisances, while they were alive, but they're philanthropists now.' He straightened an aching spine, and regarded her with a friendly grin. 'This fellow,' said Jack, patting his cadaver cordially on the chest, 'committed suicide after having forged a note for a sizable sum of money. The man who lost the money is probably at home, by this time, reading the evening paper. He is well-to-do, highly respected, and after dinner he and his wife will go somewhere for a game of bridge. But — he will never have a chance to serve his generation in a big way because, after all's said to his credit, he is just another run-o'-the-mine citizen. When he dies, the lodge will turn out in plumes and mothballs, and bury him. Maybe taps will be blown at his grave, if he was something in the war. But — *my* friend here,' continued Jack, 'is offering the medical profession some information about the left subclavian vein — but I wish he wouldn't be so darned reticent.'

Winifred eyed him steadily, her inviting lips pursed. She shook her head. It was a pretty head. She had just suffered a permanent.

'I don't know how you can do it,' she said, slowly. 'You love it, don't you? I hate it! I loathe it!' She tucked her forehead into the crook of her arm, and shuddered.

'Maybe you should be doing something else,' suggested Jack, fraternally. 'Maybe you should be at home, serving on the hospitality committee for the Junior League.'

Now Winifred was going to cry. Jack regarded her with apprehension but with interest. He had been looking ahead, in the textbooks, and presently he would be studying the various phenomena of the lachrymal glands. He didn't want Winifred to cry, but if she was going to cry he felt that he might as well note all the phases of it that could be viewed externally.

'Come on,' she entreated, brokenly. 'Let's leave these rotten old corpses — and go out and have dinner — someplace — and ——— Oh, I'm so dreadfully fed up with this terrible business.' She drew a long breath, with a sob in it, and pushed her face deep into his white smock. Jack patted her arm.

There was a sound of brisk footsteps. Professor Milton Forrester had ineptly chosen this high-geared moment for an excursion from his office into his private laboratory. He paused, outraged at the sight which smote his gaze. Winifred detached herself from Jack's shoulder, and regarded the enemy with frightened, tearful eyes. Jack felt as foolish as he looked. Tubby bore down on them indignantly.

'Well!' he snorted. 'If this isn't the last place in the world for people to make love! It's a wonder the whole roomful of cadavers doesn't sit up and laugh! Now — you get out of here — both of you — and attend to your mooning elsewhere!' He strode off, stiffly, toward his laboratory. At the door he paused to say, 'Beaven — I'm surprised at you. I had hoped ——' He shook his head, disgustedly, opened the door, and disappeared.

'Maybe you'd better run along now,' said Jack, thickly. 'I think we've done enough to ourselves, for one session.'

'I'm awfully sorry, Jack,' murmured Winifred. 'My fault. All of it. He'll hate you, now, worse than ever. Please forgive me.'

* * * * * * * *

Never had a day passed more quickly. He had gone to the anatomical laboratory at nine, presently realizing — when he glanced up to find himself alone — that it was noon. After a while the others drifted in, tied on their aprons, lighted their pipes. It was to be hoped that no one of his elders and betters would stroll over to see what he was up to. He could imagine Jim Wentworth, whom he knew slightly, glancing at his sketch and saying with a grin, 'You'd better not try to stand on your head, little one, until you learn how to walk.'

Jack was not engaged on any required problem today. He was attempting to satisfy his curiosity about something that probably had no practical value at all.

Shortly before vacation, the class had been studying the head. Tubby had called attention to the quite elaborate fan-shaped muscular equipment extending above and behind the ear, an ingenious device for which there was but little use. He had added that it was a vestigial remain of muscles which were very important and active long ago when men's ears were as mobile as the ears of dogs. Now that we had escaped from the jungle and were no longer preyed upon by an assortment of stealthy enemies, we were not required to be on the jump.

'You should easily locate, on the cartilaginous rim of your own ear,' remarked Tubby, 'a trace of the tip which used to sweep about with the swiftness and certainty of movement still displayed by the human eye.'

It was rather odd, Jack thought, that the tip of the dawn man's ear should have degenerated through disuse until you could hardly find it, while the muscles which had served the ear's necessities — a million years ago — showed no signs of atrophy.

Nobody in the class had raised the question. Tubby had volunteered no further information on the matter. The dissection had proceeded and the scheduled drawings had been made, quite as if there was nothing peculiar about the auricular muscles which had been loafing on the job for innumerable ages. The class had picked its way, routinishly, through these muscle-fibers, tagging the arteries and veins and nerves with red, blue, and black threads, as usual. And, having drawn their charts, had moved along next day to a similar examination of the frontalis.

Jack hadn't been satisfied with this ear business, and wanted another go at it for his own private information. Already the study of nerve structure had begun to be of peculiar interest to him. He realized it was rather silly to be thinking — in his first year — of going in for neurological surgery as a specialty, but something told him it was likely to turn out that way.

This probability presented an annoying problem. Had he discovered in himself a special concern for something else — internal medicine, for instance — he would be seeing less of Tubby Forrester as the years passed. If he went in for neurological surgery, the time would come when he might be at Tubby's elbow all the day long — a most undesirable situation.

Sometimes, when Tubby had been particularly mean to him in the classroom, Jack would swear that this settled it. He would leave off concentrating his attention on nerves. Next day he would be in the library, absorbed in Ransom, Whitaker, and Quain, pretending not to notice Miss Selfridge's sniff when he asked for them — as if she was thinking, 'Sonny — you'd better stick to good old Gray until you learn where all the bones are.'

It was four o'clock now. On the tall desk beside his operating-table, Jack had painstakingly drawn a good sketch of the auricular muscles — a much more complete and detailed drawing than he had done previously as a requirement. In the microscope he had sharpened the focus of the stereoscopics upon the tiny tendril of nerve-fiber, and was studying it with an absorption so complete that he was startled to find Tubby beside him.

'Nice way for a pious young Christian to spend Christmas Eve,' said Tubby. 'I should have thought you might be playing Santa Claus at some Sunday School festivity.'

Jack straightened, blinking a little as he eased out of his eye-strain.

'They wouldn't have me,' he drawled. 'Not chubby enough.' He blandly looked Tubby up and down, his eyes lingering briefly in the vicinity of the great man's midriff.

'May I venture to inquire,' asked Tubby, with elaborate courtesy, 'what you think you are doing?'

Jack nodded his head toward the drawing and Tubby, adjusting his glasses, gave it a glance.

'I thought you had already done this. I seem to recall that we passed it, some days ago.'

'Yes, sir. I was just curious about it.' Jack proceeded to explain the nature of his inquisitiveness, rather reluctantly, for he didn't want Tubby to make sport of him. It was all very well if Tubby, wanting to punish him, held him up to open ridicule before the class, savagely raking him as a prig. But he hoped for some degree of fairness and sincerity when it came to a matter of scientific inquiry.

'Far as I can see,' concluded Jack, 'the nerves in control of these non-functioning muscles are of the same structure and caliber as those of the frontalis. Why haven't they atrophied?'

'What do you want to know for?' growled Tubby, resetting the stereoscopics to his own astigmatism, and squinting at the tiny thread of nerve.

'Oh — just curiosity,' replied Jack, lamely, and half-ashamed of the confession. He wondered if Tubby would be cad enough to make some contemptuous allusion to it later in the classroom.

Tubby tucked his pince-nez back in his breast pocket.

'I see you're interested in nerves. Why?'

'I've often wondered,' said Jack, in a tone barely audible, as if he were speaking to himself. Then, with animation, 'Would you be good enough to tell me, sir, what I want to know about this nerve?'

Tubby, who had been carrying his overcoat on his arm, put it on and buttoned it.

'No!' he snapped. 'I'll not tell you!'

He needn't be so damned brutal about it, thought Jack, flushing with anger.

'I'll not tell you,' repeated Tubby — 'because I don't know. And I don't thank you for stirring the question up.' He tugged on his gloves, with quick little jerks.

'Then — I suppose *nobody* knows,' said Jack.

Tubby darted a searching look.

'Are you trying to say something smart, young man?' he challenged, his jaw thrust out pugnaciously.

'No, sir. I never was more honest in my life. I think that if you do not know, it is unlikely that anybody else does.'

'Humph!' muttered Tubby. He turned to go, took a few steps, returned, elbowed Jack away from the microscope, peered into it for a long moment, and having grunted another 'Humph,' stiffened his back and marched out of the room.

Jack turned his head to watch this pompous retreat; then grinned, and growled deep in his throat, 'Merry Christmas — Towser.'

* * * * * * * *

Noisily closing the laboratory door behind him, Doctor Forrester proceeded through the dimly lighted lecture amphitheater to his office. He had a call to make before dinner, and had forgotten the street address.

Snapping on the lamps, he drew out a large metal drawer from the cabinet of case-histories, extracted the page he sought, and put on his glasses. A good deal of misery had been boiled down into the succinct, cold-blooded phrases detailing the clinical log of William Mason, forty, carpenter, resident of Elmersville, married, no children; state charge.

Forrester's eye ran swiftly through the report, stirring afresh an indignation that — six weeks ago — had furnished him the materials for a whole day of fiery speeches.

A dozen years ago, Mason had begun to suffer burning pains in the lower part of his back. He had consulted a physician in the little town where he lived, and was given amateur massage and hot fomentations — and bromides. For more than a year he continued, with increasing discomfort, to pursue his trade. The pain becoming unbearable, he had consulted another physician in the slightly larger neighboring town of Kenwood. His tonsils and four teeth were removed. Six months later another doctor had operated on him for hernia, followed shortly by an appendectomy. Two years afterwards he was hospitalized again and an extension apparatus was applied to his legs for eight weeks.

Then they had all given it up. Mason was helplessly bed-ridden, nursed by his wife who supported them by home baking.

Three months ago, Mason, having applied for examination in the University Clinic, had made the journey on a stretcher. A careful survey of the case showed that the patient had a lumbosacral tumor of the spinal cord.

Forrester had fumed and raged when he made this discovery. Throwing all discretion and diplomacy to the winds, he had had his say about the case. By rights, William Mason ought to sue the state for damages. He had been put to unspeakable agony, he had lost a dozen years out of his working life, had spent his savings and surrendered his home. It was the state's fault. The state had licensed men to practice medicine and surgery who regarded their vocation as a mere trade — a mere source of food supply, 'like a truck-patch.' Perhaps they thought they meant well, romping up and down the country-side with their self-assured manner and their impressive little leather satchels, earning plaudits for their attentiveness, their kind words, their soothing smiles, but not knowing whether they were afoot or on horseback when it came to making a scientific diagnosis. Mason had been given the dirtiest kind of a dirty deal.

Next morning after Doctor Forrester had performed the operation — a laminectomy on the twelfth thoracic and first three lumbars — removing an incredibly large encapsulated tumor, he determined to make the shocking affair known. All that day he had recounted the steps in Mason's case for the benefit of his classes; had waived the scheduled lectures; had engaged in a furious lambasting of the State Legislature, the Medical Association, and the public's *laissez-faire* attitude toward incompetence in the most important profession.

'It all goes to show,' he had declaimed, 'what comes of a lack of training, lack of self-discipline, lack of capacity for personal sacrifice in school and during internship.

'William Mason is a typical victim of malpractice. Some

of you are unwittingly making preparations to go forth to commit similar crimes. You are eager to get out of training and set up business for yourselves. Some selfish little fluff is yapping at you to hurry up and marry her. Your parents think you ought to be earning money pretty soon. You're tired of the long hours, the strict supervision, the monotonous hospital food, the drudgery, the screams, and the stinks. So — you pop out, with your little black satchel, to rub horse liniment on William Mason's rump; or, in a brilliant display of acumen, to yank his tonsils out. A dozen years later, some sour old curmudgeon, who wasn't in such a hurry to hang out a shingle, finds an aged tumor in Mason's spinal cord.'

That had been a very noisy day in the Forrester classroom. He had raked the whole lexicon to find strong enough phrases.

'I hope you are not gathering from my heated remarks,' he had cautioned, 'that I am emotionally upset about William Mason, as an individual. The fact that he spent twelve years in abject misery is most emphatically none of my business. His aches and pains haven't cost me one minute's sleep. The world is full — has ever been full — of aches and pains. I am not the least bit sentimental on that subject. Nor is it my affair if Mason's wife had to bake cookies to support him. She might have been engaged in a less interesting occupation.

'But I *have* been losing sleep over the deplorable conditions which permit these injustices. I feel responsible. It is my duty to help prepare physicians to do something better for William Mason than sit by his bed twice a week, and look again at his tongue, and tell him to buck up bravely. I tell you — part of your shame as an incompetent is *my* shame!'

He had felt that these speeches had really done some good. It seemed that his classes were doing more serious work; not so many absences; not so many asinine replies to simple questions. William Mason had been put to a lot of suffering, but his case had served a very good purpose.

Somebody should tell the chap that. It would be interesting to observe his reaction.

Forrester glanced at his watch and was startled to find
how long he had been standing here, brooding over the
Mason incident. He noted the address — 121 South Hem-
lock. He remembered now, having had occasion to look
it up only yesterday.

The Masons had been advised to go into furnished rooms
for a few weeks, so that he might be available to the clinic.
The man would have to be under supervision for some
time. He couldn't be discharged now and sent back to
Elmersville where the medical profession would have
nothing for him but sympathy and sleeping-powders.

The streets were slippery and Forrester drove with
caution. He wore a scowl. It was rather awkward — his
feeling of obligation to have a look at Mason, this afternoon. People were so soft and silly about Christmas. These
Masons unquestionably felt grateful to him for the operation. The woman had tried to make a fuss over him in the
hospital. How often he was obliged to put up with this
sort of thing. It always embarrassed him; made him suspect that his colleagues were grinning behind his back.
Sometimes he had been required to be almost rude, realizing that he was hurting their feelings; but — he could trust
the tear-wipers and back-patters to attend to these damaged sensibilities.

He rang the bell and heard it jingle in the second-floor
flat. Mrs. Mason, a shawl about her shoulders, hurried
down the stairs. She peered at him with bewilderment for
a moment; then smiled the sort of welcome she might have
bestowed upon a relative.

'Why — it's Doctor Forrester! I never seen you without your long white coat and cap. Come in, please. Bill
will be so glad.' She closed the door behind them; and,
still holding onto the knob, lowered her voice to say,
'And oh — Doctor Forrester — you can't ever know what
it has meant to Bill and I — all those wonderful things to
eat.' The big tears ran unchecked, while Forrester stared

at her in dismay. Some blundering fool at the grocery
store — in spite of strict instructions — had let them know.

He made an impatient gesture up the cold stairway, and
Mrs. Mason piloted him through the stuffy little living-
room to the bedside.

'Well, Mason; how goes the battle?' demanded Forrester.

The sick man's eyes lighted. He reached out his hand,
which the doctor grasped by the wrist. There was a minute
of silence. Forrester did not take out his watch; had his
ear attentive to the busy little clock on the bureau.

'Turn over and let me see your back.... Bring that
light over here.... Hold it — so.' He drew up the sheet
again, pocketed his glasses, nodded his head. 'Very good.
Doing nicely.'

'Doctor' — Mason cleared his throat — 'That was an
awful fine thing you did for us. We know you are a big
man, with a lot o' folks to worry about. And we certainly
thank you for thinking of us — 'specially now.'

'It's made Christmas mighty happy for us,' put in Mrs.
Mason. 'Hasn't it, Bill?'

'I'll say. You've got a heart, Doc! You're not only a
big surgeon. You're a prince.' Bill, overcome by his own
words, wiped his nose on the corner of the sheet.

'We was almost afraid of you,' ventured Mrs. Mason;
adding, recklessly, 'One of the nurses said you was too
busy to take any store of common folks.'

Forrester was stroking his gloves onto his fingers with
impatience. He felt he had to say something to clear this
matter up.

'Mr. Mason — and Madam — I hope you will understand my exact motives in ordering this food. The fact
that it has come to you on Christmas is a mere coincidence,
I assure you. I am much interested in your case — as a
matter of professional concern. I would like to bring you
into my student clinic, within the next four weeks, with
your normal activities fairly well resumed. You can assist
me by taking proper care of yourself, and making every
effort to build up your strength. I feared that you might

try to live on poor food, for reasons of economy. I don't want any of *that*!' His voice shrilled to lecture-room pitch. He turned almost belligerently to Mrs. Mason. 'And I don't want *you* skimping on food, either! You're thin as a rail. First thing you know, you'll be flat, and then he'll have *you* to fret about. And that will detain his convalescence. I intend to see to it that you both are provided with proper nourishment. But what I have done is strictly *professional*!' He glared more fiercely at Mrs. Mason as he observed a timid smile puckering her lips. This ignorant woman wasn't getting the idea, at all. '*Strictly* professional!' he repeated.

'But — how about the holly wreath, Doctor? Did you mean for Bill and I to eat that?' She took Bill's hand as if to solicit his support of her audacity.

'Holly? Holly?' Forrester made an earnest task of buttoning his gloves. 'Humph! Well! I had forgotten. A trifle — I'm sure. The important thing is that I want you, Mason, to give me a good blood count within the next few days.'

To his wife's amazement, Bill let loose a half-hysterical haw-haw, the doctor regarding him with somber disapproval.

'You can't kid *me*, Doc — God bless yuh!'

'Nor me, neither,' declared Mrs. Mason, bravely. 'You done it out o' the kindness of your big heart. Perfessional — Pooh! We never had a better friend. Look what you done for him, a'ready! And now these presents!'

'Well — well — have it your own way,' grumbled Forrester, in the tone he often employed with psychopathic patients. Taking up his hat, he moved toward the door. Mrs. Mason said she would go down with him, but he assured her, with frosty dignity, that he could let himself out.

'Merry Christmas, Doc!' called Bill.

Forrester paused, blinked a few times, and replied, stiffly, 'Oh, yes — of course — of course.'

'Merry Christmas, Doctor Forrester,' said Mrs. Mason, tenderly.

'Yes, yes. Quite so.... Good evening.'

He closed the door and made his way gingerly down the poorly lighted stairway, climbed into his coupé, fumbled for his cigarettes, struck a match, spun his engine, and scooted off through the slush in the direction of the University Club where he was having dinner with an old bachelor crony, Linton, of the Law Faculty.

He found him in the library, deep in a big leather chair. 'Hi, Scrooge,' drawled Linton, dragging himself to his feet. 'You're late. I thought maybe you had gone caroling.'

* * * * * * * *

Tony and Bugs were engaged in a laborious discussion of what's-it-all-about-anyway when Jack returned at nine. Pausing at the open doorway of Cartmell's disheveled room, he peered into the smoke-fog and grinned understandingly.

'Come in,' said Bugs, thickly, 'and improve your mind. Important words are being uttered and much truth is coming to light.'

'"*In vino veritas*,"' added Tony, with deep solemnity.

'Smells more like whisky,' said Jack.

'The fellow has the nose of a chemist,' muttered Bugs. 'Bring a glass, Doctor, and we'll see how much *veritas* you are able to contribute.'

In dressing-gown and slippers Jack presently joined them, poured himself a small nip from the depleted bottle, gulped and shuddered, filled his pipe, and dumped the miscellaneous contents of a chair onto the floor. 'Don't let me interrupt,' he said. 'As you were.'

Bugs, sprawled on the bed, rose on one elbow, propping his head up with his hand.

'Perhaps you'd better give your family an account of your recent movements,' he suggested, paternally. 'It's very late for you to be out. Have you been down among the bright lights, observing the antics of the quick, or up in the lab, consorting with the dead?'

'He smells like the lab,' remarked Tony.

'Then we don't care to hear anything about your adventures,' decided Bugs. 'Tony and I have just passed a unanimous resolution, after a learned debate, to the effect that the medicine man has as good a right as a plumber to live a normal life; three meals regularly, seven hours' sleep — all served in one piece — a decent house to live in, preferably in the suburbs of a small village, a wife, children, flower garden ——'

'With plenty of ground,' interposed Tony, 'for vegetables and chickens — and a nice fat pig in a pen.'

'No, shir!' objected Bugs. 'I've been telling him you can't have vegetables *and* chickens. But' — wistfully — 'I'd rather like to have a pig-pen.'

Jack made a comprehensive gesture with his pipe-stem, and drawled, 'What's the matter with this one?'

'We trust you are not trying to be offensive,' said Bugs, with dignity. 'You come in here reeking of a loathsome occupation, partake of our hospitality, throw our various necessities on the floor, and then insinuate that our room is untidy. Rank ingratitude.'

'Rank is right,' agreed Tony. 'By the way — have you found out yet what made you wiggle your ears when you were a monkey, or whatever damn'-fool thing it was you wanted to know?'

'Proceed, brothers,' urged Jack. 'I should like to hear more about this country doctor, with the chickens and the asparagus and the pig — and the medicine case filled with quinine, morphine, and castor-oil. Tubby ought to be here to make a few more remarks about the progress of medical science in Elmersville.'

Bugs sat up and extended an arm in a sweeping gesture.

'Now — there you are! Let's start from there. Take Tubby, for example. What d'you suppose that old killjoy gets out of life? Bachelor. Lives at a club. On duty seven days of the week.'

'And on Sunday,' added Tony. 'That makes eight.'

'Thanks. And trying to tell people,' declaimed Bugs, 'how they ought to live.' He paused for reply.

'Well — I'm not acting as Tubby's attorney,' countered Jack, 'but ——'

'No!' cut in Tony, 'I shouldn't think you would, after the dirty treatment you've had.'

'That's all true enough. Tubby has been very unpleasant. But that is a personal matter. He doesn't like me; and, naturally, I don't like him. All that is beside the point. It has nothing to do with what we're talking about. I think I understand Tubby's attitude about the medicine man. One thing is certain: you can't be a doctor and raise chickens. I doubt whether you can be a really good doctor and have a home, a wife, social duties, children, care of a house, worry of family illness, monthly bills.'

'Yeah — but look at us!' grumbled Tony. 'Here we are, on Christmas Eve, crowded into this frowsy old rat-hole ——'

'Shay, fellah,' protested Bugs, 'enough has been said about my humble abode. If you don't like it, you can ——'

'Yeah — I know where you mean.' Tony dismissed him with an overhand gesture. 'And we'll be spending Christmas in just such diggings until it's time to move up to the top floor of the hospital annex for a few more years of captivity. Don't you think we'll deserve a home — ever?'

'It isn't a matter of deserving,' said Jack. 'It's the nature of the job; that's what we're discussing. You think that a doctor can pursue a normal life. I disagree. I've given up the home idea — for good.'

'You mean — you're going to be an old bachelor — like Tubby?' demanded Bugs, incredulously. 'You'll never get away with it. It must have been easy for Tubby. No woman would want him.'

'That's right,' mumbled Tony. 'Some gal will shout, "My hero!" — and take you into camp.'

'I have only one interest in life now,' declared Jack, resolutely, 'and that's scientific. That's *all*. Nothing else matters. I may turn out to be no good at it, but — it won't be because I wanted a home.'

'O lit-tle town of Beth-le-hem ——'

Mrs. Doyle had turned on her radio.

'Guess you're right, at that,' conceded Bugs, indulgently. 'A home is nothing but a millstone around your neck. . . . I wish the old lady would turn off that Sunday School entertainment. I never realized she was so darned sentimental.'

'A-bove thy deep and dream-less sleep ——'

Tony lifted himself out of his chair, stretched to full torsion, yawned mightily, and said he was going to bed.

'The ev-er-last-ing Light ——'

'Me, too,' said Jack. 'Good night.'

'Merry Christmas!' drawled Bugs.

Retiring to his room, Jack disposed himself comfortably in two chairs, lighted his pipe, and listened. It was not a Sunday School entertainment. Sunday Schools didn't furnish that kind of music. This was a choir of trained voices. Sunday Schools didn't have trained voices. If you wanted to hear a really good interpretation of the old hymns, you had to call in singers from secular society. It took the world, the flesh, and the devil to make these expressions of religion inspirational. The idea had never occurred to him before — not just this way. Funny thing about that. Religion's best art-forms — painting, sculpture, poetry, music, drama — had been composed and executed by people who were primarily artists concerned with art for art's sake. Same way with healing, maybe. The greatest contributors to medicine and surgery weren't the people who had been moved to holy pity by the world's distress: they had gone in for science not because they were emotionally disturbed over human suffering but because they were intellectually curious and wanted to know to what lengths of discovery science might carry them.

'No ear may hear His com-ing . . .'

Nor had the scientists been trained and encouraged by organized religion. More often than not, religion had disapproved of them. Sometimes they had had to fight their way through the prophets and priests to lay hold upon the instruments of research.

'*The dear Christ en-ters in.*'

Jack's brooding eyes narrowed in serious concentration. An interesting question, this. Just where did 'the dear Christ' come into this picture? Whose side was He on? What did He think of the whole business? Did it offend Him to see the healing of the world's diseases going forward in the hands of people who didn't give a moment's thought to the problem of 'inspiration'? Maybe the solemn wise-acres had Him all wrong. Maybe 'the dear Christ' was concerned only with having the Truth come out and do its work — no matter who found it, or how. If that could be proved, well — it certainly would upset the apple-cart; but it would make 'the dear Christ' popular with the people who were pushing civilization forward. It would liberate Him from the tight little enclosures where He fraternized with the uninquisitive and the resigned. Science would claim Him! The researchists would shout to the sentimentalists, 'He has been your exclusive property too long! He's on *our* side!' ... And they would hang His picture in the lab. In the anatomical lab, where Tubby could see it. Tubby wouldn't object. All he cared for was science. If it could be shown that Christ was in favor of science, Tubby would be for Him. And they would hang His picture in the chemical lab. It might change their tactics. They couldn't take much interest in poison gas if He was looking down at 'em and they knew He was concerned about chemical research.

'*It came upon th' mid-night clear ——*'

The sweet old lyric reached into Jack's memory and stirred him. He closed his eyes and let the pictures file by.... When he and Jean — his twin — had been little things, Father would go down stairs early, Christmas morning, to rouse the furnace. It was barely light. He and Jean would be pipping to go down and see the tree and the

gifts. But they weren't permitted; not until Father had
played a few Christmas hymns on the phonograph. They
must sit still in bed and listen. Mother would come and
put her arms around them, and they would try to be very
still.

'O ye, be-neath life's cru-shing load ——'

Nobody was ever more sentimental than Mother. She
certainly took her religion hard — and took it straight.
When he and Jean were in high school, the family still ran
the Christmas hymns on the phonograph before anyone
went down — but Father.

'Look now for glad and gol-den hours ——'

Once, he and Jean had brought home a couple of records
that weren't exactly religious — according to Mother's
ideas. One was an old English ballad that had something
in it about ale, and another was 'Noel' which she felt
had been concocted under the wrong auspices. Mother
wouldn't have it. Christmas was a religious occasion, and
you wanted to be mighty careful what brand of religion it
was, too. 'Ave Maria' wasn't quite the thing for Christmas morning, though Mother was uncompromising about
the Virgin Birth. If you didn't believe that, the whole
thing fell to pieces, she said. And maybe it did.... Maybe
it had!

'Joy-ful all ye na-tions rise —
Join th' tri-umph of th' skies ——'

They always had to attend everything the little church
had to offer at Christmas time. Grandfather had been a
Methodist preacher and it was up to the family to honor
the faith he had toiled for. It had been the pure faith,
once delivered unto the saints, and you weren't allowed to
ask any questions about it. Mother always grew nervous
and petulant when you asked questions. Faith couldn't
grow in an atmosphere of doubt.

'Veiled in flesh th' God-head see —
Hail th' In-car-nate Deity ——'

Whenever people began raising queries they opened the way for Satan to come into their hearts and make them unhappy — unhappy and unworthy. Mother was very precious. She might have been pretty if she hadn't worn her beautiful Titian hair that way. Sometimes a cute little curl would peep out from under her hat-brim and she would be prompt to tuck it back where it belonged. God didn't go in much for pretty things. He liked plain people best and preferred them to wear dowdy clothes. My Uncle! — but it had stirred things up when Jean came home, one day, with her hair bobbed. He and Jean had been half-grown before they realized that Father was fairly well-to-do. Mother didn't want them to know because she hoped to keep them unspotted from the world.

'Sing, choirs of an-gels —
Sing in ex-ul-ta-tion ——'

But they had loved her for her goodness and her tenderness. She would have crawled on her hands and knees over a road of cinders to get them something she thought they ought to like.

After Father was gone, she had redoubled her efforts to make them good. To be good meant to believe; believe the Word. No, no, darling — here is The Word. You must accept The Word — and be saved.

And when they had come home from college for Christmas vacation, in their freshman year, Mother had insisted on the early morning phonograph program, same as when they were tiny tots. This time, Mother operated the phonograph; and when it burst forth lustily with 'He rules the world with truth and grace, and makes the nations prove the glories of His righteousness and wonders of His love,' Jean, who was sitting on the foot of his bed, put both hands over her ears. It was the third year of the World War.... Then Jean — how vividly he remembered the moment — she had her comb in her hand, and had been running it through her lovely corn-yellow hair. She tipped back her head, shook her curls, resumed her combing, and muttered, 'It would be funny — if it wasn't so terribly tragic.'

Now that Mother was gone, one remembered best the sweetness of her. There was no discounting the value of her beliefs in their effect upon *her*. She had gone through hell, at the last, with her inoperable cancer, but The Word had unquestionably come to the rescue. Everybody had marveled at her calmness. You could say what you pleased about religion as an opiate; sometimes that's what you wanted — an opiate. Medical science could be grateful for some sedative strong enough to counteract pain, without doing any damage. There was no sense in sneering at religion because it made people contented with their disappointments and resigned to their incurable miseries. Religion had science licked at that point; no question.

'Word of th' Fa-ther — now in flesh ap-pear-ing ——'

It would be a great thing to be able to believe that; to be able to return — even for an hour — to the ecstasy of complete trust in this declaration. Impossible, of course. It would demand a faith that not only passed all understanding but wilfully dodged facts already well in hand. The Plan of Salvation was idealistic enough, but it wasn't working. It never *had* worked. It had helped Mother die quietly and with a smile, but it hadn't done anything to keep her alive and give her back her health. If the world was to be saved, it would have to escape from its own bigotries, diseases, slaveries. The Plan hadn't done much in this field. Science — not sentiment — was The Word.

The house was quiet. Mrs. Doyle had shut off the radio. Jack roused from his reverie and decided to write to Jean, at home in Oregon.

Dear Girl:

It is midnight here; nine with you. For the past hour I have been listening to Christmas carols on the landlady's radio. All afternoon I worked in the lab. The two things don't jibe.

I tried to get myself back into the state of mind we used to be in when we were children. I honestly wished I could. Something tells me that if you want to be happy, you'd better not begin asking questions — about *anything*. And that brings up the problem — What makes one *want* to be happy? Have you any *right* to be happy? Is that what we're here for — to be *happy*?

He sat there for some minutes, tapping his teeth with his pen; decided impulsively that this wasn't the sort of letter a man should write to his sister on Christmas Eve; crumpled the page and threw it into the waste-basket.

Chapter III

IN MID-FEBRUARY of Beaven's senior year, the capable members of the class were in something of a dither.

All examinations at the Medical College were to be viewed with deep respect, if not alarm, but on this occasion they were of momentous importance, for they had much to do with determining the internship assignments.

Obviously it was impossible for more than a few, from each graduating class, to intern in the University Hospital under the expert eye of the faculty. The hospital could absorb about ten. The rest of them were expected to make other arrangements.

Some of them, resident in far-distant places, preferred — regardless of their scholastic rating — to intern in the locality where they hoped eventually to practice. In many cases the graduate had a father, uncle, or influential friend in the profession who could be depended upon to secure for him a satisfactory berth.

The prized assignments, however, which were based on high marks, entitled the graduate to two or three or four years in the University environment where he was directly under the guidance of men who were considered mentors in their respective specialties. Out of this fortunate group, a smaller number — only two or three, each year — received still more valuable plums in the nature of apprenticeships to certain professors in whose departments they had exhibited unusual interest and skill.

These conferments of honor and glory did not always turn out to the ultimate benefit of the appointee, however desirable they appeared when announced at the convocation.

Graduate Jones, having shown a natural flair for aural surgery, would be taken under the wing of Professor Smith, the king-pin in Otology. Young Jones had access to Smith's personal laboratory where he became a little of everything from dish-washer to researchist. He stood at his chief's elbow in difficult operations; and, in certain sublime moments, assisted. He fagged for Doctor Smith with all the humility of a lackey; drove back to the house to get Smith's other pair of glasses; telephoned social messages of regret when there was some expert lying to be done which couldn't be trusted to the artless Miss Wonderly, the office secretary.

After the wistful young Jones had been sharpening Smith's lead pencils, keeping track of Smith's lecture-notes, and taking Smith's car down town to be lubricated — for a couple of years — he might be permitted to turn out, some inclement night, to minister to the chronic ear-ache of Grandma Perkins, one of Smith's private patients who had been bequeathed to him and his heirs and assigns forever by the late Professor Brown, his predecessor in the Chair of Otology.

From then on, young Jones's future was unpredictable. He might remain as Smith's associate, receiving more and more work of the sort that the chief didn't care to bother with. In this capacity there was plenty of sound experience to be had, both in aural surgery and clandestine starvation. If Smith considerately died before Jones was too infirm to be of any practical use, the latter — assuming he had made himself solid with the powers — might succeed to the Chair. Here the odds were against him, however, for there was a frequent clamor for new blood on the faculty; and some of the Directors seemed to feel that the classic remark, 'A prophet is not without honor save in his own country,' was one of the ten commandments, instead of a dismaying comment on the valuation of merit according to its geographical remoteness.

Desperate at thirty-three, Jones might tug loose to

engage in private practice, in which he might do very well if his drudgeries as Smith's valet, stooge, and bootlicker had not demolished his personality. The appointment was thought to be a plum, but it was as dangerous as dynamite and it ditched more men than it distinguished.

Tubby Forrester had been without a graduate assistant since the first of the year. Young Royce, who had held the post for five years, had gone to teach Anatomy in the deep South. Tubby had been enraged; but, having observed that Royce was determined to go, had aided him in securing a good position.

Everybody was curious to know whether Tubby now intended to tap someone for the vacant job. Unquestionably he needed an able assistant, for he was known to be up to his ears in some private experiments in neuropathology; incubation stuff that required no end of diligent and expert attention. As the matter stood, Tubby was obliged to visit his laboratory at all sorts of odd hours — holidays, midnights, mealtimes — to note the successive phenomena disclosed by his chemical concoctions.

Of course, Jack Beaven was the logical candidate for this position. Anybody could tell you that. Beaven knew so much more about the physical aspects of neurology than anyone else in the class that comparisons were merely silly. He had a peculiar genius for it. And but for their personal animosity, it was inevitable that Tubby would appoint him. That factor, however, made the problem too difficult. It was beyond anyone's imagination that Tubby would sentence himself to such constant and intimate contact with a man he had taunted and insulted; nor was it likely that Beaven would accept the job, in the improbable event of its being offered to him. Under normal circumstances it was exactly the opportunity he would most need and desire, but not at the price of enduring — every day and at close range — humiliations he could neither avoid nor avenge.

During the past year, Jack had accepted Tubby's jabs and jibes in the classroom without attempting to defend himself. On one occasion, however — only a week before the examinations — he had shown that his docility must be accounted for on other grounds than fear. The incident had not improved their personal relations.

Maxwell, grand old exponent of abdominal surgery, had done a most interesting operation on an ulcer requiring the removal of a short section of the small intestine. The demonstration was made before the senior clinic, the students giving it their rapt attention. During the operation, Doctor Maxwell explained that such was the rapidity of natural repair at this point that the suture would be complete and the intestine ready to resume its normal processes at the expiration of four hours.

He further declared that the sphincter muscle at the pyloric orifice of the stomach contracted, immediately upon the beginning of the operation, and remained taut for five hours, to prevent the contents of the stomach from proceeding into the intestine, thus giving the lesion plenty of time to heal itself before going to work again.

After the patient had been wheeled out, still unconscious, the doctor said, 'This act of the pyloric sphincter, which makes the operation possible, is to be studied in the field of Neurology. If you want to know anything about that phase of it, you must take it up with Doctor Forrester. And if he explains it so that you think you understand it, you will know a great deal more about it than I do.'

Evidently someone had queried Tubby on the subject; for, next morning, in his lecture — they were in the midst of a course on the surgery of the autonomic nervous system — Tubby made reference to the case.

'Before presenting the conventional theories held by students of Neurology, I think it might be of interest to learn your own deductions. I would like to have each of you write a paper to be submitted next Thursday. This assignment,' he added, with a sly smile, 'will afford an opportunity for those of you, who still believe in miracles, to let yourselves go, and give us a real taste of the glad evangel. I may ask Brother Beaven to read us his sermon aloud. We would be gratified if he could find a helpful moral lesson, based on this text.'

It was generally believed that Tubby would not carry out this threat. By Thursday he would have forgotten about it. But Jack decided to be prepared, in the event that he was called upon to read his paper before the class.

Having concluded his Thursday lecture, Tubby said, 'And now we will hear from Mr. Beaven. He has been requested to give us a few remarks on the wisdom of the pylorus. It is to be hoped he will add something to the sum of accrued knowledge on this matter.... Mr. Beaven, I suggest that you come to the front where your fellow-scientists may see and hear you without risking a cervic dislocation.'

Jack had enjoyed his task of preparing the paper. The subject was of immense interest to him. He spared no pains in collecting information. It was a scholarly essay, and the class listened to it with utmost concentration.

Briefly recapitulating the diagnosis, and the steps in the operation, he proceeded to discuss the peculiar emergency-act of the sphincter valve.

'It has been shown by Doctor Maxwell,' continued Beaven, 'that the sphincter muscle closed tightly, upon the instant that the intestine was severed, and remained closed until an hour after sufficient time had elapsed for Nature to complete the repair.

'Obviously, the autonomic system provided that a signal be given, arising at the point of the injury, and conveyed to the sphincter muscle. This explanation, however, does not suffice. The presence of the ulcer had already constituted an injury to the intestine, an injury serious enough to suggest that the acidulous contents of the stomach, continuing to flow past the damaged area, would make the lesion increasingly dangerous.

'No such signal was sent to the sphincter; or, if sent, it was unheeded, the sphincter having decided, apparently, that in spite of the unhappy circumstances the business of digestion must carry on. At the moment, however, that the operation began, which gave promise of a remedy for the injured area, the sphincter was willing to co-operate. Up to that time, the sphincter knew there was no use doing anything about it.'

The class was vastly entertained by Beaven's evident plan to edge over into the field of ethics. Everybody's eyes darted to and fro from Tubby's face to Jack's. Tubby's was a study. He sat with averted eyes, toying with his little moustache, listening with respectful attention.

'It has been suggested,' Jack went on, 'that the moral implications on this problem be set forth. In the capacity of class homilist, I venture to call your attention, brethren and sisters, to the extraordinary common-sense displayed by the pyloric sphincter. It is informed, through the autonomic nervous system, that something is going on in a gut which, if continued for very long, will bring the whole institution to ruin.

'An unwise, impatient, unstable pyloric sphincter would be apt to say to the damaged intestine, "It is obvious that you are no good. You are here to do your part in the digestion of food for the nourishment of the whole body. You are not attending to your business. Indeed, every additional task you are asked to perform makes you less and less able to brace up and carry on. That being the case, I shall clamp down hard, and there will be no more work of any sort for you to do. Your resignation is accepted. The funeral will occur on Monday. Friends may send flowers, or omit them at the announced desire of the relatives, and be privately damned for their discourtesy."'

Tubby unexpectedly grinned at this, and the class gave Jack the benefit of an appreciative laugh.

'But because the sphincter is wise,' continued the paper, 'with a wisdom out of all proportion to that which is commonly thought to be seated somewhere between the cowlick and the collar-button, it permits the contents of the stomach to flow through; reluctantly, and wishing the circumstances otherwise, but unwilling to close out the whole business in a mood of exasperated superiority.

'In my opinion, dearly beloved, however miraculous may seem the decisive act of the pylorus in shutting down for a period of five hours — when it had become apparent that an outside force was at work to insure the repair of the injured intestine — this phenomenon is not as difficult to understand as the patience of the sphincter in refusing to exercise drastic judgment through the days when things aren't going as they should.

'One feels that the easiest thing a sphincter can do, under such conditions, is to close up. The act that reveals its wisdom is its forbearance and restraint in the presence of another organ's disability.'

There was a momentary pause; and then, in a serious tone which couldn't quite be evaluated — whether it was spoken in irony or in earnest — Beaven added: '"Grant this, Lord, unto us all."'

Tubby arose during the round of generous applause and when it was quiet he said, 'Brother Beaven's sentimental discussion of the tender mercy practiced by the wise little sphincter valve has been most inspiring. Were it not for the fact that we might disturb our neighbors, I would suggest that we close this meeting with the Long Meter Doxology.... The congregation — without further benefit of clergy — stands dismissed.'

* * * * * * * *

On the day after the mid-semester recess, there was a convocation of the senior class. It was understood that at this assembly the list of internships would be read. Tubby, as the chairman of the faculty committee on such assignments, delivered a brief address, reasserting — and deploring — the fact that the University Hospital could not provide room for a larger number.

The place was very quiet, very tense. Those who felt they were on the border-line where their acceptance or rejection might have been determined by the mere fraction of a point, listened with strained faces and pounding hearts. Tubby pinched on his gold glasses and took up the paper.

Jack Beaven's name headed the list. There was a little gasp of surprise, and a spontaneous burst of applause. Tubby flushed slightly and held up his hand in a signal for order. For a moment or two thereafter, he stood blinking indecisively as if he might be contemplating a comment, but apparently thought better of it and continued reading. Having set itself a pattern for behavior in the reception of this news, the class applauded all the names as they were announced. Tony Wollason made no attempt to conceal his joy when, at the end of the list, he found himself among the immortals.

As for the special appointments, only two, said Tubby, were being made this year. Mr. Thomas, whose work in blood-and-skin had shown promise, would be invited to serve as student assistant to Doctor Meeker. The class offered felicitations to Thomas with a brief clapping of hands. No one knew Thomas very well. He was a mole.

Tubby tapped his papers into precise alignment, signifying that the event was about to be concluded. He took off his glasses and seemed uncertain about the manner in which his final announcement should be phrased.

'And now,' he said, with a half-derisive smile, 'I find myself about to emulate the mysterious wisdom of the pyloric sphincter.'

The class, quick to catch the significance of Tubby's allusion, burst into applause. Say what you liked about the old demon, he was a good sport! Tubby's stock was riding a strong bullish market.

Jack's face colored a little as he realized that everybody was curious to learn his thoughts.

Tubby went on, quietly.

'I am asking Brother Beaven to hold forth in my own laboratory through the coming year. He will serve as my private chaplain. He will spend the remainder of his time with one eye on my test-tubes and the other on the clock; or, when the experiment is more deliberate, on the almanac.' He paused, reflectively. 'This appointment,' continued Tubby, feeling his way, with narrowed eyes, 'may be somewhat in the nature of a surprise. If anyone ever tells you that these special appointments at the Medical College are based upon personal congeniality, or favoritism, or that they are withheld because of temperamental antipathy or private prejudice, I hope you will be able to remember that Beaven and I are at work together solely in the interest of neurological research.'

It was quite a dramatic moment. The class felt that it had been let in on a most unusual scene. The more analytical ones, who thought they knew something about psychology, guessed that Tubby — not quite up to the exactions of a private chat with Jack, on the subject of their relationship — was defining his own attitude in this open session; a strange procedure, but not stranger than many another impulsive act of the erratic neurologist.

Tubby signified that he had said his say, and bowed in mock deference toward his rather bewildered appointee. Suddenly the room was deathly still. Jack had risen to his feet. He bowed respectfully to Tubby, and said, in a steady voice, 'I shall do my best, sir. I, too, believe that "the ship is more than the crew."'

'You mean,' said Tubby, 'you don't have to like the captain in order to obey him?'

Jack nodded.

'That's what I mean, sir,' he said, and sat down.

'This,' said Tubby, 'is a good example of the scientific spirit. . . . That will be all. You are at liberty.'

* * * * * * * * *

Among the scattered members of the medical profession who, as former students and interns, had experienced shabby treatment at Doctor Forrester's hands, not many had nourished a lasting ill-will.

For the most part they spoke of him in about the same way that they remembered certain upperclassmen in college who had paddled them inexcusably on the night of their fraternity initiation. It was something to be laughed over, after a few years had passed.

There was a small number, however, to whom Tubby's ruthlessness was no joke and would never be a joke though they lived to a hundred; men who had been hectored and badgered and finally canned out of school because, perhaps quite inadvertently, they had ruffled the old cock's feathers.

Not infrequently, through the years, a chap would suddenly pack up and leave the Medical College or the hospital, unable to endure any more indignities. In such cases the fellow was likely to deliver to his intimates a malediction, swearing by all the larger gods and smaller fishes that he would get even with Tubby sometime, somewhere, somehow. But, as was to be expected from so much heat and bluster, the tumult subsided as fresher frets or more profitable engagements distracted the attention of the injured. So, Tubby had never been actually kicked out the window or torn limb from limb, as had often been unpleasantly predicted.

It was a common remark among the medics — and younger fry on the faculty, too — that eventually Tubby would get his block knocked off, but everyone knew that an earnest wish had sired the forecast and that nobody would ever go to the length of doing physical damage to Tubby, however much such chastisement might be merited.

Doctor Lawrence Carpenter, ex-member of the Medical School's class of 1920, hadn't blustered nor threatened when in the middle of his third year he had departed. He had left a brief note for Doctor Forrester stating in calm, business-like phrases that he felt he would be more comfortable in another medical college. There was a postscript which said, 'I'll be seeing you, one day, I hope.'

Young Carpenter's chief offense had been of negligible importance. He was of a wealthy family, had been accustomed to spending his large allowance freely, dressed expensively and rather flashily, lived in a ritzy apartment, and drove about in a long rakish roadster that had enough engine-power to drag ten times its weight at an unlawful speed.

Apparently it had never occurred to Larry Carpenter

that in an environment where most of the people lived modestly, if not indeed with a pathetic frugality, his reckless extravagance might excite unfavorable comment.

Fortunately offsetting this bad habit, Larry was co-operative, democratic, genial. He always pulled more than his share of the load when something was afoot requiring class funds, and did it unobtrusively. He entertained frequently and his guests were not selected either on a basis of their having or not having ample means of their own. Beyond question, some of his fellow-students envied him, but not bitterly. Frequently they ragged him about his extensive wardrobe and a few of the more audacious called him 'Gotrocks' to his face, but nobody tried to make his life difficult; nobody but Tubby Forrester.

Tubby had taken a savage dislike to Carpenter at once. It was commonly believed this aversion could be accounted for by the simple fact that Carpenter was not a very diligent student, that he took all the cuts, that he was frequently tardy, and — more particularly — that he refused to be cowed by Tubby's satirical rebukes. But, in the opinion of a few of the more discerning, Tubby didn't like the idea of Larry's financial rating. It gave him an air of independence. When Tubby wanted to administer reproach, he went at it scientifically, studying his victim's vulnerable spots and taking an unerring aim at the point where he could do the most damage. But he never was quite able to call his shots when he went after Larry. Larry would grin, as if he might be saying, 'Entertain yourself, Doc, but keep it in mind that I'm not actually obliged to stay here.' Now and again, in private, someone would suggest that Tubby was jealous. And there was no question about his fondness for good things. He dressed very well, owned a car that made most of the vehicles parked in that vicinity look like junk. When he went to Europe in the summer his stateroom was on A-deck in a five-day ship. Tubby was well-to-do, and didn't object to your knowing it.

That may have had something to do with his feeling

toward Larry Carpenter, or it may not. But, at all events, Tubby began early to ride Larry, insinuating — when the unhappy fellow had muffed a difficult or purposely confusing question — that perhaps if less time were spent on physical adornment and a little more on mental beautification his chances of graduating would be improved. When someone else had failed to answer a question, Tubby was almost sure to gaze disgustedly at Larry, and say, 'And *you* wouldn't know; *would* you?' — until, one day, Larry put an end to that mode of address by answering, impertinently, 'I wouldn't.'

But finally the time came when Carpenter couldn't stand any more, and he left. And perhaps that might have been the end of the story if Tubby hadn't persisted in his animosity. When queried by the Dean of a seaboard medical college, to which Larry had applied for admission, Tubby had let loose a reply that practically insured a rejection. Maybe Tubby thought he was merely being honest. He wrote that Carpenter was an indifferent student, which was a fact, and added that if he had less money and more brains it would be to his advantage.

Pretty well baffled but not beaten, Larry had taken the matter up with the Carpenters' family physician, who made a prompt and thorough investigation, with the result that Larry was accepted, after considerable delay. But, word having leaked that he was entering at this odd hour — within a month of the end of the college year — because of trouble elsewhere, he was received merely on approval.

Having benefited none by his unpleasant experience, he continued to live in a manner quite out of step with the prevailing economy, which did little to set him right in the opinion of an institution that already viewed him askance. So — he had a tough time there; was obliged, upon graduation, to intern in a hospital where the range of clinical material was limited; and felt that he was badly used, all around.

A dispassionate invoice of his woes might have shown

that he was responsible for them himself. Even his close friends realized that he should have known he couldn't act the playboy and expect preferments at the hands of earnest people who slaved while they skimped. In Larry's opinion, however, Tubby Forrester was the fellow who had done him in, and the more he brooded over it the more dangerous was his deepening resolution to get even.

The problem of breaking into active practice — perplexing enough under the most favorable circumstances — proved insurmountable. He was accepted on the staff of a reputable private clinic where it was hoped he might increase a desirable clientèle because of his acquaintance with the society set, but apparently his social connections had more confidence in him at the bridge-table than the operating-table, and they shunned his sumptuous office as if some lethal contagion were raging there. This finished him off.

With a half-dozen rich and idle cronies he went on an extended cruise in the South Seas which turned out to be a protracted binge. Until then, although convivial, Larry was more temperate than most of his sort. Now that he was afloat, physically and emotionally, he loosened the restraints. Whenever he was remorseful and jittery and idiotically self-piteous, he laid all the blame for his failures and excesses onto Tubby, and concocted ingenious plans for vengeance.

Sometimes, when he was at loose ends — he always got mean and quarrelsome whenever he tried to drink himself up out of a hang-over — he would mumble his griefs and confide his sinister program of retaliation, but nobody paid any attention to him, further than to tell him he was just a damn' fool, plastered to the eyebrows, which, while true enough, didn't quite cover the case. Larry meant it, even when sober.

The end of the year had come, and the Medical College had finished its work. There had been a few days' recess which the seniors had spent idly — if they were remaining — or packing their dunnage if they were leaving for good.

Commencement Week was at hand and the town was filling with visitors, parents, alumni, and wiseacres from neighboring colleges.

Carpenter, whose University class was having a reunion, had announced to a score of intimates that he was throwing a party on Tuesday night at the Livingstone Hotel. Immediately after the baseball game, they were to join him in the suite he had engaged. It was a roistering event, the management of the hotel admitting afterwards that while their house was not unused to racket and breakage, an all-time record for damage and disorder had undoubtedly been achieved. Larry saw his guests off to their rooms at dawn but he did not go to bed. For breakfast he had a large bowl of onion soup, some bicarbonate of soda, and two Scotch highballs. Then he took a hot bath, nervously shaved his chin full of nicks, and called for his car.

Arriving at the Medical College campus at eight, he proceeded to Tubby's office, hopeful of finding him there early. He was unarmed, but there was the light of battle in his swollen eyes.

Tubby was seated at his desk when Larry entered, without knocking. He was presently leaving for the University Administration Building where the faculty contingent of the Commencement procession would mobilize for the customary parade to the Auditorium, where in the absence of Dean Emery, he would read the names of the young medical men entitled to degrees. His impressive black gown, with the symbolic green snakes climbing a pole embroidered on the sleeve, was draped across the back of a chair, his gold and green and black silk hood was folded on the desk, and his mortar-board with the bright gold tassel reposed on top of it; well-deserved trappings which he had worn every Commencement for sixteen years, but was not to wear today, on account of an accident which Prexy regretfully announced when stating that Doctor Osgood would present the candidates for the degree — Doctor of Medicine.

He glanced up at the intruder, whom he failed to recognize immediately, blinked a few times, and laid down his pen.

'I see you don't remember me, Tubby,' rasped Carpenter, truculently. 'You gave me the sack, six years ago, and then pursued me with a dirty letter to discredit me.'

'You're drunk,' said Tubby. 'I suggest that you go somewhere and sleep it off. Then, if you think you want to talk to me, I shall listen to you.'

Larry lurched forward, spread out both hands on the desk, and growled, 'Well, if I'm drunk, that's your fault. And what I've got to say to you, I'm goin' to say — right now!'

'Perhaps you'd better pretend you're a gentleman,' advised Tubby, loftily. 'If you insist on talking, take off your hat, and sit down. And be brief.'

'I take my hat off,' said Carpenter, thickly, 'only in places worthy of a decent man's respect. And I haven't come here to sit down and visit. I promised myself, long time ago, I would come back here, sometime when it was convenient, and punch your nose. And this is the day. Maybe it will be rather awkward for you — my showing up just as you are getting ready to go over to the Auditorium and show off your finery, but that's your picnic; not mine. If you want to wear a lot o' colors, you might as well have a red beak and a black eye. Now — will you take it sitting, or would you prefer to stand up?'

'I'll stand, thank you,' said Tubby, pushing back his chair. 'I haven't had much experience in fighting. I've delegated all that to my dog.'

Larry moved around the corner of the desk and stood with feet wide apart.

'Better take your glasses off,' he warned.

Tubby thought so too, and laid them down deliberately.

'It's a pity to spoil that mug,' taunted Carpenter, taking a step forward.

At that instant, Tubby waded in courageously. He had spoken the truth about his inexperience in fighting. He whanged away wildly with both hands and both eyes shut. Carpenter backed off a little and took his measure; then he began to fulfill his promise. Tubby's valor was in fine fettle, but his technique was bad. He left his stomach unguarded until his wind gave out, and then he began leading with his chin. His flesh was soft and Carpenter's knuckles were hard. Presently they were in the center of the room, Tubby having felt that he needed more space, and Larry willing to accommodate him. Now there was a bad cut over Tubby's left eye and his nose was bleeding. The battle was going to be over, pretty soon. They both felt that, confidently.

Then the door opened.

Beaven had been in Tubby's laboratory to check the temperature of an incubation. On his way out he heard the sound of scuffling in the office. For a moment he stood listening intently; then opened the door. The belligerents paused to take note of his arrival. Tubby was panting hard. His face was white as chalk, and bleeding in a half-dozen places.

'Get out of here!' yelled Carpenter, as Beaven stepped between them. 'I mean to finish this job!'

Tubby leaned back wearily against the edge of the desk, holding on for support and swaying dizzily. Carpenter elbowed Beaven aside and drew back his arm to apply the final blow. Before he had a chance to deliver it, he found himself suddenly whirled about.

'So — you want in it too, do you?' he snarled, facing his new antagonist. 'Well, take *that!*' He struck savagely, but the blow fell short.

Jack didn't relish the task that had fallen to him, for it was plainly evident that the big fellow was in a drunken frenzy, but it was no time to be considerate. He saw no reason for prolonging the engagement. The chap was running wild, and would have to be put away promptly and decisively. He deliberately selected a spot on the mandible, just below the second bicuspid, where the foramen gives exit to the mental branch of the fifth nerve, and struck it a sledge-hammer blow that would have knocked the bronze image of a major-general out of his saddle. Carpenter's knees buckled under him and he dropped limply to the floor.

Taking up the telephone, Jack asked for the Medical Library. Only ten minutes ago he had left Wollason there, who had gone in to return some books, and was to wait until Jack finished his errand in the laboratory.

'Come up to Doctor Forrester's office,' he said, quietly. 'There has been a little accident. Don't say anything — and come quickly.'

Tubby had groped his way around to the other side of the desk and was slumped in his chair. He roused with an effort and watched Beaven who, down on one knee, was examining the fallen warrior.

'Is he badly hurt?' asked Tubby, huskily.

Jack turned back an eyelid, felt the pulse, unbuttoned the man's collar.

'He'll come around, presently,' he said. 'Who is he?'

'Former student here,' mumbled Tubby. 'Drunken bounder.'

'Umm,' Jack nodded, comprehendingly.

'I hope we may be able to keep this quiet,' said Tubby, with a dry throat.

'Yes, sir.'

Tony Wollason opened the door and surveyed the scene with wide eyes.

'Jeze!' he exclaimed. 'What happened?'

'Shut the door, Tony. This drunken bruiser came here and assaulted Doctor Forrester. It's quite important this doesn't get out. Give him a sniff of something and stay here with him until he is able to stand up. Then take him to Doyle's in a taxi and put him in my bed. Don't do it until you're sure the building is cleared. Everybody will be over at the Auditorium presently.'

'But, hell, Jack — how about Commencement?'

'We'll be there in time for our diplomas.' Beaven turned to his stricken chief. 'Now, Doctor, if you're able, we will go over to your laboratory, and I'll try to put you together again.' Taking him by the arm, he led Tubby out through the lecture-room and into the small laboratory where he eased him into a chair. Tubby was pale and shaky.

'Nauseated?' inquired Jack, coldly professional. He lighted the gas under a small sterilizer.

'A little,' gulped Tubby, feebly.

'Want to throw up or lie down — or both?' Jack's tone was dryly indifferent. He went to a glass case and laid out a pair of scissors, a roll of antiseptic gauze, a spool of adhesive tape, and a couple of surgical needles.

Tubby retched ominously and Jack brought him a basin. Then, going out into the anatomical laboratory, he wheeled in an autopsy-table and helped his distinguished patient to spread himself upon it. Tubby sank back with a groan. Jack began sponging the bloody wounds.

'Fortunate — you — arrived,' muttered Tubby, at length. 'The fellow — would have beaten me — to death.'

'Probably,' drawled Jack, swabbing the open cuts with an earnest antiseptic. 'That's why I stopped him. We can't have you killed, you know.'

'He came up — to try to settle — an old score,' explained Tubby, clenching his hands as the disinfectant bit deep.

'Well — I don't know how much he owed you' — Jack paused to rig a needle — 'but he seems to have paid off quite a bit of it.'

Tubby grinned sourly and closed his eyes as the needle-work began, but did not flinch.

'Took me by surprise,' mumbled Tubby.

'I don't see why you should have been surprised, sir,' said Jack, his eyes intent upon the delicate task. 'You've had several good lickings coming to you, for a long time — if you don't mind my saying so.'

'Perhaps you think *you* owe me one,' commented Tubby, painfully. 'If so, why did you interfere?'

'Because you are very important to neurological surgery, for one thing. And, besides, I want to know a lot of things that nobody else knows — but you.' Jack deliberately took up the scissors and snipped the dangling ends from a suture.

Tubby opened his eyes and stared up into Jack's impassive face.

'That,' he declared, solemnly, 'is the most cold-blooded remark that was ever made — by one man to another — in the history of the world.'

Jack rethreaded the needle deftly and resumed his work on a fresh area.

'Knowing how you feel, sir, on the subject of sympathy and sentimentality,' said Jack, 'I thank you. If our positions were reversed, you would have no very good reason for sparing my life.'

'You do yourself an injustice, Brother Beaven,' replied Tubby, squinting acknowledgment of the next stitch. 'I can make good use of you.'

Jack regarded his patient with a new interest.

'After what has happened today?' he queried. 'I shouldn't have thought you would ever want to see me again.'

'Perhaps not — if you were doing this as a personal favor. In that event I might feel at a disadvantage. But you have considered this a professional duty. You didn't want to see me killed because I have information you need. And you are sewing me up for the same reason. I owe you nothing. If our positions were — as you say — reversed, I would have taken the same attitude toward you, I think. You will be of great service to me as an assistant here in the laboratory. I shouldn't want to lose you.'

Jack sheared off a strip of adhesive from the spool and applied it to Tubby's cheek.

'I am glad to hear you say, sir, that our relations are to remain purely professional. Now that this is mutually understood, we can work together more efficiently.'

'More efficiently than what?' growled Tubby.

'Than if you were afraid I might develop — by propinquity — some personal liking for you, sir. You may safely dismiss any such apprehension.' Jack smoothed on the last strip of adhesive with firm fingers. 'Want to sit up now? How does it feel?'

'Good job,' admitted Tubby.

'Your car out in the lot?'

'Yes.'

'I'll drive you home. You live at the University Club, don't you? We'll try to get you in without too much excitement.'

'Thanks, Brother Beaven, but I don't care to accept any further attentions. You may go on now about your business.'

'I made the suggestion, sir, because we must keep this affair quiet. I don't believe you can do it — by yourself. And I don't want you worried over the chatter that might result if this got noised about.'

Tubby snarled.

'It wouldn't be any of your damn' business if I was worried.'

'Pardon me,' contradicted Jack, 'but it most certainly would be of personal concern and disadvantage to me if you were hectored by humiliating gossip. In that case you couldn't possibly be at your best. Your mind would be distracted. You are a very important scientist and I want to have access to you at your fittest. Otherwise' — he tossed a negligent gesture that dismissed the whole matter — 'otherwise — I shouldn't care two whoops in hell if everybody in the world heard about your squabble with this fellow — and laughed. Am I making myself clear?'

Tubby blinked thoughtfully for a minute and replied grimly, 'In that case, you may drive me home.' He tugged his keys out of his pocket with a hand that still trembled. 'I'll meet you — out in front.'

'Think you can get downstairs by yourself, sir?' asked Jack, doubtfully. 'Perhaps you'd better come along with me — and let me steady you a bit. You're pretty badly shaken, you know.'

'Do as I tell you!' barked Tubby.

'Cigarette?' Jack offered his opened pack.

'I'll smoke my own,' growled Tubby, fumbling in his coat pocket.

'Light?' Jack struck a match.

Tubby shook his head.

Jack grinned — and left the room.

* * * * * * * *

The problem of getting Tubby into the University Club without stirring up a lot of interest and curiosity was gratifyingly simple. At almost any other time this feat would have been impossible. But all the residents and guests were either at the Administration Building, mobilizing for the Commencement parade, or at the Auditorium awaiting it. To the doorman and the elevator boy it was necessary only to say that there had been a little accident — of no consequence.

'No, no, no,' spluttered Tubby, when the steward wanted to go up with him and make him comfortable. 'It's nothing. I'll be quite all right. If anyone inquires, tell them — tell them I'm quite all right. But — no callers; no telephone messages; no anything, until I notify you.'

Having unloaded his responsibility, Jack was undecided what to do with the car. He didn't know where Tubby kept it and disliked to inquire. It might bring on a flood of questions. So he drove on, turned the corner, and headed toward his rooming-house. Tony would probably be waiting there for further instructions.

Parking the coupé in front of the Doyle house, Jack went upstairs and met Tony in the hallway.

'How's your rambunctious friend by now?' asked Jack.

'Asleep,' said Tony. 'He got so noisy that I had to put him away. After all, we're graduating and the procession is forming right now. We ought to be there. I haven't toiled and starved for years to let some drunken bum keep me from ——'

'You and me — both,' agreed Jack. 'How much did you give him: enough to hold him until we get back?'

'Bet your life,' muttered Tony. 'I gave him the needle. He ought to be contented until two o'clock.'

'Hope you didn't overdo it.'

'No — only a quarter grain — and just a mere sliver more — to be generous.'

'Come on, then. Have you told Lady Doyle?'

Tony nodded.

They went down to the car. Jack started the motor and they pushed off toward the Auditorium.

'I've got to get some sort of message to Osgood — or somebody — accounting for Tubby's absence,' he said, anxiously. 'Can't quite decide how to do it. Anything to suggest? I asked Tubby what explanation he wanted given but he was still too unhooked to hatch a bright idea.'

'Tell 'em he was injured slightly in an explosion,' said Tony, helpfully. 'That'll be near enough the truth.' They both chuckled at this and Jack agreed that it was a good thought.

'I'll write a note and pass it in to Osgood or Shane or someone,' he said, suddenly relieved. 'That will save questions and answers.'

'Right! — and the old buzzard can fill in the details when he gets around to it,' assisted Tony. 'Gosh! — but Tubby took an awful lickin'! How many stitches did he need?'

'I didn't count 'em,' said Jack, soberly, unwilling to share Tony's sardonic glee. 'Dozen or so, maybe.'

'Did you have a good time?' pressed Tony.

'Can't say that I did.' Jack's tone was serious. 'I went to no bother to make it easy for him. But — Tubby was game. Tubby's a brute, no doubt; but he can take it!' There was a thoughtful silence. 'Funny thing, Tony: I hate old Tubby like hell; but ——'

'Yeah — I know,' grumbled Tony. 'You hate him like hell but you think he's wonderful. You hate him like hell but you follow him around like a dog — and you're near enough like him to be his son. If I'd been in your place, I'd have sewed him up with Grade-A sash-cord — and then I'd have sewed his mouth shut!'

'It's the most important mouth on this campus,' declared Jack. 'You don't have to like Tubby to admit that he's a great man. Tubby's sound — all the way through. I'm for everything he stands for, Tony. And I liked the way he took his beating — and his stitches.'

They parked Tubby's big coupé a block from the Administration Building. Jack scribbled a note, and they proceeded to the main entrance where the faculties were assembling, bright with dear-bought colors and hot with the weight of their heavy robes. Finding the medical outfit, he pushed through the dignified crowd and handed his message to Shane. Then he hurried away to rejoin Tony and his class at the far end of the long hall where the graduating medics milled about, self-consciously blowing their ragged silk tassels out of their eyes and wishing they dared smoke a cigarette.

Viewed in prospect, this graduation day had ever been a beacon light shining brightly in Jack's imagination. It would be — he had always felt — a stirring sensation to stand, at the summons of good old Prexy, and listen to the sonorous words, 'By virtue of the authority vested in me — I confer upon you the degree — Doctor of Medicine.' It promised to be a most impressive moment, to be faced with all the reverence of a candidate for holy orders. It was a bit disillusioning to find oneself pawing over the cheap black rags that lay tousled on the long tables, hunting for a gown that would reach below one's knees and a mortarboard big enough to fit an adult skull. Tony looked so funny in his No. 6 hat that Jack laughed.

'Don't know how I'm going to keep the damn' thing on,' muttered Tony.

'Vacuum pressure,' suggested Jack, dryly. 'That ought to hold it.'

In this mood they fell into line and marched to the Auditorium, well to the fore of the long parade — a full thousand — graduating from the various colleges. The big organ boomed forth Elgar's 'Pomp and Circumstance.' Somebody made a prayer. Somebody made a speech. The diploma mill began to grind. At exactly twelve-ten Shane came to the front of the platform and said, 'The candidates for the degree — Doctor of Medicine — will please rise.'

They rose. Prexy, a bit mellow, indulged himself to the extent of a brief, informal announcement before conferring the degree. They were entering upon one of the most noble, most exacting, most sacrificial of the learned professions. 'It distresses me to announce,' he went on, 'that Doctor Forrester, who was to have been with us here today, has been hurt in a laboratory explosion. Early morning — Commencement Day — when, one would think, the Doctor might find himself at liberty from his professional duties, he goes to his laboratory to pursue his important experiments; and, in the course of his work, suffers injury. I commend to you this example of fidelity. You are about to set forth on a great adventure in the cause of human welfare. You are to be envied your high privilege: you are to remember that there is no discharge in this war. . . . And now — by virtue of the authority vested in me ——'

And so — they were Doctors of Medicine. Tony had nudged Jack with his elbow when Prexy was decorating Tubby, *in absentia*, but Jack gave no sign that he thought the situation amusing.

After they had disposed of their battered finery in the Administration Building, Jack remarked that he must now put up Tubby's car; so they telephoned to the University Club for instructions, drove the coupé to the public garage where it belonged, paused at a drug store for a sandwich and a glass of milk, and took a street-car to the Medical College. It was half-past one.

'I say, Tony,' said Jack, impulsively, 'this fellow Carpenter left his car up there this morning. Maybe we'd better see what's become of it.'

'Think we'd recognize it?'

'Probably. He's from Philadelphia. Pennsylvania license, no doubt. If it's locked, we can get his keys.'

The car was not locked. Apparently Carpenter had been too intent on his errand to exercise much prudence. It was indeed a very good-looking vehicle. Tony said he would do the driving, this time. Mrs. Doyle was rocking on the front verandah when they drew up. She grinned a little and remarked that they seemed to prefer riding to walking, today. Tony told her they had stolen the other car and traded it for this one, adding that when the police arrived she should tell them the robbers had left on foot.

'You *are* a one,' conceded Mrs. Doyle, amiably.

Proceeding to Jack's room, they entered without knocking and found Carpenter engaged in producing a yawn of large dimensions. He raised up on one elbow and took stock of his guests. Then his brow clouded as he recognized Jack. It was apparent that he anticipated some more trouble.

'Where am I?' he asked, thickly.

Tony volunteered to clear things up.

'You are at the residence of a Mrs. Doyle, who earns her living by housing medical men. I am *Doctor* Tony Wollason. My young friend, in whose bed you have been languishing, is *Doctor* Jack Beaven — a fine, upstanding, resolute fellow, whose acquaintance you made earlier in the day when you were presenting your former teacher with a bam on the snoot. Do you recall?'

Carpenter nodded, grinned tentatively, and glanced toward Jack, uncertain what rôle he was expected to play.

'I'm sorry,' he muttered. 'I was drunk.'

'You were indeed,' agreed Tony. 'But — speaking unofficially, and for myself alone — I feel that you did a good day's work. And if it is customary with you to perform such services while drunk, you certainly must be a very useful citizen when in your right mind.'

'I'd rather not be kidded,' said Carpenter, bristling a little. 'It isn't very funny.'

'You have the right attitude, I think,' said Jack, soberly. 'You paid off Doctor Forrester, and now you wish you hadn't. Well — you didn't hurt him very badly, and we have contrived to keep the affair quiet. Nobody is going to know anything about it — unless you get drunk again and spill it.' He leaned against the foot of the bed and extended an ominous index-finger toward Carpenter's heavy eyes. 'And — if you do — you'll have me to settle with! As Wollason has indicated, you doubtless had cause for provocation and couldn't be much blamed for taking your revenge. But — now that you've had it — let that be sufficient. I want to go on record with a promise: if I ever hear — next week or ten years from now — that you have told what happened this morning, I shall hunt you down and break your neck!'

'That's right, Mr. Carpenter,' advised Tony, pretending earnestness. 'The little tap he gave you was a mere free sample of the standard-size wallop he administers when he's mad.'

'Shut up!' growled Jack. 'This is no time for fooling. . . . Mr. Carpenter, your car is out in front of the house. If you want to go, there's no reason why you shouldn't. If you want to use the telephone — or if there is anything we can do for you, we'll be happy to oblige.'

'Thanks,' said Carpenter, sincerely. 'You have been very kind. I'll go now. You needn't fear that I shall ever tell about this. I'm plenty ashamed of it.'

'Well — I wouldn't fret too much about it,' drawled Jack. 'Here: let me give you a hand with those trousers.'

* * * * * * * * *

Late in the afternoon Tony, rousing from a satisfactory two-hour nap, dressed with unusual care and sauntered over to the deserted Medical campus. Entering the dingy, echoing lower corridor of Lister Hall he lazily mounted the well-worn, creaking stairs to Tubby's private laboratory where he knew Jack could be found making notes on some important cultures demanding frequent inspection.

The door was ajar, so Tony came in without knocking, crossed the room to the table where Jack sat hunched over the big Zeiss, and jabbed a thumb into his industrious friend's short ribs. Detaching himself from his occupation, Jack glanced up, appraised the intruder with curiosity, and returned to his job at the microscope.

'What's up?' he mumbled, absently. 'Why do you appear in this festal raiment, Doctor Wollason? Are you to be Queen of the May?'

'It had occurred to me, Professor,' said Tony, 'that considering we have had a long and eventful day we might go down into the bright lights for dinner. If this thought commends itself to you, and your conscience will permit a brief absence from this sweet-smelling garden of roses ——'

'Where had you thought we'd go, Doctor?' asked Jack, without looking up.

'How about the Livingstone? It builds up my personality amazingly to swagger through the lobby and sprawl in those big leather chairs.'

'You mean the ones in the little enclosure marked "Reserved for Guests"? I never sit there. I'm a very proud and sensitive person.'

'There'll be no temptation to lounge in the lobby tonight. The place will be packed. Lots of little parties. Swarms of alumni. Much excitement. Sounds of revelry. Better come along. It will be good for us.'

Tony hadn't been very hopeful. His face lighted when Jack replied negligently that the idea — if one considered its source — was surprisingly sound, adding that he would be ready to go in five minutes.

'Of course you realize,' he went on, 'that I shall be obliged to return to the house for a more suitable costume. If the Livingstone is a-buzz with important social functions perhaps it may aid our personality development if we wear dinner clothes.'

'Sorry,' regretted Tony, 'I haven't a clean dress shirt.'

'You shall have one of mine,' said Jack, unctuously. 'I shall give you the pleated one. I try to do one good deed every day, thus accumulating treasures in heaven.' He closed his notebook, tossed it into the desk-drawer, and went to the closet for his coat.

'Your manner of speech, Doctor Beaven,' observed Tony, 'increasingly reveals the influence of your irreverent master.' Suddenly abandoning his persiflage, he added seriously, 'It's a solemn fact, Jack. You're more like old Tubby every day; do you know it? I can remember the time when Tubby's flippancies and sacrilegious flings annoyed you frightfully.'

'Thanks for the sermon, Padre,' drawled Jack, reaching for his hat. 'If you will now pronounce the benediction, we'll go and find you a shirt.'

'That's the sort of thing I mean; damn it!' spluttered Tony. 'You ought to snap out of that, old son, before it gets to be a habit. You're going to be talking with all sorts of patients, pretty soon; people who haven't anything left but their religion — and — and their sentiment — and they won't like it.... I'm just telling you,' he finished lamely. 'People don't like Tubby. They're afraid of him. That's one of the reasons. Better look out.'

Jack gave him a comradely slap on the shoulder as they moved toward the door.

'Tell you what we'll do, Tony,' he said, teasingly. 'We'll hang out our shingle together. I'll do the diagnosis and the treatment — and you go along to cheer 'em up.'

Tony made no reply until they were out in the air. It was evident that he hadn't enjoyed this spoofing.

'We'll not talk any more about it,' he said, glumly. 'If you want to be just like Tubby — or even out-Tubby Tubby — go to it — and joy be with you.'

'Wonder how the old boy's getting on,' reflected Jack, glad to drop the disquieting subject that had put a momentary constraint between them.

'Perhaps you'd better call up and inquire,' suggested Tony.

Jack chuckled.

'He'd probably tell me to go to hell.'

'It's a very pleasant friendship,' observed Tony. 'Anybody can see that.'

'I don't want his friendship,' growled Jack. 'I want his skill, his information, his surgical technique. If you don't mind my tooting my own horn for a few measures, Tony, I'm rather proud of the fact that I can learn valuable lessons from a man I don't like.'

Tony was thoughtful for a moment before replying.

'Well — before you canonize yourself for your magnanimity,' he remarked, dryly, 'you'd better make sure that you don't like him. I've a notion that this animosity between you two silly asses is superficial.'

'Let's talk about something else,' suggested Jack. 'What other ideas have you?'

* * * * * * * *

As Tony had predicted, they had found the Livingstone unusually active. Arriving at seven-thirty, they had made their way slowly through the noisy lobby where knots of old fellows, who had dined early, were spinning yarns and smoking big cigars. The crowded foyer was a-twitter with feminine voices; wives, no doubt, temporarily left on the beach by their learned spouses.

The congestion in the big dining-room had been somewhat relieved. A table for two was presently available.

'Know those fellows?' asked Tony, indicating the pair of diners nearest them. Jack glanced across and took brief stock of the neighbors, who were finishing their dessert; urbane, graying men in their late forties. He shook his head.

'Do you?' he asked. 'Look like doctors.'

'The one on this side is Woodbine,' said Tony, out of the corner of his mouth. 'Buffalo. Pulmonary.'

Jack nodded.

'I've heard of him. Good man. How did you recognize him?'

'Someone pointed him out to me this morning. They're talking shop, I think.'

Jack took up the menu card.

'In the humble home where I was reared,' he remarked, idly, 'we were taught that it is impolite to eavesdrop or squat at keyholes. You listen to their conversation — and tell me what they are saying — and I'll see what there is to eat.'

The waiter was at hand now and they gave him their orders. The man across from Doctor Woodbine was talking earnestly.

'— And one of these days, Jimmy, there's going to be a bomb dropped into camp. You'll see! Sometimes I think the Medical College is almost as sad a place as a reforma-

tory. You take the reformatory now. Sound enough in
theory. The state rigs up an institution for the reclamation
and development of mishandled boys; arranges for their
schooling, sports, health; provides shops, amusements,
movies. But the whole thing falls down because the guards
and teachers and overseers take a cynical view of the pro-
ject. The boys catch it. They contaminate one another. . . .
Same thing goes for the medical school. Dry old devils on
the faculty, each obsessed with his own little specialty.
Nobody interested in the humanitarian aspects of the profession. Medics get to thinking it's smart to be cold. . . .
You take the situation — right here ——' He lowered his
voice and leaned forward to mutter something inaudible
to the attentive young pair near by.

Tony quizzed Jack's eyes and grinned a little.

'Ever talk with Cunningham about this?' Woodbine was
saying. 'He has some pretty strong convictions. Fearless,
too. . . . By the way, he's making the principal speech tonight at the Ninety-Nine class reunion.'

'I know it. Wish I could get in on it.'

Woodbine chuckled; picked up the dinner-check, brought
out his wallet.

'Too bad old Tubby's laid up,' he said. 'They're of the
same class; aren't they? They might put on quite a
sprightly debate.'

The soup came on. Jack became immediately attentive
to it. The older men pushed back their chairs and left the
dining-room. Tony ventured a comment on what they had
heard. 'Most interesting,' he observed.

'Oh?' said Jack, indifferently. 'I didn't find it so. Nothing new; is it? Same old complaint. Lot o' these old has-
beens — too damn' lazy to keep up with the march of
science — trying to defend their own indolence by making
war on their betters. . . . Have an olive?'

* * * * * * * *

The foyer was practically cleared when Jack and Tony
came out of the dining-room. At the farther end of it a

close-packed little crowd was assembled, evidently listening to something of considerable interest.

'Shall we see what's up?' asked Jack. They strolled toward the overflow meeting that had mobilized about the half-open door of the ordinary. It was one of the occasions when they found it of advantage to be tall. Twenty-five or thirty grizzled old chaps — easily recognizable as doctors — were listening to a speech. This, agreed Jack and Tony, with an exchange of knowing nods, would be the Medical Class of Ninety-Nine; and the speaker, beyond all question, was Cunningham.

'Want to stay?' whispered Tony.

'For a minute.' Jack turned his head to listen sharply, his narrowed eyes aimlessly taking in the neighbors, more than half of whom were women. This would be natural, of course. It was probably the sort of speech that women would enjoy. A few feet away a very pretty girl in black satin attracted his curiosity. She wasn't seeing anything, for her view was quite obstructed, but she was listening hard. Her head was tipped back a little, her eyes were raised, her lips were parted. It unquestionably was, thought Jack, the most beautiful head he had ever seen; hair so black it was midnight-blue, bobbed — and straight bangs that covered half of an unusually white forehead. Jade eardrops. Shapely ears. He began to be ashamed of himself for staring, but the girl was so completely unaware of his scrutiny that he continued to observe her. She looked foreign. Didn't seem to belong here. Longest lashes he had ever noticed. Their curling tips almost touched her brows: the brows were gracefully arched. He wasn't hearing a word that this Doctor Cunningham was saying. He glanced out of the tail of his eye and found Tony raptly absorbed in the speech. Resolved to listen, he concentrated on the voice that sounded as if it spoke with deep feeling. Now he began to catch the drift of it.

'Menaced by the threat of over-sophistication . . .'

Jack's eyes traveled slowly back to the attractive girl. He was not naturally disposed to invoice women's physical proportions, but it occurred to him that a man would have to be a hardened atheist indeed if he could look at this girl and deny the existence of a benevolent Creator. He told himself he had no right to be gazing at her; but, after all, it was about the same as looking at a lovely picture.

Standing beside her was a woman probably old enough to be her mother, a quite distinguished figure, blonde, intelligent, poised. They seemed somehow to belong together. Jack wondered if they were related; tried to find some facial resemblance.

Suddenly the girl turned her head and looked him squarely in the eyes, surprising him in the act of offering her an admiration so utterly undisguised that his expression, he knew, was equivalent to a statement of his thoughts. It was exactly as if he had said, 'I hope I'm giving you no offense, but you are the most adorable creature I ever saw.'

For an instant, she queried him with her wide eyes — a childlike question, as to say, 'Why?' And she couldn't be blamed. She thought they had met — and she had forgotten — and he had remembered. He couldn't turn away from that inquisitive pair of eyes with a confession that he had simply been staring. So — he ventured a smile and was promptly rewarded. Without the slightest suggestion of reticence or shyness or pretence of aloofness, she returned his smile and resumed her interest in the address. Jack's heart skipped a beat. It was high time now, he felt, to attend to the meeting. Clearly — something had been said which had been of so much interest to her that she had thought he, too, had been impressed by it. That was why she had smiled, no doubt. That was why he had smiled, she may have thought. So — he listened.

You had to admit that the fellow was a convincing speaker, and meant every word he said. But — it was the same old stuff. Appeal to sentiment. Doctors must be altruists. Doctors must realize their responsibility to guide their patients into a safe and sound thought-life. Jack scowled. Tony leaned forward and whispered, 'Want to go?'

He didn't want to go, but he mighty well knew that Tony would be curious if he wanted to remain. He nodded — but did not stir.

'No matter how discriminating we may be in our diagnoses,' Cunningham was saying, 'no matter how skillful we are with our surgery, how canny with our evaluation of X-ray pictures, how thorough our pathology, our usefulness to our generation swings on one axis. When the laboratory becomes of paramount importance, and physical healing becomes the all-in-all, we are shorn of our greatest strength; we have declined to accept our highest commission. We are living in a time of amazing progress in science, and no man of our vocation dares lose one step in this onward progress; but it is my solemn conviction that when all's said that can be said about our duty to keep abreast of modern research and experiment, our job is primarily an affair of the heart. It may be tame and trite to say that love of humanity is the greatest thing in the world, but without that urge all the new patter of science is as sounding brass and a tinkling cymbal. I may have all faith in the amazing progress of our honored craft, our clever inventions, our efficient implements, our instruments of precision — but, if I have not love, I am nothing!'

It was too, too much. Jack turned to Tony and muttered, unfortunately loud enough to be overheard by the girl, 'Let's go. I've had enough of this love-bird.'

She looked up into his eyes with a baffled, beaten expression, as if he had struck her in the face. Instantly he repented of his impulsive rudeness. What if she was somehow related to this Cunningham? He wanted to apologize. For a second he lingered. Tony was pushing out through the crowd and he followed.

They fell into step.

'What did you make of that girl?' inquired Tony.

'What girl?' muttered Jack.

'Oh, well — never mind,' drawled Tony. 'You must have been pretty hard hit if you can't bear to speak of her to your closest playmate.'

'Pardon me, Tony. I was still thinking about that sloppy speech. Did you ever — in all your life ——'

Tony slipped his hand through Jack's arm and slowed his steps.

'You said to me, this afternoon, that it is a great thing when a man can learn lessons from people he dislikes; people who are antipathetic, antagonistic. I suggest that you try this out on someone else besides old Tubby. Perhaps you might learn something from Cunningham.'

Chapter IV

ALTHOUGH their mutual antipathy remained unchanged, the three years of Jack Beaven's internship (and 'apprenticeship' under Doctor Forrester) had been speeded by interesting problems in the field of inquiry to which they were devoted.

Beaven's work was exacting and exhausting. Not only was he expected to perform the usual hospital drudgeries incident to the career of an ordinary 'house-pup,' but he was obliged to toil in Tubby's laboratory where increasing responsibilities were shifted to his broad shoulders.

Tubby never went to the length of commending him for his diligence, nor did he ever voice any satisfaction over the rapid development of his young subordinate's unusual talents, but it was plainly evident — by the reckless confidence with which he left important experiments in Beaven's hands — that he had full respect for the knowledge and skill of his loyal assistant.

Their relationship continued to be frostily professional. Doctor Forrester issued orders cogently, crisply, haughtily. Jack answered, 'Yes, sir,' in exactly the same metallic tone, scrupulously respectful but devoid of the slightest trace of amiability. They never exchanged smiles or civilities; never said 'Good morning' or 'Good night'; never told each other that it was a warm day or a cold one. No comments were ever offered concerning current events, however startling. All England could go on strike, a tropical hurricane could devastate the Florida coast, Lindbergh could fly to Paris; such matters were not mentioned between them. Conversation was infrequent, laconic, and restricted to business. Had it been announced, some morning, that the world was coming to an end at five o'clock that afternoon, neither would have known or cared how the other felt about it.

But when a laboratory experiment had reached a phase where its success or failure was at stake, with a canny guess to be refuted or verified, they became intensely aware of each other and alive to the sole bond that united them. On such occasions they rubbed elbows companionably as they peered at test-tubes held up to the light, and touched heads as they studied baffling X-ray plates, growing gleeful over their findings and momentarily sharing their delight; or, if they had been foiled and deluded, raspingly muttering their damns in concert. At these times, they were in complete accord. Their normal relation of austere preceptor and taciturn disciple gave way to such a harmony of mind and mood that anyone observing them — sitting side by side, ear to ear, on their tall stools, breathlessly watching the reaction of a solution into which three drops of some potent acid had been introduced — might have thought them father and son.

One day — it was near the close of Beaven's second year as Tubby's assistant — an incident occurred which, while trifling enough in itself, indicated their mutual attitude perfectly. Jack had just succeeded, after much painstaking work, in accomplishing a very delicate adjustment in a temperamental microscope. Tubby, absent-mindedly occupied with his own business and unaware of what was afoot at his assistant's table, stamped heavily across the room, on his way out, and was suddenly stopped in his tracks by Jack's sharp command, *'Easy, there! And don't you slam that door!'*

The impudent order had popped out involuntarily. With the echo of the words in his ears, Jack's heart missed a beat. He realized that he had done a pretty dreadful thing, and glanced up expecting to face a justifiable indignation. Tubby was proceeding the rest of the way on tiptoe. He closed the door very softly behind him. Jack tightened his fingers into an astonished fist, caught his lip between his teeth, drew a quick smile that registered an immense satisfaction, and made a decisive gesture of approval in the direction of the door. '*At*taboy!' he exclaimed. It was fine! It was of the stuff that they put into grand opera!

Tubby was a brute. He hated him. In any other but their present relationship, he would have wanted to get even with him somehow for his continued meanness. But in the laboratory, when important things were in process, he and Tubby were not related as a pompous professor and an immature associate. They stood on an equal footing here, humbly serving the same master. Every personal consideration — their mutual dislike, their temperamental incompatibility, their vast difference in rank, age, experience — everything in which they differed, and everything they despised in each other was ignored when their common master made a demand! Everything else had to move onto the siding — and let Science have the right-of-way. It was quite a stirring thought.

Jack often wished he knew the nature of Tubby's feelings about this. As for himself, he occasionally pondered it, sometimes with a studious frown, sometimes with a broad grin, but always with a sensation of pride. The relation between himself and Tubby Forrester might be deucedly irritating to both of them, but this much could be said for it: Their personal animosity dignified their job. The job was bigger than they were, and they both knew it.

Always he had been strangely stirred by Kipling's declaration, 'The ship is more than the crew.' That sort of gallantry gave him a sense of exaltation. Human progress could proceed at a startling pace, he felt, if every intelligent man regarded his task with such devotion. Doubtless the sluggish movement of civilization could be explained by the half-hearted efforts of men whose attention was distracted by all manner of outside interests. They didn't keep their eye on the ball. They spent an inordinate amount of time and thought on their own affairs; associates watching one another anxiously to make sure the other fellow wasn't paid a larger salary, didn't own a bigger car, hadn't taken a longer vacation. The trouble was, obviously, that they weren't committed to their job. That was what ailed civilization: too much jealousy and selfishness interfering with the minds of the people who ordered the world's work. They didn't care a damn for the ship, so long as they got what they thought was coming to them — in rank, wages, shore leaves, pensions.

All the way down the line of human action, the machinery of progress was screechingly hot with the friction of personalities yelping for preferments. What society needed most was the equivalent of the Hippocratic oath, honestly sworn and subscribed to and faithfully kept by men who held the world's welfare in their hands. When the whole legal profession acknowledged that Justice was its God; when attorneys and judges cast aside all their personal desires, their tedious bickerings, their envies, and bowed themselves before the calm, majestic face of Justice, the public would respect the law and obediently walk in its ways. When teachers left off thinking about their jobs in terms of monthly checks and promotions, swearing fealty to the cause of Education, their disciples would be ashamed not to follow them. When the people's elected representatives in legislative halls and executive offices abandoned their duplicities, their connivances, their unabashed knaveries, their lust for applause, front-page publicity, and indiscriminate loot; when these so-called statesmen were willing to serve Patriotism with something like the selfless devotion of the men who served Science; well — the world would presently come out into the sunshine of a new day! What Civilization needed was a crew that understood the nature of its obligation to the ship!

His relation to Tubby Forrester, Beaven felt, was conducive to the highest type of service to their important task. They gave no heed to each other as persons. They wasted no time in small talk. Nothing else in the world mattered, when they were together, but their scientific research.

Sometimes he allowed his imagination to play with the

fancied scene of a captain and a navigating officer, standing
shoulder to shoulder on the bridge, in a dangerous storm,
venomously despising each other but acknowledging that
the ship was their mistress. Perhaps — when and if the
ship made port — they would sneak off to some quiet spot
and fight out their pent-up animosity. But that event could
wait. Just now, they were serving a mistress whose claims
on them were such as no other mistress could undercut or
understand. She was their God, and She was a jealous God,
and so far as they were concerned *there were no other gods
before Her*.

That's the way it was with him and Tubby. Science was
their God. Whatever might be their hostility toward each
other as persons, they put it all aside when their God spoke.
What mattered their insignificant little tiffs, or their puerile
aversions, or even their silly little *selves* when in the presence
of their Lord! It was, thought Jack, a form of worship that
really amounted to something. It rebounded into their
work — work for the emancipation of society from its pains
and discomforts; work that would set men free of their
physical disabilities. He and Tubby were religious. The
laboratory was their chapel, the Bunsen burner was their
censor of incense, the perpetual light was to be seen in the
Crookes tube, the stained glass was not in the windows but
in the depths of a high-powered microscope. The analogy
moved him to the depths. He pressed it for further revelations, even to the length of saying to himself that the poor,
mangled cadavers had been given — in the laboratory —
the right to a triumphant resurrection; not some fantastic
emergence from the grave on a 'last day,' but a glorious
opportunity to serve the world, now and here. He would
have given a great deal for a chance to say all this to Tubby,
and watch his face.

Not infrequently, memories of his childhood would sweep
over him. The family's social life had been so inextricably
tangled with the doings in their little church that it was almost impossible to review his youth without bumping into
something religious. As he looked back upon those experi-

ences now, from his present position as a servant of Science, the whole sorry business offended him. In the light of recent events, he recalled the grotesque antics of contentious sects whose discordant brawls kept the neighborhood at loggerheads. How glibly they all talked about their God! But they didn't talk the same language. The high quest that should have bound them all together — as he and Tubby were bound together — was the one and only thing that kept them apart.

If their God had really possessed them — as Science possessed himself and Tubby — they might have had rows about everything else, but not about *Him*. Had they been sportsmanly enough to agree upon a truce, in the presence of their God, like the officers on a ship or scientists in a laboratory, they might have got something that would have made them a great deal finer and more useful than they were.

But their conception of God wasn't big enough. He couldn't command their attention. He was such a frail little fellow that they had the audacity to fight before His very face! He was so impotent that in His presence they were able to remember and exploit all of their futile controversies. If He had meant anything to them, they couldn't have done it! They sneered at each other's efforts to evaluate Him. There wasn't a single unifying influence at work throughout the whole community — not even their God! Least of all — their God. That was what made them poor, cloddish, selfish, stupid. There was nothing to stir their courage or stimulate their minds. That was what ailed them: they had no *God!* The poor old home-made scarecrow that they had set up, and called God, had never done anything for them but split up the country-side into warring factions.

He remembered how, as a lad, he had earnestly wished that he could feel the ecstasy, the tug, the thrill of a Spirit that would inspire him to reverence, awe, and devotion. It was impossible.

Now, belatedly, he had achieved that sense of being

mastered by a powerful influence worthy of his best efforts.
Science was his Master! Maybe Science was just another
name for The True God. Certain quaint and cryptic bits
of Scripture, read by his father at morning prayers, clung
tenaciously to his memory. One sentence in particular, that
had widened his boyish eyes, recurred to him. 'I am inquired of by them that asked not for *Me*.' Perhaps there
was some truth in this. Perhaps a diligent inquiry into the
mysteries of Science was indeed a quest for God. At all
events, when Science was your God, you knew exactly what
to expect of Him. Science wasn't full of whims and pusil-
lanimous little prejudices and partialities. Science had no
pet children; no chosen people. You could kowtow and
genuflect and sing and pray all you liked to this God, and
try to make yourself believe that you and yours had a
special stand-in, but if you combined certain potent
chemicals in the wrong relationships, He would blow the
pants right off of you, as promptly and cheerfully as He
would pay off the most flippant atheist for the same mistake.

Some day there might be an occasion to discuss all this
with Tubby. He suspected that Tubby — down deep inside
— was potentially religious. His constant jibes at the
common prattle of the sects certainly indicated that the
subject was much on his mind.

Jack had but little time for recreation, and no social life
at all. He did not fret about it. His program had no place
in it for women, and social events inevitably threw one into
contact with them. He was strongly aware of their attraction. They disturbed and distracted him. He could easily
understand the predicament of his fellow-interns who made
short shrift of their work and committed inexcusable
blunders when under the spell of some new infatuation. The
way to insure against any such mental collapse was to
avoid women; refuse to think about them. For many weeks
after graduation he had been pestered by memories of the
charming girl he had seen at the Livingstone; but he had
resolutely disposed of her — the only girl he had ever really
longed to know.

Most of the other interns groused about the long hours required of them and made their own tasks almost unendurable. Their complaints occasionally rose to shrill crescendos of rage when peremptorily ordered to do some relatively unimportant thing at nine-fifteen — thus destroying a promised evening off duty — something that might as well be done at eight or one. For some of them it was so hard a life that they candidly discussed throwing it all up — and to hell with it!

Jack would make a mockery of their discomforts, ironically soothing them with such philosophical tidbits as 'There, there! This too shall pass.' And they would mutter, 'Old sphynx! Old mole! Old owl!' And indeed he did seem much older than the lot of them. Sometimes he made fun of their rages and sometimes showed his utter disgust, declaring they were a herd of asses, unconsciously giving the word an intonation, accent, and value so amazingly like Tubby's own use of it that it startled him.

* * * * * * * *

It had been tentatively planned that Beaven's internship and appointment as Doctor Forrester's laboratory assistant should carry on through four years. At the end of his third year, however, this program was revised. Tubby had been invited to spend the first semester in Edinburgh as an exchange lecturer in Neurological Surgery.

This invitation from the celebrated medical college in Scotland had been extended three years previously and annually renewed, but Tubby had not felt until now that he could safely leave his job.

One afternoon in early May, he came into the laboratory where Jack was staining a tissue for microscopic examination, and said, brusquely, 'Beaven — you don't imagine that you know enough about Anatomy to teach it; do you?'

'To whom?' drawled Jack, without looking up.

Tubby laid his hat and stick on the table, mounted a tall stool, scowled, and demanded attention.

Jack put down his work and listened.

'I am spending the first semester in Edinburgh. I have been farming out my duties here. How much of a mess do you suppose you'd make of the first-year class in Anatomy?

'You ought to know, sir. All the Anatomy I have I got from you.'

Tubby's lips twitched in a brief smile.

'Your damned impertinence, too, I suppose,' growled Tubby.

'Yes, sir; but I wouldn't have the nerve to try to teach that in your absence — if that's what you mean.'

'Beaven — I don't know why I tolerate you. You're as impudent as the devil.'

'Oh no, sir! But — thanks for the concession — just the same.'

'That's settled, then,' said Tubby. 'First-year Anatomy. Better bone up on it. And keep it in mind that these young cubs have to be handled patiently, at first.'

'Yes, sir — I remember how you do it.'

'You're a bit inclined to be sarcastic, you know.'

Jack grinned.

'I am told that the younger house-pups find you a pretty hard taskmaster,' continued Tubby.

'Well — they're going in for a serious business,' said Jack, defensively, 'and they may as well find it out now.'

'But don't imagine that because you yourself live like a monk and work like a slave ——'

'I've been acting on your own advice and example, sir,' interposed Jack. 'Besides — I like it.'

'Nonsense! Nobody likes such severe self-discipline.'

'How about *you?*' demanded Jack.

Tubby dismissed this query with an impatient shrug.

'What I am trying to get through your tonsure, Father Beaven, is my wish to leave here with the belief that when I return I may find the first-year class still attending the Medical School. Don't discourage these cubs. And don't make them hate you. You easily could; you know.'

The interview gave Jack many reflective moments. Was he getting hard? Was he cutting himself off from everything

and everybody? He must have come a long way on the
road to isolation if even Tubby was moved to warn him.

Reviewing his relationship to the interns, the nurses, and
the patients, he was bound to admit that he had no personal
interest in these people beyond the business that had put
them all under the same roof. He comforted himself with
the knowledge that he was courteous in his dealings with
them. But it was apparent that in most respects, he and
Tubby Forrester — for all their mutual animosity — were
as nearly alike as peas in a pod.

* * * * * * * *

Young Doctor Beaven kept the yearlings on the jump.
Tubby, returning in February, was so occupied with experiments relating to his own specialty, that he had no
inclination to resume his class-work. Occasionally he would
saunter about through the anatomical laboratory, pausing
to ask tricky questions, picking up drawings and tossing
them down; but, apparently confident that his assistant
was doing a good job, he gave himself no further concern
about it, and privately promised himself that he was done
teaching the elements of Anatomy.

The past eight years of steady contact with medical
interests had brought Jack Beaven into a maturity that
gave him the appearance of being older than thirty. There
had been no fundamental changes in him, but all of his
identifying traits had been seasoned and accented. Never
disposed to be garrulous, his conversation had become
laconic. His physical exercise, restricted now to an hour's
vigorous workout at the punching-bag in the gymnasium,
every day from five to six, was admittedly a health measure
rather than a pleasurable recreation. Occasionally he took
a long walk into the country, alone. During this past year,
because of his classroom and laboratory duties, he had been
relieved of the routine activities of internship, but he still
lived in the Hospital Annex as before.

In physical appearance he had developed into a rather
striking figure. The blondish hair, which still had a strong

tendency to be curly, was close cropped. His features, naturally rugged, gave him distinction as they matured. The deep-set blue eyes had a penetrating quality, possibly to be accounted for by the inquisitive, analytical mind behind them, and their diligent application to microscopy. His work had made him serious. He almost never laughed aloud at anything. Indeed, his cloistral life did not bring him into frequent contact with amusing episodes. His smile — when it showed — was unexpectedly boyish, but brief.

Hospital patients, after a few unrewarded attempts to be jocularly informal, gave it up. It was clear that he hadn't come to play with them. They saw that there was a chasm between themselves and young Doctor Beaven too wide and deep to be crossed. This had the effect of increasing their confidence in his skill, especially when they noted the assurance and decisiveness of every movement he made in their presence. He wasn't much of a joker, but he knew his stuff.

Nobody had to be told that Doctor Beaven was absolutely obsessed by his work. His impassive face testified that if he had any emotions at all they were under perfect control. He wasted no time in soft compliments, but when he commended anyone for excellent behavior under heavy stress his crisp words of approval were cherished.

There was very little difference in his attitude toward men and women patients. By implication, rather than direct statement, he gave women to understand that they were expected to have brains and bravery. They liked his cool confidence in their toughness and were bewildered by his cooler indifference to their coquetries. Many droll stories drifted about through the hospital, reporting brusque remarks made by Doctor Beaven to patients putting up a gallant fight. One yarn, told by a nurse, had it that he had come into a room at two A.M. to see how a young woman was getting on who had been put through an operation, late in the afternoon, to repair a broken jaw and deep throat lacerations received in an automobile collision. The conversation was reported to have run as follows:

Doctor: 'Hello' [gruffly]. 'Does it hurt badly?'

Patient: 'No, sir.'

Doctor: 'I know better. You're lying.'

Patient: 'Yes, sir.'

Doctor: 'But you have the proper spirit.'

Patient (mistily): 'Thanks.'

Doctor (whimsically): 'Lies of great men all remind us, we can make our lies sublime.'

Patient: 'Yes, sir. Thank you, sir.'

Doctor Beaven hadn't said anything further, not even 'Good night.' After the door had closed behind him, the patient, swathed in bandages, had mumbled, 'He's wonderful.'

'How do you mean — wonderful?' snapped the nurse, testily. 'Don't go losing your heart to this good-looking thing just because he was sweet enough to call you a liar when you said it didn't hurt; for that's as sweet as he's ever going to be — on you — or anybody else. That bird's arteries are filled with ice-cold lemon juice.'

But the whole hospital had a growing respect for Beaven — a sentiment compounded of fear and admiration — and predictions were freely made that he would be a very important person, some day.

'Exactly like Tubby,' was usually added.

'Except that Beaven doesn't have tantrums.'

'No; he doesn't shout and swear — but — Boy! — he's hard!'

* * * * * * * *

One morning in mid-June, Doctor Forrester summoned Beaven to his office. They faced each other, as usual, coolly and without salutations. Tubby pointed to the chair opposite and redirected his attention to the voluminous case-report he had been reading. Jack ignored the invitation and waited, absently toying with his dangling stethoscope.

'We are getting a case from up-state tomorrow that promises to be interesting.' Tubby leaned forward, smoothed out the document on his desk, and tapped it

significantly with the inevitable pince-nez. 'It is referred
to us by Doctor William Cunningham. Ever hear of him?'

Jack nodded noncommittally. For an instant he was
tempted to comment, but decided to withhold his own
opinion. One heard a good deal about Cunningham, these
days. The medics discussed him freely. He had a sound
reputation as a surgeon; was highly respected as a diagnostician; was reputed to be the most able surgical consultant in
the whole Saginaw Bay region. On the other hand, he was
considered a self-confessed sentimentalist; one of these
altruistic chaps who stewed and fretted over the non-
pathological problems of his patients; a typical example of
what Tubby scornfully called 'the goodole country doc.'

It would be interesting indeed to hear Tubby — who had
never once referred to Cunningham in Jack's presence —
offer his own appraisal of his soft-hearted classmate, who
believed that the greatest thing in the world is the love of
humanity — surely a sappy thing for a scientific man to say.

'This is in the nature of a repair job,' continued Tubby,
momentarily dashing Jack's hope for an intimate revelation.
'Some unsuccessful surgery was done on this case before
Cunningham saw it. Cunningham could unquestionably
attend to it himself, but he apparently has a good reason for
wanting to refer the case to a better guesser than he is.' The
chief paused to glare a challenge at his protégé. 'I daresay
you think *you're* a pretty smart guesser by this time; eh?
Well — we'll see.' Something had happened to make Tubby
very scratchy, this morning. Willing to accommodate his
boss with the proffer of a little controversial fuel, Jack
countered with, 'Depends on what the guess is about, sir.
I'm willing to guess that thirty-six inches make a yard,
though I've never verified it, and have it only on the
flimsiest hearsay.'

'Humph!' grunted Tubby. 'Very silly remark!... Sit
down; damn it! You make me nervous!'

Jack sat, on the arm of the chair, and lighted a cigarette.

'The patient,' continued Tubby, reconcentrating on his
papers, 'is a seven-year-old boy. Six months ago, he fell

from a stepladder, his left arm striking a picket of an iron
fence — the awkward little rascal — and one of the spikes
penetrated the medial aspect of the arm near the junction
of its middle and upper thirds. A bruise and a slight hemorrhage but no impairment of function. Simple bandage.
Next day there was a pain in the hand but none in the arm.
... Got that?'

'Yes, sir,' replied Jack, through a lazy streamer of smoke.
'Median nerve.'

'Of course!' Tubby's tone indicated that any ass should
have known the trouble was in the median nerve. 'So —
after two weeks the pain became more acute; now localized
to the medial half of the hand; second and third fingers
stiff; nails brittle and glossy; skin dry. The boy found that
the pain could be somewhat alleviated if the hand was kept
moist; or, better, immersed in a basin of water.' Tubby
paused to query — over the top of his glasses — whether
these facts meant anything to his junior.

'Of course!' grumped Jack, in a tone so amazingly like
Tubby's that the chief blinked a little.

'An operation was performed — by some doctor I never
heard of — fellow named Munson — up there some place.
It appears to have been a fairly intelligent job, but without
results.' Tubby glanced up. 'Perhaps you can guess what
this chap tried to do.'

'Well — if this is an examination,' replied Jack, slightly
ruffled, 'I suppose the man performed a peri-arterial
sympathectomy.'

'Exactly! But there was no relief. The hand now became
so sensitive that a loud noise or the jar of traffic in the street
was almost unendurable. We have scar tissue to deal with,
and Cunningham says there is a distressing pulsation.'

'Nerve probably adhering to the brachial artery,' ventured Jack.

'Sounds like it. ... Well — that's all. You know as much
about the case as I do. And my only reason for calling you
in on it' — Tubby rose, and pushed back his chair — 'is
because I have had my lenses changed and am not quite

accommodated to the correction. This nerve-suture will be a tricky job. I may ask you to do it. Take all this stuff along with you; Cunningham's covering letter — and all. Parts of the letter are personal. I haven't time to edit it and get a deleted copy for you. You will note that Cunningham's observations include a rambling account of the patient's family, a whole waste-basketful of irrelevant comments having no bearing whatsoever on the case. That' — Tubby's voice grew testy — 'that's Doctor William Cunningham's besetting sin, Father Beaven. He's a good surgeon. He's a good diagnostician. He might have been a great man; had it in him; might have been a member of this faculty!'

It was plain to see that the letter from Cunningham had stirred the smouldering ashes of an old friendship that had met disaster.

'So, you are not to leap to the conclusion' — Tubby handed the papers across the desk — 'that Cunningham is just an old blatherskite because he gossips like an afternoon tea at the Mothers' Club. He has a sentimental interest in this family; wants 'em shown special attentions.'

'Not a ward case, I take it.'

'By no means! They are quite independent. The child's mother is bringing him down. I have made a reservation for her at the Livingstone. Her sister will come later. Cunningham will be here for a day, if he can get away.'

Jack folded the bulky document, pocketed it, and walked toward the door.

'And — Beaven ——' called Tubby.

'Yes, sir.'

'I expect to be away for a few days, immediately after Commencement. You will have full charge of this case during convalescence. Bare possibility, of course, that the operation may not be successful. Might have it to do over again. If so — it's your job. . . . That's all.'

Proceeding to Tubby's laboratory, Jack re-read the case-history with care. Cunningham might be a garrulous old lady, but there wasn't anything loose or unprofessional about the case-history. Then he took up the personal letter, perusing it with expanding interest. Two or three facts about the Cunningham-Forrester relationship were plain as a pikestaff. These men had once been intimate. Something had tugged them apart. Perhaps Tubby had been annoyed over Cunningham's unprofessional attitude toward his job. Maybe Cunningham's success had taken a tuck in Tubby's pet theory. Or, Cunningham was mildly annoyed over Tubby's cold-bloodedness. At all events — they hadn't been very close; not for a long time. Not unfriendly, but not chummy; not any more. Jack marveled that Tubby had let him see this letter. It was an immensely interesting document; nice little riddle in psychology.

Waiving that problem, Jack ran his eye over the detailed information about the patient and his kin. The boy, Theodore King, was exceptionally bright for a seven-year-old. Precocious, and a bit spoiled. His mother, Mrs. Claudia King, was the widow of a man who had been conspicuous in the lumber industry. Before their marriage she had been private secretary to the president of the company, a position she had resumed after her husband's death.

Her father — as if that mattered a damn in the relief of young Theodore's nerve-adhesion — had been a sea-captain, Henry Hilton by name, running from San Francisco to Hongkong for many years; shrewd, thrifty, picturesque old chap, who had stacked up a considerable fortune and left his daughters well fixed.

'Claudia King is not required to work for her living,' clattered Cunningham, 'but for her health. You will observe that she is disposed to overplay her gem-like brilliance. All of her thinking is done in italics. She burns more carbon while asleep than most people do at full gallop. She will probably reorganize your hospital while she is with you (and do a mighty good job of it, too). Claudia is uncommonly easy to look at, and uncommonly hard to talk to; a renowned monologuist. If you feel it imperative to tell her something, grasp her firmly by the scruff of the neck with your left hand and put your right hand over her mouth —

and watch out for your fingers. Her sister, whom you will see a little later, resembles her in that they are both white, female, and adult. Otherwise they have nothing in common. The sister has a story that deserves more space than even this lengthy letter permits.'

Jack folded the letter and thrust it into the pocket of his white duck jacket, sat for a long time staring out at the window. He wished he knew the probably dramatic tale of the battered friendship between the eccentric Saginaw Bay surgeon and surly old Tubby.

An unwelcome thought suddenly smote him. Could it be possible that Tubby was asking him to have charge of the King case for the purpose of showing up Cunningham as a person of small importance professionally? Cunningham is baffled by a surgical problem and sends it down to Tubby for expert handling. Tubby sniffs, and turns the case over to his assistant. Would old Tubby be that mean? Jack's eyes narrowed thoughtfully and he shook his head. No — not even Tubby would do that! Tubby's explanation was honest, no doubt. He was having his glasses changed. That was all.

Descending the stairs, his mind so preoccupied that he made no response to the respectful greetings of students on the way up, Jack entered the library, went back to the alcove containing works on the autonomic nervous system, and settled down to a review of unique case-histories of nerve-adhesions involving the brachial artery. Cunningham's human-interest comments on the case had been utterly forgotten. The fact that the little boy was said to be bright and his young mother brilliant hadn't registered at all. The youngster might be a half-wit and his mother a shrimp and his enigmatical aunt a monster, for all he cared. The case, so far as Jack was concerned, was a problem in neurological surgery.

After an hour he returned to the anatomical laboratory and strolled among the tables until he found a pair of young medics dissecting an arm in the general field of his present concern.

'Pardon me a moment, won't you?' he said, stepping between them. 'I want to look at something.'

They deferentially made way, pleased to feel that the capable and handsome young Doctor Beaven had thus honored their cadaver. One of them, hopeful of making the most of this unexpected contact with his Anatomy teacher, audaciously ventured a bit of grim drollery.

'This gentleman came to us from one of the state hospitals for the insane, Doctor Beaven. Pete and I call him "Mr. Hatter."'

Beaven, thoroughly occupied with his problem, knitted his brows and regarded the flushing young medic with a mystified stare.

'What did you say?' he inquired, remotely.

'It was of no consequence, sir,' explained the unhappy humorist. 'I said we called this subject "Mr. Hatter" — because he was a nut, you know.'

'Oh,' drawled Beaven, absently, adding — after a long moment's intensive search with a probe — 'I should think you might find him congenial.'

The other student unsuccessfully stifled a chuckle, and Beaven glanced over his shoulder to survey him briefly.

'Very happy relationship all 'round,' observed the young anatomist. 'Thanks, gentlemen.' He turned away, conciliating them with the merest suggestion of a twinkle at the corners of his steel-blue eyes.

Mr. Hatter's attendants, rosily sensitive to the cool ridicule they had experienced, fell to work industriously, hoping the neighboring tables had missed the dialogue. After a while the more facetious one muttered, out of the corner of his mouth, 'God, I'd hate to have him mad at me.'

'Playful little feller; eh, wot?' said Pete.

'Yeah — like Tubby.'

'Well,' soberly, 'if I knew as much as Beaven knows about old man Hatter ——'

'You wouldn't know anything else.'

'Wouldn't need to.'

Chapter V

It HAD been a long time since Jack Beaven had taken any personal interest in a child. From the day he had left home to enter college, a dozen years ago, there had been very few occasions for meeting young children.

As an intern, his contacts with them had been infrequent. Most of the surgery he saw was performed on adults. And as Tubby Forrester directed his student assistant's attention more and more toward neurological surgery, the opportunities for seeing children became correspondingly farther apart. It was a rare thing for a child to show up in this department.

Perhaps if he had nourished the hope that some day he might have a home and a family of his own, he would have made more effort to acquaint himself with the mental processes of early adolescence. As the matter stood, he was as unfamiliar with the normal behavior of a seven-year-old boy as with the habits of a penguin.

Of course this lack of knowledge related only to Jack's information concerning the child's mind. A seven-year-old boy, considered physically, was a man, drawn to a smaller scale. You didn't have to explore to find his brachial artery or his median nerve. But his mind, far from being a diminutive model of a man's mind, was an entirely different institution.

Early next morning after the operation, Jack went up to see how his young patient was getting on. He felt confident that the nerve repair would prove successful. The tricky part of it — dissecting the nerve out of the scar tissue, and freeing it from the artery to which it had adhered, and suturing the nerve ends, after the neuromatous portion had been excised — had been his personal responsibility. Tubby had merely opened the field of operation. Jack had done the rest of it. And it was a good job. Doctor Cunningham had not been able to come, somewhat to Jack's disappointment. His curiosity about Cunningham had been stirred.

He had seen very little of the boy on the afternoon of his arrival. Nervously distressed by the fatigue, excitement, and jarring of the trip, the patient had been given a sedative strong enough to induce lethargy. Tubby felt that they knew enough about the history of the case. The important thing now was to let the boy rest. Jack had not seen Mrs. King. Assured that her child was in good hands, she had been driven to the hotel by Tubby himself who rarely went out of his way to accommodate the kin of his out-of-town patients. Jack was secretly amused when the nurse told him, and reflected that Doctor Cunningham's comment on the lady's attractiveness must have had some element of truth in it.

Nor had he seen Mrs. King yesterday at the time of the operation. Undoubtedly she had followed along when the lad had been taken from his room, but they had stowed her away safely before the anaesthetizing had begun. After the operation, Tubby had gone directly to the room, but Jack had not followed. After all, it was Tubby's case. At seven, Jack had peeped in, and the nurse said the boy was asleep; everything the way it ought to be; and Mrs. King had been advised to return to the hotel since there was nothing she could do at the hospital. Doctor Forrester, added the nurse, had come for her.

About six-thirty next morning the assistant in Neurology proceeded to the King room and quietly pushed the door open. The boy was awake. He seemed very small. The short fringe of damp, curling, black hair on the white forehead was soft and babyish. The eyes, extraordinarily long-lashed, were set wide apart in an oval face with a dimple in the chin.

Young Doctor Beaven went to the bedside, looked down into the questioning brown eyes, and said, 'How do you do, Mr. King?'

The child folded his lower lip between his teeth and struggled with a grin.

'How do you do?' he replied, remotely.

The Warren girl, who had been on duty since eleven, was caught with a sudden chuckle in the very middle of an open-faced yawn, and retired to the window where she regarded the maple trees with much interest.

'Does your hand hurt?'

'No — but my arm does.'

'That's good,' commented Doctor Beaven. 'I mean — about your hand. We don't care anything about the arm.'

'Oh?' said the child, wide-eyed, shaking his head.

'Did you sleep well last night?' asked the doctor, taking the boy's good wrist in his hand.

'I think so. Did you?'

'Just fairly well, sir,' replied the doctor, soberly. He drew out his watch and regarded it with full attention.

'What was the matter? Did you drink coffee? My mother ——'

'Shh,' said Miss Warren, with a high smile and uplifted finger.

Presently Doctor Beaven repocketed his watch and said, as one man to another, 'No, sir; it wasn't coffee. I am a doctor, Mr. King, and doctors almost never sleep all night. Last night, I was up several times. Sick people, you know. This is a hospital.' He gently drew down the sheet. 'I should like to listen to your heart, please.'

'Will it make a loud noise — in that thing?'

'I hope not.'

'Will you let me listen to yours when you're through listening to mine?'

'Not today. The nurse wants you to be very quiet today.'

'Don't you?'

Doctor Beaven, feeling that his suggestion about silence might be obeyed, had put the tips of his instrument in his ears, but now took them out again, and said, 'Don't I what?' to which the patient promptly replied, 'Don't you want me to be quiet?'

'Oh yes; of course. Everybody wants you to be quiet; Miss Warren, and Doctor Forrester, and I ——'

'And my mother, too, I expect,' added the boy, helpfully.

'Unquestionably. Now if you'll kindly not talk for just a minute ——' He laid the bell of the instrument on the child's heart.

'Was it still beating?' asked the boy, eagerly, when the doctor had stuffed the stethoscope back into his pocket.

'Faintly. It will be stronger, I think, after you have spent an hour or two without talking.'

'I didn't see you yesterday.'

'No. I saw you — but you were asleep.'

'Doctor Beaven operated on you, dear,' put in Miss Warren. 'We must be very quiet now.'

The brown eyes shifted to inspect her gravely.

'You, too?'

Miss Warren couldn't think of a prompt answer to that, and merely laid her finger-tips on her pursed mouth and opened her eyes wide.

'Did you see my mother?' asked the boy, returning to the doctor, who shook his head.

'Does that mean "No"? — or "Shut up"?'

'Both,' said Doctor Beaven, quietly.

There was a moment of reflection. The boy sighed.

'My mother says it isn't polite to say "Shut up."'

'That's true, Mr. King. But doctors aren't engaged to be polite. However — may I beg your pardon?'

The child nodded, enthusiastically. Doctor Beaven moved away toward the door.

'I shall be seeing you again,' he said.

'But you said you would beg my pardon.'

'Didn't I?'

'No — you just asked me if you could.'

'You certainly keep your eye on the ball; don't you?'

The boy's eyes danced.

'Do you like to play ball? I'll bet you could play football if you wanted to. Did you ever?'

'I'll tell you tomorrow — provided I get a report that you have been very quiet all day.'

'What did you do to my hand to make it stop hurting?'

'I shall tell you that, too, tomorrow, if you are obedient today.'

The child shook his head obstinately.

'It wouldn't hurt me to lie still and listen, while you talked.'

'Tomorrow!' said Doctor Beaven, firmly.

Teddy's face registered disappointment. It was easily to be seen that he was accustomed to having his own way.

At the door, the doctor turned and said, significantly, 'All the patients on this floor are men. You are one of them, Mr. King.' He gravely gave the little fellow a military salute. Teddy's lips reluctantly broke into a smile as the salute was returned. Miss Warren viewed the pantomime with interest.

'Did you like Doctor Beaven?' she asked, after the door had closed.

Teddy nodded with heavy dignity.

'You musn't ask me questions,' he said, severely. 'I'm not allowed to talk.'

* * * * * * * *

Late that afternoon, in a brief conference in his laboratory, Doctor Forrester made it clear that he would not expect his assistant to give any of his time to the King boy for the next three days.

'I am obliged to leave on Saturday, Beaven. After that, you will look after the case until the child is ready to go home.'

This wasn't a bit like Tubby. As soon as an interesting operation was performed, and its success assured, Tubby had no further concern about it. In this instance he had endeavored — rather lamely, Jack thought — to explain his continued interest on the ground of his close friendship

with Doctor Cunningham, whose patient should receive
personal attention.

There was nothing about the boy's case that required
expert oversight. Except for the natural procedure of healing and full recovery from the shock of the operation, little
remained to be done that Time and Nature would not
attend to.

'Very good, sir,' replied Jack.

'The boy's mother,' continued Tubby, 'expects to go
home on Saturday. She has a responsible position and feels
she should return to it. His aunt will arrive on Sunday, and
remain here until he is ready to be discharged; a week longer,
perhaps. You will decide that.'

It was somewhat annoying to Jack, finding himself conscious of a strong curiosity about a woman. He wanted to
see this Mrs. Claudia King, who had upset Tubby's
equilibrium. He sincerely hoped that his eminent preceptor
would not turn out to be a silly old ass. However, habit and
training would eventually assert their claims, he knew.
Tubby might be temporarily distracted, but he would snap
out of it. Mrs. King would go home, and Tubby would
resume his customary program. You couldn't make a
Romeo of Tubby.

Meantime, while the famed neurologist was enjoying
a brief season of excitement, the claims of Science would be
discharged by his faithful associate. Jack hoped he was not
smug when he entertained this valorous thought. He hated
smugness. Smugness had been the thing he had considered
most objectionable in the religious fanatics with whom he
had been associated in his youth.

As he sat there in the laboratory, after Tubby's departure,
it suddenly dawned on him that if a man didn't watch himself with care he could easily become as disgustingly pleased
with his own moral grandeur while serving Science as he
might when paying the tribute of stern self-discipline before
the face of Jehovah or whatever other tribal deity had
stirred his imagination.

It was a disturbing thought. Here was the vast majority

of the world's population obviously proceeding without any idealism, at all; not conscious of an obligation to render any kind of service or pay homage — other than a perfunctory gesture — to any sort of God. In striking contrast, here was another group, numerically negligible, spending a lifetime of rigorous devotion to the service of some Master; and, in the face of that great cost and at the sacrifice of almost everything which men have counted pleasurable, finding that their honest courage had developed a cancer of self-righteousness! No matter what kind of God you served, you were menaced by this unhealthy fungus. You went in for Art, and presently you were pleased to find that you had achieved a beauty of soul which set you apart. You went in for Religion; and, if you did it with all your might, it wouldn't be long before you would be mounting the temple steps murmuring sweetly, 'Lord, I thank Thee that I am not as other men are.' If you hoped to avoid the inevitable temptations of the aesthete and the mystic, you would better go in for Science. No trashy sentiment about *that*! No climbing the martyr's stake to sing brave hallelujahs in the flames! No self-pitying, self-congratulatory preening of feathers!

That's what he had come to think about his own life program. Science was a Master you could follow without falling victim to these nasty little psychoses which softened the minds of sentimental daubers and prayer-hounds.

Today, Beaven stood shocked in the presence of the fact that it was possible to become just as putridly self-pleased over one's abnegations in the cause of Science. He despised himself for the littleness of the thought. He had caught himself saying to himself, 'Very well. Let Tubby Forrester go and play. I'll carry on!' It was a pretty hard jolt. He went back to the hospital to pursue his rounds. And all day he kept saying to himself, 'After all, I'm nothing but a well-trained chemist and carpenter. I know where all the parts are — and I know how to fix 'em — and so does the greasy fellow on his back under the motor-car. I work in a hospital and he works in a garage. I've been taking myself and my job too seriously. Need more fresh air and sunshine. And diverting society, too.'

But he made no effort to satisfy his curiosity about Mrs. King. Nor did he call to see the child until late Saturday afternoon, when he was sure that both Tubby and the boy's mother had left town.

* * * * * * * *

Jack was obliged to admit that he was pleasantly stirred by the child's welcome. There was no question about its genuineness.

'Teddy has been inquiring for you, Doctor Beaven,' said Miss McFey. 'He feared you had forgotten him.'

'I knew Doctor Forrester was taking good care of you.' Doctor Beaven took the small hand. 'And this is a big hospital, with a lot of sick people in it. I suppose you're almost well now. Sitting up — and everything.'

'My mother went home,' said Teddy, soberly. 'Did you see her?'

'No — I didn't meet your mother. I'm sorry.'

'I told her about you.'

'So?'

'Yes — she laughed.'

'At me?' The doctor raised his brows.

'About your calling me "Mr. King." My Aunt Audrey is coming tomorrow. She wouldn't think it was funny. Aunt Audrey is very polite. She will draw pictures for me. Can you draw pictures?'

Somewhat to his own surprise, Jack nodded, drew out a pencil and a prescription pad, and quickly sketched an arm.

'There. That is the place where you were hurt. This nerve was injured and grew fast to an artery. See? That. And this made your hand hurt, because it was the same nerve that wiggled these two fingers. So — we mended the nerve, and your hand didn't hurt any more. It doesn't; does it?'

Teddy shook his head reassuringly.

'Can you draw anything else — besides sore arms?'

'You mean — faces of people, and cows, and horses, and things?'

'Umm-humm — and pagodas and rickshaws and people planting rice.'

'No. Do I look like a Chinaman?'

'You mustn't say "Chinaman" in front of Aunt Audrey. She wouldn't like it.'

Properly reproved, Doctor Beaven said he really knew better and would be careful about it in the future.

'Does your aunt draw pictures of people planting rice?'

'Yes. Lovely ones. Aunt Audrey *is* Chinese.' Teddy opened his big brown eyes wide and shook his head. 'Didn't you know?' he asked.

'No,' said Doctor Beaven, quietly. 'I hadn't heard that. Are you sure? *You* aren't Chinese. And your mother isn't; is she?'

'No. Just Aunt Audrey,' said Teddy, firmly. 'You'll see,' he added, noting the doctor's expression of amused incredulity.

'I can't think why he says that,' interposed Miss McFey.

'I expect your aunt must have traveled a good deal in China,' suggested Doctor Beaven, 'and that's why she likes the country so well. . . . Now let's have a peep at that arm. Oh — that's getting along famously.'

'No — that isn't it,' declared Teddy, oblivious to the arm. 'My Aunt Audrey *is truly* a Chinese.' He bobbed his head energetically. 'You ask her!'

'Very well,' agreed the doctor. 'You ought to know.'

'And she can eat with chopsticks same as you do with a spoon.'

'All right, Teddy. It's O.K. with me. And that's why she likes pictures of China.'

'She makes faces, too.'

'Indeed! How shocking!'

Teddy laughed hilariously.

'I mean — she draws faces. Maybe she'll draw a picture of *you.* I don't know, though. She's very polite.'

Doctor Beaven grinned, and the little boy's face was perplexed.

'I expect you're trying to say that your aunt is — is reserved. Do you know what that means?'

Teddy shook his head.

'Shy,' assisted Miss McFey.

'Umm-humm,' answered Teddy, uncertainly. 'She's not like you, or — or my mother — or anybody. Her really name is Lan Ying, but I don't call her Lan Ying except when we play. My mother doesn't like to have me call her Lan Ying.'

Doctor Beaven rose to go, feeling that we were probably getting too deep into family affairs.

'I'll see you tomorrow, Teddy. Be a good boy.'

He closed the door behind him and proceeded to the elevator, aware that the nod with which he had just now greeted Doctor Shane was indifferent enough to have been mistaken for an insult. Lan Ying, indeed! Lan Ying probably had a loose screw.

* * * * * * * *

Sunday was a busy day. Not only did Jack have his own duties to perform, but Tubby's as well, plus much extra work occasioned by the absence of several staff members in attendance at the State Medical Association's annual meeting.

With these pressing cares on his mind, the crowded hours passed with very little further thought about Teddy King — whose case did not require it — or of the lad's enigmatic relative who drew pictures of pagodas and ate with chopsticks. His imagined portrait of this lady was very sketchy. Obviously she was an eccentric maiden who had gone in for oriental things in a big way. The Cunningham letter had mentioned that her father made regular trips to China; a long time ago, doubtless. Perhaps he had taken her with him on one of his voyages to China. Or at least he had talked interestingly at home concerning the country. And, later — after the old man had died — this Audrey Hilton, with a comfortable income and nothing to do, with no home ties and indifferent to matrimony, had become a seasoned traveler.

It was easy to contrive this much of a picture. She would be about forty; tall, wiry, resourceful; expert with a camera; a self-admitted authority on Chinese art. She would be able to tell a Yuan vase from a Ming at a hundred yards, and talk your arm off about the ethereal grace of pot-bellied Buddhas.

Sooner or later he would be obliged to meet this Audrey Hilton — this Lan Ying — and make a decent show of being interested in what she had to say; for the lad's sake, and Tubby's and Doctor Cunningham's.

There was always a big jam in the hospital on Sunday afternoon. The finer the day the bigger the jam — and this was mid-June. Friends and relatives packed the elevators to suffocation and swarmed through the corridors, en route to administer candy and home worries to their sick. The doctors and nurses generally resorted to the stairways to go more easily from one floor to another. Occasionally seasoned visitors, reluctant to join the pushing pack in the sluggish elevators, took to the stairs, too.

Jack Beaven rarely saw individuals in the Sunday afternoon multitude. The crowd was all of a piece. Not often did any of these people stir the slightest interest. Now and again, he had given a bit of idle thought to this matter, wondering whether it could be true that persons — otherwise and elsewhere intelligent and good-looking — inevitably sagged into a common state of flat-faced stupidity upon entering a hospital. Perhaps there was something in the air that brought it on.

The day was gradually wearing itself and everybody else out. It was four o'clock now and the tide of visitors had begun to ebb. People were leaving by platoons. Jack had been up on the fourth floor to make sure the appendectomy he had done late last night was behaving itself. It had been an emergency affair, the patient having arrived in a party gown attended by her husband and a half-dozen friends in evening clothes. He had not told them afterward what a narrow squeak she'd had. Tubby was always saying to his classes, 'It is not necessary to inform your patient or his relatives, after an operation, that but for your remarkable skill there would have been a death in the family. Leave all that kind of prattle to the chaps who must blow about their cunning, if anyone is ever to learn of it.'

Glancing over the chart, Jack handed it back to the nurse, nodded his satisfaction, noted that the patient was sleeping normally, and proceeded on his way down to the third where a kidney drainage was becoming fretful — and not much wonder.

He had pushed open the stiff-spring swinging door leading to the stairway and was passing through when a brisk patter of heels on the stone floor informed him that he was closely followed. Obviously the heels belonged to a visitor; not a nurse. Pausing momentarily he tried to retain his grip on the door to prevent its snapping violently into someone's face, but it slipped from his fingers.

Not to be thought rude, he turned, pushed the stubborn door open with his elbow, and waited indifferently for the heels to come through. She hesitated in the doorway, gave him an appreciative smile which sobered suddenly to a half-perplexed look of recognition. Then she smiled again, perhaps with a trace of amusement at the sight of his surprised eyes. Afterward, when Jack reconstructed the details of that chance encounter, it occurred to him that he had simply stared unsmilingly into her face. His memory of her had been accurate in every detail. She hadn't changed in the slightest particular. The blue-black bobbed hair was in the same mode as before, the even-edged fringe concealing the upper half of an arrestingly white forehead. Sometimes he had thought his imagination had run away with him when he remembered her brown eyes, but now he realized that his mental picture had been correct. She was even dressed much as she had been on the night he had stared her out of countenance at the Livingstone. Her black satin blouse was buttoned to the throat where it was topped with a snug collar. An accordion-pleated white silk skirt completed the costume that sculptured a shapely figure.

He instantly decided not to advert to their former meeting. To have done so would have been to confess a recollection implying a deeper interest than he cared to admit; and, besides, it might be embarrassing to her if he imputed the same interest on her own part. If she wanted to speak of it — well, that would be another matter. In that case, he could remember their meeting.

She took a step forward, through the open doorway, and made a curiously quaint little bow.

'I'm sorry,' said Jack. 'These doors are very much in earnest.'

'They object — may-bee — to one's leaving the hospital.' Her voice was softly pitched in a contralto register, and the words were spoken slowly, precisely, without an identifiable accent but with the cautious deliberation of one accustomed to thinking in another language. Her 'maybe' was oddly stressed on the second syllable. 'May-bee.'

Jack couldn't think of anything suitable to say in response to this. He remarked rather dryly that the stairway was not often used — except by employees.

'Oh?' She raised her brows and shook her head in a manner amusingly childlike. 'Perhaps I am not allowed. I did not know. I am very sorry.'

They had come to the door which opened into the third-floor corridor. He pushed it open and signed to her to precede him.

'Thank you,' she said, again with a little bow. 'I shall go to the lift — for the remainder of my journey.'

'Not if you'd rather walk down,' said Jack, casually. 'Come along. I'll go with you. If you have a car parked, I can show you how to get out by the shortest route.'

'I am not imposing?' Again she shook her head — a gesture which seemed to accompany any query she hoped might be answered in the negative. 'Do the taxicabs — are they available there too?'

'No. They have to be called. I'll do it for you.' They had

arrived at the first floor. Jack indicated the way into the corridor.

'I should not be taking your time, sir,' she protested. He made no reply to that. Doubtless the appropriate thing to say was that he was happy to serve her, but habit was strong and he was not accustomed to making such remarks Together they walked to the Information Desk.

'Call a taxi for this lady, please,' said Jack, crisply.

'Yes, Doctor Beaven,' replied the clerk.

The girl quickly raised her head and glanced up into his eyes. Her lips parted slightly in a smile that showed very white even teeth. He regarded her with sober interest.

'It will be here presently,' he said. 'At the main entrance.'

'You have been very kind.' She bowed again. 'Thank you.'

For a moment Jack entertained an impulse to see her to the front door and into her cab, but his habit of strictly minding his own business intervened. Besides, he disliked the prospect of amusing the loquacious clerks in the front office by passing their windows with this young woman in tow. It wouldn't be in conformity with his normal behavior.

His eyes followed her for an instant. Then he retraced his course by the stairways, with the third floor as his objective. It had been a very stirring interlude. He wished he had contrived some plausible reason for learning her name. With a studious frown he tried mentally to call the roll of fourth-floor patients.

His steps had lagged. Pulling himself together with a shrug of self-reproach, he scowled over the silly moment he had had. It was quite against his principles to permit himself to be distracted — for more than an instant — by a pretty face. He had driven her quite out of his thoughts, long ago. He would do so again. She wasn't going to mean anything to him. It was the girl's exotic flavor that had made her linger in his thoughts, no doubt. A most enchanting personality, quite unlike anyone he had ever met. Who

and what was she? Something decidedly foreign, but difficult to place. Caucasian; no question about that. Euro-
pean? Probably not. No accent; not French, Spanish,
Italian. Nothing Latin: too calm for that. Russian? No.
That courtly bow: where did that come from?

He paused before the door where he had met her, pushed
it open, walked through, released it slowly, halted a moment
at the window, still in a deep study. Then a light suddenly
dawned, and with it came a slow smile.

'Well — I'll be damned!' he muttered.

Chapter VI

NOTWITHSTANDING his reputation for cold-bloodedness, Jack Beaven had not arrived at thirty without experiencing many a sharp conflict between his head and his heart. These struggles were brief but savage.

It was one thing to have mapped an ambitious program of unremitting effort in the cause of Science: it was quite another thing to conform to the severe demands of that inflexible design. The seizures of revolt did not threaten the plan very often; but, when they did, the uprising was violent.

For about three hundred and sixty days of the year, Jack was complacent over the stern self-discipline he practiced and had good reasons for feeling that his sacrifices provided their own reward. To maintain his ambition was a costly investment but it had paid him profitably. As he surveyed the current professional rating of his former classmates — very few of whom had struck their stride — it was apparent that he had been exceptionally fortunate.

Doubtless there had been an element of luck in his early and sound success. He was ready to concede that. In any of the so-called learned professions it was demonstrated, over and over again, that of two men equally in earnest, equally industrious, equally prepared, one might move rapidly into reward and recognition while his friend plodded along, doggedly perseverant, but without promise of advancement. Some little quirk of personality, perhaps quite irrelevant to the actual requirements of the job, might prove to be the deciding factor; some odd mannerism, maybe, that the man himself was hardly aware of; an over-ready open-faced smile that suggested toadyism, the involuntary disclosure of a lack of self-confidence; or an habitual pursing of the lips as if to say — 'This is it: you can take it or leave it.'

Jack had been lucky, and was appropriately thankful. But there was no denying that most of his success could be explained by his stubborn determination to let nothing beguile him from the road he had chosen to travel. Ordinarily he proceeded on this deliberately charted course with steady steps, entirely self-possessed, and assured that what he had achieved already was worth its price. And it had been very costly.

His angular pattern for living had squared his shoulders, tensed his jaw, chiseled an arc of crow's-feet on each temple, firmed his mouth, and narrowed his steel-blue eyes. His conversation was restricted to professional matters. He was increasingly economical with his words. Nobody could or did say that he was gruff. His attitude toward those whom he outranked was consistently just and considerate. He was courteous to the young interns, to the nurses and orderlies; but when he commanded that something be done it was issued in a tone clearly meaning that either the order, or the person who received it, would have to be carried out.

But there were occasional bad days and nights when Beaven doubted whether the game was worth the candle. At such times, he looked back with derision upon the personal sacrifices he had made in an effort to hold the rough road toward his goal. Where the average man, in a blue funk of remorse over his mistakes, generally lashed himself for his laziness and dissipations, Jack's sour reflections deplored the loss of the normal pleasures he had missed while serving a master who wanted all of his time or none of it.

Unswerving ambition was a thrilling thing to yodel about, if you were a well-paid grand opera tenor, dying nightly for noble principles, and rushing out — after the sublime tragedy — to fill your capacious paunch with spaghetti and

chianti; but it wasn't quite so stirring if pursued without
orchestral accompaniment.

Lonely valor was easy enough for the poets; easy enough
for the high-school valedictorian, fetching his oration to a
heart-bumping climax with the resounding shout — 'Excelsior!' Very glibly could this insufferably bright boy
mouth the classic lines recording a young hero's ascent to
greatness and glory. A gallant fellow, this youth with the
banner. Up and up and up went he. 'In happy homes he
saw the light' — but on he climbed, undetained. 'Oh,
stay,' the maiden said, 'and rest thy weary head upon this
breast' — but no, sirree, said he, said he: Excelsior! . . .
That kind of stuff. . . . A bit dismaying at the end of the trip,
however. 'There in the twilight, cold and gray, lifeless but
beautiful he lay.' And who cared a tinker's damn? The
fellow had never really belonged anywhere. The people
who hadn't asked anything better of life than to be amply
fed, decently clothed, happily married, beloved at home,
and respected by the neighborhood, thought this chap with
the grim face and highfalutin banner was a nut.

And after he had worn himself out on his solitary trek,
he at length slumped down on the tipmost top — encased
in snow and ice, banner and all — to take the count. 'And
from the sky, serene and far, a voice fell like a falling
star — Excelsior!'

Now — wasn't that nice? And who wouldn't love to go
plugging along by himself, bearing a banner with a strange
device — 'Excelsior,' perhaps, or 'Neurological Surgery';
spurning the welcoming lights shining in the windows of
happy homes; thumbing a frost-bitten nose at the generous
maiden with the hospitable breast; finally winding up at the
summit, stiff as a statue and dead as Queen Anne — but
beautiful; oh, how beautiful! A shivering angel, blowing
steam into his mittens, would softly coo 'Excelsior.' Fine
pay for the perils of the trip! Nobody else would care a
hoot. In the spring thaw, a Saint Bernard dog would nose
him out. . . . 'Lookit!' calls the pious monk. 'Excelsior.'

But Beaven took pains to disguise his feelings when

these moods (they usually swamped him for a day or two in early summer, and during the Christmas holidays) descended like a sudden fog to make him desperately restless and remorseful.

Happily, through all the years — until just now — no identifiable lights had beckoned to him from any particular window. The happy home he had passed up was a mere phantom. If he had impulsively decided to renounce his ambition and rush with all speed toward that happy home, he wouldn't have known where to find it. The maiden who called, 'Oh, stay!' lacked a name and a street address. No girl had been attractive enough to disturb him, much less detain him. This was to be accounted for by the fact that he had resolved not to be attracted. Something warned him that the surest immunity against falling in love was an attitude of complete detachment from the whole tribe of them. And — if he did have to say it himself — he had done a thoroughly good job of avoiding them.

To the effective pursuance of this resolve, Jack Beaven had practiced a technique of his own devising. He was half ashamed of it, and not for any consideration would he have confided the nature of it to a friend, however urgent his need of counsel in this field. When brought face to face with a pair of bewitchingly pretty lips, he steadied himself against disaster by looking straight through to the exact spot where the quadratus labii superiosis separated into three muscular controls employed in the enchanting act of smiling. If she pouted a little under this scientific inspection, he noted the slight twitch of the mentalis muscle at its point of origin in the incisive fossa. You could keep yourself on an even keel by performing these imaginary dissections. They were never done in a spirit of disrespect. Indeed, he felt he was doing the girl a favor if — upon observing that she was cordially disposed toward him — he could promptly signify that her charms were being wasted. He didn't like to have people take up his time, and he assumed that others should be grateful if he was considerate of theirs.

These dissections were in the nature of insurance. Destiny having decreed that you were to be a celibate in the cause of science, you had a right to defend yourself against impulses that might distract your attention. Jack always knew how to deal with the lingering memory of a provocative curve. Immediately he fancied himself in the operating room. 'Scalpel,' he would mutter to the nurse at his elbow. 'Sponge... Retractor... Forceps... Scissors... Needles.' Ordinarily this method was fool-proof and timeworthy.

On the Sunday night after his chance meeting with the girl he had every reason to believe was Audrey Hilton, Jack discovered that she was much on his mind. At six he had gone up to Teddy's room to pay his respects to the little fellow whom he had not seen all day.

'I wanted you to come this afternoon,' complained Teddy, in a tone that accused the doctor of having let him down. 'Lan Ying was here to see me.'

'Sorry, Teddy. It has been a busy day. Perhaps I may see your aunt tomorrow.'

'I told her about you.'

'And I suppose she laughed, as you said your mother did.'

Teddy's face wrinkled in perplexity.

'About my calling you "Mr. King,"' explained the doctor, smiling.

Teddy shook his head.

'No. Lan Ying wouldn't think that was funny.'

'So you didn't tell her that, eh?' drawled the doctor, absently, as he inspected the child's arm.

'He gave you a reputation as a very hard worker, Doctor Beaven,' said Miss McFey. 'I think Miss Hilton got the impression that you never slept.'

'You tell her not to worry, Teddy,' said the doctor, reassuringly. 'I get plenty of sleep.'

But not that night. At eleven he had gone to his room, made himself comfortable in dressing-gown and slippers, and begun an intensive review of a case-history — an intradural tumor which was going to be on the table promptly at nine in the morning.

He knitted his brows in earnest concentration upon the words before him, annoyed by interpolations which kept breaking into Doctor Rogers's account of a previous operation that had proved ineffective. 'I then removed another lamina at the upper part of the incision — (They object — may-bee — to one's leaving the hospital.) — and on opening the dura mater I saw on the left side of the cavity a round, dark-bluish mass about 3 mm. in diameter — (Oh? Perhaps I am not allowed. I am very sor-ree.) — resting upon the left lateral column and posterior root zone of the spinal cord — (I should not be taking your time, sir.)

And that was a fact. Realizing that these upraised brown eyes and full red lips were playing the very devil with tomorrow's duty, Jack determined to have it out with the intruder and be done with her. He tossed the bulky script onto the table, filled his pipe and lighted it, and settled himself deep in his chair, his eyes half closed.

He was in the operating-room now, and had nodded toward the door, signing that he was ready. Presently they wheeled her in. Young Linquist was at the foot, backing into the room. Harvey was at the other end, pushing. The rubber casters rolled noiselessly. Flagler was closing in, at the rear, with his portable anaesthetizing apparatus. Miss Terry was gingerly picking at a viciously hot towel with rubber-clad finger-tips, unwrapping the instruments. The only sound was the hiss of steam escaping from the valve of the autoclaves. He nodded to Harvey who drew down the rubber mask from its perch above the patient's head, and was making ready to adjust it over her face. It was all very vivid.

He put out a staying hand and regarded her almost childish face with solicitude, trying to brace himself against a sensation of tenderness. Roused by this scrutiny, she slowly opened her eyes, looked up into his with a bewildered little smile of recognition. 'Oh!' she said. 'Is something the matter with me?' She shook her head as she asked the question, hopeful of a negative reply. 'No,' he heard himself saying, firmly. 'There's something the matter with *me*. I'm operating on you to cure what ails me. Understand?'... 'May-bee,' she answered pensively.

Shaking himself loose from his painful reverie, Jack rose and paced up and down the room for a few turns, tossed aside his dressing-gown, dressed hurriedly in his street clothes, went downstairs and out into the warm June night. The policeman at the corner greeted him. 'You're out late, Doc.'

He returned from his walk about three, quite restored to his normal mind. He had been working too hard, his resistance was down, he had undertaken too many extra responsibilities in Tubby's absence. Everything would be all right again, tomorrow. One thing was certain: he wasn't going to permit an intriguing smile to make a monkey of him after all the expensive self-restraint invested in the pursuit of the only thing in the world that really mattered. This girl-smitten Beaven who had mooned and dreamed for a poignantly unhappy hour wasn't going to be allowed to double-cross this steadfast Beaven who had kept his nose to the grindstone for eight years. He took up the case-history of the intradural tumor and read it through with care, made a handful of memoranda, left a six-thirty call, went to bed — and slept.

* * * * * * * *

No effort was made to have a glimpse of this mysterious Lan Ying on Monday. At noon Jack had dropped in, briefly, to say 'Hello' to the little boy, promising to call later in the day. But he had not done so.

Time was an excellent healer of diseases. When in doubt about what to do, do nothing. While you are waiting to decide what should be done, the problem may solve itself. How often this had been demonstrated in baffling cases in the hospital. Tubby was an ardent advocate of this principle. Put the man to bed and keep him under observation for a while. Don't rush at him with pills and tools until

you're sure of your diagnosis. And give Time a chance to
do something for him.

This desire to see more of Audrey Hilton was probably an
ephemeral wish, a mere phosphorescence that would be
driven into total eclipse by the bright white lights of absorb-
ing tasks in the operating-room.

On Tuesday morning, a bit apologetic when he observed
that Teddy's feelings had been hurt, Jack went to some
pains to exhibit a friendly interest. The boy's bed was
strewn with sheets of drawing paper bearing pencil-sketches.

'Teddy has been anxious to show you some pictures,'
said Miss McFey. 'His aunt drew them for him, yesterday.'

The doctor took up three or four of the scattered pages
for close inspection, cleverly executed drawings of dwarfed
trees with branches that postured meaningfully.

'This,' explained Teddy, leaning forward with his cheek
snuggled against the doctor's forearm, 'is a very tired tree.
It has been working all night and is worn out.'

'Yes — I can see it is,' agreed the doctor.

'It seems to need some leaves,' put in Miss McFey.

'Of absence, probably,' he added, a remark that was
wasted on both of them.

'This one,' Teddy went on, pleased to be serving as inter-
preter, 'is Miss McFey, bringing in the orange juice. And
this is me, squatting, with the catcher's mitt. This is the
best one, I think.'

'So do I.' The doctor grinned over the grotesque but
deucedly lifelike personifications. He put down the trees
and took up another sheet.

'Faces,' said Teddy. 'Not really faces; just parts of faces.
Lan Ying likes to make eyes and noses and ears and chins,
by themselves. These are all mouths.'

'It's easy enough to find yours, Teddy.'

'I told Miss Hilton,' said the nurse, 'that it looked as
much like her own mouth as it did like Teddy's.'

Doctor Beaven briefly nodded, leaving Miss McFey to
speculate privately. He observed an inquisitive light in
her eyes.

'It would be very natural if they resembled each other,' he said promptly, hoping this comment would take effect.

'That's Miss McFey,' said Teddy.

'Umm.' The doctor nodded his recognition. 'Here's one that looks as if it might bite. Pretty grim, I'd say.'

Teddy rumpled his hair with white fingers and grinned uneasily.

'That isn't a very good one,' he said, reaching for the paper. 'Sometimes Lan Ying doesn't draw very good ones.'

Miss McFey was busily gathering up the sketches.

'We mustn't keep Doctor Beaven too long, Teddy. Let's clear off the bed now and give the doctor a chance to examine you.'

Suddenly the child resolved to be honest, no matter what came of it. He retrieved the page of mouths and pointed to the severe one.

'That's the way Lan Ying thinks you look,' he said, with a deprecatory chuckle. 'But that's because she never saw you.'

'And you told her, Teddy, that Doctor Beaven worked very hard,' assisted untactful Miss McFey, tactfully. 'So — she tried to draw a tired one.'

'This isn't a tired mouth,' remarked the doctor. 'This is an *iron* mouth.' He decided to make a little joke of it. 'This mouth could take a handful of marbles, Teddy, and chew 'em up into — into oatmeal.'

'Do you like to play marbles?' asked the child, much relieved to steer the conversation into a more pleasant channel.

Yes — he liked to play marbles; that is, he did a long time ago; and now we would have another look at the arm, and be on our way.

The incident was trivial enough, but he wished it hadn't happened. Clearly, this Audrey Hilton had given both her nephew and the nurse to understand that there had been no meeting. The McFey girl would know better. The drawing of his mouth might be arrestingly unflattering, but it was easily recognizable. McFey couldn't be much blamed if she was inquisitive. Perhaps she would confide the little mystery to someone else. The thought annoyed him. He could imagine the physically opulent McFey, whose red head was so full of romantic nonsense that she wasn't above making eyes at the orderlies, chattering some rubbish as — 'And she let on that she had never seen him, and he as much as said he'd never seen her, and there was that picture — the spit-'n'-image of him. What d'you know about that?'

He went up to the operating-room to make ready for a ten o'clock gall-bladder, changed to his surgical kit, and began the usual process of scrubbing up. He glanced into the mirror and studied his mouth from a fresh angle of observation. It wasn't a sullen mouth, or a cruel mouth, or a pessimistic mouth. It wasn't peevish or petulant. The worst thing you could say about it was that it looked — determined. He thrust an elbow against the control that increased the heat of the water in the basin and continued his vigorous scrubbing. Determined — that's the way it looked. A damn' good trait, too. Fine thing if more people had it. Maybe they'd get somewhere. (May-bee.)

The Chinese might not approve of that sentiment, but who were the Chinese? They hadn't contributed very much to the world's welfare. Mighty little they knew about science. You probably wouldn't see many mouths like this in China. But that didn't mean that this one was reprehensible. May-bee she hadn't meant it that way. May-bee she liked a firm, straight, indefatigable mouth.... But what difference did it make *what* manner of mouth she liked? She would be gone by day after tomorrow. He would put her out of his mind entirely. In fact, he had almost done so already. He caught his eye in the glass and queried it for a substantiation of this last remark, and was instantly informed that he was a liar.

His reflection candidly told him that not only was he trying to fool himself about his dismissal of Audrey Hilton from his mind; he had also tried to fool himself about that mouth of his. 'Determined' — he had said, complacently.

That wasn't the word for it at all. 'Detached' — that was
it. Except for his tireless activities in a small world of test-
tubes and retorts, microscopes and fluoroscopes, dissections
and operations, he lived apart. It was a dismaying world,
cluttered with pickled corpses and sick rabbits. He had
put the real world behind him so long ago that he had forgotten what it was about. It had been years since he had
talked to an old man, except to get his case-history. He
knew so little about young children that he was embarrassed
in their presence. His understanding of women was restricted to an accurate knowledge of their anatomy. His
few men friends moved about in a world not much larger
than his own, talking in scientific terms and smelling of
antiseptics and ether.

It was a detached mouth; and, in the effort to arrive at
this detachment, it had become *hard*. Not much wonder
if nobody slapped Jack Beaven on the back, or detained
him with a droll story, or suggested a few hours off duty
for a frolic.

Audrey Hilton had captured and defined that mouth
with a half-dozen pencil-strokes. She knew more about his
mouth than he did.

He held out his arms for the surgical gown and the Warren
girl slipped the sleeves to the shoulder. Their eyes met for
a split second. Her impersonal look suggested that if she
had any talent for drawing, her picture of him would be
much the same as the one that had disturbed him. Maybe
he looked like that to everybody.

* * * * * * * *

The next morning he told Teddy that he might go home
on Thursday. It was no surprise. They had been talking
about it for several days.

'When Miss Hilton comes, this afternoon,' he added, to
Miss McFey, 'you may say that I shall hope to see her
before she leaves the hospital. You will call me, please.'

From then on he went about his usual duties in an
abstracted manner, frequently consulting his watch, now

wondering why the time passed so slowly, now wishing the interview over. When three o'clock came, he found himself in an expectant attitude; starting, a little, whenever he heard the sound of a house-telephone. At three-forty-five he was in the men's surgical, readjusting an elevating apparatus for a broken hip, when a ward nurse informed him he was wanted on the telephone. His heart bumped.

'Beaven,' said Doctor Shane, urgently, 'come up to operating-room C. They've just brought in another automobile crack-up. Two of 'em. Looks bad for the girl. I haven't had a chance to examine her very closely yet, but I'm afraid her neck is broken.'

'O.K., Shane; I'll be right up.'

He wasn't sure whether he was annoyed or relieved that something had interfered. On the way to the operating-room he decided that he would ask one of the nurses to inform Miss Hilton of the emergency that had turned up. He would see her, if possible, later.

Arriving in the operating-room, it became apparent at once that they were, as Shane had suspected, dealing with a broken neck. The young woman, probably twenty-two, was dully conscious and when asked to move her arm could not do so. Several plates were made of the injury, and it was evident that considerable damage had been done to the cord. Jack decided against any operative interference but followed along to the room to observe the rate of temperature increase which would indicate whether heroic measures should be undertaken at once.

He talked to her in a very business-like way.

'What's your name?'

'Prentiss. Nancy Prentiss.'

'Miss Prentiss —— ' Jack began, seriously.

'Mrs. Prentiss,' she said.

'Oh. Then the man who was hurt with you is your husband.'

'No. My husband is away — looking for a job.'

'Well, Mrs. Prentiss, your recovery depends on your own ability to keep your head and obey orders. Your neck is hurt very badly, but I think you are going to get well — provided you lie still, no matter how uncomfortable you are, and make sure you do no further injury to this place that is broken. For the present I am going to stay right here with you — and so is the nurse. Remember that any crying, any excitement is going to send your fever kiting; and then we will have to do something very serious. If you will keep cool and be quiet, you have a chance. Are you going to work with us?'

'Yes, Doctor. May I see my mother?'

'Tomorrow.'

'She will want to see me.'

'We will explain.'

'She will take on, if you don't let her see me.'

'Thanks for telling me. If your mother is a taker-on, we can do nicely without her for a couple of days. Don't worry. We will tell her all about it.'

'She has my baby.'

'Very good. It's in safe hands. You will not need to fret about it. No more talking now.'

At nine the chart showed that the temperature was holding at 102½°. The patient was asleep under a strong sedative.

'I am going out now for an hour,' said Jack to the nurse. 'If you want me, the Desk will know where I am.'

He had had nothing to eat since morning but a sandwich and a glass of milk at noon, but the stresses of the past few hours had made him indifferent to the thought of food. Going down to the main office he put through a call to the Livingstone Hotel and presently recognized the low-pitched voice with the foreign influence giving it a cautious precision.

'Very sorry not to have seen you today, Miss Hilton. We had some unexpected trouble here, and I couldn't get away. They may have told you. I should have liked to talk with you before you take your nephew home. Is there anything I can do for you?'

'No, thank you, Doctor,' she said, carefully spacing her

words. 'I am sor-ree too that I must leave without your instructions about Teddy, his exercises, and —— '

'How would it be if I came over to see you now? I am relieved from duty for a little while.'

'Yes; you may come. Thank you.'

Hurriedly changing to his street clothes, Jack took a taxi to the hotel. Upon inquiring at the desk for Miss Hilton, the clerk said she was in Parlor Suite A, and had left word that he was to be shown up. He followed the bell-boy to the elevator, ascended to the top floor, pressed the button, and waited, wondering what manner of reception he might have.

She opened the door and he stood for a moment rather non-plussed. Teddy hadn't been fooling. His Aunt Audrey was Chinese.

In response to her deferential bow, he stepped into the room. She was dressed in a black satin jacket with a high throat and long sleeves, black satin trousers, tiny black satin slippers.

Taking his hat, she nodded toward a chair and seated herself opposite him.

'Thank you,' she said, 'for coming.'

For five minutes Beaven was strictly professional, laying out a program of simple exercises for restoring the boy's arm to its normal condition and usefulness. Audrey Hilton listened attentively, with an occasional question when his terms became too technical for her to understand.

Then there was a little pause. Beaven's errand seemed to be over, but he was not ready to go. He hesitated. He could not overcome the impulse to continue on a more personal basis.

'Teddy said you were Chinese, but I thought the child was just having fun.'

'Not really, Doctor.' Her tone was comradely. 'You knew — on Sunday — that I wasn't quite — quite ortho-dox. Oh, how severely your eyes accused me of being some-thing foreign.'

Jack smiled and nodded.

'And my mouth, too, I fear. I admit that I couldn't quite make you out, and of course it wasn't any of my business to —— '

'To solve the riddle. Certainly not. But if it interests you, at all, I shall tell you.'

'Tell me anything you like,' said Jack, encouragingly. 'I feel sure it's more than a mere masquerade.'

'Thank you. Do you want to smoke, Doctor Beaven? A pipe — may-bee?' She abandoned the straight chair where she had sat so primly, and chose a low stool, folding her arms over her knees, and watching him with interest while he filled his pipe.

'There is of course nothing unusual about an American's being born in Hongkong,' she began. 'This has happened many, many times; children of missionaries, and embassy people. But it is not often that an American child remains abroad very long. He is sent back to school. He quickly forgets the land of his birth and finds himself quite at home in the land of his — his nationality.'

'And you remained,' said Jack, 'until you became Chinese. Is that it?'

'My father was the commander of a steamship. For twelve years he went back and forth from America to China. Naturally he had opportunities to meet many well-born and educated citizens of China, on their journeys to this country on business; commercial, political. It was not always comfortable for them. Sometimes they were given the cold shoulder by Americans who had had no experience with Chinese, except those they had seen in some menial service.

'My father seemed to understand their predicament, and they probably sensed his sympathy. May-bee the word was quietly passed among them that Captain Hilton was a cosmopolitan gentleman. One never knows just how such information gets about in China. They are very good at keeping their own counsel, and equally good at sharing knowledge that might be of mutual benefit.

'There was a Chinese merchant in Hongkong named Sen Ling —— '

Jack's eyes widened a little.

'What is it Teddy calls you? — Lan Ying?'

She nodded, smiling. Responding to his evident interest, she seemed to welcome the opportunity to explain herself.

'On Sen Ling's first trip to America his feelings were hurt so badly that when he boarded my father's ship for his return he was half-ill with his humiliation. Perhaps it was his own fault, really. He had seen so many splendid things done for his servants who had been in the hospital and school of the American Christians that he thought our people here had a feeling of fellowship with the Chinese. He might have known better. If it had so happened that he himself — together with Chinese men of his own caste — were faced with the miseries of ignorant and superstitious Americans of the lowest class, he might have fed them for sheer pity's sake; but he would not have expected the Americans of his own social rating to express great gratitude over his philanthropies. He might rather have expected them to be embarrassed and annoyed by his performing charities they had neglected. They would hold themselves stiffly aloof, and he would never understand. He would despise them for their haughtiness, and all he would ever know of their civilization he would have to learn from their ignorant masses.

'So — Sen Ling, hopeful of finding a warmth of heart in the Americans, was badly snubbed. And as if it was not enough for him to board the ship for home wounded and shamed, a few Americans on the vessel took pains to let him see their contempt. My father had it from the ship's doctor that Sen Ling was ill, and he went to his stateroom. They had a long talk. My father moved Sen Ling to a cabin in his own suite, had him out on the bridge and explained the mysteries in the chart-room. And then, after the voyage, he probably forgot all about the incident; but Sen Ling remembered. After that, whenever my father's ship docked at Hongkong, Sen Ling was at the wharf waiting to bow a welcome to him; sent him gifts; invited him to be his guest. At first, my father pleaded business as his excuse for refusing to accept these invitations. But, once he had gone there, he never made port at Hongkong without calling at the house of Sen Ling where he was entertained as a dear friend. It was a palatial home.' She paused, reflecting.

'I am sure you must have seen it,' said Jack, hoping she might elaborate.

'Yes — I had always lived there until about three years ago. It was verree difficult to leave my Chinese home. For a while after coming to America I was so lonesome I thought I should have to return. I cannot tell you how deeply indebted I am to Doctor and Mrs. Cunningham for their friendship when I was so distressed. They have frequently taken me with them on little trips. The first time they did so — only a few days after I had arrived in this country — they brought me with them to a Commencement at the University.' She looked up and smiled. 'Doctor Cunningham made a talk to the members of his class at the Livingstone Hotel.'

'Yes,' said Jack. 'I remember.'

'You did not like his speech.' Her tone invited him to say why he had not liked it.

'I'm afraid I did not hear very much of it,' he replied. 'There was a good deal of confusion in the foyer where we stood. And my attention was — diverted. . . . It had been an eventful day,' he hastened to add. 'My own graduation — and a flock of rather unusual occurrences.' Then, impulsively, he confided, 'I didn't mean to offend you, that night. I have always been sorry.'

Her smile raced his heart.

'You have a good memory,' she said.

'At times.' Jack felt the three-year-old episode had now been sufficiently reviewed and hoped to restore the conversation to its previous theme. 'So — for most of your life — you've lived in China. Wouldn't you like to tell me about it?'

'Gladly — if I am not keeping you.'

The telephone rang. She rose and answered it.

'For you,' she said, handing him the receiver.

'Yes. Yes, Miss Warren. Yes; right away.'

He tossed the receiver back on the hook and turned to her with a little shake of his head.

'That's the way it goes,' he muttered. 'That' — he pointed to the telephone as if it symbolized the restrictions under which he lived — '*that* thing has a strangle-hold on me — for life!' He reached out his hand.

'I'm sorree,' she said.

Chapter VII

NEXT morning, after the departure of Audrey Hilton and Teddy, Jack Beaven received an official communication from the Board of Trustees offering him the position of Assistant Professor of Anatomy. The gratifying news arrived at a strategic moment, for the recipient was very restless and depressed.

With a consistent perversity, Tubby had chosen to arrive in town yesterday just in time to assume full charge of the migration, thus making it entirely unnecessary for Jack to accompany Miss Hilton and her young nephew to the train. Unable to have another glimpse of Audrey after having been hastily summoned from the hotel to the hospital, he had counted on a final word with her, on the way to the railroad station. He had no hope of learning the rest of the Chinese story, but there would be some comfort in seeing her once more. After that, he would endeavor to put her out of his thoughts.

Shortly before they left the hospital, Jack had gone to Teddy's room to say 'Good-bye.' The excited little boy was friendly but distracted by the confusion of packing. Audrey, at their formal handshake of parting, looked for an instant into his eyes with an expression of anxiety that suggested a candid sharing of his disappointment in leaving their acquaintance dangling with no expectation of cultivating it further.

Feeling himself decidedly in the way, Jack had left the room and gone about his business, promptly experiencing a sag in his spirits. He hadn't realized until now the extent

of Audrey Hilton's invasion of his peace. All afternoon he
kept saying to himself that if there had been an opportunity
for a few words with her alone, he might have been satisfied
to declare their brief friendship a closed incident. If he could
have had a chance to thank her for giving him a little
glimpse of her most interesting story; if he could have told
her how much he regretted the circumstances that had
broken into her fascinating narrative; if he could have
expressed the hope that sometime — who knew? — they
might meet again, it would have helped immeasurably to
bring their mutual interest to a much less disquieting conclusion. He slept very little that night and awoke in the
morning with the feeling that life was barely worth the
bother of living it.

With the arrival of the impressive document, Jack immediately felt that the universe could be viewed if not with
jubilation at least with patience, tolerance, and a willingness to arbitrate.

The University's recognition of him had not materially
altered Jack's duties but had definitely improved his status.
Henceforth, instead of serving merely as a refractor behind
the brilliant light shed by Tubby Forrester, he would be
given a chance to generate a bit of illumination on his own
account. Now he was to have better rating; a respectable
salary, too, though that didn't matter so much except for
the satisfaction of receiving wages commensurate to his
work. The money problem had never bothered him. Indeed
the modest trust fund which constituted his inheritance had
been so much more than his need of it that its reinvestment
annually had amassed a tidy sum. To have his salary
raised from seventy-five dollars per month to two hundred
— immediately effective — meant nothing more to Jack
than an acknowledgment that his services to the Medical
College and the hospital had increased in value. With no
dependents and few desires, this feature of his promotion
counted for very little beyond its pleasant implication that
he was progressing professionally; and that, after all, was
the only thing worth a moment's thought.

He was sincerely grateful that this boost had come to him at an hour when it was a debatable matter whether his profession was going to command the attention he had previously given it. Now he was able to take a fresh grip on his responsibilities, reassuring himself that his steady devotion to a policy of hard work and no play was justified. The letter had come in the nick of time. It would help him forget the girl.

Tubby, of course, was directly responsible for the appointment. Under no circumstances would the Board of Trustees have taken this action without the full approval of the Professor of Anatomy. Tubby had suggested it and had seen to it that the resolution was put through. Common decency demanded that some expression of gratitude should be promptly forthcoming; no easy task, in this case.

That afternoon, Jack called at Tubby's office, not quite sure yet about the phrasing of his appreciation; sure only that it was up to him to acknowledge the favor.

'Doctor Forrester,' he began, 'I have received the appointment as Assistant Professor of Anatomy. I — I appreciate it very much.'

'Then you'd better write to the Board of Trustees,' drawled Tubby, 'and tell 'em so.'

'Thank you,' said Jack, lamely, feeling that there wasn't much more to be added. He turned to leave the room.

'Doctor Beaven,' barked Tubby. 'It is none of my business where you live, but I understand they're crowded in the Hospital Annex. Now that you are a member of the faculty, I suggest that you move to other quarters. You can afford to, now.'

Jack felt a slow flush creeping up his cheeks. Tubby's insinuation that he was likely to be too stingy to leave his free quarters among the interns was insufferable. God knew he wouldn't have been living there if his day and night duties in the hospital had not required it. For an instant he was impelled to say as much but thought better of it. After all, he had come here to thank Tubby; not to make war with him.

'Yes, sir,' he said, shortly, and left the room.

The fact was — however indignant he felt — it hadn't occurred to him that he would now be free to live more comfortably. Doubtless the thought would have come to him presently. It would seem very queer to be setting up an establishment of his own. With the new idea in mind, he took a couple of hours off, next day, to investigate available bachelor suites in the vicinity.

Having lived for years with the bare necessities of existence, sleeping on a hospital bed and sharing a community bathroom, his mental vision of new quarters comprehended a small suite of two furnished rooms and a bath. But after having been shown a more commodious apartment on a residence street fully a mile from the Medical College it suddenly struck him that if he was to live the rest of his life alone he was at least entitled to surround himself with a few things he could call his own. The apartment was unfurnished. For the next few days, every spare hour was spent in shopping for the equipment of his new home. Once he had begun it, he gave the matter his full attention, wondering — as he saw his possessions arrive — why he had gone so long without desiring them.

The little cubicle that the apartment-house manager had — no doubt jocularly — referred to as a library was the only room left unplanned. Jack closed the door on that, deciding to wait until he could think of some use for it. The living-room was to serve also as a library. One of the bedrooms — the one with the north light — would be fitted up as a laboratory. It was a strange sensation — to be a householder.

He framed the most recent pictures of Jean and her two small children and hung them above his new leather-topped desk, wishing he had the right to ask Audrey Hilton for hers, too; wondering whether, if she sent him one, it would help or hurt. This idea was promptly dismissed as impracticable; a bit silly, indeed, in view of their short acquaintance and the improbability of their meeting again. For soft sentimentality this thought — he felt, on sober

reflection — should be given some sort of prize. Tubby
should be called in to make the award.

Undeniably, this rigging up of Jack Beaven's new establishment had slightly mellowed him. He was becoming
domesticated. Within ten days he was living at the new
address, realizing that there was something at once amusing
and pathetic about his proprietary pride as he moved about
among his possessions, trying out the big leather chairs and
the over-stuffed davenport; and wondering, as he sat at
his large desk (he had ordered some very good-looking
social stationery), who, besides Jean, he might write to.
Tony Wollason, quietly growing leaner and shabbier in a
little rat-hole of a town in Wyoming, was surprised a week
later to have a chatty reply to his Christmas greetings.
Bugs Cartmell, flat-footing for the Health Officer of Peoria,
was likewise amazed to discover that his former fellow-
lodger at Mrs. Doyle's remembered his existence. Jack
also began a few letters addressed respectively to Miss
Hilton, Miss Audrey Hilton, Audrey, and Lan Ying, tearing
them into small, precise squares and tossing them into a very
handsome waste-basket lined with metal and bound in tan
leather to match the new desk.

Transportation facilities between the hospital and the
apartment being found sluggish and unreliable, Jack presently resolved to buy a car. In a few days a modish maroon
roadster was assigned a private stall in the parking-lot at
the rear of the hospital. A freshly lettered card, affixed
to the low railing in front of the stall, said — DOCTOR
BEAVEN. This, he felt, was the most convincing certificate he had received, accrediting his arrival as a seasoned
and recognized member of the medical profession. His
appointment to the faculty had afforded him a new self-
confidence; his acquirement of a home of his own had given
him a feeling of permanence and stability. But his name,
printed in the same-sized black letters as the neighboring
names of Forrester, Shane, McCormack, Osgood, and a
dozen more — all of them his seniors — had a curious effect
upon him, deepening his resolve to give the profession that

had so early and generously rewarded him for his single-
hearted zeal a reconsecrated fidelity to prove that the honor
had not been too unworthily bestowed. The car may have
been an extravagance, but the name on the railing was a
stimulating challenge.

* * * * * * * *

It was in the last week of August that the incident occurred which drove a new wedge between Jack and Tubby.
Had anyone else but Doctor Forrester been caught in the
ridiculous situation into which Jack had come involuntarily,
the matter would have been dismissed with a laugh. But
the great man's pride was badly injured. He had been
surprised in the act of displaying a softness of heart; and
Beaven, of all people, had witnessed it. The person most
to blame for the unfortunate affair was the Prentiss baby.

The recovery of Nancy Prentiss was one of the major
achievements of Tubby Forrester's career. Cervical injuries
always registered a very high mortality rate, and Nancy
had been so badly hurt that for three days after she had
been brought into the hospital everybody — including
Tubby — agreed it would be more humane to let her die
in peace than to subject her to an inevitably futile mauling.

But when she refused to confirm the general prediction,
Tubby — who had popped in, every two hours, to inspect
her chart — began toying with the thought of attempting
an operation. Not in the memory of the eldest nurse had
Tubby seemed so indecisive. He would stand by Nancy's
bed, tapping his gold pince-nez against his teeth, his gimlety
little eyes narrowed to mere slits; then he would utter a
snort that had the value of — 'Certainly not! Nonsense!
Silly!' — and leave the room, to return shortly and go into
another trance.

At eight o'clock on the morning of the fifth day, Tubby
impulsively growled, 'Get her ready! Up she goes!'

The case attracted wide attention. A flood of gaudy and
unwelcome newspaper publicity, keenly embarrassing to
the noted neurologist, spread tidings of the 'miracle' he

had wrought. Hundreds of wistful inquiries poured in from relatives of incurables and inoperables who seemed to be under the impression that the University Hospital had gone into competition with Lourdes or Sainte Anne de Beaupré.

To Tubby's credit it was observed that while he made short work of the excited sensationalists who sought interviews, he was unusually dutiful in replying to the voluminous correspondence which their noisy dispatches had stirred up, and did his utmost to put himself and the hospital right with these people who sought more aid than he or any other man could hope to deliver.

But, however much the press reports had exaggerated the story, the fact remained that Tubby had saved the young woman's life when the chances of her survival or her death were related — according to medical annals — as one is related to three hundred and ten. Professional journals gave generous space to the case-history and the technique employed, a score of surgeons specializing in neurological surgery visited the patient, the whole hospital was proud as a peacock, and Tubby's habitual scowl gave way to intermittent flashes of good-nature, almost as rare as the operation he had performed.

From the very first, Tubby's relation to Nancy Prentiss would have made a dog laugh. It might have been unfair to speak of Nancy as scum; for scum — especially in laboratory experiments — occasionally had considerable significance and value. The girl had had about as little mental or moral discipline as could be imagined of any person living in a civilized community, and had not been provided with the emotional stability demanded by so long a grind of tedium and discomfort as her convalescence required. It was a case where the post-operative care was of the highest importance. Nobody but Tubby could do anything with her.

She was an impudent and wilful little rascal with a vocabulary of invectives that would have paled the cheek of an inebriated sailor. For unalloyed brass and impertinence, Nancy had probably never met a rival worthy of her talents until she collided with Tubby Forrester. Having capitulated with the humble concession that she had never known anyone so mean and tough, Nancy became Tubby's devoted slave and beamed on him with the fascinated eyes of an obedient collie.

Under the peculiar circumstances, Tubby became Nancy's slave, too. The whole hospital was aware of Tubby's predicament and rejoiced in it. He was called at all hours to deal with Nancy's tantrums. On these occasions the amenities they exchanged were so forthright that the nurses left the room.

Tubby had given his patient to understand, at the outset, that it was of no personal concern to him whether she lived or died, except for the single fact that he wanted to demonstrate the success of the surgical technique he had employed. Nobody had ever been quite that honest with Nancy before. One day she had had a rather mellow moment in which she confided a good deal of her brief but exciting past, and Tubby agreed with her that it would be no great loss to the social order if she failed to recover.

'In fact,' he added, judicially, 'I suppose it is an immoral act on my part to prolong your life. You are no good, Nancy, and I see no excuse for your living at all. But I'll tell you this: if you let me down, by refusing to get well, I'll — I'll never speak to you again!'

And so — the indestructible Nancy had got well enough to be taken to her mother's frowsy little cottage on the outskirts of town, after two months of grueling immobility, lying on her face, imprisoned by bandages and pillows as inflexible as sandbags.

Several times daily, during her last two weeks at the hospital, Tubby was sent for to keep her from spoiling the whole thing. Toward the last, as her returning strength increased her restlessness and exasperation over the confinement, the nurses did not elaborate on the nature of the call when they telephoned to Tubby. They just said, 'Nancy,' and Tubby said, 'Coming.'

Sometimes he swore at her most horribly, and it was

said that once in a fine frenzy he called her by a very
unpleasant — albeit by no means misapplied — name, upon
receipt of which she called him a stuck-up, pig-eyed, little
pennyfeist, an appellation undeniably impolite but — in
the opinion of many who heard about the affair — approximately correct. When savagery was of no avail, Tubby
would soothe her with rash promises. On these occasions
she badgered him into pledges of favors to be rendered
when and if she ever got out of this damn' plaster cast.
It was often wondered to what extent Tubby would endeavor to keep his word.

One afternoon in August an emergency case came into
the hospital which clearly called for Tubby's good judgment.
A painter had fallen from a scaffolding, and there had been
a dislocation of the twelfth thoracic vertebra. Having
studied the X-ray plate, Jack Beaven found the cord slightly
injured. Preferring that Tubby should see the picture
before anything was done, a general search for him was
instituted without success. Then somebody remembered
that he had been going down every afternoon to see Nancy
Prentiss, who had no telephone.

Jack drove to the house. The front door was open. He
was about to rap on it when he heard Nancy's metallic voice
issuing from a room adjacent to the little sitting-room at
the door of which he waited with startled eyes.

'C'mout o' there, damn yuh! I see yuh, a-crouchin'
behind that there tractor! Up with 'em, now, er I'll blow
yer head off!'

Nancy's enunciation was slightly impaired, leading to
the suspicion that she had been gagged. Jack opened the
screen and walked in, crossed the living-room, and stood
in the doorway. With her yellow hair done up in curl-
papers, and her jaws kneading an incredibly large mouthful
of chewing gum, Nancy was reading aloud a western shocker.
She was flat on her back in bed, her knees drawn up to lend
support to the magazine. She glanced up, grinned, and
said, 'Hello, little one. Looking for your papa?' Nancy
pointed impishly to a corner of the room not yet in Jack's

view. He stepped through the doorway and halted, unbelieving.

By the window, in an old-fashioned, ramshackle rocking-chair, sat Tubby holding Nancy's baby in his arms, with one hand steadying a tilted bottle. The impromptu nurse glanced up and glared at the intruder murderously. Jack's amazement at the sight quickly gave way to an outburst of laughter. He could no more have controlled it than his heart-beats.

'Smatter?' demanded Nancy, vigorously agitating her gum. 'Didn'cha ever see anybody feed a baby before?' But this comment failed to have a steadying effect on Jack. He couldn't stop laughing.

'Get out!' roared Tubby, his voice cracking a little with fury. Jack was suddenly sobered. Tubby seemed about to be threatened with a stroke. Nobody had ever been that mad before.

'You're wanted at the hospital,' he said, retreating.

'Get out!' screamed Tubby.

And Jack got out. After that, their relation — at no time amicable — was so strained that the hospital noticed it. In the operating-room, Tubby would say to the Warren girl, 'Tell Doctor Beaven to do this suture.' And Jack, at Tubby's elbow, would comply. Merely to say that they despised each other was to have said nothing whatsoever about it.

* * * * * * * *

Doctor Shane had hinted that he would like to see the new diggings. More than ready to comply, for the apartment was still a novelty and he was anxious to show it to his friend, Jack drove him over there after having luncheon with him down town.

'Beaven, if I were you,' said Shane, settling himself comfortably into a big tan-leather chair and fumbling in his tobacco-pouch, 'I would ask for a couple of weeks off before the new semester opens.'

'So? I hadn't felt the need of a vacation.'

'Well,' drawled Shane, nodding his head sagely, 'you'd better. Far back as I can recall, you have had no time off; at least not since you began working with Forrester. And you needn't tell me that working with Forrester is any fun. It's no secret that you and Tubby are in each other's hair.'

Jack laughed dryly and minimized the ruction with a gesture.

'We understand each other,' he said. 'Doctor Forrester's bark is worse than his bite.'

'Maybe so — but I'd rather be bit, once in a while, than barked at all the time. I know you admire Tubby's skill, and so do I. But he's hard to get along with. He's wearing to the nerves. Anybody who has to see as much of him as you do should have a leave of absence occasionally. If it was me, I'd want to be away about eight months out of twelve.'

Jack loyally mumbled something about Tubby's not being so bad, really; and, as for a vacation, he wouldn't know what to do with one if he had it.

'Don't be silly!' said Shane. 'A few days away from the grind will do wonders for you. Change of air, change of scenery. You're not quite up to par, you know. I watched you today, stirring things around with your fork and not eating anything. You've been glum as a clam lately. Maybe somebody or something has been getting your goat. I don't know. And, anyway, it's none of my business. But you'd better not start in on your new faculty job with your tail dragging. I'm telling you this for your own good; same as if I was your uncle.'

Jack shook his head and lamely repeated that he wouldn't know where to go or what to do.

'Hell!' shouted Shane, pointing in the wrong direction with his pipe. 'Any number of things to do! Take a boat trip up the Great Lakes. Toss a few mystery stories or some such tripe into a bag and go on a cruise for a couple of weeks. Come back fit as a fiddle. Brown as a bun. Full of zip. Why not go fishing? Like to fish?'

'I don't know whether I do or not. Probably not. Never did — except for grubby perch and blue-gills when I was a youngster.'

'Well — it's about time you learned. Best diversion there is. If you want to stop thinking, try fishing. Get out in a flat-bottomed boat with some old guy who doesn't know what your occupation is and couldn't talk about it with any intelligence if he did know. Live out in the open, broiling your own catch, and fighting deer-flies. Spend the evening reading detective stories. Give your mind a complete rest. Better think that over.'

The idea wasn't half bad. The past few days had been unusually trying. Tubby had been impossible. The weather had been depressing. Jack had never been quite so lonesome. The new living quarters had solved a few small problems but had presented a new one. It was going to be a great treat to get out of the crowded and noisy Hospital Annex where there was no privacy at all. You could live like a gentleman. Nobody would borrow your last shirt or swipe your razor-blades or come in singing 'Sweet Adeline' when you were short on sleep. But, it was a radical change to move out of all this confusion into the quiet of the new apartment. Lonesome? You woke up in the night, roused by the silence. The silence wasn't merely the absence of racket. The silence was positive. Perhaps you needed a cat or a dog or a geranium; something alive. Now that you had a new home, you wanted something to share it with you. And then you would get to thinking along that line. Presently you would arrive at the thought that needed to be pitched out of your mind, pretty soon, if you didn't want to go crazy; a monstrously silly idea it was, too, for it was very doubtful if she had given you a second thought. The telephone had rung, and you had answered it and said 'Good night' and left the room, and that was all. She had handed you your hat and looked up into your eyes, very soberly, and said, 'Sor-ree.' And that was all. And that was enough. And that ought to be the end of it.

But Shane's suggestion was worth considering; so he

milled it for several hours and asked for a two-weeks' leave. The request was granted without a word of debate.

'Certainly,' said Doctor Osgood. 'Quite proper. Hope you have a good time. Leave your address at the office, so we will know how to reach you.'

Jack felt puzzled and not a little chagrined. It would be most ungracious not to tell Osgood where he was going, and he disliked to confess that he had no plans.

'I thought I'd go fishing,' he said, impulsively.

'Excellent. Up north, I suppose.'

Jack nodded, wondering whether 'north' meant some particular river or lake that the fishermen knew about, or extended on to the pole.

'Cunningham writes me there's some fine bass fishing now in Spruce Lake, only an hour's drive for him. Wanted me to come up, but I can't get away just now. He would be glad to have you come, I know.'

Jack meditated a reply with averted eyes.

'I'm afraid that would be an imposition,' he said, reluctantly. 'I do not know Doctor Cunningham.'

Osgood waved the objection aside with a flick of his hand.

'That wouldn't make the slightest difference. Cunningham is a grand fellow. He will enjoy having you. And, as for knowing him, he was much pleased over your attentions to the King child. Forrester told him the operation was mainly your job.'

Jack's eyes widened a little, but he shook his head resolutely. It was a great temptation. It would give him a chance to see Audrey Hilton. But was that good sense? It was costing him a lot of earnest will-power to barricade his mind against this girl. He'd better stick to his guns. Besides, it wouldn't be very good cricket to accept Cunningham's intimate friendship and hospitality, considering how little respect he had for him professionally.

'Thanks, Doctor,' he replied, firmly, 'but it's quite too much to ask of Cunningham. I wouldn't feel comfortable about it.'

'Very well.' Osgood turned away to attend to the queries

of a waiting nurse, and Jack set out on his morning's duties in the wards. He had turned down a golden opportunity to do the thing he very much desired, but he had demonstrated his ability to make that sacrifice. His self-satisfaction squared his shoulders. He had himself well in hand, he reflected proudly.

At noon, as he was leaving the hospital, Osgood summoned him into his office. Osgood's face was beaming with an enigmatic grin. He handed Jack a telegram. It was from Cunningham.

VERY HAPPY INDEED TO EXTEND INVITATION TO BEAVEN FOR FISHING EXCURSION TELL HIM TO WIRE ME WHAT DAY HE IS COMING

Jack read the message through twice before looking up. His face was troubled.

'Mighty good of you — both,' he admitted, slowly, 'but I don't see how I can do that.'

Osgood chuckled boyishly.

'I don't see how you can do anything else,' he declared. 'It's all arranged for you. You can't wire Cunningham that you don't want to come.'

'That's true,' said Jack. He was thoughtful for a long moment. 'Well — thanks ... I'll go.'

Now that the decision had been made for him, he felt he had an adequate alibi to offer his conscience. He grinned dryly at remembrance of the droll yarn about the good Catholic who, on a Friday, having called for shark, whale, and octopus, without results, had reluctantly taken roast beef. In an almost hilarious mood, he hurried away to the laboratory to inspect his cultures. He was going to see Audrey! Through no fault of his, the matter had been determined for him. He had done his best to avoid this temptation. Certainly he had played fair with his conscience. Heaven knew he had 'asked for fish.'

There was an operation at one. He whistled a few bars of 'Sweet Rosie O'Grady' while scrubbing up. Tubby, at an adjacent basin, scowled at him and he grinned amiably.

'Losing your mind?' asked Tubby, anxiously.

'Yes, *sir*!' boasted Jack, recklessly.

'It's the heat,' declared Tubby.

'It's the humidity!' amended Jack, vigorously scouring his fingers. 'Good old humidity! Makes things grow! Yes, s-i-r!'

'You'd better pipe down,' muttered the Warren girl, holding up his surgical gown. 'He'll think you're drunk. Maybe you are. You certainly act like it.' She moved almost into his arms and sniffed him suspiciously.

'I'm going fishing,' he whispered, impressively.

'You're going crazy,' she replied, tying his tapes.

'That'll make it unanimous,' he said. 'We'll all be crazy.'

Late that afternoon, Jack drove down town to outfit himself for the expedition. It was a very disconcerting experience. The young man behind the counter in the sporting-goods store was at once misled about his unidentified customer.

'I want to look at some fishing equipment,' said the customer.

'Very good, sir. What did you have in mind? Where are you fishing?'

Jack jerked his head in a general northerly direction and said, 'Oh — up state.'

'You'll probably be looking for muskies.'

'Probably.' Jack didn't know what muskies were but if they were fish indigenous to northern lakes — which seemed a reasonable deduction — he would probably be looking for them.

'And bass,' added the clerk. 'Of course you have your rods.' This was said in a tone implying that if a prospective customer didn't even have his rods he had no business here, at all.

'Of course,' replied Jack, coldly, a bit irritated over the insinuation. The fellow had said 'rods.' What would you do with more than one rod? One for muskies, probably; one for bass, one for sharks.

'Reels in good order?'

Jack nodded. It was apparent that reels were temperamental.

'I suppose you want lines, leads, spoons, flies; eh?' The clerk turned to push the sliding-door of a tall glass case. 'Here you are, sir. If you'll step around the counter, you may look 'em over.'

'I'm afraid I've left my car parked a little too close to a fire-plug,' said Jack. 'Excuse me, please.'

As he drove away, there swept over him a feeling of mortification, not induced entirely by this episode. He was realizing how very little he knew of the sports and pastimes which constituted so large an area of almost every normal man's life. Other men could tell you the standing of all the clubs in the Big Leagues, knew what was par on every hole on every course within a radius of twenty miles, knew the names of hockey players; knew where to fish and when — and what to take along. He didn't know anything. He scowled darkly as he drove into the tight garage. He didn't know anything about anything that men were interested in. Perhaps he'd better wait for the fishing tackle; make a clean breast of it to Cunningham.

He decided that he would drive up on Friday. With an early start he could do it nicely in a day. Putting through a toll-call he informed Doctor Cunningham of his plans, thanked him for his generosity, and said that he would go to the Roscommon Hotel, upon arrival. Cunningham, boisterously genial, would have none of that. 'No, sir. Coming directly to my house! The lady may want to have a few friends in for dinner. You try to get here by six-thirty. Next morning we'll go out to the lake.'

The two intervening days were tiresomely long. He had made a wise decision about the vacation. Needed to be out of doors. Needed to inspect the strange mind of this generous fellow, Cunningham. Needed to have one more glimpse of Audrey Hilton before he put her permanently out of his thoughts. Of course Cunningham would expect him to call on Teddy and his family. No more than common courtesy

to do that. Even tough old Tubby Forrester would have
wanted to pay his respects to a patient under similar circumstances.

* * * * * * * *

The drive was delightful. It was the first long trip that
Jack had taken alone. The top of the roadster had been let
down, transforming it into quite another type of vehicle.
The whole out-of-doors was yours. The car skimmed along,
more like a speed-boat than a thing on wheels. The dawn
breeze swept by, cool, invigorating. The sky was streaked
with pink. One's nostrils dilated eagerly to inhale the early
morning earthy smell of dewy grass, moist soil, the pungent
aromatics of pine and balsam. There was a whirr of wings
as the swift car flushed a covey of quail at the rounding
curve that rimmed a pond strewn with white water-lilies.
Country-dawn sounds combined to produce a symphony
that Jack had not heard since he was a boy; the creak of
a wind-pump, the bleat of sheep, the crowing of roosters,
the lowing of cattle, fugitive bits of arias offered by meadow-
larks.

The effect of it all was exhilarating, intoxicating. Jack
was amazed to find his mind reacting to the swift rush of the
morning wind, the rapidly shifting kaleidoscope of forms
and colors as the winding road unrolled like a ribbon over
graceful hills. His mind was free, uncensored, out on its
own. With the reckless spirit of young Pippa on her annual
day off, he wanted to sing and shout.

The small towns were waking up now, and the broad
highway was sucking in — from lanes and barnyards — all
sorts of market-trucks and battered flivvers rattling toward
the day's work. The sleepy road was taking up its burden,
rousing to its responsibilities, insisting on full stops at
junctions. Now we were coming into a big town where
twenty-five miles an hour would be enough until we reached
a sign saying twenty would be enough. Big factories; red
brick, high iron fences, guarded gates, tall chimney stacks.
Hundreds — thousands of men swarmed the streets, poured

through the gateways; men in their late twenties and thirties, mostly; blue shirts open at the throat; stocky fellows; hold their own in a fight, no doubt; some tall, slim ones overtopping the stocky chaps; ought to have employment out in the fresh air; big, bulging, chicken-gizzardy Adam's apples, hollow chests, stooped shoulders, unquestionably anaemic, touch of T.B., low metabolism, red count down to the danger line; but — to hell with the diagnosis.

At the University, Remsen, ambitious entomologist, had rigged an ingenious glass house for the observation of a city of ants. Remsen wasn't quite so sure as Maeterlinck had been on the subject of the social behavior of insects. Remsen doubted whether any intelligence was required of the individual. The ant's job was cut out for him to fit his sex, or the lack of it, his size, his structure. If the ant was leggy, he had a good deal of running around to do. Some of the ants worked all day in one spot. Factory life. One little job to do, rapidly, expertly, automatically, without thinking. If you stopped to think about what you were doing, you got behind, and the ant next to you shouted a bad name. Nice occupation. Led to mental decay. But all jobs were more or less like that. Jack reflected on his own duties. Not much difference between a work-bench and an operating-table. Surgeon had cleaner hands, cleaner tools, but was just a mechanic, after all.

Presently he was out of the swarm of ants, ants making automobiles, and was increasing speed in frowsy suburbs, accelerating to pass long, lumbersome vans piled high with new cars, worse than mere road-hogs; road-hippopotami. There was very little of the pastoral now. Towns were coming fast and ugly. By noon Jack was passing through a district largely devoted to the milling of lumber. Enormous stacks of it waited to be shipped in the hulking freighters moored at great wharves. He turned off the highway and onto a cobbled street to have a better look. Heavy chains rattled over enormous pulleys, long cranes swept quarter-circles with precarious loads of sawed pine and lowered the burden into the big square hole, returning almost instantly

with twisted cables dangling, sprawling steel fingers stretch-
ing out for another handful of yellow lumber. The boat
didn't care; wasn't affected in any way by the threat of
more work to do; just sat there and let the lazy sailors smear
red paint on her rusty belly, and the fussy windlasses feed
more lumber into her capacious maw; indifferent as a cow
chewing her cud while they milked her. It might be fun to
sail in one of these unhurried old tubs. You could escape
from all drudgeries and cares for a few months. What would
that do to you? Would you come back refreshed and ready
for duty? Refreshed, maybe (may-bee), but probably not
ready for duty. It might cure you permanently of any
desire for work. No — a breathing spell of a week or two
would be better. You must not delay your return to the
other ants, or they might declare you dead — or a deserter.

So — he got to thinking about sociology, as he drove on
and regained the highway a half-mile farther. Very foolish
for people to talk about 'Social Science.' Science was
a laboratory pursuit. If you were going to be scientific you
had to work by fixed rules and with instruments of precision.
'Social Science' — indeed! Of course you could call anything a science if you didn't care how you abused the word.
Science of barbering. Science of chicken-raising. Science of
lawn-mowing. Plenty of people hoping to dignify their
petty crafts by attaching 'science' to them. Take 'Political
Science': with no two students agreed about where it had
come from, whither it was bound, or what it was good for.
'Science of Ethnology': about as practical as trying to tie
up a sand-dune with a clothesline; study of the 'character
of races' — nonsense. Let an invading nation come in and
sit down on a race for a couple of generations, and their
own grandmothers wouldn't recognize 'em. What would it
do to an American girl if she had lived from her infancy in
Hongkong?

You couldn't make a 'science' out of sociology. Why
couldn't you? You couldn't diagnose and treat the social
behavior of human ants. Why not? Maybe you could put
them through a clinic, one by one. You could say to this

fellow, 'We've gone over your case with care, Mr. Beaven, and recommend a two-years' voyage on a lumber-boat. It's going to China. China would be good for you. Cure your restlessness. The Chinese are well balanced. They do not fret.'

Never in his life had Jack's mind rambled, scuttled, galloped, summer-saulted over such a wide variety of problems. The new scenes, the release from duty, the rush of wind conspired to produce a pleasant ungirding of the brain. Perhaps it was healthful to let your thoughts loose, occasionally; relieve the tension of responsibility; let your mental belt out a few holes. Maybe the mind needed intervals of rest. Even a setting hen had sense enough to let her eggs cool off, for a half-hour every day.

At five o'clock he stopped in a village and telephoned Doctor Cunningham that he would arrive at six; sauntered back to his car, paid for the fresh tankful of gas, and pushed on. Cunningham had been more than cordial. Jack was anticipating the visit with mounting interest. It would be the first night he had spent in a private home for thirteen years. The speedometer again crept up to sixty. Cunningham had said something about dinner guests tonight. He didn't say who. A couple of doctors, maybe; and their wives. Silly thought, no doubt, but not beyond possibility that they might ask Mrs. King and Miss Hilton. Audrey. Very pretty name. Very good road. Sixty-five. Sixty-eight. Lan Ying. Absurdly sweet little toy name — Lan Ying. Seventy.

Chapter VIII

It had been a morning of surprises. Doctor Cunningham had upset the theory that you couldn't mix science and sentiment.

As he sat in Cunningham's hard-used sedan at the main entrance to Mercy Hospital waiting his host's return, it occurred to Jack Beaven that he would have to abandon his prejudices on this subject.

Under Tubby Forrester's influence, Jack had contrived a mental portrait of the typical family physician of the better sort who endeavors to treat a wide variety of cases. He had pictured Cunningham as a fair example.

Cunningham, he felt, was worthy of respect as a general practitioner who, for lack of time and the necessary instruments of research, could hardly be expected to keep himself informed on contemporary discoveries or the latest techniques employed by explorers in the field of medicine and surgery.

Tubby's urgent insistence upon scholarship and 'the scientific attitude' had been carried to the point of sneering snobbery, Jack thought. There was a rightful place in society for the family doctor. Obviously this busy man was no scientist. No matter what fine intentions he may have had, during his early days, his diversified duties in homes and hospitals would make it impossible for him to continue his studies. Gradually, inevitably — perhaps regretfully — the hard-pressed fellow would slip farther and farther behind in his scientific interests until he not only failed to make any progress but was inclined — for reasons of sheer self-defense — to adopt an attitude of derision toward the new-fangled crotchets of the experts. Jack had expected to find Cunningham exemplifying this state of mind.

It wasn't that he entertained any top-lofty ideas about his own superiority to Cunningham. He could understand this man's difficult position. Under similar circumstances, he would unquestionably pursue the same course. The family doctor, visiting — in one day's rounds — a broken hip, an incipient T.B., a chronic arthritis, a benign cyst (that he nervously hoped wasn't going to be malignant), a cerebral hemorrhage, an aneurism, a pernicious anaemia, a carbuncle, an ingrowing toenail, a chicken pox, and a carcinoma — shouldn't be asked to engage in scholarly research.

It was exactly as if some Jack of all trades, who had spent the day going about from place to place successively performing such feats as the readjustment of a hot-water heater, the repair of broken plastering, the installation of a plate-glass window, the mending of a door-lock, a thermostat, a lamp, a chair, a hardwood floor, a sewing-machine, a phonograph, should then be sneered at because he hadn't written a monograph on television.

Jack Beaven felt that he had the proper degree of sympathy for the family doctor. But — down inside himself, defiant of all the extenuating circumstances, there was a conviction that the general practitioner was, as Tubby had satirically maintained, only a benevolent soother tirelessly scattering sedatives and sunshine, courage and quinine, aspiration and aspirin, love and liniment. One thing was certain: If a man was working at a job that demanded a constant exercise of his emotions, it wouldn't be long until he suffered a deterioration of his intellect. Doubtless that was what ailed so many social workers, professional altruists, welfarers, parsons, and the like. The unrelenting drain on their emotional energy made it impossible for them to use their brains. Cunningham, of course, would be better than that. The fact that he had the respect of Tubby and Shane and the others at the Medical College was significant. However, Cunningham was a general practitioner. You couldn't be a general practitioner and a scientist.... And now Cunningham had knocked this well-established theory into a cocked hat. Jack sat in the sedan, under the shade of a tall elm, still utterly bewildered over what he had seen during the past hour and a half.

It had been an eventful morning. At six-thirty they had breakfasted together, rising early because his host had to attend to a few professional duties before leaving on their excursion to the lake. Mrs. Cunningham had joined them while they were having a second cup of coffee and a cigarette.

Jack had liked her immensely from the first moment. Her effortless hospitality had put him at ease immediately upon his arrival. She had met him with the quiet amiability of a pet cousin whose trust and devotion could be taken for granted. He hadn't been in the house an hour until he felt they were long-time friends.

She was, or rather had been, a typical Nordic blonde. At forty-five she was still pretty; a bit more roly-poly than was good for her, a bit too white for her florid type, but her sky-blue eyes were clear and uncommonly cognitive. They lighted quickly in response to drollery. They had a capacity for friendly teasing. They were also wise. It was doubtful if you could fool them very much about anything. They did not make an effort to impress you with their subtlety, nor were they snoopy, but — they took you in. You could do a pretty fair job of playing the poker-face, but you had a feeling that Edith Cunningham — in spite of her blandly disarming smile — could see right through the backs of your cards.

She unwilfully conveyed the impression of having had a lot of experience in a close-up study of human relationships. Maybe she saw through your cards because it was a deck she had played with so often that each card had its own identifying marks. She was not obtrusively inquisitive, feeding you cues for inevitable confessions and watching you — with the diligence of a cat at a rat-hole — for some unguarded remark that might be shaken into a revelation of the Hyde that was secreted within your Jekyll. Not at all! It wasn't as if she was trying to let you know that she had already gone through you with a ladder and a lantern and knew all about you from your first bottle to your last battle. There were plenty of women who made a gallant bluff at that sort of prescience, mistaking their victim's unhappy look for abject surrender when the real cause of his discomfort was a pain in the neck.

There wasn't a smart-alecky drop of blood in Edith Cunningham's body. But you sensed, almost immediately after Audrey Hilton had come downstairs to join the other dinner guests, last night, that Edith was quietly saying to herself, 'Well — what have we here? Isn't this interesting?' Audrey had quite taken his breath away. Nobody had ever been so lovely. No doubt he had stared. He had been in the library with Cunningham and young Kline and Mr. Swanson. Mrs. Cunningham appeared in the doorway and asked them to come. She stood beside him as Audrey — whom he had not expected — came down. He had tried to be collected when he greeted her. What he wanted was to throw his arms around her and hold her tight. Edith must have divined his wish. For the next time their eyes met, Jack knew she knew.

Claudia King he had not liked quite so well as he had expected, maybe because in features and pigments she most certainly did resemble her incomparable sister and he didn't want anyone else in the world — not even a blood relative — to look like Audrey. If this was an imbecilic thought, as he was forced to suspect, it was due to his mental turbulence. It was the first time anything like this had happened to him. He had had no opportunity to build up, through previous exposures and inoculations, any immunity against this strange psychosis. It was easy to locate the cause of his assorted mental disabilities manifested of late in his insomnia, restlessness, and instability. Because of his constant absorption in his work, he not only had failed to immunize himself against this kind of an attack, but it was clear to see that he had a definite anaphylaxis in regard to this particular girl. It was a problem in allergy.

Perhaps that's what explained the apparent boredom of matrimony. A man went about yearning for a wife and a home. Eventually he met the one particular woman to whom he was allergic. Having located the exact cause of his general wistfulness he married her and that cured him, precisely as a hay-fever victim may sneeze his very brains out until it is scientifically or accidentally disclosed that the dust emanating from a rug — not just any rug, mind you, but a Shiraz rug with a pattern of hexagonal panels — will touch him off. Joyfully he takes a few injections of Shiraz rug-dust and never sneezes again.

Jack Beaven had been doing a good deal of thinking about love. And since the only school of thought to which he was accustomed was essentially pathological and pathognomonic, he psyched himself up one side and down the other, growing more and more bewildered. Indeed he wondered if he wasn't getting a bit nutty. Edith Cunningham's sly grin had been very disturbing. What she had detected with the experienced eye of a diagnostician, any mere layman would presently be able to see at a glance. Perhaps the thing would come out on him in the form of a rash.

Well — be that as it might, he didn't care for Claudia. He wondered what Tubby had seen in her to make him go prancing about. She was so feverishly animated, neurally taut as a fiddle-string, almost boisterously glamorous, and hard to talk to unless you put yourself at full gallop. Maybe that's what had done Tubby in. He was such a pompous old ass that women shriveled into silence when they met him. The incandescent Claudia had probably caught him the way a pair of dazzling headlights will stun a rabbit.

Considerably to Jack's satisfaction, Claudia had made short work of him when they met, permitting him to give himself to Audrey who offered her hand, looked up from beneath long lashes, and said, 'She did not die?' — accompanying the query with that inimitable little shake of the head which meant she earnestly hoped the reply would be negative.

'No,' he had answered, 'but I found her in need of help. I was sorry about the interruption. You were saying — it was about Sen Ling, you know ——'

'I remember clearly,' she replied without a trace of coquetry. 'You had just said, to me (how quaintly childlike her lips when she made the words 'to me'), "So — for most of your life — you've lived in China. Wouldn't you like to tell me about it?"'

Jack nodded, happy that she was able (and willing) to recall the episode with such accuracy. He was prompt to let her know that he too had cherished a detailed picture of that conversation.

'And you said, "Gladly — if I am not keeping you."'

'Yes,' she assisted — 'and then the telephone rang and you skipped away.'

'I had to go,' he declared soberly.

'I know.' She regarded him with a sort of brooding smile such as she might have bestowed on Teddy. 'You were so ver-ree serious.' She pursed her lips, affecting sternness, knitted her brows severely beneath the adorable black fringe, lifted an imaginary receiver to her ear, and repeated — with appropriate pauses for listening, '"Yes... Yes — Miss Warren... Right away."'

The implications of her exact reproduction of his words had stirred him. He hoped his voice would not betray his happiness. Taking himself in hand, he tried to be casual. 'You have an excellent memory, Miss Hilton; even for names. It was Miss Warren who called me.'

She shook her head with artless honesty. 'No — names are ver-ree hard for me to remember. With us' — she turned her head slightly in the direction of her sister as if hopeful her voice had not carried — 'with the Chinese,' she amended, guarding her tone, 'names are not so difficult. They always mean something.'

'Yours, too, I suppose,' Jack had ventured.

'Of course.' She lowered her lashes momentarily. 'You will think it foolish — may-bee. Chinese names are so — so fanciful.'

At this juncture Doctor Kline, Cunningham's junior associate, had sauntered up to claim her as his dinner companion. Kline was a self-contained chap, but admiration shone in his eyes. She took his arm and gave Jack a smile over her shoulder as she turned. Edith Cunningham, now at his elbow, had led him into the dining-room, Kline and Audrey following. Mr. Swanson attended the luminous Claudia. Cunningham and the diminutive Mrs. Swanson, absurdly dwarfed alongside his six-feet-three, brought up the rear.

Having arrived at their places, and before they sat, a little hush fell. No one had signaled for it. Apparently these people, having been guests here before, knew what was coming, for their eyes were expectantly leveled at the face of their host. There seemed something almost majestic about the dynamic fellow at that arrested moment. Bowing his white head, Cunningham reverentially said a Latin grace; and, without an instant's interval, remarked, as he drew back his chair, 'I'm glad to see you're serving cold consommé, Edith. It's hot as hell in here.'

After they were seated, Jack, who could hardly keep his amusement out of his voice, said, quietly, 'I didn't know you were Catholics.'

'We aren't,' drawled Edith. 'That's just one of Bill's many whims. Thinks there ought to be some religion in the home.'

'But why in Latin?' asked Jack, smiling broadly.

'Oh — Bill thinks it's a little better taste to address God in a language you don't use for ordinary conversation.'

'Well, I'll be damned,' muttered Jack, under his breath.

'That's what I used to say,' rejoined Edith. 'But when you've known Bill Cunningham as long as I have, you won't be damned for anything he says or does. He's the most unpredictable, most inconsistent, most magnificent creature God ever made.'

Then she had gone on — with brief intervals for attention to her duties as hostess — to do some pithy biographical sketches of the small company. Ole Swanson was the third generation of his family in spruce and pine; very civic-minded. That's what attracted Bill to him. Parks, playgrounds, a small art-gallery, the municipal orchestra.

'Bill's hobby — the orchestra. . . . Are you interested in music?'

Jack had been obliged to confess that this part of his life had not been cultivated.

'Bill thinks it's very important for a doctor to have diversions,' she said. 'Remember? — of course you don't — you were too young — but in the early days of X-ray the doctors used to burn their fingers. Bill says if you don't have some aesthetic protection as an insulation — or something like that — Science will burn your fingers. He says he has some scars that he got before he found that out.'

Jack knew that his face was registering astonishment. He hoped it wasn't registering just a trace of amusement. He guessed that Cunningham wouldn't have to insulate himself very heavily to avoid being damaged by Science. His contacts with Science were probably about as remote as the average congressman's relation to statesmanship. Now Edith was speaking of Kline, the Bostonian, who had been with them for a year. She had lowered her voice for Kline was seated next to her.

'It isn't important,' she was saying, 'for every good-looking young doctor to be a bachelor, but it is mighty convenient if a good-looking bachelor can be a doctor. When the girls pester him he has the best alibi in the world. . . . I daresay you've worked that yourself, Doctor Beaven — a-plenty.'

Jack protested that the girls had never bothered him very much, to which she had replied, in the dry tone of an elder sister, 'Pish.' He had considered standing his ground on this but decided it might sound silly to be debating her playful rejoinder. His noncommittal smile had the effect of encouraging her to a further exploration.

'Claudia King would make a grand wife for you. Never a dull moment. Always something going on. No long, tiresome silences, with neither of you able to think of anything to say.'

He had glanced up to interrogate her impassive face, and she laughed a little, doubtless at the sober perplexity she may have found in his eyes.

'No,' she went on, confidentially, 'on second thought, I doubt if that would work out. Claudia is too — too dynamic. She's been managing the Swanson lumber mills, and Swanson, and Mrs. Swanson, and Effie Swanson, and Peter Swanson, and setting up her generator higher and higher to carry the load until — well — when you plug her into some quiet, pastoral scene, like a dinner party in a private home, she blows all the fuses out.... You need a more serene wife — somebody like' — she made an elaborate pretense of casting about, and Jack thought he knew what was coming — 'like her sister, for instance.'

It was a moment before Jack trusted himself to glance up. Edith's sky-blue eyes met him squarely — a bit solicitously, he thought. He was conscious of drawing a long breath.

'She's the most enchanting thing I ever saw,' murmured Edith, spacing her words. 'Naïve as a child; deep as the sea.'

Jack considered saying, 'That's very interesting,' but felt it would offend her; so he simply nodded his head. She could make what she liked of that.

'Audrey has had a very strange life,' continued Edith, shielding her voice. 'Know about it?'

'Just a little.'

'Do you know anything about China?'

'No — nothing.'

'Better inform yourself.'

There was a considerable pause before he decided, almost against his will, to say, 'Why?'

She did not reply to this. When their eyes met, she lifted her brows a little, smiled companionably, and turned to ask Mr. Swanson how the new boat was behaving.

Kline had rather completely monopolized Audrey after

dinner. Claudia had taken possession of Jack; first, to tell him all about Teddy, and then to tell him all about everything. She seemed to be on a strain. He suspected her of being in the early phases of an exophthalmic goiter; either that or cocaine, and of course it wouldn't be the latter.

'And how's Doctor Forrester, the old darling?' she inquired leaning forward eagerly.

Jack grinned in spite of himself. He'd heard Tubby called almost everything, but never a darling.

'Very well, I think, Mrs. King. I haven't seen much of him, lately, except of course in a strictly professional way.' Jack thought he might as well sound her out a little. 'We haven't had dinner together for quite some time.'

'He talks so much of you,' declared Claudia.

Jack said, 'So?' — mentally reserving the thing he really wanted to say.

'I hope this isn't going to turn your head completely — which would be very bad for you at your age — but he told me that you were the most brilliant anatomist of his whole acquaintance.'

'Thank you for telling me. I appreciate it as much as if it were true.'

'But it is true. He did say that,' she insisted.

'I didn't mean he wouldn't say so — though that, I'll admit, is rather unexpected. I meant ——'

'Oh — you're just being modest. That, too, is a sign of greatness.'

Jack was beginning to feel himself something of an ass.

'My sister likes you,' said Claudia.

'Thank you,' said Jack. 'I reciprocate.' He didn't fancy the direction of the talk, fearing he might give himself away to this pair of bright eyes.

'Perhaps you can do something for her. Tell her she belongs right here in the good old U.S.A. She was brought up in China, you know, and can't forget it.' Claudia shook her head. 'Tsch! Tsch! I don't know what I'm going to do with her.'

'Do you have to do something with her?' asked Jack, a bit brazenly, he feared.

'Well — I'm her older sister,' defended Claudia. 'She has no one else to advise her.' She lowered her tone. 'Doctor Kline is simply mad about her. And she treats him as if he were her grandfather. Everywhere she goes she's a sensation. And she sits at home all day writing letters to China; doing it in Chinese, too, damn it! It exasperates me so! First thing you know, people will be thinking *I'm* part Chink.' Her voice changed to entreaty. 'Doctor Beaven — I feel that Audrey would listen to almost anything you said to her. Do! — do talk her out of this!'

Jack mumbled something about his not being very good at minding other people's business for them and feared any intervention on his part might be mistaken for impertinence. Then it occurred to him to champion Audrey's cause.

'Suppose your sister does like the Chinese,' he said. 'Maybe the sort of Chinese she knows compare very favorably with the people she has met over here. I'm sure I don't know,' he added, more conciliatory. 'I never was there. I daresay you've been.'

Claudia shook her head, disdaining the thought.

The Swansons were rising. Mrs. Swanson was drawing her face into a smile that was the equivalent of a bread-and-butter letter, and Mr. Swanson was shaking a trouser-leg loose from a garter. Jack saw a chance to have a quiet word with Audrey.

'Before I return,' he was saying, urgently, 'I wonder if it wouldn't be possible to hear the rest of that story.'

Her face was doubtful.

'We would like to have you call,' she said. 'But I mustn't talk of China. My sister thinks my heart is too much in China. She wishes me to forget — and not talk about it.'

'Why shouldn't we take a drive?' asked Jack, a little surprised at his own impulsive suggestion. 'Then you could tell me. Would there be any objection to that?'

'It would be ver-ree pleasant,' she agreed. 'Thank you.'

'Doctor Cunningham and I plan to come in from the lake on Monday, probably about noon. I could come for you at three. Would that be agreeable?'

'Quite so. I shall be ready.'

'And you can talk about China — all you please,' he promised, lowering his voice. 'Maybe you will tell me what Lan Ying means.'

Audrey smiled companionably as she offered her hand.

'May-bee,' she said, softly.

* * * * * * * *

After breakfast, Cunningham had loaded the back seat of his sedan with food and tackle. He had a couple of calls to make before leaving.

'You may as well go along, Jack,' he said. 'Then we can be on our way. My first stop is over on the east side.'

Presently they were moving rapidly through a more modest residential district, Cunningham chattering about the case he was going to see.

'Took this child home from the hospital yesterday,' he was saying. 'Knocked down by a car. Concussion. And a lot of abrasions. For a day or two it looked like a pretty close thing. Family quite upset. Had 'em all on my hands; parents and half a dozen children; all scared because Dolly was unconscious.'

Jack wondered why they couldn't be kept out and ventured to ask the question.

'Oh, yes,' agreed Cunningham, 'we could have kept them out. That's what you would do at the University Hospital. You're strictly business, down there. But it wasn't doing Dolly the slightest damage to have her brothers and sisters come in and cry over her.' He was thoughtful for half a block, evidently organizing something he wanted to say.

'Beaven,' he broke forth, at length, 'the medical profession has done a very poor job of capitalizing anxiety and grief.'

'I'm afraid I don't understand,' said Jack.

'Well — here you have the case of a family that has gone

along for years without a major disaster. Plenty of small
perplexities; making ends meet, losing a job, having babies,
mumps, rackets with the relatives; minor irritations, but
no heart-breaking tragedies. Husband and wife take each
other for granted. Not much romance left. The children
get on their mother's nerves, and she cuffs them about. This
seeming the proper thing to do, they cuff each other. The
girls are catty and jealous; the boys are surly and cruel.
Along comes a catastrophe. Somebody in the family is
seriously sick or injured. Instantly they discover how much
they care for one another. They are all mellowed. The outburst of affection isn't directed at the patient exclusively.
The parents are bound together; ties more enduring and
endearing than the early love based largely on physical
attraction. Brothers and sisters hold hands and speak
softly. Lazy Sam runs errands cheerfully. Selfish Lizzie
volunteers to wash the dishes.'

'I suppose it does have that effect on a household,' agreed
Jack, for courtesy's sake. 'But where does the medical
profession come in?'

'Now — that's the point,' said Cunningham, indicating
it on the steering-wheel with an impressive forefinger.
'We're so intent on our fussy little programs of hospital
discipline, which I'm bound to say have been rigged up
mostly for the personal convenience of the doctors and
nurses, that we do nothing whatever to help the family get
the benefit of their lesson. We do worse than that: we try to
keep them from it.'

'A hospital without discipline would soon be in trouble,
wouldn't it?' Jack hoped there was no irritation in his
tone.

'Yes — but we've made too much of that. We've been
very short-sighted. All we're interested in is the physical
therapy. Child has broken skull. Our job is to reduce the
fracture. Never mind the family. They're not sick. They're
none of our business. We're not even under obligations to
answer their questions. Let 'em sit and wait in the reception
room. That's what the reception room is for. Bah! This

high-and-mighty professional attitude gripes me so — I can
hardly contain myself.'

Jack pursed his lips and wished Cunningham wouldn't
go any farther in his sentimental debauch.

'Of course it's important that the patient recovers,' continued Cunningham, trying to regain his composure. 'But
it's important also that the family has a chance to realize
something on this disaster. I want them to get together in
the sick-room and commit themselves — in the presence of
one another — to a new devotion to their tribe. A good deal
of our cold-blooded austerity is the nurse's fault, but she
wouldn't be quite so high-handed if she didn't think we were
approving her course. She likes to make 'em feel that she is
a professional — and knows a lot; closes the door on them;
hushes them down when they come in on tiptoe, wide-eyed
and scared. The family, instead of having a chance to express its affection, is self-conscious, silent, embarrassed.
I say to my nurses, "Let 'em in! If mean little Patsy, the
young bully, wants to have a touch of hysteria, and promise
he'll never pull hair any more, let him bawl. Chances are
he isn't annoying anybody but you."' Cunningham
chuckled. 'These nurses certainly can freeze up a home.
I tell my nurses, "This isn't a mere job. This is a vocation."'

Jack felt that he had never heard such an unabashed
defense of what Tubby had so often and so sourly con-
demned as 'sloppy sentiment.' He was both amazed and
disappointed. Cunningham had been spoken of as a sound
workman. They'd even asked him to join the faculty!
What a mess he'd stir up. The school would soon be a
laughing-stock. But — he wouldn't debate the matter.
Cunningham was his senior and his host. He hoped there
wouldn't be any more talk on this subject. Presently they
drew up in front of a rather battered house, the bare spots
in the dooryard testifying to hard usage.

'Come along in,' said Cunningham. 'I'm going to give
you a treat; glimpse of the old family doc in his natural
habitat.' He laughed boyishly. 'I've often wished I could
take Tubby around with me for a day, the old hypocrite.'

'Hypocrite?' echoed Jack.

'Sure!' drawled Cunningham. 'Pretends to be an iceberg; pretends his heart is nothing but a syringe: he may be able to spoof you fellows at the University, but I know more about Tubby's soft insides than he does himself.'

Jack, not knowing what rejoinder to make, grinned and said nothing. Some of the family had sighted the car at the curb, and the children came swarming out of the house.

'Just look at 'em.' Cunningham turned off the ignition, and chuckled with amusement over the bewildered stare on Jack's face. The youngsters were climbing onto the running-boards, all talking at once. Dolly, they shrilled, was sitting up. Dolly was eating her breakfast. Dolly had a new pup — the darlingest little pup that Daddy had got for her. They'd all given her presents.

'Well, well, get away — about a dozen of you — so I can open the door!'

'I got her some dishes,' yelled Jimmie, 'at the ten-cent store.'

Jack followed along, feeling a bit out of it. Rather undignified, he thought, Cunningham's free and easy manner with these children. They had no more respect for him than they might have had for the ice-cream vendor.

They entered the house. The woman met them. She was frowsy, shapeless, and needed a lot of dental attention, but the smile she gave Bill Cunningham was very tender; almost reverential.

'Mrs. Timmons,' said Cunningham, 'this is my friend, Doctor Beaven.'

She wiped a damp hand on her brown apron and gave it to Jack tentatively, glancing at Cunningham with anxiety in her eyes.

'No, no, no, Mrs. Timmons,' he said reassuringly. 'There's nothing the matter. Doctor Beaven is not here for a consultation. We're going fishing.'

She smiled, happily relieved. Her attitude was puzzling. Cunningham had pretended she was alarmed for fear it was thought that Dolly needed a specialist. Jack wondered if she wasn't afraid of him. Maybe it showed in his face that he wasn't quite in sympathy with all this informality. Well — Cunningham could get whatever satisfaction he might out of this kind of idolatry. As for himself he preferred a more professional demeanor. By the Cunningham technique, you probably lost in respect and disciplinary authority all that you gained in palaver and devotion.

They all went in together to see Dolly who reached up her arms. Cunningham allowed himself to be hugged. He made a brief examination, had a quick, quiet conference with the nurse, sat down in a creaking old chair, and said, 'I've brought Doctor Beaven out to hear you say your catechism.' The children drew closer about him and grew suddenly quiet. It was evident that they knew what was coming. Cunningham had put them through this quiz before, and they were anxious to prove that they remembered the right answers.

'If Dolly hadn't got well, what would have happened to the rest of you?' asked the doctor, solemnly.

'We would never have been happy any more,' they replied, practically in unison.

'So — now you're all going to be happy?'

A chorus of assent.

'Always?'

'Always.'

'No quarreling?'

'No quarreling.'

'Cross your heart?'

They crossed their hearts — and hoped to die.

'That's all, then,' said Cunningham. 'Meeting's out.' He disentangled himself from the miniature mob and led the way to the car, accompanied by his noisy constituency.

'Dolly doesn't know it,' said Cunningham, when they were in motion again, 'but her whack on the head has been worth a good deal to this family. They were the damnedest lot of little ruffians.'

It was pretty dreadful — this exhibition of mawkishness. Jack tried to think of something pleasant to say about it.

but the words wouldn't come. He was willing to concede that it was good for the Timmons family to stop wrangling, but it wasn't the doctor's business to attend to it. Maybe their plumbing was out of order, but it wasn't the doctor's business to fix it. Maybe their roof leaked. Maybe a payment was due on the mortgage. It would be nice if all their affairs were put in order — but the doctor shouldn't try to do it. While he was giving himself up to these unprofessional services, he was becoming less and less a man of science. Couldn't do everything — so science would have to be neglected. Tubby was right!

'Got to stop at my office a minute, Jack,' said Cunningham, as they swung into a busy street. 'Want to come up with me?'

Jack assented, naturally, but he would have preferred to wait below. He had no curiosity to see that office. He could easily picture it; a reception room, a nurse-secretary, a private cubicle with a desk and an adjustable chair for examinations and a glass case of instruments for minor repairs; perhaps another little coop with a cot.

They had drawn up in the parking-lot at the rear of a fifteen-story modern building. They took the elevator to the top floor. In the carpeted corridor there was a desk and a girl in a white uniform. Jack thought it odd that Cunningham's secretary was holding forth in the hall. Maybe she served as general secretary for a dozen doctors. It was immediately apparent that the girl was in Cunningham's service exclusively. His offices comprised the whole top floor!

'Come back to the laboratory, Beaven,' he said. 'I've a bit of an experiment I want you to look at before we go.'

'You have your own laboratory?' Jack was puzzled.

'Hell, yes,' called his host, over his shoulder, as he led the way down the hall. 'Think I was just a pill-peddler?'

He opened the door, and they stepped into a spacious room equipped with the latest gadgets for pathological research.

'I've been doing a little independent investigation of interstitial pneumonia,' said Cunningham. 'I got some nice smears yesterday. Stone mason. We have a lot of dusty, abrasive jobs in this country. Take a peek into that microscope, Beaven.'

Jack bewilderedly tossed aside his straw hat and went to the table by the north window. The microscope was a Beck binocular! He adjusted the delicate mechanism of the eye-pieces, and concentrated his attention on the tiny burnt-sienna smear.

'That's the best specimen I've had,' said Cunningham, at his elbow.

Feeling so small that he thought it would be more appropriate if he were at the other end of the microscope, Jack studied the infinitesimal but very significant object for a long moment. His thoughts were divided. He wished he could ask Cunningham's pardon for the injustice he had done him. Cunningham wouldn't want that. It would make their relations very awkward.

'Made your count yet — leucocytes?' he asked.

'Yes — and that reminds me I must give these notes to the girl to transcribe.' Cunningham gathered up a handful of pencil-written sheets from the table. 'Made 'em last night when she wasn't here.'

Jack, still intent on the smear, repeated, as from a considerable distance, 'Last night?'

'After you went to bed.'

Straightening, Jack regarded his host with silent appraisal for a moment.

'Do much of that? Night work — after you've been at it, all day?'

'It's more satisfactory.' The other detached himself from the disapproving eyes. 'No interruptions — at night.'

'It'll break you,' warned Jack.

'You do the same thing, don't you?'

'Not quite. I haven't your responsibilities. Besides — I'm a younger man than you. This program of yours will shorten your life.'

'Well, I'm not trying to hang up a new record for longevity.'

*   *   *   *   *   *   *   *

He was coming down the hospital steps now, almost jauntily. It was easy to see that he had already put himself into a vacation mood. Jack leaned over and opened the car-door for him.

'Sorry to have kept you waiting,' said Cunningham, spinning the old engine. 'I've a chap in there — Jim Gibson — who has been laid up for three months with a bad leg; compound fracture, infection, long and painful drainage; hasn't cared a hoot whether he got well or not; shrewish wife, wild daughter. Part of it was Jim's fault. The leg was the least of his troubles — and the least of mine. I am going to discharge him on Monday.' He exploded a sigh of recollection. 'I saw, from the first, that it wasn't any use to drain Jim's infected leg unless we drained the poison off the whole darned Gibson family.'

'I'm afraid I wouldn't be much good at that sort of thing,' admitted Jack, feeling he ought to say something.

'You would if you had it to do. It's part of the job: maybe it's the most important part. Sometimes I think my surgery is chiefly valuable because it gives me entry to the confidence of a family. We do a satisfactory piece of surgical repair, and people think we can work wonders of all sorts. They look to us with a trust they don't have in anybody else. It's flattering, but — you've got to pay for the distinction!'

They were in a brief traffic tangle now, Cunningham attending to his problem at the wheel. There was a considerable pause in the talk. When the street was clear, Jack said, 'I've never thought about it, just that way. My training has been different. It has never occurred to me to interest myself in the private lives of patients.'

'That's because you don't think of them as *your* patients. They are referred to you by other doctors. The home physician knows the patient, through and through. You get

the case because you're an expert, a specialist. You feel
that you aren't expected to know anything — or to want
to know anything — but the pathology involved.' Cunningham's eyes suddenly widened with a new idea. 'But — I
say! — Beaven; you really have a bigger chance to do something important than the old doc at home! See? The
patient has been sent to you because you're more accomplished than the family physician. *You* perform the
miracle! Old doc couldn't do it; admitted it; brought the
case to you. *You* did it! By Jove — if *you* were to show
some concern for the fellow's well-being, he'd follow you
about like a dog!'

Jack grinned rather self-consciously over this crazy
imputation of greatness, hardly knowing what rejoinder
would sound less silly than another.

'Of course,' he conceded, at length, 'I believe in social
rehabilitation, but it's a separate task. I can't attend to
that — and give the best I've got to science.'

Cunningham turned his head and faced Jack with an
almost paternal smile.

'What makes you think that social rehabilitation isn't a
science?' he asked, quietly. 'Beaven — every man's occupation should serve him mainly as an axis on which he
revolves through a given social area, in the capacity of
a constructive humanitarian. Even in an obscure job, he
makes social contacts offering opportunities. Not every
man has my chance to do something important, much less
your chance which I think is greater — for the reason I have
told you. But, if a man wills it so, he can exert a mighty
influence even as a common craftsman. One time, there
was a *carpenter* ——' He left the sentence unfinished.

'Do you believe that story?' queried Jack.

'Substantially. I expect it has been cluttered with legends
that were well-intended — but unnecessary.'

'You mean — the miracles?'

They were getting out into the open country now.
Cunningham allowed the old sedan to slow down a little.
He did not immediately reply. Jack felt that he would when
he was ready, and waited.

'Well — let's not talk about those miracles, just now,' said Cunningham, thoughtfully. 'Let's talk about ours. Yours and mine. If Jim Gibson was your case, handled according to your professional theory, you'd say to the nurse, Monday morning, "Gibson can go, this afternoon. His leg is well now." And they'd help Gibson into his pants — and call a taxi.' The sedan lagged almost to a stop. Cunningham laid his hand on Jack's knee and looked him squarely in the eyes. 'But when I discharge Jim Gibson, on Monday, I'm going to say, "*Arise — and walk!*" And Gibson's going to know that I expect something more of him than mere *locomotion!*'

Chapter IX

THAT inclement night seemed specially made for story-telling, and Cunningham knew a good one. It was the most unusual and fascinating tale Jack Beaven had ever heard; the most disquieting, too, for the farther his companion went into it the more remote was China and the Chinese, and — of course — Lan Ying.

The vacationing doctors made a ridiculous sight as they sprawled before the blazing spruce in their bathing-suits and blankets. All the chairs in the one-room log cabin, except the ones they occupied, were ranged in two rows on either side of the big field-stone chimney, grotesquely draped with soggy and steaming garments. It was raining cats and dogs, and the air — abominably hot through most of the day — had become decidedly cool.

From three o'clock on, the sky had lowered and darkened, occasionally muttering and spitting crimson fire through the folds of purple-blue curtains, a quite exciting spectacle. It seemed that a great deal was going on, what with the mounting racket of the threatened storm and the increasing recklessness of the bass.

Jack felt that he had never been through a more confusing experience, with the whole heaven staging a noisy and flamboyant show while a hard-fought battle was being waged with a plunging, diving, twisting, leaping, utterly berserk bass made of unlickable courage and coiled steel springs — undoubtedly the biggest fish ever deceived by a hand-made fly. It was found later to weigh three and one-half pounds — not tons.

Cunningham stood up and dragged in the muddy anchor

— an old plowshare on fifty feet of sash-cord. Beaven limbered up the oars and fitted them into the creaking rowlocks. The storm was gaining strength.

'It's old Richard Wagner!' called Cunningham.

'Ought to be arrested,' shouted Jack. 'Disturbing the peace.'

'It's grand! Magnificent!' Cunningham swept the tempestuous sky with an exultant gesture. Jack, reinstalling an oar that he had just yanked free of its lock by a mighty tug, yelled, 'Glad you like it!'

Whereupon Cunningham delivered an impressive oration. 'Anybody could see,' he declaimed, 'that the soul of Wagner was putting on the big show. All the Wagnerian devices were at work in the way the storm built itself up — through threats and challenges, thrusts and forays, piling crescendo on crescendo — until, the supplies having given out, it scurried back to the ammunition dump for more kettledrums and cymbals ——'

'And water,' assisted Jack.

'Then,' pursued his companion, undistracted, 'it goes into a huddle for grumbled consultation on strategy, and rushes forth again into the open field — a thousand abreast, galloping full tilt, lickety-split, hoofs pounding, turf flying, armor clanging. . . . Sheets of flame! Bursts of bombs! . . . Stupendous! . . . Tremendous! . . . It's Wagner!'

'And it's vet,' added Jack. 'Wery, wery vet!'

In the world's long history it had never — but once — rained this hard before. Jack, rowing with long strokes and budding blisters, his head tipped back to let the water in the scuppers of his panama run down his neck instead of his eyes, inquired how far it was to the mountains. Cunningham was scaling the biggest bass, raking its shining flank with an experienced hand.

'You'd better save your wind for your work,' he advised. 'You've a half-mile to go. No — you needn't look around.' He flapped the fish over on the other side and harvested another long winnow of silver scales. 'I'll stop you before you run into the dock.'

'Galley slave,' growled Jack.

'None o' that soap-box oratory.' Cunningham slit open the bass and scooped its viscera into the lake. 'I'm a capitalist.'

'Yeah — you look like one. You ought to see yourself.'

It had been that kind of an afternoon, conversationally; chaff, banter, and nonsense. Cunningham had turned out to be a rare companion. Beaven, habitually serious, was discovering in himself a capacity for play, and was delighted. After a couple of eternities Cunningham began signaling directions for landing. Cramped and weary, they climbed out onto the slippery wharf, unloaded their catch, and plodded heavily to the cabin, squashing water at every step; soaked to the hide.

Presently the host demonstrated that he was a good cook, though he didn't have to be a very good one to seem so when the huge platter of broiled fish encountered the voracious appetites developed by the day's sport.

After the noble feast had been devoured and cleared, the contented medicos replenished the fire, lighted their pipes, and agreed that the world — taken by and large — should be viewed with approval. Doubtless it had its little imperfections; but, as worlds went, drawled Cunningham, this one wasn't any worse than some and better than most.

'I'll take your word for it,' agreed Jack, lazily. 'You've probably been about more than I have.'

'No' — Cunningham was suddenly serious — 'That's my most valuable regret. All my life I've nursed a bad case of wanderlust. And I haven't been — anywhere.'

Jack admitted that he too had often wished he might push back his horizon a little but didn't intend to fret about it. 'It just isn't in the cards for me.'

'Perhaps not — for either of us,' conceded Cunningham. 'It's hard for us to get away. But I'm convinced that the man who spins around one pivot, describing a circle about a hundred miles in circumference, occasionally flying off at tangent for a day in Detroit or Chicago, but never really seeing the outside world, has missed the best part of life.'

'Maybe it isn't quite that bad,' reflected Jack. 'If it's scenery you want, our country can supply every sort there is. If it's people, well — there are plenty of foreigners here. You don't have to go to Italy.'

The other roused to support his argument. That was, he declared, the hell of it. We had all sorts of foreigners, but they didn't represent their races or nations any more than our own riff-raff could represent us abroad.

'What can you find out about Czechoslovakia,' he persisted, 'in your hospital wards? What do we learn about Italian thought — manners, aims, arts — from the ordinary run-o'-the-mine Dago who shows up at the Free Dispensary?' He paused for a long moment. 'What I want to do most, Beaven' — Cunningham lowered his voice, impressively — 'what I hope to do — some day — is to see China.'

'Why China?' Jack shifted his position and was attentive.

'I'm not thinking about the tourist's China,' continued Cunningham, ignoring the query. 'Swarms of coolies, fantastic processions, joss houses, tea houses, junk shops and junks, shrill sounds and bad smells — and then back to the cruise-boat for the hop to Honolulu. No, no! I want to see a Chinese home of the better sort. I'd like to stay a while — and get acquainted.'

'Fat chance of that,' scoffed Jack. 'But whatever put such a notion in your head?' He tried to make his voice sound careless.

Cunningham got up and poked the fire, returned to his chair, hooked a bare toe under the rung of another and drew it toward him, stretched out his legs on it, and refired his pipe.

'Beaven — how much do you know of Audrey Hilton's story?'

'Almost nothing. She told me she was brought up over there.'

'Interested?'

'Of course. Why not? Carry on.'

* * * * * * * *

Cunningham, having settled to the task of narration, spent the first few minutes reciting the part of the story that Jack already knew. The wealthy and cultured Sen Ling, wounded in spirit because of slights and rebuffs received in this country and on homing shipboard, had been tactfully conciliated by Captain Hilton, ship's commander; invited to share his suite, given the liberty of the bridge, treated with dignity and distinction. Sen Ling had been quietly grateful.

'Hilton's motives may have been a bit confused: I don't know. He may have felt that the fine old Chinaman had had a raw deal and wanted to assist him in saving face. On the other hand, Hilton was something of a diplomat in his business relations with Hongkong and may have hoped that Sen Ling's good will would be valuable to the steamship company. At all events, it turned out that way. When the captain died he was fairly well-to-do. Bonuses — and so on — from an appreciative board. Hilton, for years, carried the most lucrative cargoes of any ship in the trans-Pacific service. Sen Ling had passed the word around that Hilton was their friend.

'But that wasn't all; smallest part of it. Hilton's favor to the Chinaman had loomed so large in the merchant's mind that he invariably came down to see the ship tie up. Sometimes the captain's duties would detain him on deck for three or four hours, but when he came off there would be his Chink — waiting for him; insisting on Hilton's coming to his house to be his guest. For months these invitations were refused. The captain had his work to do; probably didn't want to go, anyhow. One day he gave in. Sen Ling had seemed very much hurt over these rejections of his hospitality and Hilton decided to humor him. That may have been for business reasons. What I'm trying to get at is: Captain Hilton never made an effort to wangle himself into the esteem of Sen Ling.'

'Maybe that's the reason the Chinese wanted him,' suggested Jack.

'Doubtless. . . . Well — after that, Henry Hilton never had to be coaxed. And it may be assumed that his motives, from that time on — whatever they may have been, in the first place — were free of any commercial interest. When he arrived, his host was always waiting for him with luxurious litters and bearers, and breezy old Hilton was eager to climb in and be carried over the winding road to the beautiful house of Sen Ling, halfway up the peak that overlooked the city.'

'He must have known instinctively how to accommodate his habits and behavior to the customs of the Sen Ling home,' reflected Jack, 'or he wouldn't have felt so easy there.'

Cunningham nodded agreement.

'That — plus the fact that Henry had been in the Chinese trade long enough to pick up plenty of information about their peculiar quirks. But Sen Ling was by no means an open book for the captain to read at a sitting. He was a deep one. Hilton had been visiting him regularly for a period of more than three years before he knew — and he found this out by sheer accident, and not from the Sen Lings — that the merchant was lavishly philanthropic. He was said to be, for instance, the largest private contributor to the English Hospital's upkeep and had staked a half-dozen or more Chinese youths to their medical education in England.'

'Why England? It was farther.'

'I'm not sure this was ever explained. Perhaps Sen Ling's unhappy experiences in the States may have had something to do with it. At all events, Hilton discovered that his Chinese friend — for all his strict adherence to the manners and motives of his own country — did not resent the intrusion of any knowledge that might add to the general welfare of China. His large benevolence to the hospital is a case in point; and, besides, it is an important factor to this story.'

Cunningham helped himself to the tobacco tin and

passed it. The fire was smouldering, and Beaven revived
it. He had a feeling that the first chapter had come to an
end. It had all been interesting enough, but he was anxious
to see Audrey come into it.

'I think it may be taken for granted,' Cunningham went
on, 'that Sen Ling's influence in Hongkong — both with
the foreigners and the Chinese — was very strong. Even
at that, he must have had a very anxious time at the turn
of the century, when the Boxer mess was on. I don't know
how he managed it, but the English Hospital in Hongkong
was one of the few institutions that carried on without any
interruption through those wild days. For about a year,
foreign trade was upset, shipping disorganized, everything
at sixes and sevens. Henry Hilton's ship, for some unexplained reason, came more nearly carrying on a normal
schedule than any other vessel doing business in Chinese
waters. The fact that Hilton was British-born had nothing
to do with it; for Chinese animosity was more vigorously
demonstrated, at that time, against England than America.

'But Henry stoutly refused, during this period, to be Sen
Ling's guest, unwilling to put his friend in an embarrassing
position. After the rebellion had subsided, their former
relations were resumed, seemingly all the stronger for the
temporary interruption. Sen Ling had four sons and one
wife. His monogamy was considered, by his intimates, as
in the nature of an eccentricity. Perhaps the fact that
Madame Sen Ling was a descendant of the celebrated King
Wan family ——'

'I say,' Jack chimed in, 'you seem to be mighty well
posted on these details. Where did you learn all this?'

Cunningham smiled, chuckled reminiscently.

'My yarn is synthetic, Beaven. It's pieced together of
bits furnished partly by Audrey and her sister, but mostly
from Ted King, Claudia's deceased husband. Ted's father
was Henry Hilton's chief navigating officer — and closest
friend — for all of a dozen years. That's how Ted and
Claudia met. This story also is not without interest, but I
shan't bother you with it just now.'

'Very well,' consented Jack. 'Be on your way.'

'Let's see — where were we? . . . Oh, yes — Sen Ling had only one wife, four sons, and enough uncles, aunts, cousins, second-cousins, nephews, and nieces to —— I am told that when they all assembled on ceremonial occasions the family made quite an impressive showing.'

'All live together?'

'In one big compound, surrounded by a high wall and gorgeously beautiful gates, though I understand that these huge establishments are rigged up so that — in spite of the population — each unit of the big family enjoys about as much privacy as it wants. . . . Well — I'm stringing this out too long. Hope I'm not boring you.'

'Don't be silly! I'm all ears.'

'Claudia Hilton was born in '96. In San Francisco. Her mother had a rough time and was not very well for several years. She was hospitalized, a half-dozen times, and the little girl was sent to a first-class boarding-school near Monterey. The Hiltons were warned that they'd better not have any more children. I don't know the pathology. Might have been any one of a dozen things, as you know.

'In 1904, Mrs. Hilton discovered she was going to have a baby. Henry, naturally, was very much worried; couldn't leave his run, particularly at that time, for affairs in China were unsettled; the whole situation — politically, commercially — loaded with doubt and dynamite. The ship's doctor, to whom Henry had confided his anxiety, suggested that Mrs. Hilton might be better off in Honolulu. So, they took her over there. She was lonely — and scared. Once, well on toward the end of her time, Henry found her — on his outbound voyage — in a grand state of hysterics, which wasn't like her, at all. The ship's doctor said they had better take her along. By the time they reached Hongkong Mrs. Hilton needed better care than they could give her on shipboard, so they put her in the hospital.'

'Sen Ling's, maybe?' guessed Jack.

Cunningham nodded.

'Yes — and the Sen Ling family was very much concerned. Henry had to sail again in a week. They assured him that they would see to it that Mrs. Hilton had every care. Reluctantly the captain put out to sea. It was before the days of radio. When he arrived in San Francisco, they handed him a cable from Sen Ling. It was brief.

'SHE IS BURIED WITH MY ANCESTORS
YOUR GIRL CHILD IS WITH US.'

Beaven gave an incoherent exclamation of amazement.

'They took her home with them?'

'They did. They engaged a nurse from the hospital. Nobody knows anything about the scene enacted when Henry next returned to Hongkong and saw his daughter for the first time. It must have been very tender. Madame Sen Ling was overjoyed to have a girl-baby in the house; probably glad her own children were boys, but naturally wistful for a girl, nevertheless. It was obvious that the baby would have to remain in China for the time being. Henry had no home now. Claudia was much better off in the girls' school than she might have been under the care of a housekeeper. Next time he came back, Henry told Madame Sen Ling that he wished to name the baby Audrey, after her mother. Madame Sen Ling smiled and ventured to glance at her husband inquiringly.

'"She should have two names, Captain Hilton," said Sen Ling. "You shall call her Audrey. We ask permission to call her Lan Ying."'

'Does that mean something?' asked Jack.

'Yes — but I don't know what.'

'She wouldn't tell you?' Jack tried to keep his tone steady.

'No — and Claudia doesn't know, for I asked her.'

Jack nearly bit his pipe-stem in two. Even her sister didn't know. But Audrey would tell *him* — may-bee!

'Beaven — I'm getting cold. Besides, I've told you about all there is, except that this girl never came back until three years ago. Claudia's objections to her remaining any longer in China had fermented until they were almost

an obsession. She thought and talked about nothing else.
Finally I was persuaded to write and say that I thought —
and it was true enough, God knows — that Audrey had
better come back, at least on a visit, or Claudia would be
sick. So — Sen Ling and his wife brought her over. They
went around the other way and spent some time in England
where Sen Ling had some business he wished to cover personally.'

'That explains something,' said Jack. 'When she was in
our hospital she referred to the elevator as the lift. That's
English, isn't it?'

'You've a remarkable memory,' drawled Cunningham
with a grin. 'However — Audrey Hilton didn't have to go
to London to learn that an elevator is a lift. Hongkong is,
as you know, essentially British. All the Caucasian children
she knew were as English as John Bull.'

'Then she did have some contacts with English-speaking
people? I gathered from some of her peculiar pronuncia-
tions that her knowledge of English was had by reading
rather than conversation. She puts quaint stresses on certain syllables — "ver-ree" and "fun-nee" and "may-
bee."'

Cunningham laughed. 'You've got that down pretty
pat, Beaven. Well — this fun-nee little trick of hers is a
hang-over from the influence of a governess the Sen Lings
provided for her. The woman was French originally; tu-
tored Audrey in French and the sort of English that a
French person would dispense. Sometimes Audrey's sentences are composed in a manner that proves she was better
acquainted with French syntax. But, however compe-
tently she handles herself in English — and French — I
have no doubt she does most of her thinking in Chinese.'

'She'll become Americanized, won't she; in time?' asked
Jack, in a hopeful tone that meant the question admitted
of only one answer.

'I doubt it,' said Cunningham, with conviction. 'One of
the unexplained mysteries is the uncanny ability of the
Chinese to assimilate the people who get caught in the web

of their curious culture. They are not crusaders, they are
not missionaries, they are not propagandists. They have
no interest in making converts. In fact, they have always
exhibited a serene indifference to the philosophy and manners of foreigners. But history insists that the people who
go to China, and stay in China long enough to expose themselves to its mind and mood, are captive. The ancient
Greeks had the same capacity. The Romans could hammer
'em to a pulp but had to admit that the Greeks had taken
'em into camp — spiritually. The time came, even while
the Gauls had Greece in abject slavery, when no Roman
could call himself a gentleman if he didn't speak Greek.
No — you'll find that Audrey Hilton will never be at home
anywhere but in Cathay. Some ways considered, it's a
great pity. Her life — judged by our views — will probably be ruined. She couldn't possibly bring herself to marry
a Chinese, no matter how deeply she might respect him —
and any American who marries her will either have to make
her over, from the ground up, which would inevitably destroy her personality — or else ——'

There was a long pause before Jack gained the consent of
his own mind to inquire, 'Or else — what?'

Cunningham made a baffled gesture with upturned palms,
and after a moment's delay, muttered, 'Or else — go
Chinese himself.'

'That's — that's too bad,' commented Jack, lamely.

They sat for a couple of minutes in silence. Then the host
rose and raked the coals together with the fire-shovel; Jack
watching him with moody, abstracted eyes.

'Thought I'd tell you,' said Cunningham.

*   *   *   *   *   *   *   *

It was by no means an easy task to inform Cunningham
of the engagement he had made with Audrey for the drive.
If it had not been such a discourteous thing to do, Jack
wouldn't have told him. But there was no dodging it. It
could be postponed but not evaded.

Best of all reasons for his reticence was his doubt whether

he had any right to be seeing more of Audrey. There could be no question about the unwisdom of his course. He was aware that in yielding himself still farther to the charm and loveliness of this enchanting girl he was taking a chance of demolishing his own plan for living; to say nothing of the injustice he might be perpetrating by disclosing — and this seemed unavoidable — his deep interest in her.

The program he had mapped for himself, many years ago, and to which he had adhered with stern fidelity, demanded a singleness of purpose — the pursuit of Science. It had been his conviction, deliberately arrived at and uncompromisingly maintained, that the work he intended to do should have his full attention. He had resolutely averted his thoughts from any wish to establish a home and take on the inevitable cares which would absorb more and more of his time and interest. The happier the home, the worse for his ambition.

In allowing himself to think tenderly of Audrey Hilton, he had not, he felt, violated his compact with himself. Nothing would come of it: he would see to that. Surely nobody could say it was his fault if circumstances — directly in line of professional duty — had thrown him into contact with this superb creature. His interview with her at the Livingstone Hotel, Jack told himself, had not been sought for any other reason than to extend the natural courtesies required by the occasion. His vacation trip, too, was soundly explainable. Had he not been advised to take it? It hadn't been his own idea, at all. Shane had suggested it, claiming he ought to have a few days of recreation for the sake of his own fitness for his work. Nor had it been his own scheme to visit Cunningham. That was Osgood's suggestion. To find a good place for fishing; that was the motive. And if Audrey Hilton was a dinner-guest at the Cunninghams,' it certainly wasn't his fault.

And he couldn't be a boor; could he? Science surely didn't expect a man to be rude, unsocial. Ordinary politeness required him to say he was sorry he had been called away in the middle of the story she was telling him. It was natural enough, was it not, to say he would like to hear the rest of it? A man could be a devoted scientist and still be a gentleman; couldn't he? And when Audrey had given an excellent reason why it would be impossible to finish her story in the presence of her sister, what else was there for him to do than suggest a private talk? It was all plain as a pikestaff. Down inside himself, his censor-mind grinned, winked, and made the objectionable noise commonly referred to as a Bronx cheer, to which he had with dignity replied by arraying his assorted self-justifications.

But it was one thing to explain to himself the casualness of his appointment with Audrey and the utter lack of design in his engagement to see her alone. It was quite another thing to say to Bill Cunningham, 'I'm going for a drive, this afternoon, with Audrey Hilton.' He couldn't line up all his defenses and excuses, and invite Cunningham to observe how naturally this had come about. It would sound very silly. And his censor-mind, chuckling, remarked, 'It would sound silly because it *is* silly, and nobody knows it better than you.'

'I'm going for a drive, this afternoon, with Audrey Hilton,' said Jack, when they were within a mile of the city.

'Edith told me,' said Cunningham. 'She had invited Audrey to go with her to a garden-party today, and she begged off from the engagement; said she'd just promised to go with you. That will be very nice. Hope you have a good time. We'll expect you to spend the night with us. Right? And dinner?'

'Thank you. I hope I'm not wearing out my welcome. I'll be off tomorrow. Back to the mill, I think. I am not accustomed to vacations. I've a guilty feeling that I'm neglecting my work.'

'In my opinion,' said Cunningham, 'any man engaged in a profession as wearing to the nerves as ours can do more work in eleven months than in twelve. No man is more in need of a regular vacation than a doctor — and no man is less able to take one.'

Jack, agreeing to this, added, 'I've often wondered

whether — instead of carrying on through a long term of eleven months, and then absenting oneself for a month, and getting rusty in one's technique — it might be more sensible to take two or three days off frequently.'

'Well — here we are.' Bill drew up in the garage-area. 'Now for a bite of lunch, and we'll be on our ways. Edith won't be here. She's at the party. One of the hostesses. We'll see her this evening.'

Making short work of his luncheon, Cunningham hurried away. Jack dressed with care in sports clothes, occasionally glancing at his watch on the chiffonier. Fearing he had forgotten to wind it, he gave the stem a few turns. It was an odd thing, he said to his reflection in the glass as he retied his scarf, how time seemed to stop, on some occasions; how swiftly it speeded, on others. Apparently the mind possessed no uniform instruments of precision for estimating time. Three minutes spent in boiling an egg and three minutes in a long-distance telephone conversation weren't the same thing, at all. A man knew, by experience, how much he could lift; how fast he could run; how far he could jump. He knew, almost to the inch, the length and breadth of his car; knew, to a certainty, whether or not he could drive through a narrow lane between vehicles in congested traffic; knew whether he could park in an opening at a crowded curb. But he was inaccurate in judging the relative value of five minutes, ten, fifteen. With only one life to live, and time being very precious, it was queer that the human being hadn't evolved a precise time-sense to assist in saving this most valuable of all gifts. His censor-mind spoke up: 'If you want to know why you're philosophizing on this subject, I'll tell you. You're averting your thoughts from this interview with Audrey because you're afraid of it. You want to see her, but you don't know what you want to say to her. You're in love with her, and you know you shouldn't be. You would like to know just where you stand, in her regard, and you hope she likes you. You believe she likes you. But — if she does — what are you going to do next?'

The roadster responded pleasantly to his guidance, promising to be on its best behavior. Audrey's street address was not hard to find, a commodious house of the bungalow type. She met him at the door, dressed for the drive. Her white flannel suit, well tailored, was distinctly American, accenting her shapeliness more insistently than the flowing Chinese garments in which he had found her on the evening of their interrupted talk at the Livingstone Hotel. A red scarf intensified the glossy blackness of her hair, and a narrow white satin bandeau bound the fascinating black fringe to a white forehead. She held out her hand and gave him a smile that raced his pulse, making no attempt to dissimulate: she was eager to have him come and entirely willing to let him know how she felt about it.

'So sorree you will not see Teddy,' she said. 'He left on Saturday for a boys' camp. So well. So happee. Shall we go?' Her dark eyes widened with the query, and she nodded her head, childishly, as if coaxing to be off. It was as if they had known each other so long that she had no reason to be reticent. Jack's heart warmed at this little gesture of trust. In some indefinable manner Audrey was — he couldn't find a phrase for it — was in his keeping. He had a glowing sensation of something akin to proprietorship.

The roadster's top had been folded down. Apparently it was the first time Audrey had been driven in an open car. The sense of freedom delighted her, and she said so. She said so with such exultation that Jack wondered whether she didn't live a rather hampered life. He asked her if there was any particular drive she would prefer to take, to which she replied, 'Anywhere.'

So, putting the town behind them, Jack chose the road over which he had just come with Cunningham, a winding graveled road that hugged the wooded shores of small lakes sparkling in the afternoon sun. The car was rolling slowly, smoothly through a heavily shaded avenue of tall firs. Audrey, with parted lips, drew a deep, luxurious breath, shook her head incredulously over the beauty of the scene and her own sensation of pure delight.

'You don't often get out into the country?' observed Jack.

'No. My sister is always engaged through the day, and I do not drive.'

'It would be pleasant if you had a little car. Then you could be more free.'

Audrey smiled half-pensively and slowly shook her head.

'Some people are not destined to have freedom,' she said. 'I think I am one of them.'

'Was your liberty restricted when you lived in China?'

'Naturally. Chinese girls, especially in homes that adhere to the old traditions, live very closely sheltered lives. However, I did not worry about it then. In America it is different. Almost everyone has more freedom.'

'But not you?' asked Jack, sympathetically.

'May-bee it is my fault,' confessed Audrey. 'I find it difficult to adjust myself to American ways. I do not know many people. And my sister, knowing how little chance I have had to be independent, leads me about with her as if I were a small child.'

'Well — we can't have that,' declared Jack, firmly. 'You will have to tell your sister that you're grown up.'

'I'm afraid Claudia would not believe it.'

'You'd better issue a declaration of independence before she smothers you.'

Audrey laughed a little, almost guiltily.

'I think I am doing that now,' she confessed. 'I feel like a culprit. Claudia would not approve of this, at all. So I did not tell her. It is a strange experience,' she added, 'to be out on one's own.'

In the mood of a fellow-conspirator, Jack surprised her by admitting that he too was enjoying an unaccustomed freedom.

'I live a very narrowly bounded life,' he was saying. 'If you are relishing your stolen hour of liberty, I can assure you that I share your sensations.'

'But do the hospital and the Medical College require you to work all the time?' she wanted to know. 'How cruel of them!'

'In all fairness to them,' explained Jack, 'my schedule of

work has been of my own making. It's a long story. I
mustn't bore you with it. The day is too fine for such dull
reminiscences.'

'Please,' said Audrey, gently. 'I want to know — if you
want to tell.'

The car slackened its speed perceptibly.

'When I entered the Medical College as a student, I had
about the same ideas concerning my future work that were
shared by the majority of my classmates. I had a natural
fondness for scientific research and looked forward to my
medical course with interest, but it never occurred to me
that I would permit my profession to dominate my life to
the extent that nothing else could have a place in my
thoughts.'

'And then something happened — suddenly?' encouraged Audrey.

'Yes — but not what you might suppose. Many people
have sworn themselves into an exclusive devotion to some
task or mission because of a tragic disappointment; unhappy love affair, maybe. That wasn't the case with me. I
had pursued the normal life of a college student but without
any entanglements that would affect my emotional gearing.
No — the thing that happened was an address delivered to
the class, on the first day, by a very brilliant and hard-
working professor. The picture he drew of a life devoted to
science stirred me very deeply. To attain the highest pro-
ficiency in that career, the professor said, one must not only
practice constant self-discipline — as to habits, hours of
work, and the abandonment of social distractions — but
must see to it that the self-discipline became automatic and
effortless.'

'I see,' commented Audrey. 'So you wouldn't have to
spend any of your time worrying about what you had given
up.'

'Exactly!' declared Jack, pleased over her promptness to
understand.

'And you did it?' she asked. 'I can see that you did.
Was it not difficult?'

'Not for long. I think I soon began to take pride in it, like a man saving money. The first thousand is the hardest.'

'And, after that, he is a miser,' she suggested, smiling.

'I suppose so,' Jack agreed. 'I never thought much about money, so I don't know just where thrift turns to avarice.'

'You would not need to think much about money — if you never went any place or did anything but work. So, after a while' — Audrey shook her head in expectation of his answer — 'you did not fret, any more, about the pleasure you were missing?'

He deliberated his reply for a moment.

'It wouldn't be quite true to say that I did not have restless days; but, in the main, I found so much interest in my job that nothing else made much of a bid for my attention.' He turned to her with a smile that promised a confession. 'Take the subject of girls, for example. There's probably nothing that can so completely divert a young man's mind as an infatuation. I resolved that to avoid this problem it would be better if I closed my eyes to the very existence of women.'

Audrey's eyes were averted as she received this information. She made no comment, and Jack went on.

'So — you see — this is in the nature of a stolen hour of freedom for me, too.' He chuckled, a bit self-consciously. 'You have run away from Claudia, and ——'

'And you have run away from yourself,' added Audrey, soberly.

'Yes — something like that.'

'But' — she glanced up with an honest smile in her brown eyes — 'You have so good an excuse, Doctor Beaven. This is, after all, a research party for you. I was invited to tell you the rest of my story about my life in China. May-bee,' she added, thoughtfully, 'you might have a Chinese patient, some time; is it not so?'

Jack studied her eyes for an instant, but they would not confess they were teasing.

'That's true,' he replied, gratefully. 'I might. Perhaps

you will go on with it now. I am most anxious to hear it.'
'It is hard to know where to begin.' Audrey's tone was
tender as she adventured upon the strange narrative. Much
of the tale Jack had already heard from Cunningham, but
he did not tell her so; listened attentively to her account of
the unusual circumstances of her birth in Hongkong and
her adoption by the Sen Lings. The car idled to a stop at
a bend in the road where there was ample space to park in
full view of an engaging vista, a silver lake rippled by the
breeze.

'Tell me something about your childhood,' encouraged
Jack, when she had done with the prologue of her story.
'I know next to nothing about life in China. Far as my
knowledge goes, you might as well have been born on the
moon. Was the Chinese language hard for you to learn?'

Audrey laughed merrily.

'How sillee!' she exclaimed. 'It was my native tongue,
you know. I suppose it was no more difficult to learn than
English was for you when you were a baby, Doctor Beaven.'
Her brown eyes twinkled teasingly as she added, 'I assume
that you were once a baby. You are such a verree serious
man, I am not sure about that.'

Jack chuckled to prove that he wasn't as serious as he
seemed, and Audrey continued with her story.

'I distinctly remember my first little shoes,' she said,
dreamily. 'They were red, with gray cats' faces painted on
the toes; so I wouldn't fall, you know. The cats made me
sure-footed.'

'You mean — the family actually believed that?'

'Oh, no.' Audrey smilingly repudiated this accusation.
'That is,' she hastily qualified, 'I am sure my mother did
not think so, and of course the wise Sen Ling did not. But
— the old myths are quite persistent, and the old symbols
are respected. Perhaps Shu-cheng may have believed in the
cats. Shu-cheng was my amah — my nurse — and had
been brought up to have faith in all of the superstitions.
Most of the instruction given to little children is done in
fairy-tales. But it is so with you, too; is it not? Perhaps we

heard more than you, about the doings of the gods, though
I am not sure of that. Your Jehovah — he opened a dry
path through the rivers, did he not, so his good friends would
not get their feet wet?'

'Yes — but not lately,' said Jack, amused.

Audrey's face was suddenly animated.

'Now — that is the difference between your gods and
ours,' she went on. 'Your gods have done their work. Ours
are very much alive and busy all the day long.'

'For instance ——' Jack's interest was mounting.

'Well — our kitchen god heard everything that was
said and reported to the other gods.'

'Was there more talk in the kitchen than elsewhere?'

'May-bee. I think there is always more candid talk in
kitchens. But perhaps the reason why they hung this god's
picture in the kitchen was because it was so convenient to
the sugar-bowl. Whenever we said anything rude or unkind,
that we did not want told to the other gods, we touched the
kitchen god's lips with sugar.'

'So his report would be more palatable?'

'Yes — and we had to pay for the sugar by performing
some errand.'

'Or having to sit in the corner, perhaps,' suggested Jack,
'meditating on your misdemeanor.'

'No,' said Audrey, seriously. 'The Chinese would never
punish a child that way. Meditation in China is not a
penalty but a privilege. The Chinese father would be
greatly distressed if his child felt that an hour of thoughtful
solitude was irksome.'

This was a new idea, but Jack agreed that it had
merit.

'The next time I have a chance to repeat this to the
parents of a small child,' he said, 'I shall give them something to think about.'

With the utmost candor Audrey rejoined, 'Perhaps you
may want to remember this when you have occasion to
discipline your own children — if you should have some.'

'Well — I'll not be having any,' said Jack, firmly. 'As

I have told you, there is no room in my life for the obligations one should expect to meet in a well-ordered home —
and I am sure I shouldn't want any other kind. I definitely
gave up all thought of that — years ago. I have no time
for such responsibilities.'

'I fear I am in the same position — for other reasons —
but good ones,' replied Audrey, after a meditative pause.
'I seriously doubt whether I could fit into the way of life
that is practiced in the American home; and, of course, I
could not consent to marry in China, however deeply I
respect the Chinese.'

'You and I have a great deal in common, Audrey. You
don't mind, do you — my calling you Audrey?'

She smiled and shook her head.

'No — but I would rather you called me by the name
I like so much better — my Chinese name, you know — the
one I have always worn, until recently. I think it would be
verree pleasant if you called me Lan Ying. I get hungry
to hear my name. Do you want to say it?' She leaned
forward a little toward him, her eyes lighting with a new
interest; and, elaborating the movements of her expressive
lips, as if she were instructing a small child, carefully
enunciated, 'Lan Ying.'

'Lan Ying,' repeated Jack, tenderly, making the name
sing, as she had done. She clapped her hands happily.

'So verree good for the first time,' she said, in a tone of
maternal encouragement. 'You are quick to imitate, Doctor
Beaven. I shall teach you many of the words I like best,
just to hear you say them. I am starved for the sound of
my own language. Perhaps you do not realize how intense
that kind of hunger can be.'

'I never thought about it before,' admitted Jack, 'but
it's easy to understand — Lan Ying — how you must feel
about that. Now that you speak of it, I do not often hear
my name, these days. My student friends, who called me
Jack, have mostly gone away to other places. I am Doctor
Beaven in the hospital and the Medical School.' There was
a long moment before Lan Ying replied.

'Shall I?' she asked, searching his eyes seriously.

'Would you like to?' He tried to say it calmly.

'If I may. I do not know. We are hardly more than strangers. Perhaps it is not done. You would tell me — is it not so? — if that would be the wrong thing for me to do.'

'Yes — I would tell you, Lan Ying.' His heart was pounding. He hoped she did not realize the exact state of his emotions.

Her lips were pursed slightly and her eyes were momentarily averted, as if she were debating whether to extend a confidence.

'Your name will not be difficult to say,' she ventured. 'In the hospital I heard Miss Warren refer to you, in speaking to another nurse, and she called you by your first name. I think the nurses do that quite often. Do you know what they call your Doctor Forrester?' Her lips widened in a smile.

Jack nodded and grinned.

'Yes — I know.'

'Does he?'

'Of course.'

She shook her head in anticipation of his next reply, and said, 'He does not like it?'

'I don't know. There are so many things that Tubby doesn't like. This may be one of them.'

'What are some of the others?' inquired Lan Ying, with interest.

'Well — me, for instance.'

Lan Ying promptly disputed this with a little gesture of unbelief.

'I heard that,' she said, 'but it surely is not true.'

'What makes you think so?'

'Because he told my sister you gave promise of becoming the most brilliant surgeon in the hospital. Would he say such a thing if he did not like you?'

'Yes — he might. One man can approve of another man's work without liking him personally. Sometimes I think that two men who dislike each other can get more work done than cronies who waste their time in friendly talk.'

'But — you like Doctor Forrester, do you not?'

'Not by a jugful!'

'And you work together — all day?'

'And all night, sometimes.'

'He never calls you "Jack"?' she asked. It warmed him to hear his name on the lips of Lan Ying. They were adorable lips. Their mobile curves fascinated him. He could not see through to the muscles that moved them: he had forgotten everything he ever knew about anatomy.

'No,' he replied, with a slightly sardonic smile. 'Tubby is never chummy with me. He is very surly and critical. It is only fair to say, though, that his reproaches are generally just and beneficial. He is a very wise man. It was Tubby who made the speech I told you about — on the first day — the speech that changed the whole course of my life.'

Lan Ying shook her head incredulously.

'You mean to say,' she demanded, in a bewildered tone, 'that you would permit the opinions of a man — whom you disliked — to set you going, for life, on a new path?'

'Why not? Opinions about such matters are not private property. I didn't have to like Tubby in order to see sound sense in what he was saying. Perhaps this sounds as if I were not very sensitive,' he added — 'and maybe I'm not. It has sometimes occurred to me that my likes and dislikes for other people are not as acute as in the case of most persons. Part of my self-imposed program is the careful disciplining of my affections and aversions. My aversion to Tubby hasn't interfered with my feeling that it is mutually to our advantage to work together. And I suppose' — he was choosing his words carefully — 'I suppose that I could regard an affection in much the same way. I might feel it strongly without letting it encroach on my duties.'

He was not quite satisfied with this speech, which he had delivered mostly for his own benefit.

'You are verree strong, Jack,' remarked Lan Ying, seri-

ously, a comment that left him feeling foolishly priggish;
but was, he felt, about the sort of rejoinder he had earned.
'And verree lonely, I think,' she added, 'having so little
interest in people — as persons.'

'Any line of scientific research,' explained Jack, dodging
the real issue of the conversation, 'is a lonely job. But' —
he brightened — 'it has its compensations. I should not
want to be doing anything else. I am quite contented.'

Lan Ying shook her head with child-like obstinacy.

'You could not be,' she demurred. Impulsively she laid
her fingers on his sleeve. 'Why do you not make friends
with this Tubbee? He is stubborn, and dislikes to take the
first step toward a reconciliation. But you are younger —
and you are not stubborn — and I know you are not bitter.'

Jack frowned a little. It was a painful subject. He
hoped they might soon dispose of it. However, it was not
at the stage where he could abandon it.

'There is nothing to reconcile,' he said, resolutely.
'Tubby and I were never friends. We have had no friendship to repair or reclaim.'

'I am sorree, Jack,' she replied, softly. 'It must have
done you both a great deal of damage — to feel that way.'
Noting his mood, and apparently realizing that there had
been quite enough talk about this matter, Lan Ying abruptly
called his attention to the loveliness of the peaceful scene
spread before them.

'Perhaps you would like to stroll down toward the lake,'
suggested Jack. He glanced at her shoes. 'I don't think
you would find it too rough. There seems to be a fairly
good path.'

She was pleased with the idea, and they set out through
the tall firs, Jack making no effort to accommodate his long
stride to the little steps she was taking. They were very
small feet. He wondered about them. Lan Ying, glancing
up, found him smiling, and asked the reason with her eyes.

'I think I heard, somewhere,' he said, audaciously, 'that
the Chinese had stopped going in for small feet. Perhaps
the rumor was incorrect.'

'Thank you,' acknowledged Lan Ying, 'if you mean what I think you mean. I am not so ver-ree big. I do not need big feet.'

'That must have been quite frightful,' reflected Jack, 'binding their girl-babies' feet, and making them hobble through life.'

Lan Ying laughed; and, halting, pointed to her heels, three inches high.

'I think women are not supposed to walk naturally in any country,' she said. 'Did you ever look under the table in one of your nicer restaurants?'

Jack couldn't recall that he had ever done so, but promised he would, next time.

'Shoes off, maybe?' he inquired.

'It is so funnee,' she said. 'The Chinese gave up their foot-foolishness, just in time to save me much discomfort; and now I have come to America to find it.'

'If I were a woman,' announced Jack, 'I would be independent, and wear what I pleased.'

'Pouf!' scoffed Lan Ying, in unexpected raillery. 'What do *you* know about women?'

He nodded agreement to this charge, though he felt he might have debated the question successfully. It may have occurred to Lan Ying that this would be a suitable place to change the topic, for she immediately gave herself to an exultant appreciation of the natural beauty surrounding them.

'How refreshing this must be for you,' she was saying, 'after such long, trying days in the hospital. It must grieve you dreadfully — all the miseries of the people.'

Jack's nod of assent was rather noncommittal. He disliked to pose as a sentimental altruist, much less a martyr.

'The miseries of the people,' he reflected, casually, 'are all in the course of the doctor's daily work. He cannot let them grieve him. The more he is emotionally upset by these misfortunes the less able he is to relieve them. The patients and their families can be depended on to do the grieving. A doctor cannot wear his heart on his sleeve.'

The metaphor stirred Lan Ying's interest.

'How funnee!' she exclaimed. '"His heart on his sleeve."'

'Didn't you ever hear that before? It's an old stock saying with us. If a person is easily moved to pity or sympathy or affection we say that is wearing one's heart on one's sleeve.'

'And it is not considered good form to pity anybody?' she asked, with widened eyes. 'And one should not show sympathy or affection?'

'Depends on circumstances,' Jack replied, judicially. 'Pity is usually ruinous. One would think that so cheap a gift as pity could have no weight at all — either for good or bad; but it can do a lot of damage. And sympathy often accents troubles that would be much less painful if the people tried to forget them. And as for affection; well, that's quite another matter, but one has to be careful where one displays affection.' He tried to make this sound dryly impersonal. Lan Ying's face was turned away, her eyes surveying the rippled lake.

'You may think it strange,' she said, slowly returning to him, 'but I have much to learn about such things. In China we do not see many persons outside the family and a small circle of close friends. Even in the household, the men and women do not associate closely or confidentially. I was brought up with women. Perhaps I have been wearing my heart on my sleeve. When I like a friend verree much, I cannot help telling her so.' She shook her head inquiringly. 'One should not do that?' she asked.

'Oh, yes,' said Jack, reassuringly. 'That's quite all right.'

Her eyes were serious as she searched his face with all the honest candor of a child.

'But — I must not say I like *you?*' she queried.

He regarded her for a moment, smiled a little, and replied, slowly, 'Well — if you were my sister — I think I might advise you not to say it; at least, not quite so — so directly.'

'Oh?' pursued Lan Ying. 'If I were your sister, I should not tell you I liked you? How funnee!'

'I think you misunderstood me. I meant — if you were
my sister I should advise you not to say that to a man
friend. He might take advantage of your frankness.'

'But — *you* would not,' she declared, looking him
squarely in the eyes.

'No, Lan Ying,' returned Jack, resolutely. 'You may
say whatever you like to me. I'll understand. You can't
help knowing that I like you, too, very much.'

'I am so glad,' she said happily. 'Tonight I shall write to
my foster-mother and tell her I now have a good friend.'

'Perhaps you will write to me too, occasionally,' suggested
Jack, privately reflecting that he was behaving rather badly.
This affair must not go any farther, he kept saying to
himself.

'If you wish; but my letters will not be interesting.
Nothing ever happens. It is so different with you. Your
life is full of activity. You do so many kind deeds.'

Their conversation had been so uniquely forthright that
Jack felt the necessity of qualifying her compliment to his
altruism. He hoped he was not to be bracketed in her
esteem as a grown-up Boy Scout. By mutual consent they
sat down on a green knoll near the quiet water.

'You do me too much credit, Lan Ying. I am not con-
sciously performing kind deeds. Patients in the hospital
are not there on my invitation, and my interest in them is
professional. If they have other than physical troubles,
that's too bad, but none of my business. The man who
comes into the hospital with a spinal tumor may have any
number of other things the matter with him, and they
ought to be remedied; but, so far as I am concerned, he is
just a —— '

'Just a tumor,' assisted Lan Ying, soberly.

'Just a case,' amended Jack. 'Maybe I've been saying
this the worst way. What I mean is: I am trying to do my
job as well as I can, without dividing my attention between
my professional duty and an emotional interest in the
patient as a person.'

'I should think you would be missing a great deal of

happiness that you are entitled to, Jack. After you have performed an operation that has made someone well again, he would be so grateful that almost anything you said to him would carry weight. I know,' she added, 'it would be true with me — if I had been sick, and you had made me well. You could advise me about anything, then; and I should listen.'

For an instant he had a recollection of the occasion when he had fancied her on the operating-table. It had been such a vivid experience that the memory sent a little shudder through him.

'I appreciate your thinking that, Lan Ying,' he said, 'but you might get poor advice. Doctors aren't supposed to know anything much — outside their own field.'

'They ought to,' persisted Lan Ying. 'They have the best chance in the world to help people. I think it would be verree sad and dull business — just cutting into people — and sewing them up again. But it would not be sad or dull if you knew you were going to give them courage and direction, after they were on the way to health again. That would be wonderful!'

Jack did not immediately reply. He had already stated his position in regard to the surgeon's task, and did not wish to defend it further.

'Shall you be coming back again, sometime, to see Doctor Cunningham?' Lan Ying was saying. Jack wondered whether Cunningham had occurred to her mind in connection with what she had said about the wider opportunities of his profession. For a moment he experienced a little surge of jealousy, the first rap of it that had ever come to him. His response to her query was so tardy that Lan Ying glanced up to interrogate his eyes. Turning to her, he extended his open hand into which she trustfully laid a small gloved one.

'Lan Ying,' he said, gently, 'I am so fond of you that I mustn't do anything to make you unhappy. I know how much delight it would give me to see you often. But — as I have told you — I am a slave to my work. I want to be your friend, but I'm afraid my friendship will add very little to your happiness.'

'You mean — may-bee — we will not see each other — any more?' she asked, in a tone that was barely audible.

'You have been so honest with me, Lan Ying, that I must be sincere with you. I shouldn't be saying this,' he went on, recklessly, 'but nobody else has ever —— ' He broke off, suddenly, freeing her hand. After a moment of struggle, he continued, resolutely steadying his voice. 'My friendship is — is a poor thing. I shall not forget you. We will write to each other, sometimes,' he finished, lamely.

She took his hand in both of hers and pressed it warmly.

'I know what you mean, Jack. May-bee I understand even better than you. Your life is all planned — and it is a verree courageous life — and there is no room in it for anybody or anything but your work. You have given up everything — so you might be a great scientist. And I should be most unhappy if our friendship worried you, or occupied your mind. But — it need not be so. We are both of us lonely people. To you, men and women are just broken machines that you must repair — day after day, night after night — all your life — until you die. Surely — a hard task. With me — I have no country, no interests, no happiness. We are both waifs — you and I.' She paused. He felt that it was a critical moment. Steady! Steady! The firm grip that had kept his emotions — his passions — on a leash for years was still there. 'And when I knew that you liked me a little,' continued Lan Ying, 'I wanted you for a friend. No one understands me — but you. And now you are afraid to like me; is it not so?' Her eyes were misty.

'From now on, Lan Ying,' replied Jack, a little huskily, 'you and I are going to understand each other. It will be a peculiar friendship, because — because neither of us will expect anything of the other — but comradeship.'

'I am so glad,' she said. 'It will be verree nice. I shall do a water-color for you to hang in your library. Would you like that?'

'Please — and may I have a picture of you, Lan Ying?'

'In my Chinese clothes, may-bee?'

'In anything — so it's you.'

'Shall we go now?' she asked. 'I must be at home when Claudia arrives.'

They retraced their steps slowly to the road, carefully avoiding a return to the subject of their personal relations. Jack opened the door of the car for her, and closed it with the sensation that he had no right to her, yet she seemed to belong to him. He opened the other door and stepped in.

He tipped the ignition key and was on the point of spinning the engine, but he paused. 'This has been the most delightful day I ever spent,' he added. 'Thank you, Lan Ying, for — for coming with me.'

She had tugged off her gloves, and now gave him her bare hand.

'It has made me happy,' she said, softly. 'I shall be content to wait — a long, long time — until we meet again. I wonder' — she drew a regretful little sigh — 'if we shall ever again be able to talk to each other — this way — apart from other people.'

'I hope so,' said Jack, unsteadily. Then, impulsively, he slipped his arm about her and drew her close to him. She made a brief flutter of protest like a captured bird, just a breathless little 'Oh!' — and relaxed in his arms, nestling her cheek against his shoulder. A whole minute passed. She stirred. Jack lifted her small hand and, bending over it, kissed it. Lan Ying's brooding eyes followed the hand, watching the caress with a smile on her parted lips. Their eyes met in a mutual confession that no words could have denied. She slowly disengaged her hand and, with eyes averted, softly pressed the back of it to her own lips.

'Lan Ying' — Jack's voice was husky — 'I haven't the slightest right to ask this of you — and if you don't want to, I'll understand — but it might be a very long time before we see each other —— ' He leaned toward her, entreatingly.

For a long moment she searched his eyes studiously, each of them separately, back and forth; inspected his lips gravely; returned to his eyes; smiled, tremulously, and said, with a childish little shake of the head, 'It would not be the wrong thing — for me — to do?'

The crow's-feet at his temples deepened.

'You mustn't ask me to decide that for you, Lan Ying.'

She turned her face away and meditated on her problem for a little while, a slow flush creeping up her cheek. Then she returned to him and said, shyly, 'You may think it funnee, Jack, but I never kissed anyone, in my life, but my sister — once — and little Teddy. May-bee I shall not do it verree well.'

He put his arms around her and drew her to him, kissed her on the adorable black fringe and the white forehead, laid his cheek against hers, finding it comfortingly warm. One small hand trustingly circled his neck. Her eyes were closed.

With a racing heart, he found her lips, and she responded — tentatively, honestly. Then, for an ecstatic moment, a great wave seemed to engulf them both. They clung to each other, startled by the discovery of the force of their emotions.

Beaven was more than startled: he suddenly realized that he was terrified. He had never dreamed that he — the controlled, scientific mind and pulse — could be so shaken. With an effort, almost of violence, he released the girl, strove to recover his self-control.

There was a moment of silence between them. Then Beaven, his voice unsteady, in spite of his effort to control it, whispered, 'Thank you, darling. You are very good to me. But — you mustn't ever let me do it again. I have no claim on you.'

She laid her palm against his cheek.

'Please do not be sorree, Jack. It was my own decision. And — it was my own desire. We will not do it — any more. Shall we go now? Claudia will be wondering.'

He pushed the starter-button, and the roadster moved slowly into the road.

'I never thought anything like this could ever happen to me,' murmured Jack.

Lan Ying was stroking her gloves onto her slim fingers.

'Nothing has happened to you,' she said, reassuringly. 'You will now go back to your destiny, and I shall go back to mine. But — we shall be friends forever; is it not so?'

Jack's eyes were on the road, as the car gathered speed.

'Yes,' he said, sincerely, 'it is so.'

Chapter X

Tubby was barking dictations to his stampeded Miss Romney when, on Wednesday morning early, Jack showed up in response to a peremptory telephone call. To his surprise, the office was folding up. Minions from the administrative office ventured in and scurried out. The much-traveled bags were piled beside the door. Jack sauntered across to the window, lounged onto the sill, and waited.

'That's all,' declaimed Tubby. 'You may go. I want to talk to Doctor Beaven. Call a taxi. I'll be down in ten minutes. And send up an orderly for my luggage.' Apparently Tubby was going abroad, if his baggage was luggage.

'Good-bye,' squeaked the girl, as she went out.

'Now, Beaven —— ' Jack took the inquisitorial chair and Tubby clapped on his derby hat to add a touch of finality to his remarks. 'As you see, I'm about to leave. Sudden decision. The Regents insist on my attending this Neurological Congress in Vienna.'

'I'm glad you can go, sir,' said Jack.

'Not sure that I want to,' gruffed Tubby. 'Not sure it is a good time for me to be off the campus.'

'I'll do my best, sir, while you're gone,' said Jack.

'There's more at stake this time. Perhaps you know what I mean.' Tubby scowled searchingly into Jack's baffled eyes.

'I'm afraid I don't, sir.'

'That's odd. Do you mean to tell me you've been on a fishing trip with Cunningham, and he didn't tell you about his lecture assignment?'

'No, sir. Not a word.'

Tubby lighted a cigarette and seemed uncertain where to begin with an explanation.

'You're going to see a lot more of Cunningham,' he growled.

'That's good, sir.'

'Quite to the contrary, that's bad, sir,' mocked Tubby. 'It is quite impossible that you should have been in intimate contact with Cunningham and not be affected somewhat by his damn'-fool ideas. They sound reasonable when he states them. They would not be so insidious if Cunningham was a second-rater. But that's the trouble. Cunningham is not a mere evangelist. He is an informed pathologist and an excellent surgeon. But — and here's the difficulty — there's only one Bill Cunningham, so far as I know. For the rank and file of doctors, his brand of sentimentality would be ruinous.' Tubby pushed back his chair and began pacing the floor. 'Ruinous!' he repeated.

'Yes, sir,' agreed Jack, honestly.

'Now — here is the problem. You will recall that we have a new member of the Board of Regents, Mr. Denman of Chicago, who has recently been appointed to the committee on Medical College affairs. Just why, I'm sure I don't know. I fail to see how his gift of one hundred thousand dollars — pumped out of an Oklahoma oil-field — qualifies him to select the special lecturers for this institution. Nor do I know why the other members of the committee have listened to him. Perhaps they feel that whoever pays the piper should be permitted to call the tune. In my opinion, this Denman — however generous — is about as well fitted to suggest policies to the Medical College as I am to be — the' — Tubby groped for an assignment appropriately remote — 'the Maharajah of Lickapoo.'

Jack considered saying, 'You might do that quite nicely, sir,' but prudently refrained.

'Denman began it innocuously enough,' continued Tubby, clipping his words, 'by suggesting a series of lectures by some man of outstanding reputation as a general practi-

tioner; something fresh from the field. Everybody agreed
to that. The new member should be treated amiably. He'd
come through with a lot of money. Perhaps he'd respond
to an encore.' Tubby's tone was bitter. 'Then — properly
encouraged — the fellow amended his own informal resolution to include an occasional clinic, and a week or two of
making the rounds of the hospital with the interns and
seniors in tow, showing them how to talk to the patients.
That wasn't so good, but nobody debated the matter. I
think they all assumed that the appointment would be
left to the discretion of the faculty. It would have been no
more than common courtesy.'

Jack stroked his jaw to efface a grin. 'The faculty' —
huh! Tubby had assumed that he himself would make the
appointment.

'Then!' shouted Tubby. 'Then! — with all this agreed
to, the bounder suggests that Cunningham — of all people
on earth — should be asked to lead the cubs around, and
show 'em how to hold hands and coo!'

'And — they approved?' inquired Jack, suspecting he
knew the answer.

'They approved — the asses! And of course Cunningham
will accept. Why shouldn't he? Honorable assignment.
He can't very well refuse. This Denman, it appears, was
popped into the hospital up there with an emergency gall-
bladder or something, a year ago. Cunningham operated.
He could and would do a good job. Denman liked him,
naturally enough. Couldn't be blamed for that. Everybody likes Cunningham. I like him. The story is that
Denman sent Cunningham a whopping fee, which he
returned with a modest bill, suggesting that the rest of the
money be presented to the hospital. And the tale sounds
authentic. That's about what Cunningham would do. Upright fellow. But — not the man for this special lecture-
ship.'

'Couldn't you have said that, sir?'

'No. This Denman is a pretty smooth individual. He
had taken the pains to remark that Cunningham and I were

old friends and classmates; it went without saying — and then he proceeded to say it — that I would be glad enough to see this honor bestowed upon this comrade of my youth. If he'd gagged me, he couldn't have taken out better insurance against my objections.' Tubby, having boiled over, resumed his seat. His tone became almost confidential.

'Now, Beaven, you will have to do your best, in an indirect way, to counteract the influence of this genial Boy Scout from Saginaw Bay. Don't offend him. Don't deride him. Don't make open war on him. But see to it that these youngsters are kept steady.' Tubby glared a threat. 'I hope I'll not find, when I come back here in November, that the whole school has gone in for faith-healing!'

'I'll try to obey your wishes, sir,' promised Jack.

'Well — you'd better. You have come into a very responsible position, and you know how you got there. I practically went on your bond when the Regents thought you were too young for this faculty appointment. Don't let me down. . . . And now — there's one more thing.'

A grizzled orderly had shuffled in. Tubby pointed to the bags and motioned him out.

'One thing more. Yesterday, I understand, we took in another polio. It's getting late in the season for polio, and this may be the last of it. I hope so.'

'But I don't have to do anything about that; do I?'

'Not unless you're interested. It's not your job — no. But you are better equipped than anyone else within five hundred miles to do some valuable research. If I could be sure we'd have some more polio — enough polio to offer a fairly wide range of clinical material — I shouldn't think of leaving.'

The bald statement made Jack wince. He had been trained to despise and distrust sentiment, but this comment was a bit too cold-blooded, even for him.

'You have a heavy schedule,' continued Tubby, obviously unaware of Jack's reaction. 'But if there is an opportunity for laboratory investigation of this thing, don't miss it. Don't miss it, even if you have to slight something else.

Give it the best you've got!' He glanced at his watch. 'I must go,' he snapped. 'Tell the Romney to lock my desk and give you the keys.' With a jerky little nod in Jack's general vicinity, he caught up his camel's-hair coat and brief-case, and marched out, leaving the door open behind him.

Hooking a rangy leg over the arm of his chair, Jack waited for the office clerk's return. He was glad the interview had occurred. It had cleared his mind of perplexity. It had helped him to the consolidation of a precarious position. He knew now where his duty lay. Cunningham had upset him. Cunningham had played the very devil with his mental habits. Now Tubby had come to the rescue of the jeopardized scientific attitude. Bill Cunningham, performing all manner of good and gracious deeds along the shoreline of Saginaw Bay, was an admirable friend and an undeniably useful citizen. But Cunningham, teaching his sentimental bedside manner to a lot of impressionable young medics, was another person altogether. Tubby — damn him — was right about that.

As for the prospect of laboratory polio, that wasn't much of an issue. There wouldn't be any more infantile paralysis; not after midsummer.

Pallid little Romney's high heels were pattering in. Jack regarded her indifferently as she cleared off the top of Tubby's desk.

'Doctor Forrester said I am to be your secretary now, while he's away,' she reported, with a twitchy little smile.

'That so?' replied Jack, absently. 'Well — you may go, and have yourself a vacation — until Monday.'

'Thank you, sir,' she said, anxiously. 'Will it be all right, do you think?' Her puzzled eyes doubted it. 'Do I have to ask anyone else?'

'You may if you wish,' said Jack, dryly. 'Ask anybody. Ask the girl at the switchboard. Ask the orderlies. But — you said you were to be my secretary and I have told you to take a vacation until Monday.'

She made a pathetic little grimace as if she were about

to cry. Somehow it didn't fit in with the starchy permanent, the snugly modish gray gown, the competent business air. Jack sat up straight and regarded her with interest.

'What ails you?' he queried. 'Somebody get your goat?'

Romney twisted the end of her nose with a small handkerchief.

'I haven't had a goat,' she replied, thickly, 'for almost two years.'

Jack grinned.

'How long have you been working here?' he asked. 'I forget.'

'Almost two years.'

'It's a curious coincidence,' drawled Jack.

Miss Romney ventured a half-hysterical chuckle.

'I needn't tell *you* anything about a lost goat,' she retorted. 'But maybe you don't care about yours. You have your guinea pigs and your monkeys.' Brittle Miss Romney had the traditional posture and mood of the admittedly licked who back up against the wall resolved to sell out dearly. Jack was amused but he admired her. Her passion spent, she collapsed into Tubby's chair. 'Now you can fire me if you want to,' she muttered, ruefully.

'Romney,' he said, soberly, 'you have had a hard day and you're upset. I'd much rather see you blow off at the whistle than explode and shatter the building. I cannot remember anything you have said. Run along now and come back Monday morning. While you're gone, you might look for your goat. A few days of fresh air and a change of scenery would be good for you.'

'I'll send my sister,' said the girl. 'She needs it more than I do.'

Jack was about to say, 'As you like,' when the Cunningham influence prompted him to inquire, 'What's *her* trouble?'

'Our mother has a cancer, Doctor Beaven. She requires constant care. Lou is practically a prisoner. I'm gone all day, and Lou carries the load.'

'You mean — Lou does the nursing and you earn the living?'

Romney nodded.

'That's pretty tough,' said Jack. 'I'm afraid you don't have very much fun.'

'Some people weren't meant to have fun,' rejoined Romney. 'Their job is cut out for them.'

'There's a certain satisfaction, though, in courageously doing one's duty; don't you think?' Jack remembered what Edith Cunningham had said about the value of a challenge to bravery.

'I expect there is for *you*,' sighed Romney. 'You work hard all the time and never have any fun; but you don't actually *have* to do it. It isn't brave when you *have* to do it.'

'Nobody *has* to do *anything*,' declared Jack. 'You — for example. You could run away from it all, if you wanted to.'

'But I'd have to take myself along, and it wouldn't be any fun.' Her eyes lighted with a sudden smile that made her almost pretty. 'I expect that's what keeps *you* from running off,' she ventured.

Jack nodded a tentative approval and rose to go.

'I'm glad we had this talk,' he said. 'You're very good stuff, Romney, if you don't mind my saying so.'

Romney's eyes were swimming and her chin trembled a little.

'Thanks,' she said, unsteadily. The tears were rolling down her cheeks now, but she managed a grateful smile. 'I'm glad to have made your acquaintance, Doctor Beaven.'

Jack softly closed the door behind him. That was an odd thing for Romney to say. Perhaps she was embarrassed. He'd been seeing her in Tubby's office every day for — how long was it? Almost two years. 'Glad to have made your acquaintance,' eh? He frowned, as the light broke. Tubby was right. Express sympathy or human interest, and presently you find yourself all milled up with people's private predicaments. Then you can't keep your mind on the business you're being paid to do. Little Romney lived a dog's life, but it was no affair of his. And the minute he

shows a glimmer of concern, she insists that he has become
another fellow than the one she'd known. 'Glad to have
made your acquaintance.' Damned impudence; that's
what it was. That's what you got for hobnobbing with the
Cunninghams.

* * * * * * * *

On his swift drive back to the University, yesterday, the
most recent appointee on the Medical College faculty had
been a seriously perplexed young man.

As he had sped along, only vaguely conscious of the
colorful landscape that had filled him with delight a few
days ago, his mental tumult suggested a complete reorganization of his aims. He resented this proposal as absurd
but he could not dismiss it.

It was quite evident that he should not have gone on
this fishing excursion. That's what came of abandoning
your program, even for a day. This brief vacation, which
was to have been a pleasantly restful interlude, now appeared in immediate retrospect as a distressing intrusion
upon his peace. He was to have come back refreshed. Instead, he was returning bewildered, asking himself how
much of his life-plan was any longer tenable; how many
of his professional duties required a drastic reappraisal.

In the first place — overtopping all his other problems —
there was Audrey. Why hadn't he been sensible enough to
let that memory fade into oblivion? Ever since that first
chance meeting on the stairway in the hospital, she had
been much on his mind. But in the natural course of events
he would, he knew, have forgotten her; or, not forgetting,
have cherished the dream as the most dear of his many
might-have-beens. As matters now stood, Audrey Hilton
was in a fair way to monopolize his mind. She had said,
'Nothing has happened to you, Jack. You will go back to
your destiny, and I shall return to mine.' And that would
certainly be a moving speech as the curtain slowly descended on the third act of a stage-play, after which the
sacrificial offerings could retire to their dressing-rooms,

scrub off the paint, put on their street clothes, and saunter out together for a snack.

But something *had* happened to him. He was returning to his 'destiny,' yes; but it wouldn't be the same destiny. One thing was clear, and in this he felt he had Audrey's full sympathy and approval: they would not marry. They would be friends forever; that would be all. And that would be torture. He would go back to his eighteen-hour-per-day job bearing this extra burden; facing more exacting responsibilities than ever before, and with a mind distracted.

Momentarily the recollection of yesterday's enchanted hour swept his heart with ecstasy. Every instant of that glorified moment was indelible. He could, he believed, have disciplined himself to forget the Audrey Hilton he had met at the hospital, and the Audrey Hilton he had talked with at the Livingstone and at the Cunninghams'; but the kiss would remain an indestructible memory. Perhaps the easy and sensible way to deal with it was to toss all of his life-program aside and let this new motive have the right of way.

Having luxuriated in this prodigal thought for a few miles, his hard-earned mental habits would reassert their claims, and demand a hearing. Did not this love-smitten Jack Beaven, who was toying with the idea of marriage, a home, a family, social obligations, domestic problems, owe something to that other Beaven who had lived like a monastic and worked like a slave to win the distinctions that had now come to him? Why had he been asked, at thirty-one, to become a member of the faculty? An unusual achievement of this sort should be valued no more for what it had brought than what it had cost! And Tubby — hateful as he had been — had engineered his early arrival into a place of preferment. What would Tubby think? What would Tubby say? What would Tubby have a perfect right to do when he learned that a girl had stepped in to claim part of his time and most of his mind?

And then — there was Cunningham. Last night, in the library, over their pipes, Cunningham had said some things that had impressed him deeply.

'Leave out the human-interest element,' Cunningham had declared, 'and a surgeon might as well be working in a garage. When you stop to think about it, Beaven, there's a good many points of similarity between a man and an automobile. Gasoline and blood serve the same purpose. Plenty of likeness between lymphatics and lubrication; the ignition system and the lungs; radiator and kidneys. The car also has eyes that get out of whack and feet needing a good deal of attention.'

'And a larynx,' Jack had added, solemnly, 'suffering from overwork.'

'Thanks. And there isn't much difference between Jack Beaven, in white duck, working on a bad kidney — and Chuck Billings, in greasy overalls, working on a bad water-pump, except that Beaven has an opportunity to add something of nobility to his patient.'

'And Chuck,' assisted Jack, obligingly, 'hasn't anything to show for his work but six dollars and fifty cents.'

'I'm not so sure about that, Jack.' Cunningham puffed thoughtfully for a long moment. 'It just happens that I didn't invent "Chuck Billings" to serve my little homily. I know Chuck Billings very well. He operates the garage where I go for repairs. I took a busted appendix out of Chuck, about five years ago. He was sure he was going to die, and I felt, too, that his prediction wasn't a bad guess. He didn't have much to fall back on. He'd been very intemperate. Very improvident. Not much good. Head over heels in debt. Floating bills all over town. Well — one day, when he was burning up, and felt that he was as good as dead, and ought to be collecting time-and-a-half for overtime, he wanted to tell me what sort of fellow he'd be if he got well.'

'When the Devil is sick, he'd be a saint,' recalled Jack, sardonically.

'Exactly! And that's the time to let him commit himself. So — we brought up one of the girls from the hospital office, who had a notary's power and seal, and we let Chuck dictate a new constitution for himself, to be effective when and if he ever asked for his shoes. He was talking his head off, anyhow; so he might as well be talking about that.'

Edith Cunningham had appeared in the doorway at this juncture.

'Intruding?' she asked.

'You couldn't,' said her husband, pointing his pipe-stem at the davenport. 'I was telling Jack about Chuck Billings.'

'Famous story,' murmured Edith. 'Jack will love it.'

Doubtless she had called him Jack because Cunningham had just done so. All the same, it had warmed him. He liked her. She was sound.

'Well — not to elaborate this too much — Chuck got well, as you have probably forecast; and, having had quite a bit of experience with death-bed confessions and promises, I thought I would make a little experiment. When it became fairly clear that the angels weren't in urgent need of Chuck, I mailed his dictated aspirations to a bang-up good printer in Detroit, and ordered a copy — thirty inches by eighteen — to be done in a dignified Gothic type, with art initials in red. It was a beautiful job. I had it framed under glass. And on the day we turned Chuck loose, I gave it to him. He was sitting on the edge of the bed, grinning. His wife was there, waiting to drive him home. I said, "Chuck, you have been such a gallant patient that I've decided to present you with a certificate. This entitles you to be — from now on — a very important fellow in this town. I hope you will accept it, with my best wishes, and enjoy all the new rights and privileges it offers you." Chuck gingerly took the thing in both hands, balanced it on his knee, and stared at it in astonishment. His lips soundlessly formed the words as he read on with widening eyes. Mrs. Billings, pleased at her husband's distinction, and bursting with curiosity, hooked an arm over his shoulder and surveyed the formidable document with a stunned expression of incredulity. It was ever so much more impressive in ecclesiastical print than it could have been in pen-writing. Chuck swallowed, a couple of times, rather noisily, as he reviewed his legally attested vows to pursue a new life.

When he had finished, he handed the thing to his wife, and said, sheepishly, "Thanks, Doc." For a long time he sat staring at the floor. Then he looked up, and blurted out, huskily, "By God — I said it!... By God — I'll do it!... O.K., Doc!"... Well' — Cunningham whipped out his handkerchief and blew a strident blast — 'I couldn't stay there any longer, so I bade them a hasty farewell and got out.'

'And then ——' Jack had asked, not very optimistically.

Cunningham straightened from his lounging posture in the big leather chair, tapped a finger on Jack's knee, and replied, 'Chuck Billings took that thing down town — *and hung it up in his garage!*'

'And it's there now!' declared Edith, proudly. 'All sorts of people, having business there, drift over to the wall where it hangs, and read it, mostly without comment. Sometimes they mutter, "Well, I'll be damned." But nobody laughs.'

'Of course,' conceded Cunningham, 'we really had a little something to work on in Chuck's case. People like him. And they trust him. Very personable chap. If he'd had a little more education and a better background, he might have gone far.'

'He has gone far, Bill,' put in Edith, 'considering where he started from.'

'The Rotary Club took him in, a couple of years ago,' continued her husband.

Jack felt he must have grinned a little, unwittingly, for Cunningham interrupted himself to defend his remark.

'I know,' he said, 'how Tubby would sneer at that. It has become the fashion to poke fun at these luncheon clubs. Well — there's many a selfish old codger who has been either inspired or shamed into something like sound social behavior by such organizations. I'll bet if the citizens of this country would turn the Government over to these derided boobs in the luncheon clubs — and let them run it for a while — there'd be ——'

'Tut, tut, Bill,' advised Edith. 'Go on — about Chuck.'

'Well — the Rotary Club took Chuck in. Proudest moment of his life, I guess. They put him on a committee to recondition delinquent boys who've done time in the Reformatory and are consequently in need of reformation. He always has three or four of these fellows working for him. Last time I was in there, I said, "Chuck, how are your problem boys making out, on the average?" And he rubbed his head with the greasiest hand in town and said, "Well, Doc; it's this way. So long as we make 'em think they're doing something important, they play the game pretty straight. If I say to Pat Reegan, 'Now this is a darned ticklish job, Pat, and if you can't do it be sure to call for me,' Pat comes through with some fine work."'

'That's the whole thing; isn't it, Bill? The challenge!' Edith's eyes were thoughtful. 'Isn't that what keeps them lined up?'

'That's what keeps us *all* lined up, dear,' he answered. 'The challenge to do something worth doing! The feeling that something is expected of us! I know this sounds trite, Jack. Sentimental small-town stuff, if you like. Maybe, with your highly specialized interests, it seems mawkish, moony, and annoyingly unprofessional. But if — while I'm taking a bad appendix out of Chuck Billings — I can put an idea into him that makes him useful and respected, I'm willing to be a hick.'

The telephone had rung, at that point, and Cunningham went to answer it.

Jack said, 'Has he done this sort of thing often, Mrs. Cunningham?'

'You mean — printing Chuck's promises? No — not just that way. I think the occasion usually suggests the method. He finds it a fascinating game; studies his patients' minds, learns their history, discovers their vulnerable spots, and plans his attack like a military strategist debating whether to launch an offensive by land, water, or air. Mostly he appeals to their courage, I think; imputes to them a gallant spirit; assumes that they are strong; makes them believe it. He gets a great thrill out of his experiments. Of course he loves surgery and his work in the laboratory. They demand a certain amount of skill. But — the other thing — revamping people's mental attitudes — that's where my husband's heart is.'

Cunningham had appeared at the door, hat in hand.

'I'll be out for an hour,' he announced. 'Hospital.'

'Want me to go along?' asked Jack.

'No, you stay here and talk to Edith.'

After the front door had slammed,' Jack said, 'Your husband is a remarkable fellow. I never knew anyone just like him.'

'Have a good time with him at the lake?' asked Edith, casually.

'Excellent.'

'Bill says he told you Audrey Hilton's story. You like her very much; don't you? I could see that you did.'

He had not been prepared for this cool inquisition. In any other tone or mood it might have sounded impertinent. Edith was asking him if he liked Audrey in much the same voice she might have used had she asked him if he liked horses or Beethoven or steamed clams.

'Very much indeed,' he had replied, frankly.

'That's nice,' approved Edith. 'You two should have a very happy life together, I think. You have so much to present to each other; your distinction, her charm; your ambition, her serenity; your ——'

'I do not expect ever to marry, Mrs. Cunningham,' Jack had interposed. 'The nature of my work does not permit it. Audrey and I have talked it all over, frankly.'

'Oh? So soon?' Edith's brows expressed amused surprise. 'Well, you certainly haven't let much grass grow since you met her. How deliciously funny! You two blessed things talked it all over, and decided not to marry! Now wasn't that heroic of you both; especially you!' She laughed.

'Sorry if it sounded heroic,' Jack had countered. 'I'm not given to heroics. We were just facing facts. I don't think either of us felt martyred.'

'Don't be miffed,' entreated Edith. 'But you are so

dreadfully serious, Jack. You invite teasing, and it's hard to resist.' She suddenly sobered. 'Please don't think I'm indifferent to your passion for work. I can guess what it has cost you to be where you are. I am sure you didn't arrive at it by self-indulgence. But isn't it possible' — she half-closed her eyes, thoughtfully — 'isn't it possible that your single-minded devotion to your work has become something of an idiosyncrasy? You've made a lot of cruel self-sacrifices. You're proud of them. You have a right to be. You love your scars. They identify you — and that's what everybody strives for; identifying marks; something more interesting than mere finger-prints. Perhaps you never actually strutted up to a mirror and said, "You're the man who's going to be remembered for having given up everything to Science; wedded to her, renouncing all others and cleaving only unto her till death do you part." But — that has been your purpose and your pride. If I'm wrong, please correct me.'

'That's one way of saying it, I suppose,' admitted Jack.

'And now a bright and lovely girl has tapped at your heart, but you haven't room for her because you think your heart is already occupied. I think you're mistaken. It's your head that's fully occupied; not your heart. You've cultivated your intellect at the expense of your emotions. Audrey would be good for you.'

'As a loyal friend — yes.'

Edith smiled knowingly, and relaxing from her argument lounged negligently into the corner of the davenport.

'I should like to make a bet with you, Doctor John Wesley Beaven.'

He shook his head.

'Not about that,' he protested.

'If I can't bet, let me at least prophesy. I'll give you and Audrey a year to find out how silly you are.'

'Are you a pretty good prophet?' Jack grinned dryly.

'One of the best. Positively uncanny — in romantic matters. First time I ever saw Bill Cunningham I mentally

branded him as my personal property. Went home and told
my mother I was as good as married.'

'Tell me all about it,' insisted Jack, thankful for the
digression.

'It was at a concert — Chicago Symphony Orchestra —
in Detroit. Bill was an intern then. He had brought Tubby
Forrester with him, hoping to distract his mind from his
trouble. Tubby had just lost his girl.'

'Girl?' echoed Jack, incredulously. 'Tubby ever have a
girl?'

'Very much so,' declared Edith.

'I can't picture Tubby in love with anybody. What
happened? Wouldn't she have him?'

Edith sat for a moment meditating a reply.

'I think I'll let Bill tell you,' she said.

* * * * * * * * *

Tubby's final instructions had the effect of stiffening
Jack's resistance to the mellowing influence of Audrey and
the Cunninghams. Back in the old routine, it was inevitable
that his accustomed mental states should prevail. In his
effort to deal vigorously with the sentimental considerations
that had briefly given him pause, he made things even
rougher than he had planned for his classes in Anatomy.

Tubby had been intolerant toward all but the most
promising. Jack had decided to be a little more considerate
of the backward and unself-confident. For the first few
days, the young professor made a point of being merciful
to the sluggish. He answered their foolish questions politely,
dealt kindly with their asininities, and refrained from disclosing the depth of his exasperation over the defectiveness
of their pre-medic training, a distinct departure from the
tradition of that lecture-hall where Tubby had so frequently
inquired — in a frenzied screech — whether the high schools
had all stopped teaching elementary Physiology. Jack tried
to be patient and conciliatory, but it was hard work. If
you put up your whip, the lazy nags slowed to a walk.

Among those who gave evidence of sound scholarship

and a willingness to work, there was one student to whom Beaven could give any amount of special attention with the full approval of the entire class. This was a good-looking and affable Chinese named Abbott who had made a favorable impression on the first day by quaintly accounting for the incongruous name under which he registered.

The circumstances had been droll. At the first roll-call when, in response to the name 'Abbott,' the young Chinese had stood at attention, Beaven had stared at him with such candid astonishment that the class had laughed good-naturedly, Mr. Abbott himself grinning broadly. Without waiting for interrogation, the suave Oriental had volunteered to explain.

'Professor Beaven' — he pronounced it 'Beeven,' which widened the general smile — 'I wish to say' — Abbott made a courtly bow — 'that the name of my family in China is "Ng." I brought this name with me to college in America, but it was difficult for my new friends to speak. My teachers and classmates could not believe there was such a name. Some thought I was taking them for what you call "the ride." In a bank I was asked what the letters "N.G." meant on the bottom of my check. It appeared that in America this was an unhappy symbol denoting that something was wrong. So, in my sophomore year' — he paused apologetically — 'but perhaps I am taking too much time with the unimportant story of my name ——'

'By no means!' declared young Doctor Beaven. 'We have heard nothing more interesting than this in a dog's age. Kindly proceed, Mr. Abbott — and do not feel hurried.' The class was delighted.

'Thank you, sir,' said Abbott, bowing. 'So, in my sophomore year, I changed my name to one less embarrassing.'

'Quite justifiable,' approved Doctor Beaven. 'Perhaps you may be willing to confide why, among all the names you had access to, you chose "Abbott."'

'With pleasure, sir. I had observed two facts about class-rolls. Frequently the students were seated alphabetically, which placed the "A's" near the teacher.'

'I was not aware,' drawled Beaven, with a quiet amusement at once shared by the class, 'that this was considered a favorable location. In my own student days, it was often thought an inconvenience.'

'The Chinese eye,' explained Abbott, 'is usually myopic. We like to be close to the desk, especially when experiments are demonstrated. But, sir, there was also another reason why it is good for the foreigner to be at the top of the roll-call. When something new or difficult is proposed, the foreigner — if called upon first — will be pardoned if he commits a blunder; because, being a foreigner, he knows no better. But if he is asked the question after many of his classmates have — have — what you call "muffed it" — the professor, by that time, is so peeved that ——' Abbott was drowned out by the laughter.

'One often hears vague references,' commented Beaven, when order had been restored, 'to the wisdom of the East without realizing to what practical purposes this sagacity may be devoted. I feel, Mr. Abbott, that you have added something important to the science of applied psychology. May I venture to speak for the class when I say that we all bid you a most cordial welcome?'

There was spontaneous applause. Abbott bowed deeply three times, twice to his young professor and again to his classmates. He had made a nice place for himself and nobody was jealous.

'Hereafter,' added Beaven, when the applause had subsided, 'you may sit in the front row, Mr. Abbott, and claim all the privileges and penalties thereto pertaining.' Everybody liked this. The episode had been a pleasant interlude. Abbott was in a fair way to become the class mascot, and Beaven's stock had risen.

With this salutary introduction, it was natural that the Chinese could receive special attention from his Anatomy teacher without exciting anyone's envy; and when, presently, Abbott began displaying an extraordinary talent in the laboratory, Beaven's marked interest in him was a thing to be expected.

Nobody knew that Doctor Beaven had any other reason for giving Abbott so much personal oversight. The secret was comparatively safe. Everything Chinese had suddenly taken on a glamorous significance. Never having thought about the mind of China with any more concern than he had for the rings of Saturn, the brilliant young neurologist found himself presented with a brand-new, age-old, fascinatingly mysterious field of investigation.

Bill Cunningham had declared that any American who married Audrey Hilton, with any expectation of their mutual happiness, would have to 'go Chinese.' It was not Jack Beaven's purpose to inform himself about China with this end in view. He was not going to marry Audrey Hilton: that was definitely understood. He and the adorable Lan Ying had resolved upon a comradeship: that was all. But to add interest to this relation it was important, he felt, that he should orient himself. The more he knew about China, the more pleasure they would find in their correspondence.

One Saturday morning, late in October, Beaven had come into the anatomical laboratory on some research errand of his own; and, noticing his pet Chinese industriously at work on a head, strolled over to his table for a friendly word with him. Although aware that Abbott had a neat sense of humor, Jack's talks with him had been consistently serious and business-like. Today he ventured a bit of facetiousness.

'I am told,' said Beaven, lounging onto a stool beside the table, 'that the Mongolian oral structure differs in some respects from the Caucasian. It's rather a pity we do not have one of your deceased countrymen in here for your benefit.'

Abbott shook his head and grinned mysteriously.

'The Chink,' he observed, 'esteems his carcass more highly than the Yank.'

'Why is that?' asked Beaven.

'Because your Yankee goes to heaven when he dies. He gets a new body. It is not important to him what they do with his old one.' Abbott laid his instruments aside and seemed prepared to pursue the philosophical topic if he had the slightest encouragement.

'You don't anticipate survival, then?' Jack queried.

'Oh yes, sir; but not after the Christian manner. When you die, sir, the angels say, "Here comes the good Doctor Beaven. Have a seat, Doctor Beaven, and join in the singing."'

Jack laughed boyishly, to Abbott's surprise.

'That's very refreshing,' he said. 'Kindly go on.'

'Thank you. And that is why Doctor Beaven does not care whether they bury his body in sacred ground or cut it up for educational purposes. But the poor heathen Chinee does not expect any personal attention, later. He cannot remember having had any special honors before he came into the world, and he does not look for any when he returns to the source.'

'So — that's the reason he makes provision for his bones?'

'It is a good reason, I think.'

'A most interesting subject,' said Beaven, sincerely. 'I should like to pursue it with you. We must have a more leisurely talk, Abbott.' He was moving away from the table. 'If you have no plans for tomorrow afternoon, about five, how would you like to come to my apartment for a cigarette and a pot of tea?'

'With your permission, sir,' replied Abbott, bowing, 'I shall bring the tea.... Allee same Chinee,' he added, relishing his little joke.

*   *   *   *   *   *   *   *

It was the beginning of a very satisfying and profitable international friendship. Abbott did not become familiar, and Beaven did not pry; but they shared each other's minds to a greater extent than either of them had thought possible. On his second visit a week later, Abbott brought a basket containing the makings of a sort of ragout, and proved himself an excellent cook, Beaven mounting a kitchen stool to observe the process. Abbott was slicing water chestnuts and talking — at his host's suggestion — about oriental customs and the Chinese mind.

China, philosophized Abbott, leaned up against the past; plastered herself fast to the past. America looked to the future.

'You expect everything of the future,' he went on, industriously plying his knife. 'We expect nothing of it. We are satisfied with things as they are; you are impatient for change.'

'The world can't have much progress — without change,' said Jack.

'Progress?' Abbott glanced up and smiled dryly. 'I hear that the English have a saying, "What we made on the merry-go-round we lost on the swings." Same with your progress, I think. Maybe a dozen lives saved in Michigan today through new inventions in surgery. As many lives lost by new invention of automobile. Airship makes it possible for important men to speed up their business transactions. Also provides new engine of slaughter. And business not much improved, I think. Radio is remarkable invention; gives you world news. Formerly the poor and ignorant did not worry about the world, for they did not know its daily troubles. Now everybody knows; everybody frets; everybody scared.'

'Well — what's the answer?' asked Jack, as Abbott put the pan on the range.

Abbott chuckled a little, without turning from his work. 'That is a typical American query; is it not, sir? You Americans always want answers. You want them immediately. You want a prescription that you can take to the Pharmacy of History and have it filled. Let all the people pour a dose before each meal; or, if there are not to be any meals, pour it at the hour when meals were accustomed to occur. The poor Chinee is in no hurry for an answer to the questions his fathers addressed to The Great Silence.'

'Doubtless,' reflected Jack, after a pause, 'it would be very difficult for the Chinese mind and the American mind to adjust comfortably.'

Abbott interrupted his work long enough to observe cannily that it would depend on what they were discussing.

'Let's suppose a case.' Jack tried to make this sound impersonal. 'Suppose that an American man, believer in scientific advancement and rather disposed to be materialistic, should form an attachment for a Chinese woman, trained to value the past more than the present or the future — what are their chances of ever understanding each other's point of view?'

Abbott gave him a quick, searching glance, and smiled.

'Perhaps they might,' he replied, 'if they loved each other. They would be unhappy, sometimes; but not so unhappy as if they had denied their love.'

'You're quite romantic,' said Jack. 'I hadn't suspected you of it, with your deep interest in scientific matters.'

'Is it your thought, Doctor Beaven, that a man who studies science is not capable of love?'

'Perhaps that's putting the matter too strongly. But is it not true that a man genuinely concerned with some exacting research might find it difficult to pay much attention to — to the affairs of the heart?'

Abbott drew a brief smile.

'Man was a lover,' he said, philosophically, 'long before he was a — a neurologist.' He turned quickly to rattle his pans as an accompaniment to his retreat after firing off this audacity.

'You seem to imply,' said Jack, trying to sound amused, 'that my question arose out of a personal interest in this matter.'

Abbott made an apologetic little bow. 'Kindly pardon me, Doctor Beaven. I thought you had intended me to know.'

'Well — now that you do know,' said Jack, 'do you mind telling me how you arrived at this conclusion?'

'Several times, Doctor Beaven, you have asked me questions showing your strong interest in Chinese life and culture. I have wondered why. China has so very little to contribute to the investigations of the laboratory. I had curiosity to learn what it was in China that you wanted. And now you have told me. But I can quickly forget that you have told me. I hope I have not been impolite.'

'Nonsense,' said Jack, half-impatiently. 'You couldn't be impolite if you tried. And your deduction is fairly accurate. I have a very warm friend — an American by blood — who was born in China and has lived there continuously until three years ago.'

'But she is — after all — an American? That should offer no problem. Her being born in China, and living in China, does not make her Chinese.'

'This is a peculiar case, Abbott. The young lady was brought up from infancy in a Chinese home. Her mother died when she was born. She rarely had a brief glimpse of her father who died when she was eight. She never spoke a word of English until she was seven.'

'Yes,' agreed Abbott, thoughtfully, 'that would make a difference. May I ask what kind of a home it was?'

'The people live in Hongkong. The man is a wealthy and influential merchant. He has been very generous with his gifts to the English Hospital.'

Abbott's impassive face brightened.

'Ah — I know. I have heard of him. Sen Ling. He has sent many students abroad for medical training.'

'That's the man,' said Jack. 'My friend was brought up in his home.'

'Then,' declared Abbott, firmly, 'she is Chinese.'

'And — probably' — Jack's tone had the flavor of finality — 'she will never be — anything else.'

'The Chinese,' said Abbott, 'are never — anything else.'

'She is in this country now.' Jack's remark hinted that Abbott's comment was debatable.

'So am I,' said Abbott, 'but me no "Melican man."'

They both laughed a little. Then, after he had paced a few turns up and down the tiny kitchen, with his hands deep in his jacket pockets, Beaven said seriously, 'Abbott, if I am to continue my friendship with this young lady, I suppose I shall have to "go Chinese."'

Abbott shook his head, discouragingly.

'You mean,' queried Jack, 'I shouldn't attempt it?'

'I mean' — Abbott sought to brighten the other's solemn face with a bit of drollery — 'I mean — "no can do."'

Jack nodded. 'I suppose you're right. But at least I might learn a few words of Chinese, for courtesy's sake; don't you think?'

'Easily.'

'Would you oblige me?'

'Gladly.'

'What does "Lan Ying" mean?'

'"English orchid."'

* * * * * * * * *

Never having considered social correspondence as anything but an affliction, Jack Beaven's pleasure in composing letters to Audrey Hilton was exceeded only by his delight in receiving letters from her.

His work had so completely absorbed him, in recent years, that he rarely had a letter other than a business communication. Every month or six weeks there would be a two- or three-page scrawl from Jean — a dutiful, sisterly, housewifely, incredibly uninteresting résumé of a young matron's dashings about, planning balanced meals, breaking in a new cook or a new pup, wiping leaky noses, taking bridge lessons and a course of lectures on Current Events — letters which began with the breathless remark that this was going to be a full day, and ended abruptly by saying that she smelt something scorching or that Junior had just fallen out of bed.

He liked Jean. He had endearing memories of their childhood together. But they had been separated for many years. Now that his whole existence was bounded by surgery, and Jean was literally drowning in domesticity, they had about as much in common as a gallon of ethyl chloride and a half-dozen cans of your best vegetable soup on the first delivery please without fail. Jack's conscience sometimes smote him when he viewed the breadth of the chasm. There had been no misunderstanding, no estrangement; just a gradual retreat from the close comradeship that had meant so much to them in their youth. He always sent Christmas presents, and was precise in remembering the ages of the children. Sometimes he would promise that he was coming out to visit them; next summer, perhaps — fully aware, as he did so, that he hadn't the slightest intention of it.

For the first time in his life, letter-writing was something other than a necessary drudgery. At Audrey's suggestion they had agreed upon a weekly letter to be written — if convenient — on Sunday night. Jack soon found this schedule too restricting, and wrote every other day. Audrey's habitual salutation was 'My dear friend,' until the letter came in which she thanked him for the orchid.

He had made haste to let her know that he had discovered the meaning of her Chinese name. Abbott had no more than left the apartment, that Sunday evening at seven, than Jack was telephoning to the little floral shop at the Livingstone, pleased to find it still open, further pleased to learn that they had some orchids. He wanted only one, and he would be down in a few minutes. On the card, accompanying the single orchid — to be shipped air-special — he wrote, 'My favorite flower — for my favorite friend. — Jack.'

Her next letter was awaited with an impatience that made his classroom hours drag sluggishly. And when it came he tore it open with the eagerness of a prisoner hopeful of reprieve. His heart thumped as he caught sight of the first line.

Dear Jack:
Thank you for the lovely orchid, and the nice note, and all the bother you must have gone to in hunting down a Chinese — a professor in Economics, maybe, who wondered why the professor of Anatomy must know the meaning of 'Lan Ying.' Perhaps he smiled, but I think he was just bewildered.

My sister told me she had a letter from Doctor Forrester,

yesterday. She did not tell me what he said. Perhaps he inquires about Teddy, who is getting on well in school, doing everything the other boys do.

My sister is not quite pleased over our friendship. She observes the coming of your frequent letters. It is not that she dislikes or disapproves of you. To the contrary, she much enjoys you. But she cannot understand a friendship that is content to remain a friendship. I told her of our firm decision about that. She is determined to see me married — and settled down securely. So long as I am your friend, I shall be indifferent to the sport of capturing a husband, she thinks.

How happy I am that I do not depend upon Claudia for my living. In that case, I should feel much embarrassed. As the matter is — while I should prefer to humor my sister in all her smallest wishes, I think it is so much more important that I should do as I please — for her sake as well as mine.

If sacrificing one's own wishes to the will of another is a good thing to do, I should be disobliging if I deprived my sister of the benefit which may come to her by letting me have my own way in the management of my life.

Jack chuckled as he read this, wondering if Audrey's logic in respect to the benefits of self-surrender was a part of the 'wisdom of the East' — or was she just having a spot of fun?

It is not good for people [the letter went on,] to exercise their wills very much in dominating the other members of their households. Slavery must be hard indeed for the slave, but it is hard also for the master. Slavery in a family would be difficult for all of them, I think. If one member of the house required the others to do his bidding in everything, great and small, it would not be long until no one of them would have a mind of his own; and then they would all lean heavily upon the strong one for support. I have often observed this in China.

I should not want ever to become a burden to my sister; so, to avoid this danger to her happiness, I must not encourage her to do my thinking for me. Eventually she will be better served if I remain entirely independent of her will except in matters where her wishes coincide with my own. Do you not think this is the kindly thing for me to do?

It was certainly a quaint way to state the old problem of the family boss. But, however funny it sounded in Audrey's bookish phraseology, her psychology was sound. Jack made a brief review of the cases he had known where a mother had completely dominated her children — not quite so ruthlessly destroying them as an outlaw tigress eating her cubs, but as effectually reducing them to a state of helplessness. He had heard plenty of tales about the heavy father, playing his thankless role as a dictator, having a grand time, making them all jump the rope while he cracked the whip. And when their personalities had been demolished, they all climbed up on him and he had them to carry, piggyback, as long as he lived, a penalty which served him right, of course, but was a pretty high price to pay for the sadistic pleasure he had had in making them lick his boots.

One thing was sure: Audrey, however sweet and gracious, wasn't going to be ordered about. Jack's anxiety on this score was relieved. The only obstacle to their friendship had been the probable objections of the competent Claudia. It was a comfort to feel that any attempted interference from that quarter would be ineffective.

* * * * * * * *

Tubby was slated to be back about the middle of November. It occurred to Jack that he might contrive to slip away during the Thanksgiving recess. Edith Cunningham had suggested it. So — now there was something for him and Audrey to write about; something to look forward to.

Cunningham's first string of lectures and clinics had been booked for the third week of October — and Jack wondered whether the chief's sudden decision to go to Vienna hadn't

been inspired by a wish to be out of town at that time —
but had been postponed, at Cunningham's own request, until
December. Perhaps he had thought it better cricket to wait
— especially for the clinics — until Tubby was on the
ground. The Regents, however — unquestionably this Denman's hand was in it — had insisted on Cunningham's coming in October for a convocation address. Denman wasn't
going to take the risk of having his friend use the soft pedal
to save Tubby's face.

So — on the third Monday morning of October, Cunningham had appeared. The Medical College Auditorium was
packed. Jack didn't like to admit it, even to himself, but
the atmosphere of the place had in it more invigoration than
he had ever sensed there on such occasions. It was warm,
friendly, inspiring. The students punctuated it with genuine
applause; hilarious applause; not the mere perfunctory
patter for duty's sake. Jack knew he had no business approving it, but it was impossible not to be swept along by it.

'You take your typical case-history,' Cunningham was
saying, midway of his address. 'Man comes into our hospital relayed to us by some baffled general practitioner from
a small town. Comes accompanied by a letter in which Doc
— wanting to give a good account of himself, if not of the
patient — has taken pains to be scholarly. Case-history
goes something like this.' Cunningham adjusted his glasses
and read, dryly: '"In August, a year ago, patient complained that his toes were sensitive to pressure. By October,
the calves of his legs were similarly affected. Shortly afterward, he walked with much difficulty, and the hands were
weak and awkward. Marked dysmetria and ataxia were
indicated by the finger-to-nose test. Extensor and flexor
movements were weakly performed. Ataxia confirmed by
heel-to-knee test. Abdominal reflexes absent. Bone vibra-
tory sense absent as high as the crests of the ilium. Pain
sensation absent as high as the third thoracic dermatome.
Plantar stimulation produced a withdrawal reflex with
a crossed extensor reflex in the opposite extremity."'

He had paused to take off his reading-glasses. Everybody

laughed, anticipating something good. Shane, who had introduced him and was seated a few feet away, contributed to the entertainment by saying, 'Shouldn't there be a report on a Wassermann, about now?' There was renewed laughter, Shane glowing happily.

'Thanks.' Cunningham turned to wave a friendly salute. 'I was coming to that, Doctor. The Wassermann reaction on the spinal fluid was — we will say — negative. Now, I think' — he glanced again at Shane — 'I'm sure you know what ailed the fellow.'

The hall grew suddenly quiet. Old Shane was on the spot. It was once when Polly talked out of turn. The medics nudged one another, bug-eyed with delight.

'Well' — Shane recrossed his legs — 'I suspect that when you did a laminectomy, you found some adhesions between the cord and arachnoid — but you'd better ask Doctor Beaven. That's his line.'

Faculty chairs scraped as Cunningham's gaze roved for Jack, seated well to the rear of the platform, as became his junior rank.

'Doctor Shane,' said Cunningham, 'has found adhesions. Do you agree, Doctor Beaven?'

'Yes, sir,' replied Jack; 'between the cord and arachnoid.'

'And a tumor?'

'Not necessarily. Of course, I'm just guessing, sir. The case-history is not very voluminous.'

'Now — there you are!' Cunningham tapped expressive knuckles on the reading-desk. 'Doctor Beaven is right. This case-history is inadequate — but not for the reason he has in mind. He and Doctor Shane have hit this difficulty smack on the button. Their operation is unquestionably sound. The adhesions would be relieved, and there is no reason why the patient should not get well — if this was all that ailed him. But the case-history, as Doctor Beaven says, is insufficient. It should go on to say, "Three years ago, the patient lost his job as an assistant bank-cashier because the president's son, having just graduated from college, needed something to do. Instead of coming out honestly with the actual reason for his discharge, it was made to appear that our man was being fired for incompetency. Because he was having difficulty in making a new business connection, the girl he was engaged to marry grew restless and after a stormy quarrel — for by this time our friend had had about all he could take, and was irritable and edgy — they parted and did not later resume their friendship. Patient therefore feels there is very little justice in the world. He is not only insensitive to palpation as high as the third thoracic dermatome, but he no longer reacts to the well-meant overtures of friends who would gladly be of service if they knew how to go about it." *Now then!* The treatment, I claim, isn't finished when the adhesions are relieved in this fellow's spine. What are you going to do about the rest of this diagnosis? While your man is convalescent from the operation, but still beastly sick in his soul, what else are you planning? You've cured his adhesions. Why not finish the job?'

Apparently the students approved this thought, or at least they were on the speaker's side, for they applauded mightily. What Tubby had been teaching was true, beyond all question. These youngsters were enraptured. There weren't a half dozen, probably, who could have made even a wild guess about the physical diagnosis. But they were keen to know how the patient should be advised, mentally rebuilt, made over into something that the Rotary Club would present with a medal. They wanted to know how to help him get another job and another girl — and live happily ever afterward. Jack scowled. He liked Bill Cunningham, but this sort of thing was no good.

There was a faculty luncheon afterward at the University Club. Jack couldn't remember a similar affair in which the honor guest had been quite so warmly received. You really couldn't stand out against the magnetic appeal of Cunningham's personality. He was a royal fellow. He was a sentimentalist — on through to the marrow. But he was a sound workman, and you had to respect him.

Early in November, Jack felt it would be comforting to

make sure about the Thanksgiving event, so he wrote to Bill and Edith reminding them of his invitation and accepting it forthwith if it was still open and convenient. He also remarked that he hoped to see as much as possible of Audrey during his brief visit.

Re-reading this letter, he thought he should add a word that might protect himself and Audrey from any embarrassment arising from the Cunninghams' naïve desire to be obliging.

'Of course,' he said, in an underscored postscript, 'you need be at no pains to isolate us. I think you know the nature of our relation. We are good friends — and that's as far as it goes.'

Next day he had a telegram from Bill.

**EDITH AND I DELIGHTED HAVE YOU
WITH US THANKSGIVING P S OH YEAH**

Chapter XI

RETURNING from Austria on the morning of November eighteenth, Tubby Forrester was staggered by the dismaying news that the Cunningham lectures and clinics — which he had made a nine-thousand-mile detour to avoid — were still happily anticipated by the starry-eyed Regents in charge of Medical College affairs.

He had calmly taken it for granted that this dangerous nonsense would have been celebrated, and — it was to be hoped — forgotten. Serene in that faith, Tubby had asked no questions and nobody had bothered to disillusion him.

It was therefore most disturbing to learn that the awkward predicament he had dodged was waiting to welcome him home. Nor did it relieve the situation to discover that Cunningham — in a unique convocation speech — had already won the loud acclaim of the students, a brilliant reception by the Faculty Club, and recognition by the Associated Press.

No one had been at any pains to cushion the shock. Remembering that the Regents' Medical College Committee was in regular monthly session that afternoon, Tubby had thought it dutiful to appear and give a prompt account of his stewardship, a report which — though received amiably enough — was immediately driven into total eclipse by Osgood's panegyric on Cunningham's address which, he declared, had done the Medical College more good in the opinion of the public, and the students more good in the opinion of the faculty, than anything that had happened since the memory of man runneth not to the contrary —

and a lot more stuff like that; laud, honor, glory, and praise, complete with hallelujahs and amen. It was pretty terrible for Tubby.

'And I suppose,' he snarled, late that night, in an unpleasant rehash of it with Beaven — 'I suppose you sat there and applauded, along with the rest of 'em.'

'Would you have preferred me to arise and publicly denounce him, sir?' countered Jack. 'Or should I have appointed myself a committee of one to scowl and sulk?'

Tubby sourly nodded his full understanding that his ungrateful associate had let him down.

'You attended the reception, too, I daresay, and beat your hands off when bright ridicule was heaped upon everything you stand for, professionally.'

Jack was slow with his reply, but when it came it hoisted Tubby out of his chair.

'No, sir,' drawled Jack. 'Hadn't you heard? After Cunningham's talk at the Faculty Club I got up and said that as an accredited representative of Doctor Forrester, I wanted to register his utter disgust ——'

'What!' shouted Tubby, bouncing up wide-eyed with rage. 'Why — you — you damn fool!'

'Be calm,' soothed Jack, with a placating overhand gesture. 'Of course I said nothing of the kind. It just occurred to me that you might like to hear how it would have sounded.'

Tubby sank back into his chair and patted his forehead with his handkerchief.

'You could have registered your own feelings,' he mumbled, 'without dragging my name into it.'

'Well,' rejoined Jack, recklessly, 'I'm willing to be your goat, here on the campus, but you'll have to excuse me, sir, if I decline to serve in that capacity at a social meeting in the University Club.'

'Do you realize what you're saying?' Tubby folded his arms on the desk and leaned forward in an attitude of incredulity. His voice shook.

Jack nodded.

'Should have said it,' he muttered, 'long ago.'

'I made you, Beaven,' said Tubby, spacing out his words impressively, 'and I can unmake you. Don't you know that?'

'It's possible — but not likely, sir,' replied Jack, with infuriating indifference. 'My position is subject to the Regents. If you wish to prefer charges against me, I shall defend myself.'

'Charges? Charges? Won't it be sufficient if I say to the Regents that we can't work together in harmony?'

Jack chuckled dryly.

'When did we work together in harmony? I've been your stooge and your whipping-boy for years, Doctor Forrester. And everybody on this campus knows it.'

From there on, for the next hour, Doctors Forrester and Beaven fairly well cleared their systems of all the pent-up animosity that hadn't filtered through in the course of their long association. At midnight they had resolved to keep their mutual disaffection from becoming a public scandal. Jack had freely conceded his indebtedness to the chief for many favors, but had declared his independence.

'There is no reason,' he said, quietly, 'why we cannot work together exactly as we have done. Our conversation tonight has not altered our relationship in the slightest degree. All it comes to is that we have been honest enough to tell each other what we have been thinking for a long time. It has cleared the air a little, I feel. If I have been brutally impudent, sir, you invited it.' He rose to go.

'Getting back to where we started, in this discussion,' said Tubby, with a detaining gesture, 'am I to understand that you approve this grand debauch of Cunninghamery?'

'No,' replied Jack, bluntly, 'you are not to understand anything of the sort. I share your opinion that Cunningham's appearance here was a backward step. I do not share your opinion that it would be sensible to protest — if that really is your opinion, which I very much doubt.'

'Are you planning to co-operate cheerfully with Cunningham when he returns for these abominable clinics?'

'I think I'll take my cue from you, sir,' answered Jack, with elaborate deference. 'If you rise up and fight him, I'll join you. I suspect,' he added, craftily, 'that I shall not be called to the colors.'

'You think I'm a coward; don't you, Beaven?' barked Tubby.

Jack laughed, almost good-humoredly.

'No — I don't think you're a coward, sir; but I was just reminded of the old yarn about a brave assembly of frontiersmen that once waited to defend a hill against a pack of Indians. When the savages were sighted, there were about ten times as many of them as the heroic band had anticipated, and one of their wise men said, "It is considered good strategy, when greatly outnumbered, to retreat. I, being somewhat lame, shall start now."'

'Very funny indeed,' rasped Tubby. 'I suggest that you accompany your crippled friend. I'll stay and fight.'

'Well, you're a pretty good fighter, sir,' said Jack, in a tone of reminiscence. 'I've seen you in action. You certainly can take it on the chin!'

*　*　*　*　*　*　*

No more polio had been reported during Tubby's absence. The two cases he had mentioned, on the eve of setting out for Vienna, had been discharged when the primary phase of the disease was passed. Jack had not seen either of them; nor did he know what had become of them. He had assumed that they were now being looked after by the physicians who had sent them in for observation.

On the next morning after their stormy interview Jack relayed the information to Tubby that an advanced case of poliomyelitis had just arrived; that Doane wanted him to have a look at it.

Tubby, after a night of bitter brooding, seemed eager to lay hold of almost any weapon for the tardy defense of his outraged dignity. Dismissing the Romney girl with a curt jerk of his head, he demanded to know why Doane couldn't handle the case himself. It was Doane's job; wasn't it?

'I think that's what Doane wants to know, sir,' said Jack. 'The case has had a lot of surgery. Doane hasn't gone into it thoroughly but suspects it has got itself rather out of the usual orthopedic bracket and needs the attention of a neurological expert.'

Tubby grunted a receipt of this implied compliment and unbent a little. After the drubbing he had received, almost any ointment offered relief. Jack, somewhat remorseful over the spanking he had administered last night, noted the effect of his tribute to the chief's ineffable wisdom and incomparable skill, and was pleased. He had dressed Tubby down and was now willing to scrub him up. Nothing, he felt, was so becoming to a victor as magnanimity.

Perhaps he overplayed this a little. Tubby retreated into his shell like a turtle, until nothing contactual remained in sight but a pair of steely, suspicious eyes. Yes — he would look at the case, when he got around to it. Beaven could go now, he said, in a tone that suggested an unpleasant destination.

Next afternoon Tubby had operated, Doane and Beaven assisting; or, rather, standing by as interested spectators; admiring spectators, too, for it was indeed a tricky job and the old boy was at his best. You could despise him with all your heart, mind, and strength, but Tubby was a surgeon; swift, sure, precise, almost prescient in his confident dissection of nerve-fiber and musculature that had suffered the distortions of a stream unbedded by a ruthless flood. When it was finished, Doane muttered, 'Tubby has a sixth sense; the sense of fixation in space; only other animal that has it is a bee.' He grinned and added, out of the corner of his mouth, 'That makes two points of resemblance between Tubby and the bee.' Jack did not press Doane for the other similarity, but thought he knew. They both chuckled, and let it go at that.

The operation, whatever it might do for the young patient, had a marked effect on Tubby. It was the most exacting piece of work he had been called upon to do for a long time, and nobody needed to tell him that you could count on the fingers of one hand all the other surgeons on earth who might have done it as skillfully. His recovery of self-confidence stiffened his spine and his strut and his stare. When he stalked the hospital corridors, attachés of all degrees — from colleagues to mop-slingers — disappeared into doorways. As for his current relation to Jack, Tubby now held himself rigidly aloof. When communication was positively necessary, he conveyed his orders through the frightened little Romney who, having slightly upholstered her angularity in his absence, had already lost a couple of pounds and a vestigial dimple since his return.

Jack was in the private laboratory, which Tubby now studiously avoided, when Romney timidly poked her head in to say, 'Doctor Forrester says that you are to look after the Buckley child.'

'Buckley?' repeated Jack, squinting at a test-tube he was holding against the light.

'The polio he operated on,' explained Romney, edging into the room.

'Oh — was that its name? I'd forgotten. Why isn't Doane taking care of it? It's his case.'

'I don't know, sir. But I've just been down to tell him that you are to look after her.'

'Come over here,' said Jack.

Romney complied, rather diffidently, glancing toward the door which had blown shut.

'Are you getting enough to eat?'

'It isn't that, sir. I'm being sent about, giving orders to people that make them mad; and then they take it out on me. I'm afraid I can't stand it very much longer, Doctor Beaven.' Apparently Romney felt weak in the knees, for she dropped into a chair, contrary to her customary attitude of deference.

'You're far too sensitive, Romney. The trouble with you is that you have the instincts of a lady. Anything like courtesy and gentility is a serious handicap in this environment.'

'I've got used to the smell,' she said, with a wan little

smile. 'And I've got used to being shouted at. But I don't like to have people mad at me for giving them messages that hurt their feelings. Doctor Doane nearly had a fit.'

'Does he think I had anything to do with elbowing him off this polio?'

'Well' — Romney made a confirming little gesture with both hands — 'you might tell him you didn't. It would please him, I think.'

'Thanks for the tip, Romney. I'll set his mind at ease on that.'

'He has been frightfully interested in the case; I mean — in the child. She's a sweet little thing, and apparently she has had a pretty rough time of it. Her father is — simply impossible!'

'You seem to know a good deal about it.'

'Well — I've been sent down there, several times, to copy the chart. Martha is in the open ward. Her father sits there by the bed, most of the afternoon, criticizing the nurses and the doctors and making himself objectionable. It makes Martha ashamed and unhappy. I don't see how she can get well under such conditions. I'll bet that if ——' She left off suddenly, and rose to go.

'You'll bet what, Romney?' insisted Jack, stepping into her way.

'You remember when Doctor Cunningham was here?' she ventured. 'I hadn't much to do, that day, and I slipped into the Auditorium and heard him.'

'I see,' said Jack, 'and you bet that if Doctor Cunningham had charge of this case, he'd do something to relieve the situation. Well — what? Tell the little girl not to care how much of a nuisance her father is?'

'I think he'd talk to her father,' said Romney. 'Maybe he's sick, too. It might be worth finding out. I must go.' She made off toward the door, and paused with her hand on the knob. 'Have I talked too much?' she asked, anxiously.

'You simply answered my questions, Romney. *Pax vobiscum.*'

'What does that mean?'

'It means "Go in peace," and I wish you wouldn't talk to me as if I were the Lord High Executioner.'

'I'm sorry,' said Romney, as she slipped through the doorway.

The episode disturbed him more than a little. During Tubby's absence they had become quite friendly. She had blossomed in the atmosphere of tranquillity, had regained her poise, had been almost gay sometimes. Now that Tubby was back, she was a tight little tangle of neuroses.

After lunch, he went to Doane and said, 'I'm informed that Tubby wants me to carry on with your polio. I think you know I had nothing to do with that, and am simply obeying orders. I should have greatly preferred that the case be left in your hands where, in my opinion, it properly belongs. But — my opinion not being worth a diddlededee — I suppose I'll have to take over. Anything you want to tell me?'

Doane was quite decent about it, though it was easily to be seen that his morale was in need of a tuck or two. He posted Jack on what they'd been doing, reviewed at some length their annoyance over the attitude of the child's father; and, together, they went into the ward to have a look at the case. On the way, Doane said, 'Incidentally, we just brought in something that looks to me like polio from the same part of town. Horrible neighborhood. Ambulance had to be towed out of the mud.'

Thomas Buckley was seated by the bed, a sharp-nosed, darting-eyed, undersized, shabby, snappish fellow, who drew a surly grin. Doane introduced Jack, who made short work of his nod.

'H'are yuh, Doc,' sneered Buckley. 'How's tricks?'

'The next trick,' said Jack, with quiet contempt, 'is ours. You may report to me, in the private laboratory in Lister Hall, in a half-hour. I shall instruct an orderly to tell you where it is. And if you don't show up, instructions will be left at the front office that you are not to be admitted into the hospital again.'

'The hell you say!' snorted Buckley. 'This is a state institution!'

'Correct,' said Jack, crisply. 'But not all of the state institutions are hospitals. I advise you to do as you're told.'

'Huh! All right, Doc,' said Buckley, with a truculent grin. 'I'll be there.'

* * * * * * * *

Quite warm under the collar, Jack examined the embarrassed little girl and proceeded to Lister Hall, up the stairs, through the anatomical laboratory where orderly rows of white-shrouded cadavers waited patiently for Monday's painless operations, and into the adjoining room where he had spent such a considerable amount of his time for years. Recently he had devoted more than the usual number of hours per day to research, rarely going to his apartment until midnight.

He examined a few virus-cultures, made some notes, looked at his watch, organized the speech he intended to deliver upon the arrival of the irascible Buckley. Presently there was a tap on the door; not the arrogant thump he had expected; a quite timid little rap, indeed. He opened the door, and his visitor hesitated on the threshold.

'Come in,' said Jack, coolly.

'My God — it stinks up here!' observed Buckley, weakly.

'You probably feel that way about it,' replied Jack, dryly, 'because of your unfamiliarity with the necessities of the medical profession. Sit down, please.' He pointed to one of the tall stools. 'I am rather surprised, Mr. Buckley, that you have found our anatomical laboratory offensive. We had been feeling that you considered yourself somewhat of an authority on medicine, surgery, nursing, and hospital management, judging by the freedom with which you have been offering criticisms. That's what I want to talk to you about.'

'Could I have a drink of water?' asked Thomas, irrelevantly.

Jack uncorked a bottle of ammonia.

'Sniff that,' he recommended. 'We'll postpone the water. I hadn't supposed you were so sensitive. You don't talk like a delicately geared person. Stomach out of order?'

'It's out of work,' grumbled Thomas. 'It hasn't had enough to do, lately.'

Jack mounted the other stool, offered his guest a cigarette which was sullenly refused, and lighted one for himself.

'You mean you're not eating properly? Why is that? Can't digest your food?'

'Can't afford it. But that's no affair of yours, Doc. I'm not up here to panhandle you. Go ahead and say what you got to say — so I can get out o' this.'

'What you probably need is a few square meals, Buckley. If you're broke, why don't you go down town to the Community Chest people? That's what they're for. They'll help you.'

'We're not beggars,' growled Thomas. 'And I don't care to have investigators snooping around in my house. Well — tell me why I'm up here, and be done with it!'

The stern lecture which awaited Buckley seemed in need of revision. The fellow was starving. Maybe that was what made him so mean. Cunningham's comments on the inadequacy of case-histories recurred to Jack's mind.

'Unemployed, I suppose,' he queried.

'Yeah.'

'What can you do? What have you done?'

'What do *you* care? You haven't any work for me, so what's the use asking?'

'I wasn't inquiring out of sheer curiosity.'

'What else?' demanded Buckley. 'I haven't come to consult you about my health, and you have no work that I can do. Why the devil should we waste our time with questions and answers?'

Jack grinned a little.

'Your time doesn't seem to be very valuable,' he drawled, 'and I'm willing to give you some of mine. Go ahead! Let yourself out! Maybe it will be good for you to tell somebody.' And, as Buckley — his face twitching — sourly debated a reply, Jack found himself saying, 'I know it isn't any fun to talk about your troubles.'

Thomas scrubbed his bony chin with the back of a thin hand and pulled a reluctant grin.

'I'll take one of your cigarettes now, Doc; if you don't mind.'

Jack offered him a light and he puffed for a moment, drawing deep inhalations until his eyes swam with vertigo.

'Doc — you're a specialist,' he began, at length, with a comprehensive gesture that took in the whole array of scientific instruments in the room. 'In a way — so am I. I'll bet you have to be mighty particular when you use that thing.' He pointed to one of the big microscopes. 'Can't do much guessing. Well — I was trained for one of those jobs where you don't guess, and I lost it because I was in competition with guessers. See what I mean?'

'No,' said Jack, crisply, 'I'm afraid I don't. You'd better tell me some more about it.'

'You know anything about how airplanes are made?'

'Nothing. Was that what you were doing?'

'Doc — maybe you wouldn't believe it — but when airplanes are put together the business of fitting the parts is such a nice job that the rivets are tooled to a thousandth of an inch. They're so valuable that they keep 'em in a safe, same as you'd see in a small bank. And when they're fitted, you have to heat 'em to exactly the right temperature or they won't go into the holes in the aluminum alloy.'

Jack's eyes were bright with interest. He crossed his rangy legs, rested an elbow on his knee, cradled his chin in the cup of his hand, and leaned forward attentively.

'That's very interesting,' he said. 'Go on, please.'

Buckley's face had lost its expression of truculence, and his voice had modulated to a tone of honest sincerity.

'When you drive 'em through,' he continued, 'and have flattened 'em out on the other side, you use a dental mirror to inspect the second head and see if it's a perfect clench, all the way 'round. It's kind of a careful job, Doc.'

'I see it is,' agreed Jack, respectfully. 'It's either exactly right — or it's wrong: that kind of a job.'

'Yeah. . . . I used to keep saying to myself,' Buckley went on, reminiscently, 'before I was a foreman, and was still driving rivets — and, mind you, Doc, I'm no softy, either — "If this tears out, somebody who thought the ship was O.K. will be killed, maybe." It was always on my mind when I was driving rivets.'

'Pretty heavy responsibility. You had the right attitude, I think.'

'Then I was made foreman. Well — we got very busy; lot o' army and navy orders; had to bring in new help; most of 'em young fellers who'd never learned to do things right. Some of 'em had had a little experience working with steel and tin. They were used to putting up gutters and spouting. If the joints didn't fit by a quarter of an inch, they would whack 'em with a hammer until they were pretty close, and the paint would cover up the cracks. Well — building airships wasn't that kind of a job. You couldn't hold 'em together with paint — if you know what I mean.'

Jack grinned and said it sounded reasonable.

'Of course, they all belonged to the union. And so did I. Had to, in fact. Well — there was a lot of the work that I couldn't pass. I kept showing 'em how it must be done to get by, but they didn't care. Then I got mad and began firin' the lazy bums.' Buckley sighed and made a hopeless little gesture with outspread fingers. 'You can guess the rest.'

'I'm not sure that I can,' said Jack. 'You mean — *you* got fired for being too exacting?'

Buckley chuckled and shrugged.

'I got fired for punching a union inspector on the nose. He had come into the shop, waddling his shoulders like a traffic cop when he's going to give you a ticket, and began growling a lot o' "What-the-hell?" You know about how he'd do it, Doc. And I went crazy. I never was much in a fight. But I just happened to swing this one right, and the feller dropped like a beef. Well — of course the boss was on my side, but there wasn't much for him to do. The company expected him to get the work out, somehow, so he had to fire me. The union forced him to it. And I was so mad I tore up my union card, right there in the shop, before all of 'em, and told 'em I didn't want to have my name mixed up with a mess o' lousy hoodlums. And, of course that didn't do me any good when I went scouting for another job.'

'No — I can see that,' said Jack. 'What do you live on, now?'

'Well — my wife makes little pot-holders — so you don't burn your fingers, you know. And I peddle 'em.'

'Where do you live?'

Buckley motioned with his head and glumly replied, 'Up at the edge o' town. A few cheap little houses up there, just this side of the reservoir.'

Jack frowned studiously.

'Were you living there when Martha took sick?'

'Yeah.'

'I understand there was another polio brought in from that district yesterday. What sort of neighborhood is it? The ambulance was mired in the mud. Had to be hauled out.'

Thomas's eyes were horrified and his face worked convulsively.

'No, Doc! No! That's not what ails the Collins girl! She had had the flu, and they were afraid of pneumonia! If they say she has infantile paralysis, they're crazy!'

Jack regarded this outburst with undisguised astonishment.

'We'll see,' he said, quietly. Stepping to the telephone, he asked the office where they had put the Collins child. While he waited, Thomas slipped off the stool and shambled toward the door.

'If you're through with me, Doc, I'll go,' he said, unsteadily.

'Not yet,' demanded Jack. 'You wait a minute.'

Thomas leaned his back against the door, and waited glumly.

'Connect me, please,' the doctor was saying. . . . 'Slattery, are you nursing this Collins case? . . . Is it polio? . . . That's what I heard. Wanted to verify it. . . . What? Focalized in the right arm — same as the Buckley child? I find they came from the same neighborhood. Yes — very odd. . . . No — I wouldn't think so. It's a mere coincidence. . . . No — that's too utterly fantastic, Slattery. . . . Doctor Doane handling the case; isn't he? He's there now? Let me talk to him. . . . Doane — this is Beaven. Does it strike you as a queer thing that your Collins polio and my Buckley, coming in from the same district, exhibit the same phenomena? . . . That's my guess, too; coincidence. However — it's worth an investigation. We'll look into it, tomorrow, and ——'

Jack heard the door close, softly, hung up the receiver with a bang, and started in pursuit of the fleeing Buckley. He overtook him in the lower corridor, grasped him by the shabby coat-collar, and brought him to a sudden stop. Buckley sagged against the wall, retching with nausea.

'Let go,' he begged, weakly. 'That stink-hole made me sick.'

'Not so sick that you couldn't run — like a wild animal. You've something on your chest, Buckley, and you're not leaving here until I know what it is.' Jack's tone left no doubt about his determination to see it through.

'All right, Doc. I'll tell you, if you promise you won't squeal.' Then, suddenly savage, the shaken fellow shrieked, 'If you do, you'll wish you hadn't!'

Jack replied sternly that they would consider all that when they got to it; and, taking the trembling man by the arm, slowly steered him back to the laboratory, poured him a minute dose of brandy, and said, 'Now — take your time — and tell the truth — and tell it all. Soon as you begin to lie, I'll begin to know it. You're not a very skillful liar, Buckley. I don't know what you've done that's given you this fright and guilt but, whatever it is, you'd better tell me, rather than the police.'

'The Collins girl makes three,' muttered Thomas. 'Our Martha, and another kid named Mead. These Meads just moved in, a few weeks ago. I don't know them very well.

I knew the fellow that lived in the house before. Name of
Billows. He moved to Detroit. Got a job as a steam-fitter.
He was mighty handy with tools — same as me — and
broke — same as me.' He paused, for a long moment. 'And
a mighty tough egg. Good fellow to leave alone.'

'I suppose he got you into trouble,' guessed Jack. 'Well
— go on with it. But — before you do that — what became
of this Mead boy?'

'He's at home. His folks don't believe in doctors.'

'What makes you think he has infantile paralysis?'

'Maybe he hasn't.' Thomas brightened a little. 'He had
a lot of fever, and now it's all settled in his arm. I heard you
say something about these kids having crippled arms.'

'Which arm?'

Thomas was tardy with his answer.

'Same one,' he admitted, reluctantly.

'We'll have to look into that,' said Jack. 'I'll notify the
health authorities about the Mead case. . . . Now — go right
on and tell me how you think you figure in this matter.'

'Maybe I don't,' said Thomas. 'But this is what happened. There wasn't any water in our houses, and the old
hog who owned 'em wouldn't pipe it in. Several months
ago, he took sick, we heard, and sent a boy around to collect
the rent; so — he didn't know what was going on. One of
the neighbors up the road had a well, and was mean and
grouchy about our tramping in there, half a dozen times
a day; so — this fellow Billows said we'd do our own
plumbing.'

'You mean — you tapped into a water main?'

'Yeah. It wasn't much of a trick.'

'Just your house and Billows's?'

'Four. Collins and an old fellow named Bowers did the
digging, and for that we let them in on it, too.'

'Oh?' said Jack, suddenly enlightened. 'When you heard
about the diagnosis of the Collins child, you began to make
some deductions. You think it's in the water. I suppose you
tapped into the main between the reservoir and the filtration
plant. Right?'

Thomas nodded.

'Well — the whole affair will have to be investigated,' said Jack, 'promptly and thoroughly. And I don't see how you and these other men can evade your responsibility in this matter. However — now that you have made an effort to correct it, I should think you might get off with a stern lecture at the City Hall. I'll do what I can for you.'

'A fat chance o' that!' growled Thomas. 'There's more to it than I told you. This Billows fellow — he just lately got through doing a stretch in the pen — isn't going to be arrested any more without making somebody pay for it. He stole that pipe, over in Wheaton.'

'You helped him? How did he get it over here?'

'He had something on a fellow, in Wheaton, that owned a truck. Made him haul the pipe here. You start something that exposes Billows, and he'll squeal on the other fellow. Then you and me will both be taken for a ride. See? Let me go, Doc! I'll shut off the water, so there won't be any more trouble; and you 'tend to your own business.'

'But this *is* my business, Buckley. The result of this investigation may be of tremendous interest to science. We might make some discovery that would help to explain this terrible disease! Do you mean to tell me that you wouldn't risk a little something — to save hundreds of children from suffering like Martha's?'

Thomas shook his head and drew a surly frown.

'You wouldn't find out anything. You docs are helpless as a lot o' kittens. You'd go up there to the reservoir — and puddle around — and write up a long-winded article, full o' big words — and nothing would come of it — except, maybe, you'd get your bean busted with a piece o' gas-pipe, and I'd go to the big house to make skillets.'

Jack was unbuttoning his white coat. Buckley's eyes followed him as he opened the clothes-closet.

'Well — I'll be going, now,' he said.

'I'm going with you,' said Jack.

Buckley growled.

'Goin' to squeal; are you?'

Jack tugged on his raincoat.

'Come on,' he said, not unkindly.

Buckley came to his feet and slouched along after him, through the anatomical laboratory, and down the stairs, and out to the parking-lot.

'What you turning this way for?' he demanded, as the car headed toward the business district. 'Goin' to turn me in?'

'We're going down to a restaurant, Buckley, and have something to eat. I missed my lunch today, and I'm hungry. So are you.'

'I'm not eating off o' you.'

'Well — then you may sit across the table from me and watch me eat — and I intend to have a sirloin steak and a baked potato.'

'O.K., Doc. I'll have one. By God — I need it!'

'Of course you do,' said Jack, almost companionably.

'You're all right, Doc. I'll hate it when you're found in a ditch, somewhere with a cracked skull.'

'I believe you would, Buckley. You're not a bad sort. By the way — how do you like your steak? Medium rare?'

'Yeah.' Thomas ventured an ironic chuckle. 'That's the way my steaks have been, for the past couple o' years; *damn* rare!'

* * * * * * * *

As Jack passed the desk in the third-floor corridor, late Tuesday afternoon, the Warren girl said, 'Telephone for you, Doctor Beaven. Miss Romney.' She handed him the receiver, and he took it up with an apprehensive scowl.

'Doctor Forrester,' came Romney's clipped syllables, 'wants me to tell you that he has just had a telegram from Doctor Mercer in New York, asking him to speak at their annual dinner of the Medical Association Friday night. The banquet speech was to have been made by Doctor Carter of Baltimore who has come down with flu or something.'

'And why does Doctor Forrester want me to know that?' asked Jack, not very pleasantly.

'Well — just a minute,' stammered Romney.

'I wanted you to know that,' came Tubby's voice, 'so that you will be on duty in my absence. I'm leaving here tomorrow night.'

'I had expected to be out of town, sir, on Thanksgiving Day.'

'You won't be, though,' said Tubby. 'You'll be right here. How's your Buckley case coming on?'

'Normally.'

'You're not out of the woods yet. These repair jobs, involving scar tissue, have a bad habit of flaring up, as you know.'

'Doctor Doane will be here, sir.'

'I committed the case to you; not Doane. I expect you to stay with it!'

'Very good, sir,' snapped Jack.

But it was far from good, and the rest of the day's work was done perfunctorily and with distaste. At six, thoroughly indignant over his disappointment, Jack drove to his apartment, debating whether to telegraph to Audrey and the Cunninghams, or explain to Bill on the telephone. He knew it was childish to be so badly upset. My word! — hadn't he yet learned, after all these years of last-minute cancellations of appointments, that this sort of thing was an integral part of a doctor's life? And wasn't it because of just such threats to one's freedom that he had determined not to have a home? Audrey would be disappointed, but she would know he had been telling the truth about the peculiar demands of his job.

He tossed aside his hat and coat; and, taking up a pad of telegraph blanks, began the composition of a message to Audrey. Then a new idea occurred to him. At first it seemed quite preposterous. Claudia wouldn't consent to it, even if local arrangements could be made; but it was worth trying.

He thumbed through the classified section of the telephone directory, looking for a catering firm; found a name that he remembered having heard and seen many times;

called them up, asked for the manager. He was expecting a guest on Thanksgiving. Could he arrange to have dinner prepared and served in his apartment at seven-thirty in the evening? They were very sorry, but all the competent help they had were already spoken for. It would be quite impossible.

Jack was dismayed over this prompt frustration of his impulsive plan. He paced the floor, trying to solve his dilemma. Suddenly a brighter thought suggested itself. Why not attempt to bring in a Chinese cook and serve the sort of dinner that would remind Audrey of her home? Abbott would know whether this was feasible. He called the house where his favorite student lived and briefly explained what he hoped to do.

'If you will permit me, sir,' replied Abbott, 'I shall come and cook the dinner.'

'I couldn't think of asking you to do that, Abbott.'

'It would be a great pleasure, sir. I shall bring a helper along.'

'That's most kind of you, Abbott. I'll take you up on it. And you arrange everything; will you? We will want chop suey — and everything.'

Abbott was heard chuckling.

'No chop suey, Doctor Beaven. If you wish to remind your friend of what she ate in the house of Sen Ling, she would be as much surprised and amused over your chop suey as you would be if Sen Ling, hoping to please you, served you with a platter of hot dogs. If you please, sir, I shall prepare the dinner.'

Jack was elated. He put through a long-distance call to Audrey, and after an anxious moment of waiting, heard her voice; explained that he couldn't leave; was stirred by her sincerely regretful, 'Oh — I am so sorree!'

'But,' he went on, earnestly, 'you are coming to see me — if you will. I shall make a reservation for you at the Livingstone. We will take a drive in the afternoon. And dinner will be served here at my apartment.'

'Would that be —— You would tell me — is it not so —

if I should not do that?' asked Audrey, in a lowered tone.

'Perfectly in order. I shall have people come in to attend to the dinner. Madame Grundy will be entirely satisfied.'

'Oh? This Madame Grundee — she will be there? That is good. Claudia will not object, then, I know. I shall tell her.'

'I wouldn't say anything about that, if I were you. Your sister can be assured that you are in safe hands. And you know that, don't you, dear?'

'Yes, Jack,' softly.

His heart responded to her confidence.

'Then you will come? Your train leaves at eight tomorrow evening.'

'Very well. I am so glad. Thank you, Jack. How nice of you to send for me.'

'I shall meet your train Thursday morning, Audrey.'

'May-bee you will not know me. I see you have forgotten my name.'

'No, dear, I haven't forgotten. And that reminds me of another thing I want you to do for me. Please bring along a Chinese costume — to wear at our dinner.'

There was a thoughtful pause.

'But — your other guest — this Madame Grundee — who will surely wear American clothes — might she not think it strange if —— '

Jack laughed.

'Madame Grundee, my dear, is just a name personifying a stiff code of conventionality. You will be my only guest.'

'Oh — that will be verree nice.' Her tone had brightened. Jack could picture the smile. 'Shall I telephone to Mrs. Cunningham that you are not coming — and that I am going?'

'Please; that I am not coming up. You may do as you like about the rest of it.'

'Oh — but she will want to know that, too.'

'Yes — I expect so.'

'She will be glad, I think.'

'I must let you go now, dear. We will have a wonderful time.'

'Yes. I know.'

Chapter XII

ARRANGEMENTS having been completed for Thanksgiving's bright events, Jack made himself comfortable in lounging pajamas and slippers, lighted his pipe, and consulted his anticipations. Deep in his mind he discovered some misgivings.

It was all very easy to say to oneself that the incomparable Lan Ying fully understood and approved the terms of their friendship, expecting nothing further to come of it than had been mutually agreed upon. Indeed she had declared that this idealistic pact was not only desirable but inevitable.

But neither his own nor Lan Ying's feeling about this matter quite answered all the questions involved. Whatever they themselves might think of their relationship, the fact remained that he was putting her in a very awkward position in the opinion of her friends; more particularly Claudia King. Claudia might feel that her sister's invitation to spend the holiday at the University implied serious intentions on the part of her host. He did not relish the prospect of seeming to trifle with Lan Ying's affection, and it was dismaying to face the risk of anyone's thinking that he had failed her, after having shown so much interest.

In considering this problem, Jack found himself reappraising the decision they had arrived at in regard to the eventualities of their friendship. Viewed in the warm glow of his remembrance, Lan Ying was, at this moment, the most important fact in his life. Ever since their last meeting, the memory of that enchanted moment when she had so trustingly and tenderly permitted his kiss recurred with the frequency of a theme-tune in a symphony. No matter how intently he might be occupied with some riddle of professional interest, this singular ecstasy would pour in over him like an unexpected tidal wave. At first he had said to himself that this emotional experience would undoubtedly fade out under the stress of his duties and responsibilities, but it had not done so. And the thing he had just now planned to do was not likely to help matters very much.

Well — maybe he didn't want to dim that vision. Maybe the only solution of the problem was to let their affection run its normal course into marriage. They needed each other. As for his own self-discipline, it served no good purpose unless it was effortless — or approximately so. The self-discipline that fretted and walked the floor and preoccupiedly sharpened lead pencils when professional obligations clamored for attention was a form of martyrdom that had no practical outcome.

On the other hand, it would be a damaging abdication of all his hard-earned merits if — at this phase of his career — he should impulsively decide to alter the whole course of his life in response to an emotional appeal. It wasn't simply a matter of determining to what extent the responsibilities of a home might interfere with his work: the problem went deeper than that. What would it do to his personality, if — after years of costly devotion to a program that had meant more to him than a religion, more than patriotism — he should say to himself that, the god he had served with such singleness of heart was not so important as a certain woman who had played the deuce with his imagination?

The telephone rang. Abbott had called up to say that he and his helper would arrive in the apartment at five Thursday afternoon. They would bring everything with them. All was arranged. Doctor Beaven could safely dismiss it all from his mind. And Doctor Beaven, grateful for this assurance, heartily wished he might also dismiss another problem closely related to this event.

'It would prefer me,' added Abbott, whose syntax occasionally went awry on the telephone, 'if I might be considered your servant for the evening. Kindly do not tell your guest that I am a student in your college.'

'Very well, Abbott,' replied Beaven, 'if that will make you feel more comfortable. I hope I may be able to repay you, somehow, for this fine courtesy.'

'It has been paid, thank you,' said Abbott.

The florist who kept an exclusive little shop adjacent to the Livingstone Hotel was sending three dozen chrysanthemums. He was also delivering a corsage of orchids to Miss Hilton's suite at the Livingstone where the room-clerk was holding the best accommodations in the house for her arrival. Yes; he remembered Miss Hilton, and they would see that she had every attention.

Jack's spirits brightened, and for a little while he considered only the pleasant success of plans for Lan Ying's entertainment. He strolled about through the rooms. It would be a strangely sweet experience to have her here in his apartment. His quarters would take on a new significance. It would never be quite the same after she had blessed the place with her dear presence.

The telephone rang again.

'Doctor Beaven speaking,' he said, hoping he was not about to be summoned to the hospital for work on some emergency case.

'This is Winifred Gillette, Doctor Beaven,' came a remotely familiar voice. 'Do you remember?'

He remembered and inquired about her graciously enough, though he hadn't given her a moment's thought since the day she had told him, at the close of their first year in school, that she had decided not to come back. She had not particularized her reasons but he could think of at least one reason that was ample. Winifred didn't have what it took to be a medical student; or, if she did, it was not conspicuously on display in the classroom.

'And what are you doing now?' Jack thought he should inquire.

'You couldn't guess.' Winifred's voice deepened to a rich contralto; and, after a brief pause for guessing, she carried on. 'Well — I married, the next year after I left school, and things didn't go right ——'

'Sorry,' said Jack, when she hesitated.

'Oh — it might have been much worse,' she replied cheerfully. 'We just gave it up and had ourselves a divorce. Nothing complicated about it. No job, no property, no alimony, no children, no love — and no regrets. So — now I am back here taking the Nursing course. I thought I should call you up — you always were so nice to me — and let you know where I am — and what I'm up to.'

Jack's brows had contracted a little as he wondered whether she really had told him what she was up to.

'Are you liking your work?' he asked, in the tone of a mildly interested uncle.

'Umm-humm,' she said, uncertainly. 'Of course I'm nothing but a slavey, this year. If anybody has a swelled head that he wants to have reduced, this is just the place for him.'

'I know,' said Jack, sympathetically. 'However, a nurse has to learn discipline, first of all. I suppose the junior year is as good a time as any — to get the hang of it.'

'I remember how you felt about discipline.' Winifred's voice sounded as if she were smiling teasingly. 'You certainly never slighted your work. I expect it paid, all right. Oh — I've kept track of you. Congratulations, Jack — if a little worm of a student nurse may take the liberty. Do you still work twenty-four hours a day?'

This was indeed a nice cue. Jack's gathering frown relaxed somewhat.

'Yes,' he replied, soberly. 'It's like anything else that one tries to do effectively. The farther you go, the harder you work. I have very little time to myself.'

'No — I suppose not,' said Winifred, as if she might be adding, mentally, 'And none, of course, for poor little me.'

'Thank you for calling up,' said Jack. 'It has been pleasant to hear from you.'

The conversation having now reached the phase where it could be spoken of in the past-perfect, Winifred was forced to admit its finality, thanked him for listening, wished him good luck, and said 'Good-bye' with a wistful little circumflex intonation that left no doubt of her disappointment over his casualness. Jack remained for a moment where he was, seated on the arm of a leather chair, reviewing the dialogue; especially his own contribution to it. The farther you went in any business, the harder you had to work. That was true. It was the firm voice of his essential self, speaking partly to feather-headed Winifred; but mostly to flutter-hearted Beaven. He decided to conciliate his conscience a little by running over to see how Martha Buckley was getting along. Very restless, he took a turn up and down through the rooms. They had already reacted to the impending visit of Lan Ying.

Lan Ying! Audrey! It was so much more natural to call her Audrey, and it was so much more to her liking to be called Lan Ying. And because of her wishes, Jack tried to think of her as Lan Ying, though bound to admit that the Chinese name only accented her remoteness from the interests which constituted his life.

Until now the cold and empty fireplace had served no purpose unless to emphasize ironically the dispiriting fact that the apartment was a lodging; not a home. Summoning the janitor, Jack arranged for some dry hickory to be brought up, and a fire laid. Then he pushed the chairs out of their prim positions and coaxed them to act as if somebody lived here.

Standing before the small group of framed photographs on the wall beside his desk, he tried to view the family pictures through the eyes of one seeing them for the first time. With folded arms, pipe in hand, he took stock of them as a stranger. Lan Ying would unquestionably notice a strong resemblance in Jean. 'But not the same lips,' he might be disposed to add to her comment, pretending to be still a little upset over the alarmingly faithful sketch she had made of his severe mouth. But perhaps it would be just as well to keep off the subject of lips. Hers were so lovely, so expressive, so desirable.

She would look studiously at the picture of his mother. It might be interesting to read her thoughts. Any woman could see at a glance that his mother's beautiful Titian hair — flattened hard against her temples — was rebelliously curly in spite of its discipline. With a woman's instinct — plus the 'wisdom of the East' — Lan Ying would wonder what sort of battles had been fought between those joy-loving curls and the uncompromisingly puritanical eyes. Doubtless she would be able to see that when the eyes met the curls in the mirror there could be but one outcome. The eyes wouldn't give an inch. From the picture they looked straight at you, not crossly, not haughtily, but with calm self-possession. The eyes said, 'There are two possible ways for people to think and act, a right way and a wrong way. The good life goes straight. It takes no interest in by-paths, undulations, pastel shades. You may take your pick, but it must be black or white, up or down, right or left: no trifling, no trimming, no hedging. Hear the Word, pay the price, avoid the appearance of evil; no ruffles, no bangles, no curls; for the Lord knoweth the way of the righteous, but the way of the ungodly shall perish.'

Her eyes said all that and her lips confirmed it, lips very much like his own. Jack had always thought that it was his mother's inflexible religion that had firmed her eyes and lips. That was the trouble with religion. It narrowed your outlook. If you took it straight, it shut you off from the loveliest and most lovable things in the world. But was it only religion that would bottle you and cramp you and blind you? Science would do exactly the same thing to you! Jack wondered if Audrey, having looked into his mother's eyes, might not turn and search his own.

The telephone rang again. It was the McFey girl.

'You asked me to keep you informed about the Buckley girl. She's rather restless.'

'What's your last temperature reading?'

'Just under a hundred. About the same as yesterday at this time. Anything you want me to do about it?'

'No. I'll be over after a while.'

Jack hung up the receiver and frowned. Now wouldn't it be just like this young daughter of the obnoxious Thomas Buckley to turn a few cartwheels?

Driving to the hospital, he found his polio uneasy but not to be worried about. The normal post-operative discomforts were present; that was all.

He decided to tarry for an hour, just to make sure. He went up to the interns' lounging-room and leafed through the medical journals, finding nothing of much interest. Fond of analyzing his own motives, he wondered whether his resolve to spend an unnecessary hour of overtime tonight was not in the nature of a votive offering to some unidentified god — as if to say, 'I'll sit here for an hour, when there's no necessity for it, just to make a small advance payment on the favor I hope you will grant me, and it's to be expected that you will be a good sport and remember that I want Thanksgiving Day free.'

It occurred to him that this superstition, in one form or another, influenced almost everybody on occasions of strong desire to execute some purpose. Perhaps the superstition was rooted in an instinct. If so, it had a great deal to recommend it. For instincts were not to be sneezed at. He decided he would leave when the clock struck eleven. He would have one more look at the restless Buckley and call it a day.

* * * * * * * *

He had wondered, as he paced the station platform, awaiting the arrival of Lan Ying's train, how much progress their friendship might make today under circumstances permitting more freedom than they had previously enjoyed. This question he faced with confused sensations of hope and apprehension.

With a rapidly beating heart he watched the gray plume of steam and smoke rising above the small, black mechanical toy, a mile away; watched four determined wisps of white cloud shoot into the gray plume, and in another second heard the screams of the locomotive; watched the thing grow bigger, noisier, until it swept past him, followed by a long string of clanking, hissing, acridly pungent cars. The train screeched to a stop; opening doors slammed against vestibule walls, porters tossed out baggage, tossed out stools.

Presently Jack sighted her and hurried to greet her. She raised a small gloved hand in instant recognition. And he knew that this thing they had called 'friendship' was something else. She gave him both hands and a smile that made him exultant.

'Lovely!' said Jack.

'Yes; isn't it?' agreed Lan Ying.

'I meant *you*!'

For a minute they returned to earth while identifying the bags and giving orders to the red-cap to follow along; then, tucking her hand under his arm, Jack led her to his car, proudly possessive and assured that he must be the object of much envy.

Presently, smiling down into her happy eyes — Lan Ying sat so close to him that when he shifted the gears his wrist brushed the softness of her Persian lamb coat and was warmed with a lingering glow — Jack said that his favorite colors were black and white and coral. Lan Ying replied that it was very early in the morning — is it not so? — for any talk about art, but agreed with him that coral was friendly. She touched her finger-tips to the gay little red feather, snugged the little black toque down tighter until the merest edge of the even black fringe still showed against her white forehead, and drew the white silk scarf closer about a white throat. The black fur coat obviously had been made by a sculptor who acknowledged the superior wisdom of the Creator and rejoiced in His handiwork and was willing to follow the pattern faithfully.

There were but very few guests at the Livingstone. Nothing was going on at the University during the holiday.

The dining-room offered a choice of breakfast-tables. They had chosen one in the corner where Lan Ying's view embraced the little park and a slice of the marble Alumni Building. She inquired whether it was a tomb, and Jack informed her. Whenever she asked such questions, he was almost startled; and, on these occasions, he wanted to call her Audrey — just to summon her away from the Chinese ties that held her fast.

'Oh?' she said. 'So this is where they all meet when they come back — the graduates.'

'No, my dear,' he replied, whimsically. 'They meet at the stadium; the football field. This is just the building where they keep the portraits of former University presidents, and I believe the Secretary of the Alumni Association has his office in there, too.'

Then she wanted to know what the Alumni Association did for the alumni, and Jack didn't know. He guessed that the University just kept track of them so they could be easily reached when some more money was needed — for new buildings, maybe, or for the endowment fund.

'Gifts of money are very important in America; is it not so?' asked Audrey. Jack nodded. 'People without much money must feel themselves at a great disadvantage,' she reflected. Jack agreed that this was unhappily true, but unavoidable.

'It would be nice,' she suggested, 'if people without money but with talents could present something they had made with their hands.' And so they fell to talking about the value of art-forms, Audrey wishing that there might be some other standard than dollars by which the worth of art objects could be estimated. 'Sometimes,' she went on, 'I read in the newspapers that a very wealthy man has just given a celebrated painting to an art museum, and it almost always says the picture cost him four hundred thousand dollars — or some great amount of money. And the people flock to see it because it was so costly to the rich man who gave it. And I think,' she added, 'this kind man should be appreciated. But would it not also be inter-

esting if the people were told how much of himself — in
time and thought and experience — the artist had invested?
May-bee it could not be measured in cash, but its cost
may have been very great.'

Jack was prompt to agree to this, deploring the importance of money in American thought.

'One of the stories which my Chinese foster-father loves
best,' said Lan Ying, reminiscently, 'is of an artist who
spent fifty years painting a beautiful vase to present to
the Emperor. The artist lived in a village and his workshop
was open to the highway. The news spread that he was
devoting his life to the vase for the Emperor. And every
day, not only the little children of the town, but travelers
on the road, stopped in to watch, and honored the artist
for his great patriotism. At length the vase was ready for
the kiln, and many people came to see the lovely treasure
taken from the furnace. But when the brick door was
opened, it was found that the delicate vase had broken in
the firing. And the artist was disconsolate. Being a poor
man, he had nothing to offer to his Emperor but his talent
as an artist, and now his work was destroyed. And he
fell ill of grief. At length the lord of the province heard
the story and he came, one day, in his golden litter, to
visit the unhappy man to whom he said — after bowing
verree low before his bed — "I am told of the vase you
painted for the Emperor. It has been said that through
these many years old men and little children, neighbors
and strangers, have gathered to watch you make this
graceful expression of your patriotic love. No doubt they
went away feeling that they too should express their
gratitude to the Emperor in some outpouring of their
strength or skill or talent. And now you lament the loss
of the lovely vase, and feel your life-work has been wasted.
But I say to you, my friend, *you have presented the vase
to the Emperor.*"'

'Sweet story,' murmured Jack — 'and sweetly told.
Not much wonder you are so exquisite, my dear. Brought
up on such idealism, you could hardly fail to be' — he
hesitated — 'exactly what you are — a beautiful soul.'

'Oh?' she said, lifting her eyes inquiringly. 'Then you do believe in souls?'

'Well,' said Jack, 'I believe *you* have one. I believe you *are* one!'

They had lingered for a whole hour over their coffee. At Lan Ying's suggestion, Jack gave a more detailed report about Abbott than he had been able to do in his letters. She had been much interested in Abbott's comments on American life. Many of his observations had not occurred to her before, and she was amused.

'Americans do not realize,' she was saying, 'that the Chinese have great sacrifices to make when their children leave home to attend college in the States. The Yankee says, "How lucky for this boy!" Well — may-bee. But it is hard for the family to let him go so far from home, to remain away for years, and come back in different clothes, eating with a fork, and complaining that his bed makes his neck stiff.

'Perhaps you may think that when young Sen was ready to go to England, his father and mother were glad the house of Sen Ling could so honor itself by sending its favorite son to be brought up by aliens.

'Of course I was then too young to realize fully what it meant to them but old enough to be deeply impressed by the ceremony enacted in the Hall of Ancestors on the day before young Sen sailed. The family — all of them; some two score, may-bee — assembled in the dimly lighted hall. And there, with much dignity, Sen paid homage to his forefathers, taking the incense from the hand of Sen Ling and offering it before the venerable statues.'

'It must have been very stirring,' commented Jack, 'and very sad. Almost like a funeral.'

'But without tears,' said Audrey. 'It was verree quiet. Nobody cried. May-bee they did when they were alone.'

Jack remarked that the Chinese must have their emotions under excellent control, to which Lan Ying replied that this national trait had been exaggerated in the American mind.

'We are not quite so stoical as you think,' she went on. 'The Chinese are not insensitive, not repressed. They know how to play, and there is much foolery in the family life; many practical jokes; much laughter; much friendly teasing.'

'I thought the Chinese father was a martinet,' said Jack, 'expecting his wives and children to creep into his august presence on all fours, with abject apologies for their existence.'

Lan Ying laughed and shook her head.

'You have been reading American novels about China,' she said. 'Most of the Chinese father's majesty is on the surface. Certain traditions relating to the obeisance to be paid to the head of the house are observed, but it is most droll to see this dignified performance as it is actually rendered.' She paused, and her lingering smile testified to amusing reminiscences.

'Tell me, dear,' said Jack. 'I am mightily interested.'

'Well ——' Her mobile lips promised an interesting revelation. 'One day, when I was about six, Sen Li, who was probably nine, and I went hand in hand before Sen Ling, and bowed deeply before him. And little Sen Li said, "Honorable parent, thy unworthy child and his wretched sister have made a toy boat with small sails. The boat upsets when the wind blows. Would the honorable father tell his worthless son ——" And I broke in to say, "We want something ver-ree heavy for the bottom of the boat, honorable father." And Sen Ling said, most gravely, but I know he was much amused, "We will go and see the boat."' She paused. 'He was such a darling — my foster-father; so wise; so dear.'

'It must be a difficult illusion for the Chinese father to support,' said Jack. 'I should think he would break down completely, and laugh.'

'He may laugh — to himself,' said Lan Ying, 'but he maintains his outward dignity. This is not for the purpose of dignifying himself any more than his son. The Chinese are wise enough to know that a father cannot dignify

himself by belittling his child. This is the verree great
difficulty about interesting the Chinese in the Christian
story of an all-powerful Father consenting to the whipping
of his Son. They do not like the idea.'

'No,' remarked Jack, shortly, 'and one doesn't have to
be Chinese to find that difficult.'

'Oh?' Lan Ying's pretty brows expressed surprise. 'I
did not know.' She shook her head, perplexed. 'Are you
Christians bewildered about it, too? Of course — you
would be.'

'Some of them are,' said Jack — 'when they stop to
think of the implications of the story. But most people
seem to accept what they've been taught, without making
intelligent inquiries. It's much easier; and that goes for
almost everything they think they know.'

'But — Jack — they can't be blamed. Only a few ever
have the time and self-confidence to pretend themselves
philosophers. They really have to rely on the old traditions
that comforted their fathers back in the times when the
myths were fervently believed and fought for.' Lan Ying
paused for a moment meditatively. 'My foster-father once
told me that the old religious myths are like the moon.'

'The moon?' Jack's eyes were puzzled.

'When the sun is bright, nobody is concerned about the
moon,' explained Lan Ying. 'But when the night comes on,
and everything is dark, there appears in the troubled man's
sky a pale light. He cannot see very clearly by it, but at
least he may grope his way. Sen Ling said the old religious
myths were like the moon; nothing any more but a dead
mass of cold craters that once shot forth fire; now merely
a mirror feebly reflecting light.'

'Marvelous!' exclaimed Jack. 'An illustration that fits
like a glove! Dead myths! Dead craters on a cold moon!'

Audrey gently touched the back of his hand with the
tips of detaining fingers.

'Yes,' she agreed, nodding her head slowly, 'dead craters
on a cold moon, but reflecting light from afar; light from
something or Someone that is still very much alive, aflame

purposeful, powerful. And no matter how dark the night —
how pale the moon — the troubled man is glad to know
that the sun is still there, and will shine on him — again —
tomorrow.'

Jack searched her introspective eyes with admiration
and amazement. She seemed so childlike, so disingenuous;
and yet, at times, Lan Ying disclosed ideas indicating a
seasoned maturity of mind. He smiled, and tried to say
that to her, tactfully.

'But they are not my ideas, Jack,' she replied. 'I learned
to think about these things when I was a little girl — sitting
on a low stool at the feet of my foster-father.'

'And what does that make you, Audrey? A Buddhist,
maybe?'

She lifted a lovely shoulder slightly to shrug the seriousness out of his query.

'The Sen Ling family — for hundreds of years — have
been Buddhists; ceremonially, at least. I never found out
how much of it they really accepted. They did not fret
over their religion. They took it along with the weather.
The hard questions were all the same as the cold days;
not their fault; not their responsibility. My foster-father
once said to me, when I was asking questions, "It is our
good fortune, Lan Ying, that the Great Teacher never
conducts examinations. The most comforting thought
about the riddle of the universe is that one is not required
to solve it."'

'Is that Buddhistic?' asked Jack.

'Yes — it is typical of the Buddhist mind.'

'And yours — too — I think.'

Her reply was confused, half-inarticulate.

'I do not know,' she murmured. 'May-bee not. May-
bee not entirely. May-bee not at áll. I do not know.'
She shook her head confessing complete bafflement; then
smiled, and added, 'May-bee I am a pagan. May-bee I
just believe in the sun and the sunshine.' There was a
considerable pause. 'May-bee you will think this strange,
Jack, but I believe I could be a Christian if they would let

me have just their Christ — standing in a blaze of sunshine.'

'And you wouldn't need a moon,' assisted Jack.

'Yes,' she said, softly. 'At night.'

Deeply stirred, Jack made no immediate response; sat
regarding her with such candid affection that her lips
parted in a smile. After a moment, he said, 'I should be
much interested in your own reaction to the Christian
story, dear. Did you hear any of it when you were a child?'

'More than you might suppose. The good Sen Ling
decided, when I was eight, that it was in order for me to
learn the religion of my people, so they sent me to the
Mission Sunday School. My amah strongly objected because the other children were not of our ——' Audrey
groped for a phrase that might be at once honest and
modest, and Jack solved her problem by saying:

'I know what you mean, my dear. Please go on.'

'And I would come home from the Mission Sunday
School and ask questions about the things I had not understood very well.'

Jack laughed, and remarked that this would make a very
funny situation. Audrey laughed too, and said, 'Funnier
than you could possibly guess. I did not realize then how
funnee it was, at eight.'

'Please try to remember, Audrey,' said Jack, eagerly.
'Your people were Buddhists, and you came home from the
Christian Sunday School to have them explain the mysteries. I never heard anything more interesting. Tell me
about it.'

Audrey sat with dark brown eyes thoughtfully averted
for a moment, and then smiled.

'Once — I recall this particularly, for it made a lasting
impression on me — I was telling my foster-father why
Jesus died on the cross. I was quite full of it, for I had
never heard that story before. In fact, I was a little shy
about telling the good Sen Ling I had learned it, for my
amah — who had accompanied me, and sat by me in the
class — was very indignant and had said, on the way

home, that it wasn't the kind of story that should be
told to little children; about cruel men driving nails
through a man's hands and feet.'

Jack nodded approvingly.

'Your nurse had good sense,' he said. 'Not much
wonder she didn't like it.'

'I suppose so,' rejoined Audrey. 'Shu-cheng was so
particular about shielding us from tales of brutality when we
were little. She said that such stories left scars on our
minds. Most of the stories she told us were personifications
of flowers talking to one another about the bees — and the
little wood-people who came into the garden at night to
play.... Well — on this day I came home and told my
foster-father why Jesus died on the cross.'

Jack was impatient to have her proceed.

'What attitude did he take, Audrey? I fancy he was
much upset.'

'No,' she replied, slowly, 'not upset. Most respectful;
most serious. He had not asked me to tell him. I volunteered to report what I had heard. I sat before him on a
low stool and told him all about it. You see — I loved him
so much and had such great confidence in him that I knew
he would answer my questions fairly.

'I sat before the good Sen Ling and told him that Jesus
was God's Son, and that made Jesus a God too, and He
had died. And Sen Ling gravely bowed his head and
replied that he knew about that, but added, "God's Son
Jesus came to life again, Lan Ying. Did they not tell you?
If not, perhaps they will, next time. You must be patient.
It is difficult to explain the story of a religion in a short
hour. Jesus died — but he came to life. The teachers will
tell you that, I know."'

'Mighty sporting of a Buddhist,' observed Jack.

'Sen Ling,' remarked Audrey, 'was much more concerned with being fair and honest than with being merely
religious. I don't think he worried much about Buddhism —
or any other ism. You see — the good Sen Ling felt that
a man should be — first of all — a gentleman.... So — I

told him, in my childish way, about Jesus dying on the bloody cross to make everything right, because the first man who ever lived had disobeyed a god and that made everything wrong for him and his children and all the people for hundreds and hundreds of years. I said the first man's name was Adam, and the god had made him out of dust that he found in a garden full of animals. And this dust-man got up and named all of the animals and ate an apple from the wrong tree. And a long time afterward the god let a big crowd of people kill his son Jesus so that everything would be all right again about Adam's eating the wrong apple.'

'God!' muttered Jack, under his breath. 'When it's put that way ——'

'I know,' went on Audrey, evenly, 'it is not a pretty story when you put it that way. And it is not quite fair. There is a great deal more to it than that, of course. A wise philosopher could make something better of it; but — that is the story I brought home to Sen Ling.'

'Was he disgusted?'

'I do not know,' she said, after a pause. 'If so, he did not disclose it. He sat for a long time in silence, slowly tapping the arms of his tall chair with his long fingers, and then he arose and took me by the hand and we went out into the garden and sauntered along the path to the round pool where there are many goldfish playing under the lily-pads. And we sat down on a stone bench. And, after a while, my foster-father said to me, "Lan Ying, the missionaries are not bad people. They are good to the poor, and they are busy with kind acts. And they are so eager for you to know about religion that they have told you things a little girl could not hope to understand. It is not time yet for you to be worried about the gods. It is enough that you should play with the kittens and help Sen Li fly his kites. You are too little, Lan Ying, to wonder about such matters as a god thinking everything would be all right after his son was killed to pay for a man's eating a bad apple."'

Jack drew a long, slow intake of breath, almost audibly,

and shook his head, his eyes narrowed. '"The heathen in his blindness!"' he muttered.

'And I said, "But — my honorable father, Adam ate the wrong apple because a lady who had been made from one of his ribs gave it to him. A big talking-snake told her about the apple." And Sen Ling said, "Let us not worry about that, Lan Ying. It must have happened so long ago that we need not care. We will watch the goldfish, and not fret about the god and his apple. You go and ask your amah for some crumbs. The fish are hungry."

'And I remember how glad I was that the good Sen Ling had explained everything without explaining anything, and I laughed and said, "How fun-nee — for the god to worry so much about his apple. My honorable father — do our gods worry about their apples?" And Sen Ling said, "Yes, my daughter, we too have gods who worry about such things as apples. But — it is not our worry; it is theirs."

'And I said, "But — my honorable father, if you were a god and had made a man out of dust, and he had eaten an apple, you would not curse him, and give up Sen Li to die with nails in his hands so everything would be all right again — about the apple." And my foster-father said, "I cannot make a man out of dust. Go, now, and ask Shu-cheng for some crumbs. We will feed the goldfish."

'And so ——'

Jack's eyes watched her lips as they said, 'And so,' smiling tenderly, his heart beating faster.

'And so,' continued Lan Ying, 'I went to the kitchen for the crumbs and we fed the goldfish, I on my hands and knees bending over the pool and my foster-father standing tall and stately beside me.' She laughed a little as she remembered. 'I distinctly recall the reflection of my face in the water. You could not possibly have told me from a Chinese child, with my chubby cheeks and little black bangs and the quaint smock gaily embroidered with pigeons. I saw my foster-father mirrored in the water. His face was verree serious and each hand was tucked into the other sleeve; this way. And I wondered if he might not still be thinking about our conversation. So I ventured to say — as I scattered the crumbs close to the noses of the fish — "It was too bad about poor Jesus."

'"Yes, my daughter," said Sen Ling, "it is indeed a sad story. Jesus was a good man." "Was Jesus as good as Buddha?" I inquired. And Sen Ling said, "They were both good men, Lan Ying, and wise men."

'It was some time before I made up my childish mind to risk saying, rather shyly, "The teacher said that we must believe what Jesus taught, but not what Buddha taught." And Sen Ling replied, "Our teachers will tell you the opposite, my child, but I think that neither Buddha nor Jesus would have approved of such words. They were both gentlemen."'

'You were most fortunate, Lan Ying,' said Jack, when she had paused. 'I wish I might have been in such competent hands. It seems very strange: in China, you were informed that Jesus was a gentleman; in our own country, I was led to believe, as a small boy, that Jesus was a sissy. It must have been a great privilege, my dear, to have sat at the feet of Sen Ling.'

She did not reply to that for a little while; then, rather uncertainly, she said, 'Sometimes I wonder, Jack. The best things I learned from my foster-father are, I fear, the verree things that make it difficult for me to live happily in this country.'

Jack nodded, and said he could see how this might be true. 'One day,' pursued Lan Ying, 'not long before they brought me to America, I saw him sitting under his favorite pear tree, and I sat down on the grass near him. After a time, he smiled a welcome, and said, "I was thinking of you, my daughter. You are soon to live with people who strive mightily. You will be much confused, I fear, by the speed and tumult with which all of their works are accomplished." And I said, "My father, I shall carry this garden with me — in my heart; and when everything is whirling fast I shall go there for meditation."

'"It will be well for you to do so, my child," said Sen Ling. "But — you should also learn to strive somewhat, or you will be lonesome, and your new friends will think you queer." And I said, "You mean — I must run fast and make much noise?" And he smiled at my foolish words, and said, "No — you need not run, or make loud noises, but you must learn to have what they call 'convictions,' and stand up for them." And I asked, "Convictions about what?"'

Jack laughed, and said this was the funniest thing he had heard for a long time. Lan Ying smiled briefly in response to his amusement, and went on.

'"Well," said Sen Ling, "you will live in a certain city, and all of the people there will say that it is the best city in the land, and when they ask you if you do not also think it is the best city in the land you should say it is indeed. For if you should say you do not know — not having been in all the cities — they may think you are unfriendly. And you should promptly choose a political party." And I said, "Which one, honorable father?" And he said, "It makes very little difference, my child; for political parties, everywhere, are merely crafts in which men are engaged for their own profit. But you should choose one of them, preferably the one favored by the people with whom you live." And I said, "But, my honorable father, should I not study the aims and beliefs of all the political parties, so I might know which of them represented my own thought?" "That will not be necessary," said Sen Ling, "and indeed you will be better served if you do not study about any of them, for you will be expected to favor one of them to the exclusion of all others."'

This brought a laugh from Jack, in which Lan Ying did not share. Her face was serious.

'And I said, "But, my honorable father, you have taught me not to be partisan, and I like your way much better." And he said, "You will always like our way better, Lan Ying; but I wish you to be contented with your friends, and they will not like you if you do not strive. You must

never say, in America, that Buddha Gautama was a wise
and great man, like Jesus." "But I think he was, honorable
father," I replied. And Sen Ling said, "You may cherish
that thought, privately, Lan Ying, in the garden — in your
heart."'

A strange silence fell between them for a moment.

'I'm just realizing, my dear,' said Jack, quietly, 'that
there are depths to you which I cannot know. But,' he
added, 'I shall try my best to understand, and you may be
sure that while I haven't had the spiritual experience en-
titling me to sit in your garden, I shall stand guard at
the gate.'

'You are so good to me, Jack,' she murmured, softly.

'Shall we go now?' he asked.

Audrey gathered up her belongings.

'For the drive in the country!' she said, happily. 'I have
been looking forward to that.'

Jack looked his pleasure over her comment. Neither of
them had ever referred to the tender little episode which
had made their other drive into the country a memorable
event. It delighted him to feel that she could anticipate
another drive with such obvious happiness.

'I shall be back for you in an hour,' he said, as they
parted.

* * * * * * * *

And now they were driving in the country. Jack had gone
to the hospital at ten to make sure his patients would not
be needing him for a while. The Buckley child had spent a
very uncomfortable night, but was showing every sign of
normal progress; temperature ranging between ninety-nine
and a half and a hundred, but nothing to be anxious about.

The day was perfect, specially prepared for their enchanted trip; just enough snap in the air, to harmonize
the coral of Audrey's cheeks and lips. The gold sunshine
had been donated by September, the blue sky pretended
it was June. The maples and oaks knew it was November.
The tall firs didn't care when it was.

The tires hummed on the asphalt.

'Did your sister approve of your coming?' he asked. They had not talked yet about the circumstances of Audrey's sudden departure for this journey.

'I am afraid not,' she said, soberly. 'She felt it was most unconventional.'

'That's a very big word,' drawled Jack. 'Are you sure you can define it?'

Audrey made a show of earnest concentration, with knitted brows and tightened lips.

'"Unconventionality" is something we told our inexperienced sister she must not do, because Doctor Forrester would not like it,' she said, bookishly.

'And how does Doctor Forrester come into this picture?' Jack inquired, making a poor attempt to disguise his annoyance.

'I am not quite sure. Claudia thinks that Doctor Forrester will be displeased.' She hesitated for an instant. 'Does he have something to say about — about your friendships?'

They had reached the top of a hill. There the road had been widened to a parking-space for the accommodation of travelers who wished to pause for the panorama. Jack angled the coupé toward the stone parapet and shut off the ignition.

'Of course you know, Lan Ying,' he explained, deliberately, 'something of the relation sustained between Doctor Forrester and me. We do not like each other. But — professionally — we depend upon each other a great deal. Doctor Forrester has given me every possible opportunity to advance, and I am deeply in his debt for this privilege. I have done his bidding, like a slave, for several years, and I suppose he would be at least inconvenienced if I left him, or gave him less of my time. He regards me, I think, somewhat as a turf enthusiast might regard a two-year-old colt that gave promise of ability on the track. The colt is given careful handling, a scientifically prepared diet, and the right amount of exercise; but the time comes when it is expected to pay for all the bother and expense it has caused. If I should die, Tubby would probably miss me. And if anything happened to distract my attention from my job; well ——'

'But I am only a brief distraction,' broke in Lan Ying, smiling. 'Surely the young race-horse should have a day off, occasionally, when he does not have to mind the rules. May-bee he could run all the better for having had a day in the pasture.'

Jack confirmed this opinion with an enthusiastic nod.

'Tubby, however, would doubt the wisdom of a day off. He never breaks training, himself. It sounds a little as if your sister had discussed our friendship with Doctor Forrester. Do you know?'

'Perhaps,' she replied. 'I mean — perhaps they discussed it. I do not know.'

'I am sure you must be thinking it very strange,' said Jack, 'that I should permit this man to intrude so deeply into my personal affairs. We are not friends. But we are both servants of the same hard taskmaster — a master who means a very great deal more to us than our aversions, our animosities, and our stubbornness. I have told you something about that. Perhaps I should tell you a little more. There was one night, about a year ago, when — at Tubby's suggestion — I had secured a valuable specimen of spinal fluid from an incipient case of meningitis. I shall not bother you with the technical details, but this specimen was of special importance because we had made the diagnosis somewhat earlier than is customary ——'

'I think *you* made the diagnosis, Jack,' said Lan Ying, loyally. 'Is it not so?'

'Well — it was my guess; and Tubby confirmed it. So — we did the spinal puncture slightly in advance of the time when such research is ordinarily possible. For an hour, that night, we alternately studied the baffling little speck in the microscope. Then, Tubby unbuttoned his laboratory smock and slipped out of it. "Carry on, Beaven," he said. "Your eyes are better than mine. If either of us discovers anything new, it will have to be you." I couldn't help feeling sorry, for it is a fact that Tubby's vision is not what it was. I should have known better than to offer a word of sympathy, but I blurted out, "I'm sorry, sir; but — after all — it's *your* experiment; and, if I can assist you any in the detail work, I'm glad enough to stand by." Tubby said nothing until he had put on his coat and hat. Then he growled, "It is *our* experiment, my son" — and left the room. Slammed the door after him.'

'Lovely!' exclaimed Lan Ying.

Jack met her unexpected comment with a stare of surprise; then, assuming she had spoken ironically — which wasn't a bit like her — he drawled, 'Yes; *wasn't* it?'

'I must write that to my foster-father,' she said. 'He would be verree much interested.'

'If he's interested in abnormal psychology, he might like it. Next morning,' continued Jack, 'I ventured to greet him in the operating-room almost as if he was a human being, and he barely grunted. That night — it must have been one o'clock — I was having another go at that meningitis smear when I heard the click of Tubby's key in the lock. I didn't look up. He stood at my elbow for a long time. Then he said, "Getting anywhere?" And I said, "No. Want to look?" He took off his coat and I gave him my place on the stool before the big Zeiss binocular. It had been raining hard for hours. I noticed that the bottom of Tubby's trouser-legs were wet and muddy. He must have spent a good half-hour at the microscope. Then he sighed deeply and prepared to leave. "Keep on trying, Beaven," he said. "We'll never have a better chance."

'"You're wet, sir," I remarked. "Are you on foot?"

'"Flooded my coils," he answered, grudgingly.

'"Let me drive you home," I said.

'"I can get a taxi," he growled. "You're not employed here as a cab-driver."'

Lan Ying's eyes were wide with interest.

'Splendid!' she cried. 'My foster-father will think that this relationship is worthy of his meditation.'

'Your foster-father will probably decide that Tubby and I are both crazy.'

'By no means!' She laid a slim hand on Jack's arm. 'Here are all the great ideas! Sometimes they are conceived and developed by persons we do not like; persons who object to us; persons bitterly disliked by us — but *great ideas!* Is it not then a mark of greatness in ourselves if we can recognize the greatness of ideas that are in the keeping of people we despise?'

He regarded her with tenderness.

'That was a good thought, Lan Ying,' he said, gently. 'You have a very busy little head — and a very pretty head.'

She shook the pretty little head deprecatingly, and replied, 'You like the Chinese bangs: is it not so?'

Jack ventured to touch the edge of the blue-black fringe with his finger-tips, and nodded approval.

'Sometimes — when I was a little girl,' said Lan Ying, softly, 'my foster-father used to touch me on my forehead — just that way.'

'You are very fond of Sen Ling,' said Jack.

'And I think he would like you,' she murmured. 'Sen Ling is so verree much interested in courage.'

Jack thought this an odd remark. It had not occurred to him that any element of courage had been discussed. While he was debating this, Lan Ying went on. 'My foster-father often said there were two kinds of courage: the courage demanded by self-restraint, and the courage manifested by audacity.'

'And which kind did he like best?' asked Jack, feeling that he should keep Lan Ying going.

'Naturally, my foster-father knew more about the courage demanded by self-discipline, for that is Buddhistic. The Buddhists make a speciality of caution and resignation. But — he also admired the courage that is audacious.'

'For instance,' pressed Jack.

'Well — do you remember the old myth about the people who built the tower, hoping to reach up to the gods?'

'Yes. They never finished it; did they?'

Lan Ying shook her head.

'When they found out what good bricks they were making,' she continued, 'they changed their plans and decided that the tower was to be a monument to themselves. And — as soon as they left off building up to see the gods, and began working for themselves, they could not understand one another, any more. So — the tower was abandoned.'

'And that,' assisted Jack, with a brief chuckle, 'accounted for all the different languages in the world.'

'It is a fantastic explanation of the various languages,' said Lan Ying, 'but my foster-father says that all the people in the world would be speaking the same tongue — and understanding one another — if they were not so eager to build monuments to themselves. But — that is not the part of the story that interests Sen Ling. It was the audacity of the original idea. There was nothing unusual about the failure of the tower-builders, or their misunderstandings. Sen Ling likes the first part of the myth — where the people voted to build up to the gods, with brick!'

'A very silly aspiration,' commented Jack. 'One would think that an ancient tribe with enough ingenuity to make good brick might have sense enough not to tackle such a crazy scheme.'

'Now — there — that is just the point!' Lan Ying's eyes sparkled. 'That is the way you get the great accomplishments! Crazy schemes! Silly aspirations! But — the gods give men these funnee ideas. Is it not so?'

'But why?' Jack's lips registered dissent. 'There's no occasion for the gods to get into it, at all; neither a God, nor a whole flock of gods. Human progress is a gradual adaptation to circumstances; a gradual improvement on the techniques of meeting life's demands. You take the wheel, for example. Some early fellow discovered accidentally that he could transport a big stone by pushing it across rolling logs. After that; well — they just kept on making better wheels. The gods didn't have to hand anything down. The primitives didn't need a divine revelation to produce the pulley. Once you had a wheel, the pulley was inevitable. Some bright fellow made a simple pulley and his grandson laughed and made a multiple pulley. No gods required.'

Lan Ying agreed to all this with a smile that promised further argument.

'Now — Doctor Beaven — you must let *me* pick a case!' she said, archly. 'One day, some early fellow wished to sail his boat out of the sight of land; and, fearing he might be lost, he said, "I shall now make a little round box, with a needle in it that will always point north." Does it not seem as if the gods may have had to furnish that crazy idea? Your Columbus: did not the gods sail with him?'

'Columbus wasn't looking for America, Lan Ying,' objected Jack. 'That was an accident.'

'May-bee he thought it was,' she persisted. 'May-bee the man who discovered the compass was trying to make something else.' Her brown eyes grew serious. 'May-bee *you* will meet with a strange accident — sometime,' she added, softly.

'That would be very thrilling, Lan Ying.'

'My foster-father told me that the great Monsieur Pasteur was led into his discoveries by trying to find out what ailed some sick silkworms. May-bee you will be looking for a way to mend a man's damaged hand, and say something to him that will make the man over into a verree important person.'

'Perhaps I should leave that job to the mental healers,' said Jack, dryly. 'I'm not working in that field, Lan Ying.'

'But — may-bee that other job *is* in your field, Jack. You first mend the man's hand — and then tell him how to use it most effectively. I think that if you restore a man's hand, you have a better right than anyone else to advise him what to do with it.'

Jack regarded her with an indulgent smile.

'Lan Ying,' he said, 'you do have the largest assortment of queer notions.'

'Did you find what you were looking for, Jack,' she asked, suddenly reverting to the story he had told her a few minutes earlier — 'the secret in the big microscope?'

'No,' he replied glumly.

'Did the patient develop a verree bad case?'

'Yes. Boy about nine. He died.'

'How verree sad for his family.' Lan Ying was much distressed. 'Had he a father and mother?'

'I'm afraid I don't know that, dear,' confessed Jack. 'It was Tubby's case. I simply did the puncture, you know. The main part of my job was in the laboratory.'

'Was he a bright little fellow — like Teddy?' persisted Lan Ying.

'I really didn't have a good look at him.' Jack's tone was apologetic. 'When I came to do the spinal puncture, they had him turned face down, of course.'

'And they didn't tell you' — Lan Ying shook her head, incredulously — 'anything about him?'

'Well — no. Naturally, they wouldn't, unless I inquired; and there was no occasion for my knowing that. I didn't see any of his kinfolks.'

'Just the little speck in the big microscope?' murmured Lan Ying, disappointedly.

'Yes; but — see here, Lan Ying,' Jack protested, defensively, 'if we could find something in that little speck; something that might help point the way to a discovery of some remedy for the boy's trouble; something that might benefit hundreds, thousands of people — isn't that enough of a job to occupy one man's full attention?'

'May-bee — but I was just thinking how verree fine it would be if you should have sat by the little boy's bed and said to him, "May-bee you are helping us to something that will make other children well and strong."' Lan Ying's brown eyes quizzed his face wistfully.

'Do you think that would register — with a small boy?' asked Jack, doubtfully.

'It might be worth trying,' said Lan Ying, softly.

Chapter XIII

JACK had left Audrey at the Livingstone shortly after four. She had insisted that he should not come back for her in the evening. She would take a taxi to his apartment about seven, leaving him free to attend to his hospital duties and dress for dinner without hurrying.

At six-thirty he was ready for her, pacing up and down in his living-room, pausing in his march to move a chair, pat a pillow, straighten a row of books. Time crept. It pleased him to discover that the clock on the mantel was almost two minutes slow.

Abbott, with his Chinese helper, was busy in the tiny kitchen. He had politely but firmly made it clear that the only duty expected of Doctor Beaven — in respect to the dinner preparations — was to refrain from offering his assistance. There was a quiet air of mystery about these proceedings, and Jack surmised that the fewer questions he asked the more popular he would be in the opinion of his impromptu oriental ménage.

When it had struck seven he was nervous with eagerness as he stood at a front window looking down the street. Presently he saw a cab coming. It made a circle in front of the apartment house and drew up at the curb. He had a brief glimpse of a white coat. Turning from the window, he went to the hall-door to await a signal from below. The elevator rumbled. Its metal gates clicked. The bell rang. And there she stood — and here she came, through his doorway, into his house. Her lips were parted in a happy smile as Jack greeted her. It was an enchanted moment.

She had turned when he reached for the lovely white coat
and his hands had touched her cheeks. Glancing up over
her shoulder, she said, 'I should have worn a mandarin
with this dress, Jack, but I felt it might be too conspicuous
at the hotel.' He laid the white fur-trimmed coat over his
arm and surveyed Lan Ying with frankly admiring, rather
serious eyes. Her beauty was so distinctly exotic that for a
moment he could find nothing to say. Rich rose-brocaded
satin; the frogged jacket mindful of her adorable shapeliness
but topped with a severely tailored but exquisitely embroidered collar high on her white throat; a long, narrow skirt of
the same material that revealed the tips of black satin slippers, slippers with low heels, apparently, for when she looked
up into Jack's eyes he felt himself towering above her. The
only jewelry she wore was a pair of jade ear-drops.

'Well?' said Lan Ying, shaking her blue-black head
slowly. 'You asked me to — you know.'

'Yes, my dear,' he finally found himself saying, 'and it's
beautiful. I never saw you quite so lovely.'

'Nor so comfortable,' she added. 'It is a verree friendly
dress, Jack. I am glad you like me in it.'

He had led the way toward the almost too energetic fire
and signed her to a huge tan-leather chair which she re-
jected with a teasing smile.

'It is much too big,' she said. 'Besides, you must let me
stroll about — and see your house. Such a nice place, Jack.
Have you a dog or a cat or a bird or a bee — or do you live
quite alone?'

It had given him a very queer sensation when, having
left her for a moment to dispose of her coat, Jack returned
to find Lan Ying sitting at his desk. She glanced up to say,
'I am making myself at home; is it not so? Here, I think, is
where you sit when you write such verree nice letters to me.'

He had stood behind her chair, regarding her with tender
eyes. He touched her shoulder and she lifted it a little in
response.

'I never enjoyed writing letters before,' he said.

'That is Jean, I think.' Lan Ying had risen to inspect the

family photographs. 'She is much like you, Jack, only not so — so serious. She will visit you, some day, may-bee?'

'May-bee,' responded Jack, teasingly.

'You will ask me to come — when she visits you?' Lan Ying's entreating little nods made her seem very child-like.

'Yes — and we will have a party. I think you might like my sister. This is my mother. I believe I told you that she died very shortly before I came here to attend the Medical College.'

Lan Ying slipped her small hand through his arm, sympathetically.

'That probably accounts for the first run-in I had with Doctor Forrester,' continued Jack. 'I had come almost directly from my mother's funeral. She was a very devout person. And when Tubby began to unload sour ironies about the orthodox beliefs, I wasn't quite prepared to think it was amusing. Mother had staked everything on the literal truth of the old legends. And they had been a great comfort to her, I know.'

'It is too bad he did not know that,' remarked Lan Ying. 'May-bee he would have been more kind. You know what I think?' she asked, abruptly. 'This Tubbee — he is verree religious; verree sentimental. He is afraid it will make him what you call "sissie"; is it not so? He wishes to deny it to himself, so that he can be a big, strong, hard man!' Lan Ying drew a ludicrously long face, deepened her voice, and raised on tiptoe in a very unsuccessful imitation of a big, strong, hard man. Jack chuckled, but she carried on earnestly.

'My honorable foster-father often said to me that when a man blusters and makes loud talk he is trying to persuade himself he is not a coward — and when he pretends to be verree hard, he is afraid of his own spirit of kindliness.' She queried Jack's eyes for a moment, and continued. 'May not this Tubbee be in a big battle with his own heart?'

'I never thought of that,' said Jack. 'If so, he has his emotions under very good control.' And then, recalling the only occasion when he had surprised Tubby in the performance of a soft act, he told Lan Ying the amusing story of Nancy Prentiss's baby, playing up the scene for all it was worth. It surprised him that she listened with so much seriousness. She smiled, but it was quite apparent that the story was more significant than silly. She made a quick little gesture of full understanding.

'That should settle it!' she declared, soberly. 'Your Tubbee is afraid of his own spirit. He thinks a man cannot be a good scientist — and have any feelings. He is probably crazy. Is it not so?'

Jack studied her lips and nodded his head judicially. If Lan Ying preferred to think that Tubby was crazy, it was all right with him. He had often thought so, himself.

'He may be crazy — at some points,' rejoined Jack, 'but he is a great scientist.'

'You should know,' said Lan Ying deferentially. She was studying his mother's picture now. 'I think she must have suffered, Jack.'

'Not when that photograph was taken, dear. She did, later. What you see there is not pain, but duty; religious duty.'

Lan Ying looked up steadily into his face with appraising eyes, and returned to the picture.

'It is the same mouth,' she said. 'May-bee it should be called a "duty mouth." Verree strong, Jack.'

'My mother's life,' he explained, deliberating his words, 'was singularly devoid of the little recreations and diversions on which most people rely for their happiness. In her opinion, to fear God and keep his commandments was a full-time job. She never had any fun. Religion was her whole occupation.'

Lan Ying's eyes brightened with comprehension.

'And you noticed that, even when you were a little boy, I think, and decided that you would not have anything to do with religion because it had made your mother unhappy. Is it not so?'

'Doubtless. I grew up feeling that the practice of religion was very grim business.'

'But you still had the "duty mouth,"' pursued Lan Ying.
'You needed a Master to serve with all your heart, mind,
and strength; so you became a disciple of Science. It is all
verree clear to me now, Jack. I am glad you showed me the
picture. It explains so many things.'

Jack wished the subject had not come up.

'I am not sure,' he said, defensively, 'that my mother's
life was positively unhappy. I think she found a great deal
of satisfaction in the performance of her religious duty.
That was the aim of her existence. Nothing else ever mattered. Sometimes, when Jean and I were half-grown children in high school, we would bring home phonograph
records of popular songs; and, when we were done playing
them, Mother could be heard — and she had a very good
voice, too — clearing the air of these frivolous sentiments
with some such quaint and doleful ditty as "We'll work —
till Jesus comes."'

Jack's brows contracted in an effort to recover the lines,
Lan Ying regarding him with amused bewilderment.

'One of the verses went, "Thi-yus world's a wil-der-ness
of woe; this world is not my home. We'll work, we'll work,
till Jesus comes; we'll work, we'll work, till Jesus comes;
we'll work, we'll work, till Jesus comes; and we'll be gathered home." Jean and I used to laugh — and then we'd be
ashamed of ourselves and try to make it up to her some way
by being unusually helpful.'

Lan Ying smiled over this reminiscence; then, sobering,
she remarked, 'Of course — that picture of life is not attractive, but — well — there was a promise of nice pay —
at the end of it. After all the hard work, your mother confidently expected to be "gathered home." Now — with
you ——' She hesitated, frowning a little as she fumbled
for the right words.

'Yes?' encouraged Jack. 'With me ——'

'With you, there is no promise of pay — here or elsewhere. Plenty of hard work, day after day. Plenty of other
people helped; their injuries healed, their diseases relieved.
But — poor Jack gets no pay. He does not know the peo-

ple, except by their hurts and damages. No,' she added, after a reflective pause, 'I think your mother was happier than you. She worked — but she was going to be "gathered home."'

'She well deserved to be,' said Jack, gently. 'Let us hope that she was.' His tone suggested that this matter had now been brought to an appropriate conclusion. Divining his mood, Lan Ying nodded approval and smiled her willingness to talk about something less serious.

'Dinner is served,' announced Abbott, in the doorway. Lan Ying's eyes widened with surprise.

'May-bee this is a Chinese dinner,' she ventured. 'All but *you*, Jack.' She laughed. 'I should have brought the mandarin coat, after all. You might have worn it.'

He drew back her chair and seated her with a warm sensation of possessorship, took his place opposite, and for an instant there was a little constrained silence between them. Jack was momentarily indulging the illusion — at once pleasant and painful — that they were together in their own home, sitting down to a customary evening meal. Lan Ying seemed to have read something of the sort in his eyes, for the pensive little smile on her lips welcomed the idea and pronounced it hopeless. It was a very expressive mouth.

She leaned forward and inhaled the fragrance of the dish before her. Abbott was at her elbow now, offering rice wafers. Looking up inquisitively into his face, Lan Ying murmured a rapid and lengthy sentence utterly unintelligible to her host; and Abbott, with a deferential bow, replied briefly. Then she asked him a question which he answered in a word. Her eyes were misty. Jack was bewildered and for a moment felt alien. Lan Ying, collecting herself, hastened to explain with an unsteady voice.

'Forgive me, Jack,' she said, softly. 'But — do you know what this is?'

'Has the flavor of orange; hasn't it?' His tone was purposely casual. 'Some sort of orange soup, I should say — if there is any such thing as orange soup. I never tasted any before. Is it made the way you like it?'

'It is perfect! And it is the first I have had since I left
China. It stirs tender memories of my home, Jack. May-
bee I should not have spoken to your man. I quite forgot
my manners, and told him how glad I was to have it
again.'

'Takes a good while to say that in Chinese,' observed
Jack, with a sly grin. Lan Ying flushed a little.

'I am afraid I asked him if Doctor Beaven really liked
Chinese food — or was he serving it just to humor me?'

'And Abbott said ——'

'Abbott!'

'Yes: His name was Ng when he came to this country and
he changed it to Abbott.'

'How funnee!' Lan Ying laughed merrily. 'How did he
happen to pick that name? Tell me some more about him,'
she urged. 'He does not in the least seem like a servant.'

Jack hesitated, remembering his promise. He realized
now that the mystery of Abbott's name invited explana-
tions.

'You may ask him, when he comes in, if he has any objection to my telling you.'

Abbott reappeared, presently, removed the soup service,
and brought in an exquisitely designed plate of lotus root,
cut in the shape of medallions, cooked with duck and
shrimps. Lan Ying gave a little exclamation of surprise and
delight. While Abbott was serving her, she turned loose on
him what sounded to Jack like one melodious word of two
hundred and ninety-six syllables; adding, immediately, to
her host, 'You do not care, I know, if I speak my own language, for a moment.' Abbott, slightly flustered, had made
no reply. He was serving Jack, now.

'You may tell the lady, sir, if you wish,' he consented.

So, Jack proceeded to clear up the mystery, Lan Ying
listening with rapt attention.

'I wonder,' she said, 'whether he may not have heard,
some time, of my foster-father. The good Sen Ling has
been so verree much interested in the training of young men
for the practice of medicine.'

'Oh yes,' replied Jack, recklessly. 'He knows about Sen Ling.'

'How funnee — that he should tell *you!*' Lan Ying's lips puckered into an enigmatic smile, and it was now Jack's turn to be somewhat disconcerted.

'Well,' he began, insecurely, 'you see ——'

Lan Ying nodded.

'Yes,' she assisted, 'I think I do.'

'Abbott and I were having a long talk about China, and Chinese interest in modern medical research, and I happened to ask him if he had ever heard of Sen Ling.'

'But you did not tell him about me.' Lan Ying shook her head slightly, inviting a negative reply.

'He wormed that out of me,' confessed Jack. 'You Chinese have a trick of discovering what you want to know; and so verree politely too.'

Lan Ying thought this quite amusing.

'It is true,' she admitted. 'The Chinese disarms you with his studied courtesies, and gets what he wants — indirectly. May-bee I can think of some examples.' Her face brightened. 'You might be interested in a story we are all fond of in the house of Sen Ling. Young Sen had been begging to go to England for his schooling, and his father said, "But you have had so little experience. You are a mere boy. How could you hope to take care of yourself among foreign people at your age?"

'And young Sen said, "Will my honorable father give his inexperienced son some test of his poor wits?"

'And Sen Ling said, "It shall be as you wish. You may put me out of this room — by your wits." So, young Sen bowed his head and was thoughtful for a long time. Then he said, "Honorable father, it is difficult. But — if you will go out of the room, I think I can bring you in, by my wits." So ——'

Jack loved the way her lips curved around that deliberate 'So.' The lips pretended to chastise his teasing smile with a brief pout before they continued.

'So — Sen Ling agreed to this and left the room, and as

he went through the open doorway, young Sen arose and
bowed and said, "My honorable father, you have asked me
to put you out of this room, by my wits. I humbly report
to you that you are now out." Is that not delicious?' She
laughed merrily. 'And so typically Chinese.'

Abbott had come with jasmine tea, candied kumquats,
and sesame-seed confections. Jack, vastly entertained by
Lan Ying's narrative, hardly noticed what was being served
to him.

'Sen Ling must have felt rather foolish,' he said.

'No — Sen Ling was verree proud!' she declared. 'That
was a great day for him, to see his child exhibiting some
cleverness. That is where the real glory of the father-son
relationship in China shows brightly, Jack. The father is
not envious of his son, and this makes the son proud to say,
"My honorable father!" The good Sen Ling often said it
was this mutually respectful relationship of parents and
children that had made China one indivisible unit — in its
inner life. I have heard him say he wondered why the
Christian people had not given more attention to the value
of this bond which their great teacher recognized when he
said, "I am in my Father, and my Father is in me."'

'Your good Sen Ling seems to be amazingly well versed
in Christian lore,' observed Jack.

'Deeply,' affirmed Lan Ying. 'You see — he is not religious like the priests, who must collect funds for the
temple. Sen Ling has always maintained that good people,
all over the earth, would believe and practice much the
same principles if left to themselves. But the priests everywhere must raise money to support the temples, so they
make it appear that their own religion is the only right one
and all the others are wrong. They do not improve their
religion to make it seem better than the others; but belittle
the other religions, so that their own may seem better by
contrast. My foster-father, who was just a layman, could
think straight about these things because he did not have
to fret about the upkeep of the temple.'

'That certainly puts all of the contentious sects on the

spot!' muttered Jack. 'I wonder if Sen Ling has not arrived at the seat of the whole trouble. Here are the constructive idealists of every nation, thinking much the same thing, hopeful for peace, common courtesy, social justice, and the good life; but kept apart, alienated from one another, because the priests —' His impromptu speech broke off inconclusively.

'The great Buddha,' said Lan Ying, 'built nothing of a material sort, and what little organizing he accomplished was limited to the guidance he gave to people who wished to walk in "The Way." According to the story, he found God while sitting at meditation under the shade of a banyan tree; and, all his life, after that, he was a homeless wanderer. And the great Jesus, he built no temple. I think he, too, lived out-of-doors mostly: is it not so? Sen Ling often talked about these things. He would say, "This Jesus knew what the temples were doing to men's religious aspirations." I have heard my foster-father recite the story of Jesus' comments when some people of another province asked him which was the right temple for them to attend. He said, "The time will come when neither in your country's temples nor mine will men worship God; for He is a spirit."'

There was a little silence before Jack ventured to respond to this. It had been a very long time since he had given any thought to these enigmatic phrases. They seemed to carry a new significance when relayed from China.

'So — your Sen Ling thinks the temples — all the temples everywhere — really impede the practical usefulness of religion,' he said, his eyes asking for a confirmation.

'May-bee I should not venture to speak for my foster-father, in reply to that,' countered Lan Ying, cautiously. 'It is a strong statement. Sen Ling was always most temperate in his speech.'

'But he thought the priests of all religions were — whether they realized it or not — a menace to the good life; did he not?' persisted Jack.

'I think,' responded Lan Ying, slowly, 'Sen Ling was

unhappy for them. He always spoke of them with respect, sometimes with pity. He often had long talks with them and was verree generous whenever they asked him for support. I think he felt that they were mostly honest and sincere. But they were caught in the machinery of the temple. The ancient traditions held them fast. There was not much they could do about it.'

'Of course — they could go out on their own,' argued Jack.

'And be discredited and misunderstood. That takes much courage.'

'Jesus did it,' Jack found himself saying, somewhat to his own surprise.

'Yes,' agreed Lan Ying, 'but not for long. And not many men are so brave as that.'

Jack wondered if priests shouldn't be as brave as soldiers in an army, and voiced his thought.

'A sincere priest should be willing to lose his life, if necessary. Don't you think so, Lan Ying?'

'May-bee — but many a man would be willing to lose his life, who would not be willing to lose face.'

'You mean — lose face with the organization — and the temple?'

'If the medical profession was making big mistakes, Jack, and you should tear up your doctor's license and go out on your own, what would become of you? May-bee the doctors would make things verree difficult for you. And the people, too. They would lose confidence — and you would lose face. May-bee it is much the same with the priest and his temple. Sen Ling often said that there was no remedy in sight.'

'And what do *you* think about it all, Lan Ying?'

She shrugged slightly and shook her head.

'Why should *I* have opinions about it? Have I not enough little worries of my own, without making myself unhappy over *that?* May-bee that is the way everyone feels.'

'Well,' drawled Jack, with satisfaction, 'the laboratory is

a good enough temple for me. I don't say that our laboratory is better than anyone else's, or that the work being done in other laboratories is futile. In fact, I happen to know that there are plenty of better laboratories than ours and I wish that ours could be improved.' He chuckled dryly and added, 'How's that, Lan Ying, for the proper attitude toward competitors?'

She studied his eyes, thoughtfully, for a long moment.

'May-bee the time may come, Jack,' she remarked, gently, 'when neither in your laboratory nor theirs will you find what you are really seeking. May-bee Science is a spirit, too. I do not know.' She drew a self-reproachful little sigh. 'I think I have been talking too much — about things I do not understand. Please forgive me.'

'On the contrary, dear' — Jack's tone was reassuring — 'I think you have a very tidy mind, and the things you have been saying are of importance. Perhaps I haven't quite kept up with you, though, in what you have just said — about Science as a "Spirit." Wouldn't you like to go on with that, a little way?'

'It is verree difficult,' she replied, her perplexity showing in her narrowed eyes. 'I am not sure what it is I want to say. We were speaking of God as a spirit. He requires no house, no walls, no machinery. Perhaps it is good for people to build a beautiful temple where they may sit in quiet meditation, surrounded by things of great beauty, lovingly made by skillful hands. But God is not limited to the temple. People may find Him elsewhere, for He is a spirit. . . . Now — you have said that Science is your god, and the laboratory is your temple. Very good. But ——'
She floundered helplessly, and murmured, 'I do not know.'

'I think I see what you are driving at, Lan Ying,' said Jack. 'Buddha and Jesus found God out in the open — under a tree, along the road, by a waterfall, on a mountain, in a flower. Now, that's very pretty, and any pagan will approve. Buddha and Jesus found the old temples suffocating. And we scientists find the laboratories suffocating, too. But our case is different. We have to stay there, whether we like it or not, because our instruments of research are there. Our god is not emotional and he does not take any stock in *our* emotions. He deals with hard facts and has respect for us only so long as *we* deal with hard facts.'

'May-bee emotions are hard facts, too,' ventured Lan Ying. 'May-bee your Science-god would like you to look into that.' She smiled brightly, signifying that she was prepared to abandon the serious phases of their discussion. Jack was pleased with her decision to carbonate the heavy talk.

'Wouldn't you like to have some hot tea?' he inquired. 'I'm afraid Abbott has served this lukewarm.'

'It is verree good, I think. Tea should not be served hot. Heat destroys the flavor.'

'Doubtless you have a more sensitive palate than mine, Lan Ying. In fact, I am quite sure you have — in respect to *everything*. I wish I had your neural reactions, your keen sensitivity. Believe me — I could make good use of it in my microscopy.'

Lan Ying smiled indulgently, laid aside her napkin, and made no reply.

'Shall we return to the living-room?' suggested Jack.

'Shall we be seeing Mr. Abbott again?' inquired Lan Ying.

'Probably not. Want me to call him?'

'Please.'

Jack rang the bell and Abbott appeared, bowing.

'Miss Hilton would like to speak to you,' explained Jack.

'How soon will you be going home to China?' asked Lan Ying.

'Two years — three years — four years: I do not know,' replied Abbott, vaguely. 'I have no plans.'

'When you do go, would you find it a burden to call on my foster-father, Sen Ling, in Hongkong, and convey the regards of his unimportant daughter?'

'It would be a great honor,' said Abbott, bowing very low.

'Sen Ling is greatly interested in doctors. You might enjoy his acquaintance.'

'A very high privilege. Thank you, Miss Hilton.'

Lan Ying rose and bowed to Abbott as if he were a prince, and Abbott outdid himself with the bow he made in return. Jack watched this dignified pantomime with amused interest. Then, disregarding him, the two of them definitely went Chinese, Lan Ying delivering a sentence that had the general flavor of an amenity appropriate to a leave-taking, Abbott responding with much dignity.

Preceding Jack from the dining-room, Lan Ying — who seemed rosily flustered over something that had happened— glanced up over her shoulder to remark, 'We were saying "Good-bye."'

'I guessed it was something like that. How do you say it in Chinese?'

'I told him I hoped that he might rest in peace, a verree long time from now, with his ancestors.'

'And then,' guessed Jack, 'he probably said much the same thing to you.'

She did not reply at once; sauntered across the room; studied the titles of his books; seemed eager for a fresh topic of conversation. Jack's curiosity was stirred; and he said as much.

'He was verree polite, Jack, but he did not rest me in peace with my ancestors, as he was expected to. He made me a wish — a verree nice, very hopeless wish.... I see you have the Life of the great Doctor Osler. Should I read it? Is it difficult?'

Jack laid his hand upon her arm.

'What was it Abbott wished?' he asked, gently.

Lan Ying shook her head and continued to inspect the bookshelves.

'Not going to tell me?' persisted Jack.

'No — please.'

'Was it — anything relating to me?'

'To us,' she answered, barely above a whisper.

Jack drew her closer.

'Perhaps he wished that we could be together — always.'
Jack's voice was unsteady. 'Was that it, dear?'

'Something like that,' murmured Lan Ying.

For an exultant moment, they clung tightly to each other.

'I wish that too, darling,' said Jack, deeply stirred.

Lan Ying did not raise her face, even when, with his
hand beneath her lovely chin, Jack would have turned it
to his eager lips. She held her head tightly against his
breast for a moment. Then she gently drew out of his arms.

'Let us not make this too hard for each other, Jack,' she
urged, looking up into his face earnestly. 'We must remember our resolution.'

'I have forgotten it,' Jack's whisper was husky. 'Lan
Ying — Lan Ying —— '

The sharp ring of the telephone startled them both.
Jack frowned.

'I think I'll let it ring,' he said, indecisively.

'You had better answer it,' advised Lan Ying. 'It might
be something important.'

He went reluctantly to the telephone.

'Yes? — this is Doctor Beaven.... Yes, Miss McFey....
Oh — that's too bad.... Delirious, eh?... What's she running now?... Well — that's too high.... I'll be there
presently.

'Damn it, Lan Ying, I've got to go to the hospital. One
of Tubby's patients. I would ask you to wait for me here,
but this is the sort of thing that may keep me tied up all
night.... Now you see the kind of life I live.'

'It is all right, Jack. What else can you do? You must
go, at once. Will you call a cab for me?'

'I'll drive you to the hotel.'

He found her coat, and his own. At the door, his hand
on the knob, Jack turned suddenly and held out his arms.
Lan Ying, advancing, was in them before she was aware.
But she did not draw back.

'I can't go, darling,' he whispered, almost fiercely. 'There
is so much more we have to say.'

'May-bee it is better so, Jack. It has been a lovely visit.

Thank you for being so good to me. I shall be verree glad
to remember.'

She lifted her eyes now to meet his, and he kissed her.

'You said — we must not do that — any more,' whispered Lan Ying.

'I know, darling. We mustn't.' He kissed her again,
and this time her arms crept up to circle his neck. There
was a moment when they were the only two persons in all
the world.

Lan Ying kissed him gently, and withdrew her arms.

'Come,' she murmured, breathlessly. 'You are needed.
We must go.'

He did not release her.

'Life is very cruel!' he muttered.

She laid a small, cool palm on his cheek, tenderly.

'No,' she said, with a little sigh, 'life is verree good.
And our friendship is verree precious. Let us be thankful.'

* * * * * * * *

Perched on a tall stool by the north light in Doctor
Forrester's laboratory, Jack Beaven was examining a smear
provided by the Buckley child. The smear had not been
hard to get, for the infected lesion was draining freely.

Doctor Beaven was unhappy about Martha who, though
not registering quite so high a temperature as she had last
night, was still a very sick girl. But in all other respects the
promising young neurological surgeon was in a state of
unprecedented rapture, warmed and vitalized by the memory of his recent experience. He felt himself in a new world.

It was difficult, this morning, to concentrate on a problem
demanding precision. Jack had let Abbott do the blood-
chemistry but had decided to inspect the smear himself.
His thoughts raced about aimlessly. And as he adjusted
the stereoscopics of the big Greenhough binocular he
whimsically wished there was a pair of small knurled wheels
leading into his head — one directly above each ear —
which might be as easily and effectively regulated for the
focusing of his mind. It was too bad about Martha Buckley,

but nothing so sweetly stirring had ever occurred as the parting from Lan Ying, last night, at his apartment.

How understanding she was! That note, sent to the hospital at midnight by a messenger — who but Lan Ying would have had the thoughtfulness? He had been sitting beside Martha's bed, watchfully waiting for better signs, and the note had come up.

'Dear Jack,' she had written, 'it is likely you may not feel safe in leaving your patient in the morning to see me off on the train. You have enough on your mind without wondering how you are to dispose of me. I am just as anxious as you are that you may do your duty. This comes first. You will never need to explain that to me. Thank you for everything. I shall write as soon as I am home again.

'LAN YING'

Surely a girl of that sort need not be thought of as an obstacle to one's professional efficiency. She would always understand. She would not only understand, but she would offer the finest type of comradely co-operation. He could safely ask her to marry him. The McFey girl, having observed his arrival in dinner clothes, had murmured her regret and sympathy over the necessity to summon him, and he had made short work of her solicitude. After Lan Ying's note had come, he had said to McFey, 'You're tired. Better sneak down and get a cup of tea. Take a half-hour to it. I'll be here.' And McFey had thanked him gratefully, adding, 'I think it is a shame you had to come back tonight!' And Jack had rejoined, in a tone resonant with pride, 'It might be worse. The trouble about these emergency calls is that one's abrupt departure disappoints others. I have been dining with people who understand.' It was a pretty long speech for Jack to make, and McFey had been very attentive; also seemed a bit bewildered, apparently feeling that there was something back of it which might be of great interest. She waited, bright-eyed, for further comments. Jack had obliged her by adding, 'Friends like that are worth having; don't you think?' McFey had nodded enthusiastically and said she certainly did. And then she had tarried a little in the hope that his incredible garrulity might continue, but he had terminated his remarks suddenly with 'Well — hop along now, and have a breathing spell.' After she had left the room, Jack had read Lan Ying's note again. She had said exactly the right thing at the right time. He was very proud of her.

This morning he was still rejoicing. He had sent her a note expressing his appreciation of her attitude toward his job; had closed it with 'You are a wonderful girl, Lan Ying!' Perhaps it was just as well, he thought, that he was unable to accompany her to the station. Their parting had been perfect.

He filled his pipe, and, neglecting to light it, stared out at the gray sky. A few early snowflakes were falling. Jack had never welcomed winter. Slushy streets, bare trees, and a bleak sky depressed him. The drabness seemed to percolate through into one's very soul. It was more difficult to sustain a patient's morale during the sunless days when there was so frail a reason why anyone should make an effort to rise up and rejoin such a dour and dismal world. And then there was the ventilation problem. If there was an institution in dire need of fresh air it was a hospital, and in winter the difficulty in getting enough invigorating air while maintaining a temperature suitable to persons of depleted vitality was almost insurmountable. Any way you looked at it, a doctor's winter was a bore and a nuisance.

But today there was something almost gay about these snowflakes. They did not threaten you with long weeks of tiresome stuffiness but promised to provide an appropriate setting for the comforts of your own blazing fire. It would be fun to hear winter howling around the corners and swishing sleet against the windows, if you had someone you loved sharing this snug security. He had now definitely decided to ask Lan Ying to be his wife. It did not occur to him to wonder whether she would consent. He took that for granted. She had made no secret of her feelings toward him; was cheerfully willing to be his 'friend forever' if that was his wish; would be equally willing to marry him if he proposed it. His firm resolution to remain single, for the sake of his work, had better be abandoned. He could break that resolve now without feeling that he had committed a crime against his own life-plan. It had become clear that Lan Ying, far from interfering with that design for living, would improve his chances of professional success. Indeed, if he were to give her up now the memory of what he had lost would torture him forever. Self-discipline, if it served you to any good purpose, must become automatic. If you fretted over your sacrifices, you had better not make them — so far as your work was concerned. Yes — he was going to marry Lan Ying, as soon as it could be arranged. And it wouldn't require very much arranging.

Lan Ying would be watching these snowflakes from her car-window. Perhaps she, too, would be glad to see them come. Maybe she would be sharing his thoughts, wondering how it might seem to have a home and a hearth of her own. It was not inconceivable that Lan Ying had formed some ideas about his stern resolution on the subject of marriage. He smiled happily over the recollection of last night's glorious events. He had kissed her and she had reminded him of their pact. He was never going to kiss her again. And now he had kissed her. And having admitted that he mustn't do it, he had kissed her again. And Lan Ying, though zealous to keep her end of the bargain, had wrapped her arms around his neck and stood on tiptoe to be kissed again. That's what *she* thought of their lofty aspiration to remain merely good friends. A little shiver of ecstasy ran through him. How ridiculous of him to have imagined he could live without Lan Ying.

* * * * * * * *

That afternoon at four, he left word that he had to go down town on important business. Perhaps it was foolish to do this thing so impetuously, but now that he had come to a definite decision he wanted to record it somehow; wanted to burn the bridges behind him.

It might be some time before he would have a chance to see Lan Ying, but it would be a comfort to prepare for that event. He would carry the ring in his pocket. The thought warmed him. The ring would be hers. He would be carrying something of hers in his pocket; something symbolic of all that they had come to mean to each other.

He had had very little occasion to visit the exclusive jewelry shop in the Walton Building, and they did not recognize him. Nor did he identify himself until it came time to write a check in four figures.

Late that night, wearied by a crowded evening at the hospital, but in a fine glow of pride over his new possession, Jack sat at his desk with the beautiful ring in his hand, holding it in his palm caressingly, slowly tipping it to the light, marveling at its kaleidoscopic moods, its exquisite revelations of lambent orange and green, its sudden flashes of white fire.

Chapter XIV

AFTER dinner Tubby strolled out to the club car, lighted a cigar, and gave himself to the organization of his address to the Medical Society.

Of course they would want him to relate some of his experiences at the Neurological Congress in Vienna which he would be glad enough to do, for the conference had been of immense interest.

Doubtless somebody, who knew him pretty well, would bait him to comment on Bill Cunningham's widely publicized convocation speech. He would have to be careful. Deeply as he resented the intrusion of Cunningham's influence and the inevitable effect it would have on his own work, it would be a serious mistake to betray to that company the exact state of his feelings.

For two reasons, he must attempt to deal with the matter rather casually, as if it were of no great consequence. It would be unfortunate if the New York crowd suspected a serious rift between him and his old crony. And if he lost his temper while talking about Bill's silly theories, it might convey the impression that he himself was under fire and on the defensive.

And neither of those things would be true. Cunningham's invasion would be a seven-day wonder, after which everybody would forget about it and business would go on as usual. It would be a mere flash in the pan. And it wouldn't be true to imply that he and Bill were unfriendly. They had meant too much to each other; it would take more than a clash of opinion to disrupt the old ties.

If he were prodded into an expression of his feelings in regard to Bill and his practice, he must make certain that no word or sign of disrespect or annoyance should creep in. It might be well to give this conciliatory mood a preliminary workout. He would say of Bill Cunningham that he was a royal fellow, a loyal friend. And it would be true. He wasn't going to indulge in any reminiscences, but he would indicate that their youthful association had been mutually cherishable.

Having decided on his course of action, Tubby thought for a long time about the close relationship he and Bill had sustained as fellow-interns. No matter how irritated he might be over the unpleasant situation that had arisen in the Medical College, he would never be able to forget Bill's stabilizing influence on him when he had experienced the shock that had reappraised his world and sent him out to be quite another person than he had thought.

Tubby could meditate on that event now — at a distance of more than three decades — without any emotional discomfort. The deep lesion had been slow to heal, but it had healed. Once in a while the scar tissue around the fracture was a bit troublesome — like a cracked patella on a foggy morning — but for the most part the damaged area was insensitive. Sometimes, when a case like William Mason's came into the hospital, revealing a long grind of unnecessary and inexcusable suffering due to an ignorant diagnosis and futile treatment, the memory of his own tragedy would flare up, and for a few days all persons having business with Tubby were advised to walk softly and humbly in his presence, and speak only when spoken to.

But even on these occasions he did not grieve over Laurel: he would be too much occupied with his hatred and contempt — noisily detonated with the violence of a rusty old bomb accidentally molested on an abandoned battle-field — when some unforgivable case of malpractice reminded him of Doc Fetterbaum.

Tubby did not often think about Laurel any more. She belonged to his youth, and he had early arrived at a maturity that viewed youth as an inconvenience which any sensible person should put behind him with all possible dispatch. Were Laurel restored to him today, as she was when she left him, he wouldn't have known what to do with her. She would have been young enough to be his daughter, with a dozen years to spare. He had not even looked at her picture for ages. All through his college course and the Medical School and the first three years of his internship, it had stood — easel-fashion — on his chiffonier. After her death, he had slipped it into the lower drawer of his desk. He couldn't bear to have it in sight.

It wasn't a very good picture anyway. Laurel was too naïvely honest to take a good picture. She couldn't pose. Her chief charm was her unexpectedness, her childish audacities, her inability to conform to the angular patterns of conventional behavior. If you failed to record this natural tendency to caprice, in doing a picture of Laurel, you hadn't captured her at all. The old photograph showed her in a costume that didn't give her the slightest chance to be herself. They should have got her picture on the tennis court, hot and tousled, with her mouth open, and her amazing vitality popping her seams. Tubby's secreted photograph of Laurel showed her dignifiedly posed as one of the last exponents of the 'Gibson' era; a wasp waist, multitudes of ruffles, big sleeves, a tight collar that rammed her ear-lobes with whalebones, an enormous hat set at a rakish angle that gave the lie to the humorless smile. Doubtless the fellow had said, 'Now — just a little happier, please,' — and had taken off the camera-cap and counted ten, very slowly, while Laurel had become more and more unhappy. Indeed, Laurel in her coffin had been less unlike her vivacious self than Laurel in the photograph.

Tubby twisted in his chair and stared out into the night as the comet he was riding roared and screamed through a little nebula, glanced at his watch, and nodded thoughtfully. This was Springville. The last time he had stopped off was when his father died. There was no reason for coming here any more. Of late years, when he passed through

the town, he didn't even look out at the window; probably
wouldn't have done so tonight if Bill Cunningham had not
revived the old memories.

Laurel's family had moved from Pittsburgh to Springville when she was sixteen. Her father had come as the new
ceramic engineer at the Elmwood Pottery where half the
men of the town and many of the young women were employed. Tubby had been a senior in high school then,
definitely headed toward medicine. In fact, he had been
headed toward medicine since he was twelve. Doc Fetterbaum had been responsible for that decision. Tubby's
mother had been on a decline for many months with anaemia. Had her illness occurred now, it would have been a
mere routine matter to put her on her feet promptly with
a proper diet and skillful dosage of liver. Of course, Fetterbaum couldn't really be blamed for not knowing what to
do about the case. Nobody knew much about anaemia at
that time. Doc had called at the house two and three times
a week, and was almost a member of the family before the
end came. He would keep saying, 'Milt — you must be a
doctor.' And Mother would smile wanly, and listlessly
remark, 'Yes — Milton talks about it sometimes.'

There were two other doctors in Springville, but they
didn't stack up very high. Fetterbaum was busy day and
night. You had to say that for him: he wasn't lazy. (But
neither was Satan.) And everybody liked him; waved a
hand to him. 'Hi, Doc!' He knew almost every man in
town by his first name, and a good many of the women;
had delivered at least a third of the children over a period
of fifteen years; remembered which ones had had scarlet
fever, mumps, and measles; remembered even the names of
their dogs and cats. Doc had owned one of the first automobiles ever seen on the streets of Springville, a Winton
that was cranked in its midriff and had a door at the rear.
He was amazingly versatile, omniscient, ubiquitous. He
sang bass in the male quartet at the Presbyterian Church.
It was a good quartet, too. Doc was also a deacon or something, and whenever a new parson was to be looked for

(they came and went pretty fast), Doc was the scout who went to investigate promising candidates. He was a Mason and an Elk, Chairman of the Board of Directors of the Civic Improvement League, a director of the First National Bank, and President of the Library Association.

His general practice comprehended everything that could possibly be the matter with anybody. His diagnoses were swift, and he never so much as thought of calling a specialist into consultation. Before the Springville Hospital was built, practically all surgical cases — except minor repairs and normal obstetrics — were sent to Buffalo, and through those days Doc's mistakes were mostly limited to the field of internal medicine. Then came the hospital, Fetterbaum's own idea. And there was nothing the matter with the hospital. Everyone said it was a credit to the town, and it would have been so if Doc Fetterbaum had not been quite so fond of surgery. There wasn't anything he wouldn't take a shot at. He had even operated a pineal tumor in the days when there were only four men in the United States (and Fetterbaum was not one of them) who would have attempted the job. Nothing interested Doc so much as to spread out some fellow-citizen and do an exploratory. Had justice been served, his penitentiary sentences for shameless and wanton malpractice — if laid end to end — would have kept him in prison until the Day of Judgment.

But Doc Fetterbaum was so popular that nobody cared to risk a criticism of his professional activities. It was quite beyond thought that the other doctors would protest, to no purpose except to incur a charge of jealousy. Everyone said he was far too good for the town and might make three times as much money in a big city, which was probably true.

Tubby had not thought about Doc Fetterbaum with such calmness for thirty-two years. Fetterbaum was the one proper noun that touched Tubby with the certainty of an electric shock and sent him careening into a red rage. Tonight, for some unaccountable reason, he was remembering the obnoxious fellow as he had known him in his own boyhood. He recalled that he had come as nearly idolizing Doc

Fetterbaum as any human being he had ever met; would have jumped off the top of the Springville water-tower if Doc had told him to. He relived again his sensations when Doc came down to the station to see him off for his first year at medical school. 'Remember, Milt,' Doc had said, impressively, 'I am counting on you. I'll be thinking of you, every day. You're going to be a fine doctor.' And Tubby again heard himself saying, unsteadily, 'I only hope I can be half as good a doctor as you.' (As good a doctor as Fetterbaum — the damn' quack!) That had been quite a dramatic moment. Tubby had stood on the rear platform and watched the little group at the station fade out, saw — and with much pride — Doc's protective air as he moved toward his car with Laurel by his side. He would drive her home and tell her, on the way, that Milt was destined for a bright future. She didn't know, then, that Doc Fetterbaum was going to murder her, one day, with his brassy ignorance.

Tubby let his memories ramble back to the first time he had seen Laurel. There was a flock of young girls sitting on the grass watching the tennis. He had been pretty fast on his feet at eighteen. After the game he was trundling his bicycle across the high-school lawn and had overtaken the bevy of freshman girls ambling toward the street. He had said 'Hello,' impersonally, and they had said 'Hello.' They were all munching peanuts. One of the girls — a taffy-haired, freckled, blue-eyed stranger, whose intentions to be a grown-up woman, one of these days, were attractively on record — had held out her paper bag toward him. 'Peanut?' she said, hospitably. He knew instinctively that she hadn't done it to be fresh. She wanted to make friends; that was all. So — he had helped himself, at her suggestion, and fallen into step beside her.

'What's your name, kid?' he had asked. It wasn't considered common or crude, in those days, for youngsters to call each other 'kid.' Husbands and wives called each other 'kid.'

'Laurel Hughes. We've just moved here.'

'Hope you like us. My name's Forrester.'

'Yes — they told me. Gee — I wish I had a serve like yours.'

'You play tennis?'

'I haven't had much chance to, yet. Have another peanut?' Laurel had steadied the bicycle while Tubby fumbled in the bag.

'Want to come down here early, some morning? Maybe I could coach you a little.'

'Gee — that would be marvelous, Mr. Forrester!' Her wide eyes had shone. 'I'm afraid it wouldn't be much fun for you.'

'Tomorrow — about eight?'

'Tomorrow's Sunday.'

He agreed that tomorrow was Sunday and said they would do it some other time soon. 'Of course,' he had added, 'we might sneak down here about six o'clock, before anyone's awake — if you could do it without getting into trouble at home.'

'My folks wouldn't care, Mr. Forrester. I'll come — if you want to.'

'My name's Milt. Sounds as if your folks weren't very religious.'

'Well — they aren't silly about it. But — Gee! — can I call you Milt? I'm only a frosh.'

'Sure,' Tubby remembered saying, beneficently. 'That's all right, Laurel. I never knew anybody named Laurel. Pretty name; isn't it?'

'I guess so. I never thought much about it. I'll tell my father you said that. He likes my name too.'

'Your father a good egg?'

'Peach!'

'Mother?'

'You bet! She's lovely! There's more difference in age between my little sister and me than between my mother and me!'

Tubby was trying to puzzle this out when Laurel, laughing at his perplexity, explained, 'Gretchen's my step-

mother, and little Gretchen is my small sister: she's three.
You any brothers and sisters?'

'Older sister. She runs the house. My mother's dead.'

'Father?'

'Yeah,' Tubby had replied.

'Oh,' said Laurel. 'Have some more peanuts.'

That's the way Laurel was — even as an inexperienced
youngster. You didn't have to go to much bother when
you explained things to her.

'Oh — he's all right,' Tubby had been moved to say in
an attempt to be loyal. 'A little bit snappy sometimes. I
guess he didn't have much fun when he was a kid. He
doesn't play very much.'

The little knot of girls were waiting at the corner. Laurel
said, 'I must catch up. See you in the morning. 'Bye.'

''Bye, Laurel. Better not say anything to the other kids.'

'But I can tell my folks?'

'Sure! Bring 'em along if you want to.'

'Gee! That'll be wonderful! My father likes me to take
walks with him, Sunday mornings. Thanks, Milt.'

''Bye, kid.'

''Bye.'

* * * * * * * *

Laurel had been too guileless to be coy. From the very
first, she made no secret of her feelings. Within a few weeks
it was an understood fact that she was his girl. The other
high-school youngsters grinned, but it was no fun to tease
them: they were so candid about their mutual devotion.

Looking back upon those distant days, Tubby wondered
if he hadn't been an awful nuisance to the Hughes family.
His own home was anything but interesting. His father
was a dour, taciturn, albeit not ungenerous person who
spent most of his evenings doing difficult problems in
calculus after long days in his greenhouses and gardens at
the edge of town where he specialized in expensive tulips.
Tubby's sister Minnie — christened Wilhelmina — was an
apathetic old burden-bearer at twenty-four, who occa-

sionally remarked that she wished she had never been born, a tardy aspiration which nobody ever tried very hard to talk her out of. Minnie was neat as a pin, and about as entertaining. There was no occasion for frugality, and Minnie could have anything she wanted; but she never wanted anything.

So — young Milt Forrester had spent much of his time at the Hughes's where he presently came to have the same freedom enjoyed by their red cocker spaniel. If the chops hadn't been ordered in time to catch the late afternoon delivery (Gretchen had never taken any prizes for household management), Milt would ride down town on his bicycle and get them, and if Gretchen had forgotten to tell him to order an extra one for himself he would have the thoughtfulness to correct this oversight. But if he was a pest, the Hughes household had not certified him as such; at least, not with enough emphasis to make him aware. He ran innumerable errands, repacked leaky faucets, helped Laurel with her Latin, reported the telephone out of order, drowned the superfluous kittens, seeded cherries, burned leaves, shoveled snow, and split kindling. By common consent he was a member of the family in such good and regular standing that Mr. Hughes — without looking up from his evening paper — would tell him to go down and poke up the furnace, and little Gretchen would nonchalantly back up to him for buttoning.

Except for the inevitable Christmas card from Kansas City, he had not heard from little Gretchen for a half-dozen years, until a couple of months ago when she had written to express her feelings about young Jim's chance to go to college.

There had been a quadrennium, a long time ago, when his correspondence with little Gretchen had required an enormous amount of time and thought. When the Elmwood Pottery had folded up, and Gretchen's father had lost his job, Tubby had sent her to Wellesley, after which she had married a not very promising chap and had drifted out of his life. During her college days, she confided all her problems to Tubby, soliciting his counsel in her choice of studies, her brief but frequent love affairs, and her little jangles with the Dean of Women. She faithfully reported how much she had spent last month, and for what, itemized down to the last nickel. She even sought his advice about her clothes. But after her marriage — which Tubby suspected was not very successful except in the rapid accumulation of a family — Gretchen's letters were increasingly wider-spaced and less difficult to answer. When the youngest of their too many children had died, she had told him all about it, and he had replied that he was very sorry, though he couldn't help feeling — privately — that the baby was probably just as well off to have died before realizing that the family was too large before his arrival. He had wished, afterward, that he had been a little more tender in that instance; but Gretchen's letter had come when he was unusually busy and he had been obliged to dictate his reply to his office secretary.

Tubby drew out his memorandum book and penciled a reminder that he must be sure to communicate with Gretchen this Christmas. Damn it! That was the way it went when you tried to help people turn a sharp corner. Then you had 'em on your hands forever, and they were hurt if you didn't promptly and exhaustively answer their letters when they told you all about their big and little days; their hopes, their fears, and — what was still harder to deal with — their endless expressions of gratitude which placed him in the silly rôle of a sentimental old Santa Claus. If they'd only be content to accept your assistance, dignifiedly thank you for it, pledge themselves to do their best — and thereafter let you alone! Couldn't they realize that you had other things to do besides listening, through all eternity, to their grateful paeans of praise? Soon as you did something for someone — mostly for the utterly cold-blooded purpose of getting them and their perplexities off your mind — then you could expect to have a lot of love and devotion hurled at you, and if you didn't reply with large basketfuls of similar mush, they would send you pensive queries beseeching you to tell 'em what they had done to offend you!

Tubby bit the end off another cigar, and scowled darkly. There was Gretchen's boy, for example. He should have answered that letter without delay. It had been all of two months since this young Jim had written a dozen pages of lushy appreciation from Columbia, addressed to 'Dear Uncle Milt.' Damn it! He couldn't spend all his time writing letters; didn't know what to say to such people, anyhow. Jim's letter had made him feel like a hypocrite. He certainly hadn't experienced any seizures of love for this youngster; had volunteered to help him through college for the practical reason that if he was given a decent education he would be less likely to be a burden on somebody later. And then comes this maudlin letter. Tubby rummaged in his pocket for it; had brought it along, for the sake of the street address; might want to call Jim up, while he was in town. If the fellow should happen to notice, in the papers, something about this Medical Society banquet, he'd probably think he had been abused if he received no communication from his 'dear Uncle Milt.' Tubby opened the letter and frowned.

DEAR UNCLE MILT:

You can't help knowing that what you are doing for me is the same as saving my life. I wouldn't have been afraid or ashamed to work at a trade or behind a counter, but I don't believe I should ever have been very happy, for I'm crazy about electrical engineering and a fellow can't get anywhere with that unless he is trained for it. I am just as grateful to you, Uncle Milt, as if you had rowed out to me in a boat and rescued me from drowning. I never said any prayers until lately. But every day I do that, now. I'm not sure whether I say prayers to you or for you; but I say them, sir, and I think they are good for me, whether they do you any good or not.

Tubby folded the letter, and shook his head. Damn it! You had to do something about a letter like that! But what?

You mustn't call the boy up and say, 'This is Doctor Forrester speaking.' That would give him a chill. You couldn't say, 'This is your Uncle Milt.' Hell! He wasn't going to be anybody's soft and silly old Uncle Milt!

They had done all their switching and bumping in Buffalo and were gathering speed again on the next lap of the journey. Tubby yawned, stretched, and made his way back to his compartment; undressed, laid out his speech-notes on the bed, and prepared to put in an hour's work on them. He wanted this speech to be good. He stacked up a flock of pillows behind him, and attacked his job.

The first entry made him grin. 'Attic treasures.' That would be ample to remind him that he had talked recently with the chief of the fire department, during which conversation he had inquired what was the most frequent cause of conflagrations, and the chief had replied, 'Things in the attic that are too good to throw away but unfit for any use.'

This would make a nice point of departure. Plenty of doctors had their heads stored with old ideas that had cost a great deal in time, money, and mental labor. But, however much had been invested in them, they constituted a hazard. Tubby was going to have a spot of fun here. He would describe the inflammable treasures in the old garret. The more solidly dignified the family, the more hazardous possessions would have been accumulated; great-grandfather's brittle old rocking-chair, grandmother's diaries, Uncle Paul's rocking-horse — all equally useless and harmless until touched off by a stray spark. He wasn't going to elaborate the moral too expansively. The illustration would be able to take care of itself without any preaching. The fact was that the largest accumulation of once costly but now obsolete notions were stacked up in the heads of substantial, prosperous, highly respectable doctors who had arrived at the stage where they never acquired a new idea and never abandoned an old one.

If it wasn't such a painful recollection, he would recite the story of Doc Fetterbaum. But he wouldn't be able to talk about Fetterbaum without getting embarrassingly en-

raged. All the same, it was a case that could be duplicated
today in almost any town or city — the fellow who, by
various philanthropies, civic-mindedness, cordiality, and
tireless exercise of his sympathies, had won the full confidence of hundreds of people, but in actual fact was a
menace to the community because of his brazen ignorance.

Tubby sat for a long time with the notebook open but
disregarded, reviewing that little group of desperate days
when, hastily summoned home by the news of Laurel's
serious illness, he had promptly suspected and then verified
the Fetterbaum blunder that cost her life. She had been
quite unconscious when he arrived at the little hospital.
Fetterbaum, cooing sympathetic phrases, had admitted his
helplessness; and, by that time, there was nothing he could
have done had he been the best doctor in the world.

According to the history of the case, a simple appendectomy, a week earlier, had been so strongly indicated that
any competent diagnostician should have known it at a
glance. But he had stalled along with ice-packs and sedatives. Then, when all the danger-signals were flying so
high and wide that anyone could have seen it was a case
requiring better surgery than Fetterbaum was capable of,
he had waded in and touched off a peritonitis that spread
like a prairie fire.

Of course, nothing that Fetterbaum could have done or
said, in that tragic hour when Laurel went out, would have
soothed Tubby's feelings. But he took the position that
this was just 'one of those things,' unfortunately likely to
turn up once in a while; nobody's fault; something unpredictable. And then Fetterbaum had had the bad judgment
to add, piously, with his hand on Tubby's shoulder, 'It's
our common lot, Milt. We can't be prepared for such sorrows, but they come eventually to us all.'

Tubby's fists clenched as he relived that hot moment.
He had said nothing until now; afraid to say anything for
fear he would impetuously say it all. But Fetterbaum's
attitude of spiritual counselor, at this moment of tension,
was more than could be borne.

'I don't want any of your sympathy!' Tubby had shouted. '"Can't be prepared for sorrows!" You'd better let somebody else mouth that kind of prattle, and ask yourself why you weren't prepared for surgery.'

Doc had stood, pale and shaky, stunned by the sudden outburst; probably the first time he had ever been grilled. Mr. Hughes had taken Tubby by the arm. 'No, no, Milt,' he had muttered. 'That won't help it.' And Gretchen, holding out his hat and coat, and urging him to come now, looked as if he had committed some shocking crime.

'No!' Tubby had gone on, indifferent to their quiet caution. 'No — it won't help it. I know that. He will be doing the same thing again tomorrow. Because he doesn't know any better — and doesn't care. *Butcher! Quack!*'

Doc had made no reply; just stood there, white as the sheet they had drawn up over Laurel's blotched face; pretending he must be patient with the insane sputtering of an undisciplined young fellow's grief. That night Fetterbaum had come around to the house, but Tubby wouldn't see him. His father had slipped quietly into the bedroom where Tubby sat alone, and had said, 'Doc wants to talk to you, son.' And Tubby had replied, 'There's nothing he can say that I want to hear.' 'He has always been mighty good to you, Milt. I'm afraid you'll be sorry.' But Tubby had been glumly obdurate. He was all through with Fetterbaum.

A couple of days later he had to endure the funeral. It was not only a very trying ordeal, but it had changed his ideas about many things which, until now, he had taken for granted without examination.

Tubby hadn't given much thought to religion. The churches were recognized institutions that doubtless served a good purpose.

In his adolescent mind they had been bracketed alongside the school, the public library, the waterworks, and the county court house. As a boy he had gone to Sunday School but had dropped out when he was eleven. There was no discipline in the younger classes, and it made him ashamed to be a party to the weekly bedevilment of a gentle-mannered Miss Runkel who seemed grieved over their disorder and inattention; and, inasmuch as it wasn't much fun to badger Miss Runkel, who never said anything that was of the slightest interest to him personally, he had stopped going. In fact his father, having learned that the place had so little consideration for the elementary decencies, had peremptorily refused to permit his further attendance.

Occasionally, when he was half-grown, he reluctantly accompanied Minnie to the 'socials,' mostly for the reason that she would have a large basket of provisions to carry, and he was expected to help her. He had almost never attended church services, which he felt were intended for elderly people. As for funerals, he knew very little about them: couldn't recall that he had ever listened to anything said on such occasions.

At Laurel's funeral, he listened, and was shocked at the quite obvious impotence of the church in its efforts to deal with so grave a disaster as his. The Reverend Blossom was unquestionably a kind man who went about doing good. Everybody made that comment. He had been in Springville long enough to have earned public confidence and respect, and his name was prominent on all the welfare committees. Mr. Blossom and Doc Fetterbaum practically shaped the policies of such movements in the town.

Tubby's overwrought mind had emerged from its state of stampede and was now prepared for whatever restoratives anybody might offer. His defenses were all down. Nothing that anyone could say today would excite his controversy. He was seriously in need of help.

Mr. Blossom, in the impressive uniform of his sacred office, began reading some very quaint and more or less contradictory sentences from a small black book. Tubby had lifted his heavy eyes and paid wistful heed. He knew it was the church's chief business to handle such matters. He had always known — without anyone's telling him — that the church's 'socials' and picnics and bazaars and amateur concerts, which furnished Minnie with the only diversions she enjoyed, simply represented the church at play. Now he would have a chance to see the church in action; doing its real job; offering spiritual guidance; and God knew he needed it.

'I know that my Redeemer liveth,' read the preacher, impressively, 'and that he shall stand at the latter day upon the earth. And though after my skin worms destroy this body, yet in my flesh shall I see God.'

Tubby didn't know what that meant, so he sat with bowed head and waited for something more intelligible to come along.

'When thou with rebukes dost chasten man for sin, thou makest his beauty to consume away, like as it were a moth fretting a garment: every man therefore is but vanity.'

This couldn't possibly apply to Laurel who was innocent as snow. It was true that the past few days had consumed her beauty, but it wasn't her sins that had devoured her. Laurel hadn't been a bad girl. He could testify to that. She was just a wholesome, happy, good-natured kid. Tubby wasn't expecting the church to tell him why she had died; he knew that: Fetterbaum had killed her, unintentionally, of course, but Fetterbaum was responsible. Fetterbaum was a kind man who went about doing good, up to the very point of performing the real job he claimed as his vocation. And now the church was trying to make out that God had consumed Laurel's beauty as a rebuke for her sins. Or was that what the prophet or somebody had meant when he wrote the little black book? Or was it supposed to mean anything at all?

'For we consume away in thy displeasure, and are afraid at thy wrathful indignation.'

Tubby felt pretty sure that Laurel hadn't known God was mad at her about anything. She wasn't afraid. There never had been a happier girl in the world. As the solemn voice droned on, Tubby could hardly believe his own ears. The church had invited him to come in here for consolation, and it had only increased his mental confusion. 'Every man is therefore but vanity.' What did that mean? — Every man is vain, or every man lives in vain? Probably the latter, for the clergyman had read, 'He heapeth up riches and cannot tell who shall gather them.' Surely a low estimate to place on human effort: it might apply to a rich miser, but it hadn't anything to do with Laurel. Why, reflected Tubby, hadn't the minister read Bryant's 'Thanatopsis' instead? That was pure paganism, of course, but it was beautiful and honest — and you knew where you were. You were a child of Nature. You weren't a frightened child of a displeased god. You were a simple and humble brother of the trees and flowers and rivers. Nature wasn't mad at you. She was carrying out a long-term program of birth and growth and dissolution. You were a member of an innumerable caravan en route to the silent halls of death. Why not accept the decree; and, when the summons came, lie down to pleasant dreams? Unless — of course — somebody had a better suggestion, and apparently the church did not.

Shaking himself loose from his reverie, Tubby had become conscious that the minister was reading now about the future life. The dead would all sleep until a last trump would bring them all out of their graves, incorruptible. In his topsy-turvy state of mind, Tubby was temporarily attracted to the word 'trump,' which he had never heard except under circumstances which seemed to make it rather anachronistic in its present setting. By the time he was through ruminating on this, the service was about over.

The undertaker's people had made several tiptoed trips to and fro, carrying flowers. Their procedure was stealthily efficient. Mr. Blossom didn't have any very definite ideas about where Laurel was going, but the undertaker did. So, presently, Laurel — who had always lived so eagerly, radiantly, joyously — was slowly trundled down the aisle while the organ ground out the most depressing music ever heard.

At the cemetery, the church simply gave the whole problem up with a pessimism so candid and conclusive that

Tubby felt a sensation of utter hopelessness. There didn't seem any good reason for one's living, at all.

'Man, that is born of a woman, hath but a short time to live, and is full of misery.'

Tubby, who had no religious convictions, knew this wasn't true. Life had its problems, but it wasn't quite that bad. If the church had absolutely nothing to say that could inspire or console a man in bereavement, common honesty suggested that it should confess its ignorance and impotence; but surely there was no reason why the church should make things out to be a lot worse then they really were. Laurel's life had not been full of misery. She had been as gay and happy as a lark.

'Deliver us not into the bitter pains of eternal death.'

But that, again, had nothing to do with Laurel. Tubby had turned away, after the benediction, with a sense of heavy depression. Life didn't seem worth the bother. Maybe that was the state of mind the church had hoped to create on these occasions. It said, in substance, 'Your loved one is gone; but, after all, what's the difference? Life is short and full of misery, and everybody would be better off dead.'

He found it hard to resume his normal habits of thinking. He had thought of the churches as belonging in the same category with the public utilities and the various public services. Your house caught fire and you telephoned for the fire department and it came. Maybe it couldn't put the fire out until it had done a lot of damage: maybe it couldn't put the fire out, at all. But it tried. The firemen didn't just stand there, in their uniforms, and sadly remark, 'Oh, well; it wasn't much of a house, anyway. And all houses either burn up or fall down, sooner or later.'

Your beloved died and you went to the church to find out what should be your best course of thinking on the subject. The church had the material property and general equipment suggesting that it was prepared to deal with you on this occasion. But apparently the job was too big. Mr. Blossom was a good man, but this sort of thing was too

much for him. Perhaps he should have said so. Tubby felt
that some of the public services on which people relied with
almost pathetic confidence needed to be looked into. Fetterbaum had back of him a fine little hospital, trained nurses,
plenty of implements — but see what he had done! Blossom, too, had enough machinery and tools — but — oh,
well, what was the use thinking about it any more?

It was good old Bill Cunningham who had rescued him
from complete despair. Tubby had telegraphed, and Bill
had come at the first moment he could effect a release from
his internship duties, arriving two hours after the funeral.
Tubby, dispirited, had met him at the station; and Bill,
after their handclasp, had said, 'I want to go in here and
make a Pullman reservation. You'll be ready to go back
tomorrow night; won't you?'

And Tubby had replied that he had thought of remaining
at home for a week or two — until he felt a little more like
working again.

'You're not going to do anything of the kind,' declared
Bill. 'There's nothing for you to do here — but sit and
brood. And Laurel wouldn't want you to do that. Suppose
she *knew?*'

'Do you believe that?' Tubby had inquired, earnestly.

'Well — I don't know anything to the contrary. I don't
think we're supposed to know anything about it. Maybe it's
part of the game — our not knowing. But — if Laurel *does*
know, I think she'd be better pleased if you carried on like
a good sport.'

They had stopped at the Hughes's on the way home; and
Bill, instead of muttering some sad conventional phrases,
had said, 'I expect you were pretty proud to have had a
girl like Laurel. Tubby has told me a lot about her.' And
Mr. Hughes had brightened a little. And Gretchen had got
out a recent snap-shot of Laurel sitting on the end of a
diving-board in her swimming-suit.

'Great girl!' said Bill. 'You must have had a lot of fun
with her!'

And then they had all talked about Laurel's vivacity

and her pranks and how much everybody liked her, almost
as if she wasn't dead, but merely away on a long voyage.
Bill didn't seem to realize that he was saying the wrong
things in a house of mourning, but the Hugheses realized
that he was only an amateur in the business of offering
consolation; didn't know enough about such matters to
follow the rules; hadn't had enough experience with bereavement to understand that you oughtn't to talk about the
dead as if they were still alive — somewhere. They stayed
so long that Minnie telephoned to inquire whether Mr.
Cunningham had arrived, and left there with the promise
that they would be back for lunch tomorrow.

The family had followed them out to the car. 'Little'
Gretchen — she was nearly twelve then, an elfish, much-
indulged child — was keeping so close to Bill that he gave
her his hand as they sauntered down the walk.

'How long can you stay?' she asked, wistfully.

'Tomorrow night. Have to go back to work, Gretchen.'

'It's awful — Laurel's not being here when Milt is home.'
Her voice wavered and her eyes filled up. 'But she's never
— never coming back.'

And Bill had had the audacity to say, brightly, 'Don't
fret, Gretchen. Maybe you'll see her again sometime.
Funny things happen.'

Gretchen shook her head and dabbed at her eyes with a
soggy little handkerchief.

'I'm going to miss her so!' she cried. 'Laurel was so
good to me. She taught me to swim and skate and play
tennis — and everything.'

'Well — there you are!' said Bill. 'There's a good deal
of Laurel that didn't go away. Every time you swim and
skate and play tennis — and everything, that will be Laurel;
don't you see?'

'I'll try to,' Gretchen had mumbled, brokenly.

Then they had said 'Good-bye' all around, repeating
that they would meet again tomorrow. Tubby had felt
much improved. It seemed that a big weight had been
lifted.

'Glad you turned up, you old bum,' he had muttered. 'God! — but this has been a hard day. And the most awful thing about it all is that it needn't have happened. Fetterbaum practically murdered her.'

'Well — it has happened,' Bill had replied, quietly, 'and you can't unhappen it by being bitter.'

Tubby often thought of Bill's curious invention — 'unhappen.' Whenever, through the years, something decidedly unpleasant or unfortunate had occurred, Bill's phrase would come back: 'You can't unhappen it.'

* * * * * * * *

They hadn't been seeing much of each other for several years. Of course that was partly to be explained by the fact that Bill had his own home. Tubby wasn't a very good visitor in a private home; hated small talk; despised the necessity to chatter for sheer sake of seeming amiable. And then, too, he and Bill couldn't be together for more than fifteen minutes until something would be said to provoke the old argument.

Last time they had met — couple of years ago, at the State Medical Association in Grand Rapids — they had sneaked off to a down-town café for dinner, and had successfully staved off their usual controversy for a whole hour. They had had a good time until they got to grilling each other, Tubby accusing Bill of being a sloppy sentimentalist, and Bill accusing Tubby of being nothing but a high-toned mechanic. They had pretended, when they were done with it, that the raillery was all in fun; but each knew that it was a fortunate provision to have had an eight o'clock engagement in the hotel auditorium.

'How's Mrs. Cunningham?' Tubby had inquired dutifully, when the soup was being served.

She was very well, thank you; very much occupied with social affairs; hopping about among the two dozen things she belonged to; good to the poor, bad at golf, worse at bridge.

'I was just thinking about the time you made her mother

sick,' said Tubby. 'I'd been invited to come along with
you for dinner at the Whittakers'. We were hungry as
panthers, and clawing into our food as if we'd just been
rescued after a month on a raft. And just to make pleasant
conversation, Edith's mother turned to you and twittered
amiably, "Were you given anything interesting to do today,
Doctor Cunningham?"'

'We got quite a thrill out of being called "Doctor,"
didn't we?'

'It was ecstasy! Well — you replied, with your mouth
full, "We operated an abdominal tumor, Mrs. Whittaker;
big one, about the size of that roast." Do you remember?'
laughed Tubby.

'A most unhappy comparison,' admitted Bill. 'I didn't
quite realize what I had done until Mrs. Whittaker pushed
back her chair and excused herself.'

'Yes — and then, after an embarrassing silence, Edith
said she would go and see if she could do anything for her
mamma. And that left us with her old man.' Tubby's
eyes sparkled. 'Do you recall what he said to you?'

'He was a dry old chip, was Professor Whittaker. A man
couldn't teach Geology for twenty-five years, and have
much cartilage left in him. Yes, Tubby, I remember. He
said, "Mr. Cunningham, the next time you perform an
operation on our dining-table, perhaps you'd better just
amputate a leg — or something less mussy than an abdominal tumor." And then *you* said — damn your dis-
loyalty — you said, "Next time, Professor Whittaker, we'll
let Bill be the patient and we'll do some brain surgery."'

'Right!' said Tubby. 'And then the old boy regarded me
with an astringent stare and drawled, "Oh? — I hadn't
realized the student brain was sufficiently developed to be
subject to disease." And you said, "I guess that'll hold you
for a while."'

'But it didn't. You had the brass to go on from there,
chattering about brain structure, so that when Edith and
her mother got back, there you were, delivering an enlight-
ening lecture fresh from the anatomical lab. You always

did stick to your work, Tubby; in season and out of season.'

'Well — why shouldn't I?' Tubby had replied, soberly. 'The surgeon's job is important enough to occupy his full time — twenty-four hours a day.'

'I used to think that,' said Bill.

'And it accounts for your success. If you've stopped thinking that, so much the worse for you. Single-minded devotion to professional duty: that's the idea I try to get into the skulls of the young asses who'd rather study anatomy at the floor-show in the Blue Grotto. Believe *me*, I ——'

'You needn't elaborate,' interrupted Bill. 'It's common knowledge that you're a slave-driver, and proud of it. I wonder if you get the results you're after. Be honest, now, Tubby.'

'Not often; but often enough to justify the method. Now you take the case of young Beaven, my assistant. Brilliant fellow. But it has taken a lot of milling to make him what he is. It's an interesting story.'

Whereupon Tubby had indulged in a detailed recital of the curious relation between himself and his promising junior.

'If you're asking *me*, Tubby,' drawled Bill, 'I should say that you two fools have dragged your old feud quite far enough. You'd better kiss and make up before your quarrel gets to be campus talk.'

'Can't change things now,' declared Tubby, obdurately. 'And anybody interested can easily see that it has been the making of Beaven. When he arrived for his first year he was so indifferent and impertinent that he needed a complete reorganization.'

'And you reorganized him, good and plenty; kept at it; still keeping at it.'

'But can't you see?' Tubby tried to keep his voice from shrilling. 'He has turned out to be the most brilliant student we've had in a dozen years. I rode him hard, and he said to himself that he'd show me. The more I ridiculed him, the harder he worked. I was afraid to take off the heat for fear he would miss the only thing that was driving him — and get as lazy as the rest of 'em. Don't you understand?'

'Well — I hear what you're saying and I know what you mean — if that's understanding. But I don't share your view. I can't see how you could do this able youngster any damage with an occasional word of commendation on his fidelity to you and the job.'

Tubby twisted his head and shook it in prompt negation.

'You don't know this chap, Bill. He's pretty deep, and he has a lot of pride; not the sort to be easily conciliated. Once, not very long ago, when we were doing a tricky bit of pathology together, I ventured an amiable comment and he gave me a stare that would freeze your blood.'

'Perhaps it was just a look of astonishment,' remarked Bill, dryly. 'Sometimes people stare when they're amazed.'

'No — we've made our bed and we'll have to lie in it. I expect to do Beaven every good turn possible, so long as he sticks to his knitting. If he can stay on the rails — the way he has been going — he will be heard from. If nothing turns up to interfere with the program he has laid out for himself, he can have anything he wants and I shall do my utmost to help him to it.'

'Program? What sort of program? What are you trying to make of him, Tubby? Another eminent, highly refrigerated mechanic; like you?'

Tubby snorted, and stabbed at his apple pie.

'At least he'll not develop into a sweet and sticky sentimentalist,' he growled.

'Like me,' assisted Bill, chuckling.

'No offense intended,' said Tubby, 'but your theories are impractical in a medical school.... By the way — do you realize what time it is?'

'I know. We must go. It has been good to have a chat with you again, Tubby. We must do it often.'

But they hadn't done it often. It was tacitly agreed that the less they conferred the more pleasant would be their memories of each other.

Tonight, as Tubby reviewed that conversation, he wondered if it might not have been better if he had taken Bill's counsel and shown Beaven a little more friendliness.

Of course it was now quite too late for any hope of conciliation. He couldn't suggest letting by-gones be by-gones, and take the risk of having Beaven gloat over a decisive victory. It gave him a sickish sensation when he remembered Beaven's cool impudence and the contemptuous defiance in his eyes.

Well — the cub would learn a thing or two before long. He'd find out what sort of position he had maneuvered himself into. The proper procedure now was to leave him severely alone; pay him no attention; ignore his existence; show no concern for anything he was doing; put him in Coventry; let him sweat. One of these days, he'd come creeping back with an apology — and then; well — then — we would see.

Chapter XV

EVERYBODY whose mood reacted to bad weather had found this third day of December very dispiriting. Since early morning it had been raining pitchforks from a low, slate-gray ceiling. The long icicles that had decorated the campus oaks and elms had been slimmed down to mere medicine-droppers. Chimneys debouched sooty coal-smoke into the murk. The street-lights had come on at noon, drawing jaundice-yellow pencil-marks across the wet asphalt.

About two, a capricious wind-storm had risen, increasing in savagery until by mid-afternoon it was running berserk. Faculty unbrellas prudently reefed and jibbed while fool-hardy student umbrellas tugged their shirts off over their bared ribs and defied the gale to do them any further damage. Hissing tires spattered muddy water over soppy trouser-legs and highly vulnerable silk stockings.

All classes were to be dismissed at three-forty-five to permit voluntary attendance at a special lecture in the Medical College Auditorium. Special lectures usually faced a dull market. Medics had quite enough required work to do without bidding for any unnecessary punishment. It was a fairly safe bet that at three-forty-five today whoever had a cosy room to go to would proceed to it with dispatch.

At least this had been Tubby Forrester's private prediction. He had no mean desire to see his old friend Cunningham humiliated, but it would be good for Bill to observe the utter undependability of the young cubs who had cheered his brilliant convocation speech on a fine October day when everybody was expected to be on hand. Great was Bill Cunningham's faith in humanity at large; in medicine men particularly. The sight of an empty hall might be a timely lesson for him. It would help him realize, a little more clearly, what a professor was up against in endeavoring to inspire and instruct a lot of irresponsible crackpots who hankered to wear white duck and be called 'Doctor.'

Tubby had been watching the calendar with uneasiness and perplexity. As the day for this first lecture of Bill's series drew nearer he had tried to think up a good reason for absenting himself. He might have found an apparently valid errand out of town but for the fact that he had just returned from many weeks in Vienna and the more recent jaunt to New York, and didn't care to have the Regents inquiring whether he was still on the University pay-roll. If he remained on the ground, he would have to attend Bill's lectures. He couldn't risk the charge of petty jealousy. But when he considered the prospect of sitting on the platform, pretending to be hospitable, amiable, amused, cooperative, while Bill genially ridiculed the things for which he had so urgently contended, Tubby pinched his eyes and lips tight shut — and shuddered.

It had comforted him a little, this morning, to see the rain. The wheat-fields needed a good soaking in December. It practically guaranteed a fine harvest next season. The farmer legislature would look more favorably upon increased appropriations for the University. By early afternoon the day had become so unprecedentedly bad that Tubby's spirits rose. He was almost pleasant to Romney when time came for the lecture. No one but an irredeemable fool would slosh through this storm to attend an unrequired event in the Auditorium. Tubby was not only willing but almost eager to watch Bill Cunningham confront a dismaying battery of vacant seats.

Always precise in his habits, Tubby knew to the second how long it took to walk to the rear entrance of the Auditorium. At three-fifty-two, Romney boosted him into his raincoat and handed him his umbrella. He marched forth with self-confidence. The anatomical laboratory was shelling out medics into the corridor. Tubby scowled as he watched them scurrying down the stairs; lazy devils; as pleased as little children over a chance to duck their work and go galloping home.

The descending procession broke in two, permitting Tubby a generous open space, fore and aft, on the stairway. Outside, however, where the rain and darkness abolished caste-lines, the eminent neurologist found himself jostled by a milling pack of students, all enroute to the Auditorium. He could hardly believe his eyes. He had a strong notion to return to his office. The storm would be a sufficient excuse. Or would it? Rejecting the temptation, he strode stiffly along, bucking the wind, elbowed by the crowd; proceeded to the stage-door of the Auditorium, glumly grunted to arriving colleagues, mounted the stairs, and came out upon the platform where the members of the faculty were lounging toward the seats to which their respective ratings entitled them. They deferentially cleared the way for him. Shane, who was to preside, beckoned to him. Four chairs were in the front row. Tubby's was at the end. The next was Shane's. Cunningham, on the other side, was talking to Osgood. Bill rose quickly, as Tubby approached, and they shook hands cordially. Then they sat down and Bill resumed his interrupted reply to some question of Osgood's.

Shane leaned toward Tubby and smiled a little.

'We've a capacity house,' he said. 'Very gratifying.'

Tubby pursed his mouth and nodded perfunctorily. It was indeed a capacity house. Biggest crowd he had ever seen at such an event. If a big crowd was any satisfaction, Bill ought to be much pleased. You could collect a big crowd by setting fire to a chicken-coop. If you wanted to estimate the population of the town, have a dog-fight.

The spacious hall was packed to suffocation with half-drowned students, all seemingly in festive mood. There was a general buzz of conversation which Tubby didn't approve. Sounded like a high-school rally. Very undignified. By the Great Horn Spoon, they didn't take any such liberties in his lecture-arena, you could bet your bottom dollar! Tubby was disgusted. A sort of pungent steam exuded from the audience — a noxious blend of damp hair, fresh sweat, hot rubber, soaked leather, carbolic acid, iodoform, and nicotine.

'Very stuffy in here, Shane,' growled Tubby. 'Better have some windows opened and let the stink out.'

Shane, pleased to find an occasion for obliging the chief at a moment of considerable stress, decided to act upon this suggestion. It might placate Tubby somewhat if he could feel that he was giving orders and getting prompt obedience. Rising, he walked to the reading-desk. The buzz died down as suddenly as if he had closed a door on it. The audience lifted its chin attentively.

'It is very stuffy in here,' said Shane, hoping Tubby would note the exact quotation. 'Will the gentlemen near the windows do something about it?'

Nobody stirred. Either there were no gentlemen present (Tubby's guess) or each waited on someone else to pry himself loose, or it was generally felt by those adjacent to the windows that it might rain in on them. At all events, nobody moved though almost everybody grinned. After delaying for a brief moment, Shane, apparently feeling that he had done his duty up to the point of making a fuss about a small matter, decided to proceed with the introduction of the speaker. The size of the crowd, he declared, indicated the nature of the welcome to which Doctor Cunningham was so incontestably entitled. This was greeted with such spontaneous and prolonged applause that Shane thought he might as well let Bill go to it without any additional lily-gilding. He sat down, and Cunningham, bowing to Shane and the faculty, leaned an elbow on the reading-desk, and began.

'It is indeed stuffy in here, gentlemen. And apparently you don't care. Neither do I. The place smells like a dog-kennel, but it reminds me of old times. I would give a great deal to be back in this atmosphere and repeat my student days.'

Then, for no very good reason, there was another round of applause. Cunningham liked 'em; liked even the smell of 'em. They knew his friendliness was honest. He was one of them. They would have fought for him against all comers.

Tubby was disgusted but he was convinced. He pushed his chair about, presenting an impassive — though slightly flushed — profile to the audience. His eyes roved up and down the faculty. They were grinning like so many Cheshire cats. Beaven, too, he supposed. He made another survey of his colleagues, looking for Beaven. His eyes grew quizzical. Beaven wasn't there.

* * * * * * * *

Beaven had forgotten all about the Cunningham lecture. He had gone to the private laboratory shortly after three, and since then time had stood still. He had made a startling discovery. He was not excited. Rather, the revelation had stunned and stilled him. He hadn't accommodated himself to the new idea yet.

In his shirt-sleeves, with a green-visored white linen cap drawn snugly over his close-cropped blondish hair, Jack sat on a tall stool, his rangy legs crossed, his heel hooked on a rung, a cold pipe in his hand, dazedly staring at Celeste who regarded him with reproachful eyes and an occasional shrug. She seemed apprehensive of danger, fearful of being touched; and at Jack's slightest movement she retreated a little, baring her teeth. A lay observer, ineptly opening the door upon this scene of a coatless young Viking in a workman's cap, solemnly exchanging stares with an unhappy monkey, would hardly have suspected that scientific history was in the making here.

Every few minutes the bewildering fact would take a fresh grip on Beaven, as if it were shouting the news at him for the first time. Something inside him kept saying, 'Well! — why do you sit there like a statue? Can't you see what you've got? Don't you realize what this means? What are you going to do about it? Why don't you run out and tell somebody?'

Had it happened a couple of weeks ago, he would have hurried to find Tubby. He couldn't do that now. Tubby would freeze up and declare he wasn't interested in any of Doctor Beaven's projects at present. It would delight Tubby to have a chance to say just that, and add that he was very busy.

After a while, Jack knocked out his pipe on the rim of the stool, and refilled it, Celeste watching him with resentment. The thing was incredible, but it had been demonstrated beyond doubt. It was not a mere coincidence. For the past eight days, Jack had experienced frequent seizures of chagrin when he contemplated what manner of disgust the chief would exhibit if informed that the life of a valuable Macacus Rhesus was being jeopardized in the performance of an utterly idiotic experiment.

Any green freshman medic — Tubby would have snorted — could tell you that if you did a spinal puncture on Jenny Collins, the wretched little alley-rat from up near the reservoir, and injected this fluid into the medulla of Celeste, the susceptible Brazilian monkey, the chances were about ten to one that your monkey would proceed through the usual phases of poliomyelitis. In the final phase there would probably be a localization of the strep. (Only Tubby wouldn't have said strep, but streptococcus; for he hated slang and shop abbreviations.) And then you would get a pronounced lesion, almost anywhere, probably in the nether extremities. But — Tubby would have said, scornfully — to waste a perfectly good monkey in an effort to discover whether the lesion would focalize in the musculature adjacent to the right elbow — simply because the Collins child's paralysis had settled there — was a distressing confession of imbecility. It would be interesting to have Tubby come in here now. It would be amusing to watch his face.

For five days after the inoculation, Celeste had run high temperatures, as was to be anticipated. During that primary phase, she had been alternately restless and drowsy, irritable and sulky. refusing food and resentful of attentions.

Then there had been a cessation of fever, an improvement in disposition, and a partial recovery of appetite. So far, so good. The case was normal and without special interest, as Jack had predicted. He was not concerned with the phenomena displayed through the first 'hump' of the disease. Now that the eighth day had arrived, he was filled with curiosity to see what might happen. Another phase was imminent. There would probably but not inevitably be a paralysis. If so, it might localize anywhere.

This morning, Abbott had been taken off his other duties to keep an eye on Celeste. It was the first time that Abbott had been asked to make notes on an experiment in pathology without knowing what he was looking for. Jack had had two good reasons for not telling him. In the first place he was half-ashamed to let Abbott know what the experiment was about; and, still more importantly, he did not want Abbott's judgment to be influenced by a hint that certain curious phenomena might show up. Had he said, 'Keep your eye out for sensitiveness in the right front leg,' Abbott might have imagined he saw something there. That was the chief trouble with experiments. You started forth with a theory and then observed only such facts as would bless the hypothesis. Nothing unique about that sophistry, however, as applied to laboratory research. Half the so-called wisdom of the world had been accumulated by such adventitious techniques. Rig up your conclusion first, and then catch and break a pair of premises to harness, mount the box, and away we go — with a new creed, a new diet, a new political science, a new theory of social uplift.

Abbott had been told to stay in the laboratory from ten to three, leaving then to attend to his internship duties. He had done so, and had left his memoranda on the table beside Celeste's cage.

Jack's eyes had widened as he read the entries. Item by item, they ran as follows:

10 A.M. — She has been licking her right front leg; not nibbling at it, as to relieve of fleas, but as if tender and sore.

11 A.M. — She is still much concerned about right front leg. Resists examination. Very petulant.

Noon. — Endeavors to bear weight on right front leg but is unsuccessful. She is frightened now.

1 P.M. — An infection seems to be focalizing in right front leg, probably affecting musculature served by ulnar nerve.

2 P.M. — No marked change. Same manifestation as above. P.S. Not very nice day.

3 P.M. — Infection appears to be definitely localized in the pronator teres. P.S. I go now.

The hour-by-hour observations had been increasingly significant, but it was not until Jack arrived at the last entry that he realized the full import of Abbott's discriminating comments. The whole affair had now been boxed into a very restricted area. Little Jenny Collins would probably never recover the full functioning of her pronator teres; and, as for the Buckley child, her pronator teres was definitely out of commission, and right thankful she was, too, that it had lost its agonizing sensitivity.

Of course it was impossible at this moment to make a wild guess about the practical value of this strange discovery. One thing was crystal clear, however: the strep in the city reservoir was of a special type. Hereafter it was going to be a mistake to refer to 'a poliomyelitis streptococcus' as if there were just one breed, as in meningitis. The Mead boy and the Buckley and Collins girls, and now Celeste, had been attacked by a strep that showed an individual characteristic. Whether the information would be of any immediate use was a question that could be answered only by experiment; but, in the study of a problem so baffling as polio, *any* new facts might prove valuable.

Jack wanted to tell somebody at once. He wished Lan Ying knew enough about pathology to understand the importance of this discovery. Perhaps he could write to her about it. She wouldn't say, 'I told you so,' but she would be verree glad that his humane interest in poor Buckley's problems had led to a strange revelation in the laboratory.

It would not satisfy Lan Ying to be told that the discovery was accidental. Lan Ying didn't believe in accidents. Such revelations were handed to you by Somebody from Somewhere; part of a Plan, may-bee.

Celeste whimpered and elevated her upper lip unpleasantly.

'Too bad, old lady,' muttered Jack, offering her a drink of water which she testily refused. 'It hurts — but you're doing something fine for your human posterity, if that's any comfort to you.'

* * * * * * *

At half-past five, Jack decided to call it a day. Peeling off his shirt, he went to the capacious porcelain basin in the corner and began a thorough scrubbing up. Polio wasn't something to be trifled with, not even in its secondary hump; not even by pathologists.

The telephone rang and he answered it.

'Beaven? This is Cunningham.'

'Good!' said Jack, suddenly swept with embarrassment over his failure to attend the lecture. 'Where are you?'

'At the hospital. I've a message for you.'

'Thanks. I'll be right over. Ten minutes.'

Cunningham's voice lowered.

'If you don't mind, I'll come up. It's rather a private message.'

'Very well. I'll wait. Find your way, all right?'

'Sure.'

Jack began putting on his clothes. Private message, eh? Now what could Bill Cunningham want to tell him privately? Something about Lan Ying? Something about Tubby? He opened the door.

Presently he heard footsteps in the anatomical laboratory. Cunningham's big frame filled the doorway. He was well dressed in gray tweeds and wore a companionable smile. They shook hands.

'Missed you,' said Cunningham, playfully reproachful. 'Did Tubby give you some difficult pathology to do, so that pure science might be going forward while sentiment was raging?'

'To tell the honest truth,' replied Jack, contritely, 'I forgot about it. And when you know why I forgot about it, you'll forgive me.'

Cunningham slapped Jack on the shoulder and told him to skip it. 'What I came to tell you, Jack — Audrey Hilton's in town. Thought you'd like to know.'

Jack's face brightened.

'How come?' he asked, mystified.

'Well — Edith decided at the last minute that she wanted to come with me. Audrey happened to be at the house for luncheon. Edith said, "Why don't you go along? You can be company for me while Bill is busy at the Medical College." She was a bit reluctant, but Edith talked her into it.'

'That's — that's fine,' stammered Jack. 'Thanks.'

'You see — Audrey gets pretty lonesome up there, and Edith felt it would be good for her to have a change of air.'

'Quite right, sir. It was a happy thought.'

'What are you doing this evening, about dinner-time? Want to join us at the Livingstone?'

'*Do* I?' Jack was radiant.

'See you at seven, then.' Cunningham put on his overcoat. 'Shane's waiting to drive me down.' He stooped and peered into Celeste's cage. 'What you got there — besides a sick monkey?'

'Polio. Let me tell you something. A strange thing has happened. We've had three polios from the same district. All developed a paralysis in the right arm. I have suspected contaminated water. I did a lumbar puncture on one of the cases and gave it to this monkey. Look at her!'

Celeste was nursing her right elbow, and whimpering. Cunningham put his hat down on the table and looked for a long minute. Then he straightened, stared at Jack in a sort of daze, and said, under his breath, 'You don't believe that, do you? It doesn't make sense!'

'That isn't what ails it, Bill,' declared Jack, unconscious of having called Cunningham 'Bill' for the first time. 'The

baffling thing about it is that it *does* make sense! Look —
let me show you. It will only take a minute. I want you to
have a glimpse at these case-histories.'

They lined up at the tall desk, and Jack spread out three
sheaves of papers.

'Now we're not going to bother about anything up to the
time of the actual localization of the paralysis in each of
these cases. Here's the first one.'

Ten minutes passed; fifteen; twenty. Cunningham read
on. The telephone rang. Shane said, 'Is Doctor Cunningham ready to go?'

'I'll see, sir.' Jack put his hand over the phone and said,
'It's Doctor Shane. Shall I tell him to wait?'

'What?' asked Cunningham, from a long distance. Jack
repeated the question.

'Tell him to go on without me,' mumbled the other, taking up the third sheaf of reports.

'Better take off your coat,' advised Jack. 'It's hot in
here. Celeste doesn't like drafts.' He laid a hand on
Cunningham's overcoat collar, and he let Jack tug it off his
shoulders without lifting his eyes from the paper. At seven,
the telephone rang again and the office said Mrs. Cunningham was inquiring for her husband. Was he there? He
answered the phone.

'Sorry to be late, dear,' he said. 'I'm with Jack Beaven.
We'll both be over there in a half-hour.'

'What has kept you so long?' Jack heard Edith say.
'You must be very tired. Is anything the matter?'

'No — nothing is the matter — but something very important has happened. Beaven has just come upon a new
fact about polio that will put the literature on that subject
into the museum.'

'What does Forrester think about this?' asked Cunningham, returning to the desk.

'I haven't told him,' admitted Jack, his eyes averted.

'You haven't *told* him!'

Jack shook his head.

'Tubby refuses to have anything to do with me. Ignores

my existence. Waiting for a good chance to have me fired.'

'What's the big row?'

'Well' — Jack hesitated for a moment, reluctant to air the details of their quarrel — 'It's nothing new. It has been cumulative. Lately it came to a head. Tubby pestered the worm until it bit him.'

Cunningham nodded and said he could understand that.

'But,' he expostulated suddenly, 'you can't leave Tubby out of *this*. You've got to tell him! You'll break his heart.'

'Heart?' echoed Jack, bitterly.

'Sure! Tubby has a heart. That's his trouble. He has been at war with his own insides for years. It all dates from the time he lost his girl; shocking case of malpractice by a doctor who knew everything but medicine and surgery. It did something to Tubby. He went crazy on the subject of incompetency in the profession. It's his life mission now to train men to be scientists. That's why he's such a slave-driver. But — Tubby is really a soft-hearted fellow, when you get to know him.'

'How long does that take?' inquired Jack, dryly. 'I've hardly been out of his sight for nine years. . . . No, sir; I'm not going to invite another insult from Tubby Forrester. He said he had no further interest in me or my work. So be it. And if he has to learn about this polio experiment when he reads it in the medical journals, he won't have anybody to blame but himself.'

Cunningham laid a hand on Jack's shoulder and looked him squarely in the eyes.

'I shouldn't do that to Tubby if I were you. All he lives for is his professional pride; his reputation as a scientist. Don't make him look like a monkey. It would kill him.'

'He needs a few killings; damn him!'

They were at the laboratory door now, Jack impatiently rattling his keys, eager to have done with the unpleasant discussion.

'Your animosity goes pretty deep, my boy,' warned Cunningham. 'Better get rid of it before it becomes malignant.'

'How do you mean — "malignant"?' growled Jack.

'A grudge is like a parasitical growth. Passes through much the same phases. In its primary stage it is usually benign. Operation is simple, safe, effective. But if you let it eat into you deep enough, it becomes inoperable.'

'Rather a fantastic metaphor,' muttered Jack, dryly.

'It's not a metaphor! It's a sound scientific fact! An incurable hatred is a malignant disease. I'd as lief have an inoperable cancer!'

'Shall we go?' snapped Jack, restlessly.

'Yes — but just one more thing, and then I'm ready to drop the subject. You know, maybe better than I, the part that the endocrine glands play in all our mental states and our consequent behavior. Sudden apprehension of danger throws into the blood-stream a secretion that serves as a stimulant and an astringent, very useful in the event of a fight or a flight. But if this sense of fear and danger is prolonged, this constant glandular secretion changes a man's character; makes him furtive, stealthy, suspicious, antisocial. You believe that; don't you?'

'Yes, sir,' agreed Jack. 'That's a fact. And then—what?'

'It is also a fact, as you very well know, that hot indignation releases into the blood-stream secretions of a similar nature; varies only in that it contains less stimulant and more astringent; tightens a man's fibers for the defense of his rights, his self-respect. But — if that indignation settles into a permanent grudge, you get much the same effect produced by prolonged fear.'

'Nothing personal, I hope,' said Jack, ironically.

'No — not yet,' said Cunningham, soberly, 'but — I thought I'd remind you that this is a fact.' His voice dropped to a tone of kindly entreaty. 'Don't be miffed, Jack. I'm much interested in your welfare. You believe that, too; don't you?'

After a thoughtful moment, Jack's moody face cleared.

'Yes, Bill,' he said, warmly. 'I know that. And — thanks for the tip. Sorry I was slow to take it.... Come on. Let's go.'

They hurried down to the dark and muddy parking-lot and climbed into Jack's roadster. By the time they had reached the Livingstone garage, they were in lively spirits, Jack full of suppressed excitement over the prospect of seeing Lan Ying; Cunningham rejoicing in the memory of his reception at the Medical College and anxious to share it with Edith.

Their dinner companions were waiting for them in the lounge.

'It's about time!' said Edith, maternally, giving them each a hand.

'My fault,' admitted Jack, breezily, as he pressed toward Audrey. 'So glad you're here, darling,' he said, grasping her extended hands. 'You're very beautiful.'

'They wanted me to come,' she explained, softly. 'I hope I shall not be a bother. I know how busy you are, Jack.'

Edith and Bill joined them, arm in arm.

'Did you ever see anything lovelier, Jack,' challenged Edith, 'than our Audrey — in that coral gown?'

'Gorgeous!' exclaimed Jack; then, remembering his manners, he added, 'And I think your black velvet is stunning!'

'Rather!' boomed Cunningham, loyally.

Edith negligently flicked protesting fingers.

'A woman who can't wear black velvet,' she drawled, 'can't wear *anything*.... Come, Audrey, let's feed the animals while they're still in a good humor.'

She and Bill led the way into the dining-room. The head-waiter, preceding them, had drawn back two chairs for the ladies. Edith archly ignored hers and moved to the next one.

'I'm not going to sit away across the table from Bill,' she explained, when they were seated. 'I haven't seen him for such a long time — and we might want to hold hands.' She gave Jack an impishly meaningful wink. Her husband, noting this by-play, remarked, out of the corner of his mouth, 'Next time, I'll leave you at home.'

Unwilling to be teased, Audrey laid her small hand, palm

up, beside Jack's. Promptly meeting her mood, he wrapped
his strong fingers around it and smiled into her eyes, Edith
and Bill following the little pantomime with silent amusement.

'Very nicely done,' approved Cunningham. 'It's your
round.'

'Pish!' said Edith. 'It's no fun to hold hands — on top
of the table.'

Apparently, they weren't going to be embarrassed by
any reluctance to see the little game through. Edith said
'Bravo!' when Jack, undaunted, tugged Audrey's hand out
of sight. The next instant, her smile had an expression of
bewilderment as she noted the sudden change in Audrey's
face. Audrey wasn't playing now. Her mobile lips had
rounded into an inarticulate 'Oh!' Then she slowly turned
her eyes to Jack and gave him a misty, tender, little smile.
His face was very sober, his eyes full of entreaty. Bill and
Edith were holding their breaths. Jack and Audrey seemed
not to realize that they were being observed. They were
alone together.

'Yes?' whispered Jack.

'Of course!' whispered Audrey.

Jack drew a long, happy sigh.

'Well — for the love of —— What's going on over
there?' exploded Cunningham.

Audrey, her face illumined, pressed the back of her fingers
against her lips; then extended her hand for inspection.

'How wonderful!' murmured Edith. 'Bill — they're
engaged! Look! And you never told us!'

'When did *this* happen?' asked Cunningham, lifting
Audrey's hand to the light.

Audrey glanced at Jack, and they both laughed a little,
rather nervously.

'Just now,' said Jack, proudly.

'Jack does funnee things,' said Audrey. 'Is it not so?'

'*I'll* say he does funnee things!' said Edith.

Cunningham pointed a finger across the table.

'Do you mean to say,' he demanded, 'that you had the

nerve to buy an engagement ring and put it on a girl's hand in a public dining-room — without knowing whether she would accept it?'

'It was not quite that bad,' murmured Audrey.

'Bless you!' said Jack.

Cunningham quietly muttered that he'd be damned, pinched his glasses on his nose and picked up the menu-card, the waiter at his elbow having sighed audibly.

'And so will I,' agreed Edith. 'My William and I will both be damned — and seeing we have to eat, in the face of this — this cataclysm — I'm having the cream of mushroom soup.' She turned to Jack. 'It won't make any difference what *you* take, my child. It will taste like ambrosia, I expect.'

The dinner had eventually been ordered and, with a good many interruptions, eaten. Doctor Cunningham had relieved the emotional stress by drawing, with his wife's help, an hilarious picture of how *he* became engaged. How, having once refused him sternly, Edith had taken him to walk in the park on a Christmas Eve, had lured him to a secluded but snowy bench, and had proposed to *him*, had kissed him soundly ('What a pity there are so many people in this dining-room!'), and had announced the engagement to her family before he had recovered consciousness!

That story, interesting though it was to the Cunninghams, was completely lost on Audrey and Jack. Those two young persons were dwelling in a rosy world of their own, which generated its own light and needed no illumination from any other star.

'Edith,' said Doctor Cunningham, with a wink at his wife, 'do you notice that all the waiters walk on their hands?'

(Darling Audrey, why did we waste so much precious time?)

'Yes, Bill, and the roof is falling in, too.'

(O Jack! I am so happee!)

'And — look, Bill! Here comes the fire department!'

(The ring fits, doesn't it, darling?)

'Doctor Cunningham, you and I are the most superfluous people on earth!'

(Yes, it is exactlee right, everything is exactlee right.)

'Never mind, Mrs. Cunningham! We have each other!'

(Beloved! Beloved!)

When the dessert had been disposed of, and the coffee poured, Cunningham thought it safe — and perhaps advisable — to bring the lovers back to earth. Pocketing his glasses, he said, 'This has been a very eventful day for Doctor John Wesley Beaven. He's engaged to be married, and he has made a spectacular discovery. I think you girls should hear about this polio experiment.'

He launched upon the story, feeding it to them in lay language, so far as possible; occasionally pausing to explain some difficult phase of the pathological procedure. When he was done with it, Audrey turned to Jack.

'And how did you discover that it was due to the bad water?' she inquired.

'That's a long story,' he replied, reluctant to get into it.

'Please,' begged Edith.

So — he told them about Thomas Buckley's confession; reviewed the circumstances of the rather dramatic interview that had produced Buckley's tale of the stolen plumbing; brought the story down to date — and added, 'Now you know as much as I do.'

'What do you intend to do about it, Jack?' asked Edith, apprehensively. 'You're dealing with some mighty tough characters. Better be careful.'

'Of course,' agreed Jack; 'careful, up to the point where prudence might interfere with the proper treatment of these cases. There's a boy up there who should be in the hospital.'

'That's the City Health Department's job; isn't it?' inquired Bill.

'Ordinarily — yes,' assented Jack. 'And if I can't get the Mead child under proper treatment, I may have to call in the authorities. The Meads, I understand, are peculiar. I should like to save Buckley from the penitentiary if possible; not a very attractive fellow, but he has been badly used.'

'If the Health Officer comes into the picture, will you have to tell him about the irregular plumbing?' asked Edith.

'He'll find it out,' put in Bill, 'if he presses the proper investigation.'

'Then these hoodlums will think you reported on them,' said Edith. 'Isn't that a rather dangerous risk?'

'Well — we can't be thinking too much about that,' said Jack. 'If we can get along without exposing the plumbing scandal, all well and good. If we can't, it will have to come out.'

'We don't want to see Jack hurt,' said Edith. 'Do we, Audrey?'

Jack found himself curious to hear her reply, for she had taken almost no part in the conversation. He was surprised to find her face alight with pleasure.

'No — we do not want to see him hurt,' said Audrey, after a little delay, 'but — we are verree proud: is it not so?'

Jack felt a glow of mingled satisfaction and embarrassment.

'I hope,' he said, casually, 'that I can get through this affair without having to be a hero.'

They had finished their coffee and were about to retire from the dining-room when a party of a dozen or more men filed in and gathered about a table obviously reserved for them.

'The Regents,' said Jack, in a whisper. 'Today is their monthly meeting.'

'I see Tubby's with them,' observed Bill.

'And he has recognized us,' said Edith. 'He gave us a good looking-over when he came in, and appeared to be unhappy about us. I think he might have come over to say "How do you do?" to me — the ole meanie.'

'That's because I'm with you,' explained Jack.

* * * * * * * * *

At the hour of Doctor Cunningham's clinic, next day, Jack was endeavoring to reason with the Meads. If he

could get the boy Donald back into the hospital or even
under proper medical attention at home perhaps there
would be no necessity for stirring up the City Health
Officer to an active interest in the matter which had become
so annoyingly involved.

He found the Meads obdurate. They belonged to a silly
little sect that enjoined them against any resort to medical
aid. It was true that they had given their grudging consent
to Donald's hospitalization a few weeks ago, under heavy
pressure by the neighborhood, but remorsefully maintained
now that the little boy's lame arm was doubtless a divine
chastisement for this temporary breakdown of faith.
Everything that happened, deposed the fanatical Mrs.
Mead, was the will of God, including infantile paralysis —
'if that's what this is.' Donald was sick because they had in
some way offended God. Mr. Mead added that he and his
wife were in daily supplication that God's face might again
shine upon them, so that Donald's lame and useless arm
would be made whole. They further remarked that Doctor
Beaven himself would be well advised to seek the Lord
while it was yet day, though they weren't very optimistic
about the success of this recommended quest, for it was
quite possible that Doctor Beaven had sinned away his day
of grace.

Reluctant — for a couple of excellent reasons — to push
the plumbing affair out into the open daylight unless forced
to do so, Jack patiently explained that what Donald's arm
needed, at this stage of his trouble, was complete rest,
nourishing food, and the sort of nursing to be had only in
a hospital. It wouldn't cost them a cent. That's what the
hospital is for, he said. And this business of urging the boy
to exercise the damaged arm in the hope of restoring its
strength was the worst thing that could happen to him.

At one stage of the interview, Jack felt that his argument
was making an impression. The Meads glumly listened.
Jack warmed to his task. When he came to the first full
stop, hopeful of having won their consent, Mrs. Mead
quietly but firmly declared that Donald's case was none of

Doctor Beaven's business; that they hadn't asked for his advice; that he had better return now to his ungodly interference with God's will and leave His true believers in peace.

Jack then rose to go, remarking, 'Your attitude leaves me no alternative but to inform the Health Officer, Doctor Yarnell. It will be his responsibility, after that. If you can talk him into permitting Donald to remain here at home, I shall wash my hands of the whole affair. If he insists on better care for Donald, you will be expected to obey his orders.'

'We are taking our orders from God,' said Mr. Mead, fervently.

'I think Doctor Yarnell will have something to say about that,' replied Jack, trying to suppress his exasperation.

Returning to the hospital shortly after five, he put through a call to Doctor Yarnell, briefly reporting the situation at the Mead home, but omitting any reference to the bad water or the pirated plumbing. The main thing was to get Donald under treatment. Buckley had promised to shut off the water. The neighborhood would return to the use of the well.

Young Yarnell, eager to exhibit his efficiency and give a good account of himself to a Medical College faculty member, lost no time in performing his errand; hustled Donald Mead to the hospital; bustled about through the neighborhood; breezed back to his office in the City Hall; encountered a couple of reporters. The story broke too late to catch the evening papers, but it made the eight o'clock news broadcast. There had been several cases of infantile paralysis in a shabby little district near the reservoir; cause unknown. The City Health Department was making a thorough investigation to determine the origin of the epidemic.

Of all this, however, Jack was unaware. Having made his report to Yarnell he considered his duty done for the present. Indeed, the whole matter had been dropped from his mind, temporarily. He was entertaining Lan Ying and

the Cunninghams in his apartment that night. A caterer
had been secured who had promised to attend to everything.

Arriving home at six-thirty, Jack had been pleased to see
that preparations for dinner were progressing in capable
hands. He went about through the apartment making sure
his house was in order. Lan Ying would unquestionably be
viewing his quarters tonight with a new interest. Perhaps
he might read in her eyes a wish that certain changes could
be made. Maybe she would be reluctant to alter anything.
It might be good sense to dispose of all this household tackle
with one ruthless swoop and let Lan Ying start at scratch
in the fascinating task of equipping a home. Well — they
could begin their life together here, and plan for the future.

The guests arrived at seven and were shown to his bedroom to dispose of their coats. Jack and Bill returned to the
living-room where Edith immediately joined them.

'Audrey,' she remarked casually, 'is having trouble
getting her galoshes off. It's a man's job, really.'

'Of course,' agreed Jack. 'I shall go to the rescue.'

When he had disappeared, Cunningham cupped his hand
under his wife's chin, and looked her in the eyes with a pretense of severity.

'You are a sweet little liar,' he rumbled. 'Audrey didn't
wear galoshes.'

'She should have,' said Edith. 'I told her to.'

'I should be interested in knowing what sort of yarn you
invented to detain her.'

Edith was sauntering across to the bookcases, Bill trailing
along after her.

'It's really none of your business, Doctor Cunningham,'
she answered negligently, 'but, remembering what happened
to the curiosity-cursed cat, I'll tell you: I said that Jack
wanted to see her for a moment alone.'

Cunningham nodded and said he supposed that statement wasn't so far from the truth. After a few moments, he
glanced at his watch and remarked, 'Think they'll be back,
or should we tell the help to serve dinner?'

Presently they drifted in, both talking at once and putting on a fairly good show of self-possession.

'Do sit down, won't you?' said Jack with exaggerated heartiness. 'I've been telling Audrey to make herself at home — as we used to say when I was a boy.'

After the manner of a lint-picking mother, Edith solicitously tugged out the handkerchief that peeked from his breast pocket, and flicked at a little round patch of white powder on his coat, murmuring sweetly, 'And how she did!'

'Edith,' said Edith's husband, sternly, 'you are unbearable.'

Dinner was announced then, and they proceeded to the little dining-room. Audrey noticed that at the place assigned to her there was a small glass bell. The Cunninghams observed it too and smiled.

'If I am the hostess, Jack,' said Audrey, 'may I ask Doctor Cunningham to say the blessing?'

'Please,' said Jack, bowing his head. It would be interesting to hear Bill's Latin grace again.

Cunningham hesitated for an instant and then said, impressively, 'God bless this new home. Amen.'

No one said anything for a little while. Then Edith remarked soberly, 'Some day soon, you two will get a license and have a legalized wedding ceremony, but I have a feeling that Bill has just now married you.'

'You are both verree good to us,' murmured Audrey.

At nine — the four of them were in the living-room — the telephone rang and Jack heard the terrified voice of Thomas Buckley.

'It's out!' piped Buckley.

'What's out?' asked Jack.

'This young smart aleck Yarnell got it out of Collins. And then he talked to old man Bowers. But neither of them knew the pipe had been stolen — so that part of it wasn't spilled. Then he asked my wife what she knew about it and she told as how I had helped with the plumbing job. Told about Billows, too. It was on the air an hour ago. Billows won't waste much time in making a get-away, but he's a very mean fellow. He'll find time to pay somebody off for squealing. What shall I do?'

'Do nothing — for the present,' advised Jack. 'Don't think of running away. That would amount to a confession of guilt, and you're in enough trouble without announcing that you're afraid to answer questions. Tomorrow, you and I will see Doctor Yarnell, and I shall tell him you confided the whole story to me.'

'That sort of leaves you out on a limb, don't it, Doc?' Buckley's tone was solicitous.

'A bit awkward, yes; but I'm not going to let you down. Come to the laboratory, early tomorrow morning, and we will talk it over.'

For a moment after he had hung up, Jack remained at his desk, debating the course he should take. Perhaps Cunningham could provide some good counsel. He returned to his seat beside Audrey on the davenport. The three of them couldn't help knowing there had been news of a disturbing nature.

'Well, everybody in the world has heard the story about the irregular plumbing,' said Jack, 'so we don't have to worry any more whether to report it or not. It was in the news broadcast tonight. Doctor Yarnell nosed it out, suspects that the contaminated water may have caused the polio, but doesn't know that the pipe was stolen. Buckley is in a dither for fear his crooked friend Billows — who lives in Detroit — may leap to the conclusion that the whole story has been told. He thinks Billows, who is a hot-headed, reckless badman, may come popping over here before the law gets after him, and settle his account with his former neighbor. I have told Buckley that I would meet him in the morning and make an effort to square him with the Health Department.'

'But that doesn't square him with this Detroit hoodlum,' said Cunningham. 'If anything, this Billows fellow, when he learns that Buckley has turned state's evidence — or what amounts to that — may have an additional reason for avenging himself.'

'Was your name mentioned in the broadcast?' asked Edith.

'I don't know. Probably not.'

'I hope you manage to keep out of this mess, Jack,' she said, anxiously.

'But he'll have to stand by this poor devil Buckley,' said Cunningham. 'Buckley's the man who made it possible for Jack to do his polio experiment.'

'I think that, too,' said Audrey, softly.

Jack slipped his hand along the cushion to hers. Audrey loved serenity, but she was no coward. His love for her deepened. A woman of such fiber, he felt, would bring out all the strength that a man possessed.

* * * * * * * *

Buckley did not appear the next morning, and when four o'clock had come without tidings of any sort, Jack decided to drive up and see how the land lay.

Mrs. Buckley was alone and apprehensive that something had happened to Thomas. He had arrived home about ten-thirty, last night, after she had gone to bed. She had been drowsily conscious that he had sat for a long time reading a newspaper. About two, she had roused; and, noting that Thomas had not yet retired, went out into the little living-room to investigate. And Thomas was not there.

'No,' she replied, when Jack wondered whether Thomas ever prowled about in the night, 'there was no place for him to go at that hour. Of course, he was worried. He might have gone out to take a walk; but it was raining. I'm scared about him, Doctor. I'm afraid he has come to some harm.'

'If Thomas had any reason for wanting to run away,' said Jack, 'where would he be likely to go?'

Mrs. Buckley pursed her thin lips cautiously.

'He had no cause to run away,' she replied. 'Not as I know of.'

Jack believed her. She wasn't quite bright enough to deceive anybody. Thomas had not told her about the stolen pipe or the Billows menace; probably had realized that the secret wasn't safe with her.

'Maybe I'd better notify the police,' she added, confirming Jack's belief that she knew nothing of Thomas's culpability.

'I should wait a little, if I were you,' he advised. 'Thomas may show up at any time. If he does, please let me know. I suppose you have inquired in the neighborhood.'

'Yes. I guess everybody was to bed early, except over at the Collinses', and they hadn't heard anything out of the ordinary. Mrs. Collins was quite sick last night.'

'Anything serious?' asked Jack.

'Mebby. She's very miserable. Sick to her stomach today; something awful! — what time she isn't just a-layin' there, asleep with her eyes open; lots o' fever. But they haven't had a doctor. Guess they're scared of doctors since this City Health fellow was up.'

Jack decided to have a look. Collins peered suspiciously through a crack of the door, but opened it hospitably enough when he recognized Jenny's physician. Doc was invited to see what ailed the missus. He went to the bedside and stood for some minutes making a general survey of the wretched woman's appearance. He felt quite sure, without further examination, that he knew what this was. There was a special characteristic, as difficult to describe as a flavor or a scent or a tint, but instantly recognizable by the experienced diagnostician as an acute polio. Perhaps it was mostly in the eyes. Any other cause of fever usually brightened the whites of the eyes to a sort of shiny porcelain. Polio puffed the lids, and the eyes sent out darting little flashes of fear and resentment.

'What 'pears to be ailing her, Doc?' asked Collins, anxiously.

Jack led the way out of the room.

'She has infantile paralysis,' he said, firmly. 'May I send the ambulance up here for her?'

'Gosh, Doc, that's terrible,' whimpered Collins. 'Is she a-goin' to be paralyzed?'

'I don't know. We'll do what we can — and then we must wait and see. I shall have a place ready for her. After you get her off in the ambulance, you go to a drugstore and get this prescription filled. It's for *you*. Zinc sulphate. I want you to swab out your mouth with it and gargle. Better get another order of it for Mrs. Buckley. I understand she has been in here.'

'Gosh, Doc. I haven't a cent,' admitted Collins.

Jack handed him ten dollars.

'Spend the rest of that for groceries,' he said, 'and divide with Mrs. Buckley. She is on short rations too. Buckley is not at home. Perhaps you knew that.'

Collins nodded an unkempt head.

'But you don't know where he is,' pressed Jack, pursuing Collins's evasive eyes.

'Nope,' declared Collins, 'not a thing. I don't keep track o' Buckley.'

* * * * * * * *

However sorry he was for the ailing Mrs. Collins, Jack was ablaze with zeal to make an experiment. Perhaps it was only a hundred-to-one shot that a serum placed immediately in the field likely to be affected would build up an immunity against this identically localized paralysis, but it was well worth trying. He would get the virus from Celeste and make a serum for injection into Mrs. Collins's arm while her infection was still incipient.

It was quarter after five, and there had been an understanding that he was to join the Cunninghams and Lan Ying at the Livingstone for dinner, but if the antitoxin experiment was to be made at all it would have to be made at once — dinner or no dinner. As he drove past Lister Hall, enroute to the parking-lot at the rear, he saw Cunningham surrounded by a group of medics. Apparently the afternoon clinic had just ended. He brought the car to a halt. Cunningham detached himself from the little knot of students, and said, 'Are you ready to go down town with me, or coming later?'

'I can't go with you to dinner tonight,' said Jack. 'Got to stay on the job.' Briefly he explained what he meant to do. Its urgency was obvious.

'I should like to be in on this myself, if you don't mind,' said the other. 'We'll phone to Edith that we're not coming, and they can have their dinner without delay.'

'Glad to have you stay,' said Jack. 'I'll park the car. Here are the keys to the lab. You can use my telephone. I shall be with you in a few minutes.'

Cunningham had been slowed up by his student admirers, and he and Jack met on the stairway. They entered the laboratory. Jack turned on the lights and crossed to the clothes locker, while Cunningham telephoned to the hotel. The clerk was saying that the ladies were not in. They had left a message saying they had gone over to Detroit on a shopping expedition and might be a little late for dinner.

'You tell them,' said Cunningham, 'that Doctor Beaven and I have been detained at the hospital and may not be through before nine or ten. They should proceed to their dinner without us.'

'Better take off your coat, Bill,' advised Jack, 'and make yourself comfortable. I have to keep it pretty hot in here for Celeste.'

Cunningham paused at the cage and peered in.

'I say, Jack,' he called, 'come here!'

They looked into the cage together.

'Asleep,' said Jack.

'Asleep — nothing!' muttered Cunningham. 'That monkey's dead!'

It was a fact. The monkey was dead, at a moment when she was about to come into her own as a contributor to an important scientific experiment.

Jack could think of no words to express his bereavement over the loss of Celeste than the hopeless ejaculation, 'Oh, hell!'

He was putting on his coat. They would go to dinner now. With one sleeve dangling, he paused, glassy-eyed.

'Look!' he exclaimed. 'I'm going to get some fluid from the Collins child, and make a serum for her mother.'

'Good!' approved Cunningham. 'That's still better.'

'Come on,' said Jack. 'We'll do it now.'

In a few minutes they were standing at the door of the private room where little Jenny was still isolated. The time had passed for the communicability of her trouble, but she was very nervous and easily upset; not ready for the confusion of an open ward. The nurse came out into the hall.

'Slattery, this is Doctor Cunningham.'

It was no mere formality when the Slattery girl told Doctor Cunningham she was glad to meet him. The whole hospital was agog with strange stories about the Cunningham clinics. General rumor had it that the man exercised a peculiar magic in dealing with difficult patients. McFey had been in, an hour ago, reporting an occurrence of the day before. The doctors were mostly in full sympathy with the Cunningham tactics, but they were good-naturedly giving the old boy some difficult nuts to crack.

McFey's life had been made unpleasant, for a week or more, by the constant complaints of one Pfeiffer — who was at that stage of a compound fracture of the ankle where the patient wanted to get inside the cast and scratch. He was a testy chap to begin with, and every day added to his surliness. McFey had thought it would be fun to see Doctor Cunningham and Pfeiffer together, and had suggested to Doctor Osgood that a call would be appreciated.

According to McFey's account of it, for Slattery's benefit, Doctor Cunningham had come in and without giving Pfeiffer a chance to harangue him about his discomforts, had said, confidentially, 'You're the fellow with the compound fracture of the ankle; aren't you? I want you to do me a favor. We have a chap down at the end of the hall who needs a bit of bucking-up; thinks he's ruined for life; ought to have a chance to look at some good sport who's been through a lot of hell. Miss McFey, let's put Mr. Pfeiffer in the wheel-chair and I'll take him down for a little chat with this man Tatlock.' Pfeiffer had stammered that he wouldn't be any good at that sort of thing, but Doctor

Cunningham had breezily overruled him. The grim joke of the thing was that Tatlock's leg had been broken in three places; they had it trussed up in a complicated contraption that rivaled the Inquisition machinery. Doctor Cunningham slowly trundled Pfeiffer down the hall and into Tatlock's room. 'Hello,' muttered Tatlock, through clenched teeth. 'What's *your* trouble?' Pfeiffer had swallowed, a couple of times, dryly. Then he grinned foolishly and said, 'Nothin', pard. Just — got bumped a little. Just — just pushed in to say Hello. Must go now. So long.' Then McFey had wheeled Pfeiffer back to his room. He had had nothing to say on the way. She asked him whether the trip had tired him and he shook his head. 'Did you buck up Mr. Tatlock?' asked McFey. '*Boy!*' he muttered, with a shudder. 'I expect he's not very comfortable in that cradle,' said McFey. '*Boy!*' exploded Pfeiffer, wincing and shaking his head as if he had taken some shockingly nasty medicine.

Equally entertaining had been McFey's report to Slattery concerning the Bretton girl's experience. Bretton had been having a rough time with Tatlock. The poor devil couldn't be blamed, of course, for being sullen and rude and unco-operative; had made up his mind he was going to be a hopeless cripple. Bretton had doubted the wisdom of bringing Pfeiffer in. It probably wouldn't do Tatlock much good to see someone who was well on the way to recovery. And she still doubted whether it was the thing to have done, after the brief interview was over. But presently the light dawned for Bretton. Doctor Cunningham had tarried. 'I hope you don't mind my bringing Mr. Pfeiffer in,' he said. 'You see, his trouble isn't all in his ankle. He has let the thing get on his nerves. His patience is all used up. I thought it might be good for him to have a glimpse of somebody who is badly hurt, but keeps his misfortune confined to his leg.' Tatlock pulled a rather doubtful grin, but Doctor Cunningham wouldn't let it be a joke. He took up the chart, ran his eye over it, nodded with satisfaction. 'I must go, now, Bob. Thanks for accommodating me. Maybe I can do something for you sometime.' Tatlock's eyes brightened. 'You're welcome, Doc,' he said, companionably. 'Come in again, any time.'

Slattery was glad to meet Doctor Cunningham. It was the truth: he was the sort of person who instantly inspired confidence. If you were in the doldrums, you would probably believe any splendid lie he told you about your courage.

'You're wanting to see Jenny Collins?' she asked, turning to Beaven.

'Yes. Want some blood. Want to make a culture. It's for the child's mother.'

Slattery's face registered anxiety, and she ventured an apprehensive 'Tsch, tsch.'

'She'll go positively into hysterics,' she declared. 'The little thing hasn't had the least mite of discipline, and she really has taken an awful beating since she's here; blood tests, spinals, and everything. Whatever you say, Doctor Beaven — but you're in for a big fight, I can tell you, if you try to do this while she's conscious.'

Jack suddenly turned his eyes toward Cunningham with a significant grin.

'I think you said you would like to be in on this experiment, Doctor Cunningham. How about getting a nice little specimen of Miss Collins's blood? We'll say that's your share of the job.'

'If I'm to do it, I should like to know a little more about the case. This child has a paralyzed arm, and you've another case or two much like it. Neighbors, I understand. There's another girl, isn't there?'

Slattery mentioned the Buckley child.

'What is her first name, the Buckley?'

'Martha.'

'Very well. You sterilize the syringe, wrap it in a towel, and lay it on the table beside the bed. I'll follow along presently.'

'You will not need me,' said Jack. 'I'll go and see how Mrs. Collins is making it.'

'Tell the girl on the desk here to find me a fresh pillow,' said Cunningham. 'Slattery's busy.'

'Pillow?'

'Yes; to carry in with me. They're never alarmed if you arrive with a pillow under your arm or a red apple in your hand. It always starts a diverting conversation. Did you ever notice that, Jack? Anything that disarms them, especially if you're a stranger. I've sometimes had pretty good luck in distracting a patient by seeming very much preoccupied with my own affairs rather than showing any concern for his.'

'Such as ——'

'Well, I have occasionally stopped, just inside the door, when I knew the patient had noted my arrival, and have gone down deep in my trousers pocket and brought up a large handful of small change which I have proceeded to count, anxiously, while moving to the foot of the bed. It is obvious that at the moment I don't care a hoot about the patient. Generally he is so relieved that he wants to joke with me. Had I lost a nickel somewhere? Was my father a Scotsman? Would I like to borrow a dime?'

'But you can work that only once on the same fellow,' said Jack.

'Maybe you don't need to work it more than once.'

Jack laughed.

'Got any more little tricks like that?' he asked. 'It's quite interesting. I suppose you go about with your pockets full of puzzles.'

'No — that's too obvious. You'd never hook any sensible person in that manner. . . . Slattery is probably ready for me now. I'll see you later.'

He entered the room, carrying the pillow. Slattery's face was full of curiosity.

'Jenny,' she said, 'this is Doctor Cunningham; came to visit you.'

'Got enough pillows, Jenny?' asked Cunningham. 'I have a few extra ones.'

'Sure!' sneered Jenny. 'What'd I want with any more pillows?'

'Oh, all right,' he said, indifferently. 'I'll give it to your mother.'

Jenny blinked a little, and raised up on her good elbow. 'She's got pillows.'

'At home, yes,' said the doctor.

'Isn't my mummy at home?'

'No, she's here. She's sick.'

'Bad sick?' Jenny screwed up her face and began to whimper.

'Pretty bad, yes. But she will be better if we can get the right kind of medicine. Would you like to send her some?'

Jenny grinned a little through her tears.

'She can have all of it.'

'No,' said the doctor, 'you'll have to make some — a special kind.'

'I can't make medicine,' scoffed Jenny.

Cunningham sat down by the bed.

'Funny thing about medicine,' he said, half to himself. 'We get the stuff it's made of from the queerest places. Some of it comes from the juice of flowers and weeds, and the bark from trees; and some of it is made out of iron and gold and silver and coal.'

Jenny was quietly attentive, and the doctor went on.

'Sometimes it's made of blood. That's the best kind.'

A shadow quickly crossed Jenny's face at the mention of blood. She winced and withdrew her finger from Cunningham's friendly hand.

'We had a monkey here, named Celeste, who had just the kind of blood we needed for some medicine to give to your mother, but Celeste died this afternoon — so we're looking about. There were only three people in this hospital who had the right kind of blood.'

'Who?' inquired Jenny, with a dry swallow.

'Martha Buckley — and Celeste — and you.'

'Monkeys aren't people!' piped Jenny, waspishly.

'You would have liked Celeste, I think,' said Cunningham. 'She was only a monkey, but she was a very nice

monkey. Now that Celeste is gone, that leaves Martha
and you.'

Jenny began to cry; softly, at first. Then she buried her
face in the pillow and mumbled, between sobs, 'You're
going to hurt me! You're going to hurt me — bad! Somebody's always hurting me — with big sharp needles and
things.' Her voice rose to a shriek. 'I won't let you! I
won't! I won't!'

'Very well,' said the doctor, gently. 'That settles it,
then.' He patted her hand. 'Don't cry. It's all right.
I thought you might want to do this for your mummy, so
she can get well. But — if you'd rather not, we will get
it from Martha. I expect she will be glad to give up a
spoonful of blood so that her little friend's mummy will
have a chance to be well again.'

Jenny's hysteria was subsiding, the sobs still racking her
thin chest spasmodically. Her eyes were full of terror.
Suddenly she forced a small white fist hard against her chin
and cried out, in a squeaky little voice, 'I'll do it! I'll do
it!... Oh, please don't hurt me! Oh — I can't! I can't!...
But — I'll do it!'

Cunningham ran his fingers through her damp curls and
said tenderly, 'You are a grand little girl, Jenny. I'm
very proud of you. And when we tell your mummy what
you did for her ——'

He reached for the syringe. Slattery pushed up a sleeve
and dabbed at the slim arm with an antiseptic. There
was a tense, silent moment. Then Cunningham glanced up
over his shoulder and said, 'Slattery, this baby has got a
lot of good stuff in her. I'm certainly glad to make her
acquaintance.' There was another moment of silence
broken only by Jenny's labored breathing as she braced
her frail will against the pain.

'There!' said the doctor. Miss Slattery rubbed the spot
and drew down the sleeve. Jenny wiped her eyes with a
corner of the sheet and tried to smile.

Jack had slipped into the room and stood inside the door
silently observant.

'You said I was a baby.' Jenny's lip trembled.

'Well — that was a mistake. You aren't a baby. You are a grown-up lady. But you aren't too big to have a very beautiful doll to play with. It's going to be here — tomorrow. It is a gift from Doctor Beaven. He will bring it to you.'

Jenny's eyes drifted across to Beaven who was standing at the foot of the bed.

'Will she open and shut her eyes?' she demanded.

'Yes, ma'am,' promised Jack, solemnly. 'She will do everything that any doll can do.'

'Tomorrow?'

'Afternoon.'

'Honor bright?'

'Without fail.'

Chapter XVI

NOT infrequently the Medical College Committee of the Board of Regents asked a faculty man or two as dinner guests. On the occasions when Tubby was invited he enjoyed himself immensely. He had a discriminating palate, and old Cremshaw, the chairman, always saw to it that the rations were edible.

Moreover, the conversation was sprightly and Tubby was encouraged to contribute to it generously. Weary of wrangling among themselves all day, the Regents welcomed Tubby's dry satire and audacious impudence. Sometimes they guffawed with glee when one of their number, serving a hot verbal drive at the veteran professor, had it back immediately in his own court — neatly within bounds, but quite out of reach. Tubby knew what was expected of him at these affairs and he took pains to see that they were not disappointed.

But Tuesday evening's dinner with the Regents had been one of the most unhappy events of his life. To begin with, he had spent a thoroughly wretched afternoon. Had Bill Cunningham come to the Medical College as a stranger, turning the institution upside-down, infecting the student body with the idea that it was more important to 'live in a house by the side of the road and be a friend to man' than to earn a reputation as a sound pathologist, Tubby would have fought him in the open with all his might and no holds barred. But everybody knew that he and Bill were lifelong friends. He didn't want an open break with Bill; and, even if he did, it would have been

mighty imprudent in the face of the Cunningham popularity.

Tubby had never felt so utterly forsaken, so out of
place, as when he had sat on the stage of the Auditorium
aware that the whole Medical College, to which he had
given his life's full devotion and for whose high rating he
had been largely responsible, was unanimously and hilariously applauding a type of medical practice with which he
had **no** sympathy at all. He had had to sit there and
take it; and pretend to like it.

After the speech, while the faculty was swarming forward
to felicitate Cunningham, Tubby had briefly remarked to
Shane that he had an appointment, had pushed through
the pack and trudged down the back stairs and out into
the rain, trying not to hear what the medics were saying
as they ganged their way to the street. There was no
urgent reason for his return to his office, but he went there
mechanically, hung up his raincoat and umbrella, and
fumbled through a small pile of late afternoon mail without the slightest inclination to open any of it.

He had thought Romney should be leaving, for it was
after five, but she was still at her desk in the corner typing
a case-history. She did not look up. Tubby tried to
think of something for her to do. He wanted to exercise
what was left of his damaged authority. So low was he
in spirit that it wouldn't have surprised him if meek
little Romney, given an order, told him to go jump in
the river.

Maybe she knew what had become of Beaven. Tubby's
bitter hostility to Beaven had relaxed a bit during the
past hour. With uncommonly good sense the chap had
apparently decided that the neatest way to accept the
Cunningham lecture was to ignore it. Tubby wished that
he himself had been as wise. Beaven, unable to approve
the popular stampede to Cunninghamery, had stayed away.

Tubby cleared his throat raspingly, and Romney recognized the raucous noise as one of the amenities employed
by the chief in summoning her to his desk.

'Do you know where Doctor Beaven is?' he demanded.

'I think he is in the laboratory, sir. Shall I see?'

Tubby nodded and twirled his watch-chain restlessly.

'Shall I tell him you want him, sir?' asked Romney.

Tubby did not reply immediately. He had been about to shake his head; then changed his mind. He was growing very tired of his feud with Beaven. It made him uncomfortable to be dodging the fellow; and, besides, it was deucedly inconvenient to be without his assistance. He had begun to realize what a large number of tasks Beaven had lifted from his shoulders; half-forgotten duties that had lately been dumped back on him. He missed Beaven; missed him in the operating-room. Sooner or later this quarrel would have to be made up. Perhaps this was as good a time as any. They had something in common today: they were both disgusted with Cunningham. Maybe if they talked about that, it might be a move toward amity.

'Yes,' said Tubby, crustily. 'If he's there tell him I want to see him.'

Romney slipped out on her errand. In another minute she was back, a little bit flustered as if reluctant to report.

'Doctor Cunningham has just gone into the laboratory, sir. Shall I tell Doctor Beaven to come now — or wait until he is at liberty?'

'Let it go,' grumped Tubby. Scowling darkly, he pocketed his letters, slammed his desk drawers, put on his raincoat and the hard wet hat, and stalked out. He had never been so completely depressed. It was almost as if his little world had come to an end.

He drove back to the University Club and went up to his suite to change for the Regents' dinner. It would be late, and he liked his meals on time. There was some consolation in the fact that Cunningham wasn't to attend. He had been invited, Shane had said, but had declined because of another engagement; obviously an engagement with Beaven. That was rather odd. He hadn't supposed that Cunningham and Beaven were so thick.

Time was dragging. Tubby didn't know what to do

with himself. He took off his street clothes and pulled on
a dressing-gown. He unfolded the evening paper, glanced
at the headlines, and tossed it aside. It occurred to him
that he had not opened his letters. He rummaged in his
coat pocket for them and drew his chair closer to the light.
One of the letters was from Claudia King. What, reflected
Tubby, could that silly woman be wanting now?

'Dear Doctor Forrester,' wrote Claudia. 'For some time
it has been on my mind to ask your counsel about a matter
that concerns my sister. I have hesitated because I know
how busy you are. But this problem has now become urgent
and I am at my wit's end.

'It is possible that you know of Doctor Beaven's interest
in Audrey. I would have no objection to that if his intentions were serious, for he is a fine fellow. But he has made
it plain to Audrey that he does not expect to marry her.
She is very much in love, I think. It isn't fair. My sister
has not had a normal life. I remember telling you about
her unusual upbringing in China. She doesn't adjust to
our ways. It breaks my heart to see how lonesome she is
and what a poor prospect she has of living happily here.
Perhaps this might be remedied if she married some congenial man who would offer her an interesting home and
a share in his social and business interests.

'As the matter stands, she has given her heart away
without any compensation. Doctor Beaven offers her
nothing but his friendship. I can't think that this is a
very sound arrangement for either of them. It goes without saying that if he is in love with Audrey (and he would
hardly have asked her to spend Thanksgiving with him
if that were not true) ——'

Tubby's eyes hardened. So *that* was what ailed Beaven!
It was this girl, who thought of herself as a Chinese! She
had been filling his head full of ideas. The whole thing
was plain as a pikestaff. It was crystal clear. Beaven had
fallen in love, or thought he had, which came to the same
thing; knew he hadn't any right to permit this distraction

to break into his work. The situation had made him
wretched; made him edgy. That accounted for his savage
impudence. He was exasperated over his own dilemma.

Flexing his jaw angrily, Tubby took up the letter again.

'I have thought of taking this up with the Cunninghams,'
Claudia was saying. 'Audrey sees a great deal of them.
But it's no use. Apparently they are doing all they can
to throw Audrey and Beaven together; persuaded her to
go with them to the University this week while Doctor
Cunningham is lecturing.

'I have wondered if you might not want to go into this
problem with Doctor Beaven. You have done so much
for him. Surely he will listen to your advice. Tell him what
a frightful mistake he is making. Forgive me for annoying
you, but I have no one else to confide in. Please — won't
you do something?'

Tubby flung the letter down on the desk and walked
the floor. Nice business for Bill Cunningham to be in!
It wasn't quite enough for him to be down here with his
abominable lectures and clinics. He had to aid and abet
in confusing Beaven; playing match-maker; furnishing fuel
and opportunity for an infatuation that might have cured
itself if he and his clever wife had kept out of it.

'Surely he will listen to your advice,' Claudia thought.
What nonsense! All Beaven needed, in his present state of
mind, to send him utterly beyond reach, would be a nice
little spot of advice. Tubby could visualize that scene.
He would tell Beaven he was ruining himself, jeopardizing
his career, disappointing the man who had made him —
and Beaven would unquestionably tell the man who had
made him to pick himself up by his hip-pockets and go
galloping off to hell. No — you couldn't advise Beaven —
not any more; certainly not on a matter so personal as
this. Tubby was heart-sick; had a notion to flick the
Regents' dinner, and go to bed.

That impulse, however, was promptly disposed of.
Tubby's stock was temporarily low, but there was no

sense in announcing himself bankrupt. To absent himself from the Regents' dinner might create the impression that he was sulking; had had a humiliating experience and was now at home licking his wounds. No, sir; he'd have to eat, drink, and be merry with the Regents.

But, by nine-thirty he was wishing he hadn't come. He couldn't think of anything he wanted to say to his dinner companions. Nobody baited him. In fact they were all of them infuriatingly polite, considerate, as if he had come in a wheel-chair with a shawl around his neck. By some perversity he had been seated between Shane and Denman who talked across him about the spectacular popularity of Cunningham and the amazing turnout in the Auditorium on such a viciously bad day. They even had the crust to ask Tubby if he didn't think it was remarkable.

'I see now,' Denman was saying, 'why Cunningham isn't with us.' He jerked his head in the direction of the foursome in the middle of the dining-room. 'Having a little party of his own.'

'Who's the attractive young brunette?' asked Shane. 'Relative of the Cunninghams, maybe? I notice that Beaven is appreciating her charms.'

'That girl,' said Denman, 'has a story. Born and brought up in China. I met her last summer at the Cunninghams'. Most interesting. Decidedly oriental in her outlook.'

'Oh? So that accounts for the straight black bangs,' remarked Shane. 'Mighty becoming, eh?'

'It isn't just the bangs,' said Denman. 'They're sort of symbolic of her whole state of mind.'

'Chink?' queried Shane.

'One hundred per cent,' said Denman. 'Has the Chinese indifference to occidental ideas of progress, makes merry over our mechanical gadgets, thinks we're all running around in circles — wearing ourselves out with worry and work.'

'Well — that doctrine might be good for Beaven,' suggested Shane. 'He works like a dog.'

'It has been the making of him, too,' put in Tubby, 'and he knows it.'

'Quite so,' agreed Shane, quickly. 'Quite so.'

Tubby would have liked to pursue this matter a little farther, but it was evident that they wouldn't debate it with him. They were bent on humoring him tonight, as if he were an old man whose remarks should be accepted with a 'Quite so, quite so,' no matter how preposterous they were.

It was that sort of evening, all the way through, and Tubby was glad when old Cremshaw pushed back his chair, slapped his knees with a gesture of finality, and said he knew they'd all had a good time — which was a lie.

All next day — after an almost totally sleepless night — Tubby fretfully debated what course he should pursue. His hope of making common cause with Beaven over their mutual dissatisfaction with the Cunningham program was now quite pointless. Beaven might not be in full sympathy with Cunningham's ideas, but it was evident that he was very fond of Cunningham, the man. Beaven's relation to Tubby was exactly the other way about. There was no use trying to talk to Beaven now about anything; much less offering him advice about his purely personal affairs. Nor would it do the slightest bit of good to talk to Cunningham.

That night, in his room, the idea suddenly came to Tubby that he might put it up to the girl herself. It wasn't a very promising prospect. A young woman in love would find it difficult to efface herself for the sake of her man's future. She might be willing to sacrifice her own happiness to save him from disaster, but she would be an exceptional girl, indeed, if she consented to the proposition that her love was interfering with his work. Her normal reaction would be to declare that her love couldn't interfere with his work; that — quite to the contrary — he could do much better work if contented and cherished.

However, there was at least the ghost of a chance that this Hilton girl might pursue a different course of reasoning

than the selfish little flibbertygibbets toddling about the
campus looking for an athletic dance-partner who might
turn out to be a permanent meal-ticket. This Audrey Hilton
was reputed to be oriental in mind. Tubby wasn't quite
sure what sort of mind that might be, but there was a
general rumor that the Far East took great pride in its
spirit of resignation, non-resistance, and peace at any
price. The Oriental was a disciple of the gentle Buddha,
who had been either too tranquil or too indolent to bestir
himself. According to the shrines, the Light of Asia was
more of a glow-worm than a firebrand. Buddha sweetly
smiled and sat. From the pictures of him, you couldn't
have brought him into action with dynamite. If the Hilton
girl took any stock in this sort of thing, she might be persuaded to give Beaven up without a protest. Maybe it
was worth a trial.

Tubby meditated on this for two hours, and decided he
would do it; he would do it tomorrow; he would try to
make an appointment with her for a private talk.

* * * * * * * *

It was an easy trip to Detroit — only an hour away.
Edith Cunningham had suggested, shortly after breakfast,
that they might run into town and do some Christmas
shopping. Audrey cheerfully consented. The day had been
pleasantly spent, though Edith remarked on the return
trip that she was very tired and had a headache.

Calling at the desk for their room-keys, Edith was
handed a message.

'They're not coming to dinner,' she said. 'They are tied
up in something at the hospital. Far as I'm concerned,
Audrey, it's a good thing. I'm a wreck. Would you mind
very much, darling, if I didn't come down? All I want is a
cup of tea and a hot bath.'

Audrey, too, had been handed a message. It was in a
sealed envelope, bearing the embossed device of the University Club. She did not open it.

'Anything I can do for you?' she asked, solicitously, as
they parted at the elevator.

'No — nothing. Don't worry about me. I'll be all right. See you in the morning, dear.'

Disposing of her hat and coat, Audrey investigated the note. Her eyes widened as she read the signature. It was from Doctor Forrester.

'Dear Miss Hilton,' it began. 'There is a matter of considerable importance which I should like to discuss with you, preferably in private, at your early convenience. I have tried to reach you today by telephone but learned that you were out of the city for a few hours. Perhaps you will call me up, on your return. I shall be at the University Club after five o'clock.'

It was rather a frightening prospect, this interview with Doctor Forrester. Audrey frowned with perplexity. Of course she would have to reply — somehow. It was not to be dodged. For Jack's sake, she must consider Doctor Forrester's request as little short of a command.

She put through the call and sat waiting, apprehensively. The gruff voice, when it answered, was not very reassuring.

'I am Miss Hilton. I have your note. I am quite willing to talk with you. You may come here, if you wish, now — or any time this evening. We are going home tomorrow.'

'You have no dinner engagement, then?' asked Tubby.

'No, sir.'

'How would you like to have dinner with me, here at the University Club?'

Audrey hesitated. If Doctor Forrester wanted her to dine with him, he must be in an amiable mood. Perhaps it might be to Jack's advantage if she humored him. How very pleasant if she could help to heal that old quarrel.

'Thank you, Doctor Forrester. I should be glad to do that.'

'Shall I come for you — or send for you — about eight-thirty?'

'I shall come in a taxi, sir, and spare you the trouble. Eight-thirty?'

'I shall be waiting for you in the reception parlor, Miss Hilton. Thank you for consenting to come.'

Much relieved, but still a bit anxious, Audrey prepared to go to Tubby's impromptu party. She stood before her wardrobe thoughtfully and decided on modish black satin, the jade necklace, the jade bracelet. She laid out also the jade ear-drops, but voted them down by a narrow margin.

Promptly at eight-thirty she was shown to the door of the reception parlor, Tubby in dinner clothes coming forward to meet her. It was a pretty stiff smile but agreeable enough to assure Audrey that he probably wouldn't bite her head off until they were a little better acquainted. She offered him her hand and he bowed over it with grave dignity. Without pausing for any conversation, Tubby presented an elbow of the old school and Audrey laid her hand in the crook of it. They marched to the dining-room in silence, Tubby staring straight ahead as they passed down through the long, rather dimly lighted hall to a table in a far corner where two white-jacketed waiters were expecting their arrival. It was quite remote from the other diners at tables near the door; so sequestered, indeed, thought Audrey, that she might easily be murdered here, and the crime remain a mystery.

Tubby proceeded, without small talk, to consult her wishes about the dinner. Pinching on his gold-rimmed glasses, he glared at her over the top, and asked her if she wanted a cocktail. She smilingly shook her head.

'But you want one, I think,' she said. 'Perhaps you will find me a little fruit cup.'

'For the entrée,' queried Tubby, with a dry smile, 'would you like a vegetable dinner? I understand you affect oriental habits, Miss Hilton. I would suggest a steak — but perhaps you do not eat meat. Does your religion enjoin you against killing animals for food?' It was evident that Tubby was going to insist on making her seem an alien.

'I do not believe I could, Doctor Forrester.'

'Pardon?' Tubby leaned forward quizzing her eyes. It was very amusing and Audrey had difficulty in keeping a straight face.

'I never killed an animal for food, sir,' she said, naïvely. 'But if this beef is already dead, I think I could eat some of it; thank you.'

After that, Tubby did not emphasize her oriental background; but treated her with exaggerated deference as if he feared he might unwittingly offend some strange foreign quirk. Audrey thought she knew, now, which way we were headed. She wasn't the girl for Jack. She was different. She wasn't regular. It would have been fun, she thought, to ask solemnly if she might have a pair of chopsticks.

Tubby deliberately built up a nice entrance for his argument. Miss Hilton, he supposed, must have had a most interesting life in China; must have found it extremely difficult to accommodate herself to our uncouth American ways; must be looking forward to an early return to a country so very much more tranquil, so very much less confusing. It was almost as if he were offering her a one-way steamship ticket.

Yes, Audrey had agreed, she had enjoyed China and the warm friendship of all those in her foster-father's house, but she had no intention of returning; certainly not to live there. America was now her country.

'But you don't like it here; do you?' demanded Tubby. 'We're much too occupied with our machinery; aren't we?'

'Are you?' asked Audrey. 'I do not know much about such things.'

They had arrived at the dessert before Tubby abandoned his various strategies and came out into the open field.

'The fact is, Miss Hilton — and this is what I wanted to talk to you about — it seems fairly clear that you now hold the destiny of a very important young man in your hands.' He put his spoon down on the plate and leaned forward with his elbows on the table. 'This man Beaven has in him the making of a great scientist. I have watched his progress for years. He is not only a man of exceptional talents but very strong character. He has consecrated himself to his work, enduring hardness like a soldier, giving up every youthful pleasure, renouncing love, home, recreations, social pursuits, so that he might give full time and his whole mind to his task. And it is a noble task! It is not too much to hope that he may provide the means for the amelioration of much human suffering.

'And now — at the moment when he is just beginning to reap the first fruits of all this self-sacrifice, *you* arrive on the scene. Please!' — Tubby's voice was unsteady, passionately in earnest — 'please let me talk to you as a father might counsel his child. I can understand Beaven's infatuation for you. You are a very winsome young woman. I do not want to like you, because you are standing in the way of Beaven's career, but I do like you. You are most attractive, desirable, adorable! If you weren't so thoroughly lovely, I might be less concerned. Your charm is a liability.

'But — and this is my only ground for hope — you are sensible, I think, and unless I am much mistaken about you, you are very strong. So — I appeal to you, in a spirit of fair play. I wish you would give Beaven up. Hand him back to his important job. He is distraught, restless, unhappy. His mind is divided. His work is slipping. He is losing ground. You think he loves you. Perhaps he does. But he loved his career for a long time before he loved *you*. How much will he love you, five years from now, when he discovers that the goal he set for himself, years ago, and pursued at so great cost, is beyond his reach?' Tubby paused and sighed deeply.

'Of course, you can have him. He will not be able to resist your affection. If you ask him, tomorrow, whether he would rather have you stay — or disappear from his life, he will unquestionably urge you to stay. This problem is not for Beaven to solve: it's *your* problem, and if you solve it at all you must solve it alone! Perhaps the greatest contribution you will ever have a chance to make, in behalf of the world's welfare, is a prompt and firm decision to clear the path for this man you love!'

Audrey had been trying to maintain her poise, but

Tubby's entreaties were beating her down. She felt very helpless, cornered, weaponless. Except for themselves, the spacious dining-room was empty. The last of the late diners had left more than an hour ago.

'Or *do* you love him,' demanded Tubby, urgently, 'loyally enough to step out of his way?'

Audrey blinked back the tears and stared into his steely eyes, frightened, overpowered.

'Do you honestly think I should?' she asked, half to herself.

'I do!' declared Tubby.

She turned her face away and tried to control it. Could it be possible that Tubby was right? She painfully recalled that afternoon at the lake when Jack had so firmly, almost fiercely announced that his life belonged to his work; that he had no right to love anybody. Perhaps he still felt so about it. Maybe he was secretly unhappy, as Tubby said. Was it true that she had led him into a situation he had tried to avoid?

'And I think,' Tubby was saying, as if he read her mind, '— I *know* that you have some grave misgivings about all this. Is that not true?'

She returned her baffled eyes and slowly nodded her head.

'You are a brave girl!' Tubby's voice was husky. 'I felt it. I'm glad I had the courage to take this up with you. Now I leave you to decide on your next step. You will know what to do. Perhaps you may feel that the easy way out is to return to China for a year or two, long enough to give Beaven a chance to pull himself together.'

There was a long silence. Audrey, with her elbows on the table and her small fists pressing hard against her throat, again nodded her head. Her eyes were closed and the hot tears were seeping through her long lashes.

'Verree well,' she said. 'I shall go — to China.'

Tubby bowed.

'Is there anything I can do for you, my friend?' he asked, almost gently.

'No — nothing — thank you.'

'Are you able to go — I mean — financially? May I help you?'

'Please don't say anything more,' begged Audrey.

'I meant it kindly,' said Tubby.

Audrey's attention was stirred by a man rapidly approaching their table; a desk clerk, probably, for he was not in uniform.

'You are wanted on the telephone, Doctor Forrester,' he said, evidently agitated.

'I thought I left word that I was not to be disturbed,' said Tubby, crossly. 'You take the message, or tell them to call later.'

'If you please, sir,' insisted the clerk, 'it is very important. It is from the hospital. I told them you could not be bothered. But someone has been badly hurt.'

'You tell them I'll be over there in a half-hour.'

'But, sir,' persisted the man, 'it's Doctor Beaven — and he is not in the hospital.'

'What?' Tubby pushed back his chair and without a glance at Audrey marched swiftly after the clerk. For a moment Audrey sat stunned and trembling; then, with a painful little cry, she rose and followed him.

He was in a telephone booth when she overtook him. The narrow door had been left open. Audrey's knees were trembling. She leaned against the edge of the door for support; then she crowded in so close beside Tubby that her cheek pressed hard against his arm. With parted lips and every fiber of her tensely alert, she listened.

It was a woman's voice, talking from the hospital. They had had a mysterious telephone call from Wheaton. It appeared that Doctor Beaven had been summoned out there on some pretext, and had been in a fight. Then the men who fought him had run away. 'And the man who called up would have to run away, too,' he said, but he didn't want to leave Doctor Beaven to die. He says you must bring along two hundred dollars to help him get away. Then he will tell you where Doctor Beaven is — somewhere out in the country. You are to drive out on

Highway Number 6, the Wheaton road, and carry on until you come to the high school.'

'Just a minute,' interrupted Tubby, hoarsely. He turned to Audrey and muttered, 'Get a pencil and paper — quickly: over there — at the desk.'

She was back in a moment, laid the memorandum pad on the narrow ledge, and handed Tubby the pencil.

'Go ahead,' he ordered. 'High school. Then what?'

'On the top step, you will find Doctor Beaven's surgical kit, empty. That's to let you know they aren't faking. You are to put the money into the satchel, and leave. In fifteen minutes you are to come back. In the satchel you will find directions leading you to Doctor Beaven.'

'Get out the ambulance!' said Tubby. 'Tell them to come here at once and pick me up! I'll be waiting at the front door!'

'No,' said the girl on the telephone. 'That's another thing. No ambulance. No police. You're to go in your own car. . . . Is there anything we can do, sir?'

'Nothing, I suppose — but get a room ready, and wait for further instructions.' Tubby's wobbly voice sounded like that of an old man. He staggered against Audrey as he came out of the booth.

'I must go,' he muttered. 'You can find your way back to the hotel.'

'Please!' begged Audrey. 'I'm going with you.'

'No — no — no!' said Tubby, firmly. He was moving toward the elevator, Audrey clinging to his arm. 'I say — no! It's too dangerous! Can't tell what you might run into, out there. No need of your taking this risk. Nothing you can do.' He shook himself loose and stepped into the elevator. The door closed quietly.

For a little while, Audrey stood there dazedly wondering what to do. The clerk came to her and asked solicitously if there was anything he could do for her. She shook her head and walked slowly in the direction of the check-room where Tubby had deposited her fur coat. She heard the telephone ringing at the desk, and the switch-

board operator saying, 'Right away, sir.' Immediately
the same voice was saying, 'Bring Doctor Forrester's
coupé to the front door — at once — immediately —
pronto!'

'Shall I get you a taxi, Miss?' asked the clerk, visibly
upset over her apparent bewilderment.

'No, thank you,' she said. The porter opened the heavy
front door for her, and she stepped out into the open
vestibule. It was snowing now. She drew her collar up
about her throat, and waited. Presently a big blue coupé
drew up to the curb. A garage attendant got out, leaving
the engine running. He gave Audrey an inquisitive stare
as she opened the door.

'This is Doctor Forrester's car, ma'am,' he said, respectfully.

'Yes,' she replied, 'I know.'

Tubby, bundled up to the chin, came down the steps,
jerked the car-door open, and climbed in.

'I thought I told you that you weren't going!' he said,
fiercely.

'I *am* going!' said Audrey. 'I am as much interested in
him as you are! I shall keep the promise I made you — but
I am going to him — now!'

* * * * * * * *

It hadn't been much of a trick to make the serum. Jack
was ready to administer it shortly before eight o'clock.
Cunningham, seeing no reason why he should remain any
longer, announced that he was going across to old Tony's
for his dinner. It would remind him of old times.

Mrs. Collins whined a little when she saw the young
surgeon arrive with a formidable instrument in hand, and
he challenged her courage by saying, 'This is a serum,
made from Jenny's blood. She was glad to let us have it
when we told her it was for you. Aren't you proud of her?'

With this job attended to, Jack noted with satisfaction
that the whole evening was before him. Lan Ying would
be waiting for him. Returning quickly to the laboratory

to change to his street clothes, he heard his telephone ringing before he had unlocked the door. He hurried in and
answered it, hoping it might be Lan Ying or Edith.

The call was coming in from a pay-station. The coin-bell
rang four times, at close intervals; two quarters and two
dimes, maybe; one quarter, two dimes, and a nickel, perhaps.

An unrecognized voice said, in a low tone that seemed
anxious not to be overheard, 'Doctor Beaven? I'm a
friend of Tom Buckley's. He has met with an accident,
out here in Wheaton, and wants to know if you can come
over and fix him up.'

'How badly hurt?'

'Bad enough.'

'Bleeding?'

'Yes — plenty!'

'It probably is urgent, then. Better call in a local doctor
to stop the hemorrhage, and I'll be over in the morning.'

'He won't see anybody but you, Doc. Says you'll know
why. Are you coming?'

'Very well. Where is he?'

'At a house in Wheaton. I'll tell you what you do,
Doc. Drive right into Wheaton on the highway. I'll
meet you at the edge of town, and pilot you in. Then you
won't get lost.'

'What's the nature of his injuries; bruises, cuts, fractures?'

'Yes. Pretty much all o' that. Thanks, Doc. I'll be
looking for you in half an hour.'

Jack hung up the receiver and stood for a moment reviewing the conversation. It hadn't sounded like the voice of a
tough; but, considering all of the circumstances, there was
no question but this summons should be regarded as a
possible bid for serious trouble. Buckley had been terrified
at the thought of what might happen to him. Evidently
he knew what he was up against. Perhaps Buckley was
more deeply involved than he had admitted. Probably
had a flock of reasons for not wanting any new people —

not even another doctor—to become interested in his affairs.

Quickly changing to his street clothes, and assembling an emergency surgical kit, Jack hurried out into the rainy night, and climbed into his roadster — the only car left on the lot. As he neared the police station, he slowed down, indecisively. Common prudence suggested that a man should have some protection on an errand of this nature. That's what the police were for, wasn't it? He brought the car to a full stop directly under the lights that served the main entrance, but immediately abandoned the idea. If Buckley was in a scrape, it wouldn't help him very much to have a cop coming into the picture. Jack pushed on, resolved to see the affair through without assistance.

The decision pleased him. He stoutly maintained to himself that he wasn't the least bit smug over it; had no inclination to dramatize himself as an audacious young hero; but there was a certain satisfaction in being able to drive voluntarily into what might turn out to be a very dangerous situation. At first he had not given much thought to the possibilities as they might affect him personally. But now he began to reflect that if anyone had injured Buckley for 'squealing,' he, himself, might be attacked for the same reason. The farther he went the larger loomed this fact: he and Thomas Buckley had a common enemy.

But he had no inclination to turn back. He was glad of that. The speedometer moved up to sixty. The tires sizzed on the black asphalt. He had the road practically to himself. A curious exhilaration accompanied his consciousness of danger. Every sense was alert, aware. This physical phenomenon interested him deeply. Bill Cunningham had spoken of it, the other day, but hadn't told him anything he didn't know about it. Many a time in the classroom he had drawled carelessly that the sensation of fear and the knowledge of impending danger set the adrenals going at full speed, pouring their mysterious tincture into the blood-stream, making the soldier more keenly alert, tightening his muscle-fibers, saturating him with such powerful astringents that his mouth was parched and dry.

'Of course,' he could hear himself saying, casually, 'the primary purpose of this emergency adrenalin, suddenly dumped into the blood-stream, is to provide a more prompt and sure coagulation of the blood in the event of an injury resulting in a hemorrhage. Nature,' he was accustomed to add, whimsically, 'Nature has her moments when she is almost considerate.'

Jack felt now that he could amplify his classroom comments on this subject. He had verified the textbooks, and had discovered something more. This emergency shot of adrenalin, administered by Nature, had also the value of a stimulating intoxicant. 'If a man could live constantly under the influence of this heady stuff,' reflected Jack, 'he would be quite a fellow.'

He became so absorbed in an examination of his own mental processes that he was barely conscious of the speed at which he bowled along the lonely highway.

Life had been pretty carefully marked out for him, hitherto, every step of the way. There had been the usual conflicts of the school playground, and the rough-and-tumble of the athletic field in college, but nobody had ever attacked him with a sinister purpose. Such sturdiness of character as he had come by, through the years, had been largely the product of self-restraint — a negative virtue, admittedly. It startled him a little to reflect that this was the first time in his life that he had deliberately hurled himself into a situation brimming with menace. He wasn't congratulating himself, but he realized that to have taken some less resolute course, tonight, would have impoverished him. Little Jenny Collins was nothing but an alley-rat. You had no right to expect anything of her. But in a stressful moment Jenny had been willing to face the music, and he had complimented her. If he had flicked tonight's problematical errand, he reflected, it would have been very difficult for him ever again to look into a pair of frightened eyes and challenge them to be courageous.

Nature — in spite of her cruelties, her mistakes, her wanton wastefulness, her indifference to the world's malformations, misfortunes, and miseries — wasn't a bad old girl, at that. If you showed the slightest disposition to co-operate with her, when she poured out the adrenalin, it was an experience well worth having.

A black-lettered signboard flashed by. One mile to Wheaton. Scattered lights grew more numerous. Jack began slowing down. He found himself rapidly overtaking a car that held to the middle of the road, a battered old sedan, traveling at a snail's pace. At once he surmised that he was being met by the man who was to direct him to Buckley. The driver thrust out an arm and beckoned him to follow. Jack tapped his horn, a couple of times, to indicate his receipt of the signal, and the leading car increased its speed.

They drove through the sleepy little town of Wheaton and a mile beyond where the pilot car turned south on a graveled road. There were about five miles of this. Then, at a country crossroads, the gravel gave out, and the road was muddy. Both cars proceeded with caution. After another mile, the pilot car came to a stop at the entrance to a lane. A man with a flashlight stepped forward and opened the right-hand door of Jack's car.

'Here you are, Doc,' he rumbled. 'Get out, and I'll lead the way. I'm afraid you're goin' to find it a bit muddy, but you can't drive up this lane.'

There was nothing of menace in the fellow's tone or behavior. He was making no effort to disguise himself. His implied apology for the mud was encouraging.

'Will it be all right to leave my car here in the middle of the road?' Jack inquired. 'Doesn't anyone ever come this way?'

'Not often. Not this time o' night. Leave your lights on.'

'How's Buckley?' Jack was following along through the sticky mud, the driver of the pilot car bringing up the rear. He had not yet seen this fellow's face. The man with the flashlight was doing the talking. It was his voice that had telephoned.

'A little better. He had quite a bit of trouble tonight,

and I think he's expectin' some more. Haven't got a gun on you; have you, Doc?'

This query was rather disquieting. Jack wasn't certain why it had been asked. Perhaps it would be a mistake to reveal that he was defenseless.

'Had you thought,' he said, 'that I would be likely to start out into the country, this late at night, unarmed?'

The man at the rear chuckled unpleasantly and decreased his distance. After that they plodded along in silence for about a hundred yards. Then they came to a small gate set in a dilapidated fence, heavily overgrown with unkempt shrubbery. They entered through the open gate and approached an unpainted, one-story house. Judging by what he saw, in the dim glow of the flashlight, the place had been long neglected; probably untenanted.

A rectangle of obscured light, defining an ill-fitted window-curtain, indicated that the room to the right of the front door was in use. The remainder of the house was dark. The man in the lead opened the door into a narrow, bare hall. Jack bumped into the banister-post of a stingy stairway. The three of them were at close quarters in the gloomy little enclosure.

'I'll take your hat and coat, Doc,' said the spokesman. 'Tom's in there.' He nodded toward the door of the room from which the light shone. For an instant Jack hesitated about taking off his coat, but decided that if there was to be any commotion he might be as well off without it. He opened the door to the lighted room.

In the center was a home-made table covered with soiled paper dishes and the remnants of a meal. Thomas Buckley, seated on the other side, near the old-fashioned cooking-stove, was still eating. He glanced up, grinned sheepishly, and mumbled, 'Hello, Doc,' with his mouth full. Jack guessed that Buckley had been missing a few meals and was making up for lost time.

'Thought you were hurt,' rasped Jack. 'What's all this about?'

'They'll tell you, Doc,' said Buckley, munching his steak.

The other men had now followed into the room. Jack set his surgical kit down on the floor beside him and surveyed his companions with interest. The man who had carried the flashlight was probably forty. He was a little over average height, and well built. It was not an unintelligent face; lean, determined, deeply lined, innumerable crow's-feet about the eyes, a corrugated forehead from which the hair receded thinly. He wore a new suit of blue overalls and was apparently well dressed underneath, judging from the white collar and neatly tied scarf. He looked like a person who had lived a pretty rough life, but he was not a hoodlum. The other chap was slightly younger, shabbier, stockier, slower, and it was obvious that he was playing second fiddle.

They sauntered across the room, sat down on the old kitchen chairs near the wall, and regarded Jack with interest. The brighter one lighted a cigarette. They had not asked their guest to sit down. He remained standing, awaiting information.

'You see, Doc,' began the older man, 'it's this way. My friend, Tom Buckley, made a bad mistake the other day when he let it out that we'd done some plumbin' in those lousy little rabbit-hutches up by the reservoir. So, we picked him up and brought him out here, just to make sure he wouldn't do any more talkin' for a while. First off, we had decided — Rusty and me — that we'd beat hell out of him for squawkin' and then take him away somewhere and lose him. But after he told us that he'd let you into it — about where the pipe come from, 'n' all — there didn't seem to be much point to our closin' Buckley's loose mouth unless we were pretty sure that you'd be willing to forget what he told you. See?'

Jack nodded.

'But what I do not see,' he countered, 'is the occasion for your bringing me out here, to this infernal mud-hole, in order to make your statement. I should think you could have come to my office and said all that without putting me to quite so much bother.'

'Now — wouldn't that have been a slick thing for me to
do?' railed the spokesman. 'No, Doc, we hated to cause
you so much trouble, but we weren't making any dates
to see you at your office. We've been in the jug before — Rusty and me — and we're not going in again.
See?'

Jack said he saw, and the other continued.

'All you have to do, Doc, is to keep your shirt on and
obey instructions. We think we've arranged it all so that
nobody's goin' to get hurt. That is — we hope so — bar-
ring accidents. This half-starved little louse here' — he
gestured with his head toward Thomas, who was now
industriously picking his teeth — 'is leavin' tonight on a
long trip, maybe to Florida, and he's goin' to stay down
there for a long time, and grow himself a nice big moustache,
big enough to cover his mouth. Rusty is goin' to drive
him down. And I think it would be kind of decent, Doc,
if you would lend them your car, though that wasn't the
reason we asked you to come over. That was a new idea
we had just before you got here.'

Jack found himself growing restless under this harangue,
and glanced about the room, taking stock of its doors and
windows.

'Now I hope you ain't plannin' to run out on us, Doc,
before we've told you why you're here. That wouldn't be
polite. And, speakin' of politeness, I haven't introduced
myself. I'm Ted Billows. I'm the boy that stole the pipe
— me and Rusty. He didn't have much to do with it,
except to truck it over there, but that'll be plenty when
the P.A. looks into his record. We didn't commit a very
serious crime, and I suppose a crooked lawyer could get us
off with a light sentence. But I jumped a parole, one time,
and have done two stretches in the big house, and I don't
care to get too chummy with the cops.

'I expect you'd like to know where you come in at, Doc.
Well — this is to notify you that you're to forget everything
this wormy little rat told you, or we'll be right over there
to take you for a ride!' Billows leaned forward, belliger-

ently, and clenched his fist. 'And if you don't like this idea, my handsome young feller, you just say so, and we'll give you a sample — right now! See?'

The Rusty person stood up, at that, and shambled around the wall until he was to the rear of Jack who turned about to keep him in view.

'Frisk him, Rusty,' ordered Billows. 'We don't want any fireworks here — if we can help it.'

'You needn't bother,' growled Jack. 'I haven't a gun.'

'Better look, anyhow, Rusty,' advised Billows, rising. 'He might have one, and get excited. And I think I'll take a squint into that cute little black satchel, too.'

Rusty moved forward and ran his hands down over Jack's hips and said, 'I guess he lied about havin' a gat.' Billows grinned, and stooped to pick up the surgical kit. Then the unexpected suddenly happened to him. Possibly had the odds not been against him, Jack would have preferred to deliver the blow when Billows was standing erect and on guard, but it was no time to be overly fastidious about such matters. It was a savage upper-cut, swiftly but accurately swung, and aimed for the point of the jaw. Without pausing to mark the score, Jack turned on the astounded Rusty, who was coming tardily into action, and struck him full in the face. Rusty came at him like an animal, half dazed, and clawing for a clinch. With both hands raised, Rusty was leaving a very sensitive area exposed between the third and fourth buttons of his shabby waistcoat. Jack found it with a thudding right. When it registered, Rusty involuntarily hugged the sickening pain; and, while thus engaged, took another bad wallop on the nose that staggered him. He was bleeding freely and one more well-placed pop would probably be enough. Jack had heard nothing further from Billows, and assumed that he was taking his time for recovery. He decided to finish with Rusty. Then he heard the legs of a chair scrape along the floor.

'Look out, Doc!' screamed Buckley.

There was a terrific crash. Jack had one split-second of
sensation that something had exploded in his head.

* * * * * * * *

They were a badly frightened little group.

It was very quiet in the room. The three of them squatted
in a semi-circle about Beaven's head, their faces pale and
anxious.

'What the hell did you do that for?' whispered Rusty,
mopping his mouth with a bloody handkerchief.

'Shut up!' croaked Billows.

'Think we'd better blow?' asked Rusty. 'This bird's
a-dyin' — right now!'

Buckley slumped onto his hands and knees, and was
noisily sick.

'You guys stay here,' muttered Billows. 'I'll go for a
doctor.'

'Yes, you will!' sneered Rusty. 'Gettin' ready to beat it,
are you — and leave us a-holdin' the bag?'

'O.K.,' said Billows. 'You go for a doctor, and I'll stay.
Take the louse with you.'

'I'm not goin' for a doctor,' growled Rusty. 'Everybody
knows me over here.'

'Then I'll go,' said Billows. 'Buckley, you're so damn'
well acquainted over at the college: who's a good doc to
call up? We'll get him started, and then we can clear out.'

Thomas sat up dizzily.

'There's an old guy named Forrester. He's this fellow's
boss, like,' said Thomas, weakly.

'Roll him over,' said Billows. 'I want his keys. I'm
goin' to take his car.'

'Yeah? And you ain't comin' back. Goin' to let us sit
with it!'

Billows made no reply to that. They eased Beaven over
on his side. The contusion on his scalp was bleeding. There
was a spreading pool of blood on the floor. Billows rummaged through the pockets and found the keys, scrambled
to his feet, hurried out, and slammed the door.

Rusty stooped down with his ear close to Beaven's mouth and listened.

'He's still breathing,' he whispered, 'but it's mighty weak. Let's get out o' here. I'm not goin' to be found when the docs and cops come. Get into the guy's pill-bag Buckley. See if you can't find a plaster, er sumpin'.'

'Where is it?' mumbled Buckley, hiccoughing. 'It ain't here. Billows took it! What do you know about that?'

They heard a motor spin.

'Come on!' said Rusty. 'We can't do anything for this bird. Get your coat.'

'He might die!' protested Thomas.

'That's what I'm a-tellin' yuh! We gotta beat it!'

They pulled on their coats, tiptoed out of the house, closed the door, and slithered through the mud toward the road. It was snowing. They turned up their shabby overcoat collars.

'Where are we going now?' asked Thomas.

'We're a-goin' to drive south till we run out o' money and gas — and — after that — I don't know. Every feller fer himself, I guess — after that.'

Chapter XVII

THEY had covered the first dozen blocks without conversation. The streets were very slippery and the big snowflakes, splashing against the windshield, made driving difficult. It was clear that Tubby had resolved to ignore the presence of his unwelcome passenger.

It was equally clear, however, that he was acutely aware of her, for when she drew her fur coat closer about her knees and shivered, Tubby, staring straight ahead, muttered sullenly, 'There's a robe back of you. Better wrap it around your legs. You're not dressed properly for this trip.' Then, dissatisfied with this show of interest in her comfort, he added, 'You shouldn't have come. I told you not to. You're likely to get into trouble. You'll be only a bother.'

'Want some of this?' inquired Audrey, offering him a share of the robe.

'One can't drive with one's feet tangled up,' grumbled Tubby. 'You ought to know that.'

Audrey said she was sorree, tucked the robe about her, and relaxed into her corner. They were making better time now, having passed the last of the city traffic signals. The pointer on the speedometer dial had moved up to forty-five.

'I can't imagine,' said Tubby, glumly communing with himself, 'what possible reason Beaven had for getting into a fight with hoodlums.' Audrey offered no comment on this, and after a moment's silence, he growled, 'You wouldn't know anything about it, I suppose.'

'A little,' she admitted. 'Jack discovered that several cases of infantile paralysis had been caused by bad water

which some men had brought into their houses secretly.
They had laid the pipes themselves, and had stolen the
materials. He was threatened not to tell about it.'

'And how did it get to be Beaven's business to investigate
this matter?' demanded Tubby. 'I thought we had a City
Health Officer who nosed out the source of epidemics....
Rather odd — Beaven's not informing me about this.'

Audrey made no reply; and Tubby, permitted to draw
the conclusion that she did not see anything odd about it,
continued, irascibly, 'Very queer, indeed! If he was in
trouble, why didn't he come to me? He tells *you!* Nothing
you could do! Maybe everybody in town knows about it —
but me. But when he gets into a scrape — then I'm let into
the secret. He's glad enough to send for me.'

'Did he send for you?' asked Audrey, quietly.

'Well — I'm the one who has to go to the rescue. It all
comes to the same thing; doesn't it?'

Unwilling to debate this phase of the problem, Audrey
did not answer. Tubby, indignant over having been
slighted, was stating the present dilemma in the worst possible way, but there was an element of truth in what he was
saying. Audrey felt honestly sorry for him. It was his own
fault that Jack had not confided in him. And Jack was not
responsible for his having been turned out on this risky
mission of rescue; but it was a fact that Tubby had not
been asked for advice and it was also a fact that he was now
on his way to offer belated help. Three or four miles slipped
under their wheels, Tubby sternly scowling at the road.
Audrey broke the silence.

'Did you bring along some bandages — and things?'

'Certainly!' muttered Tubby. 'There's a surgeon's kit
in the locker. Had you thought I might come out on an
errand like this with empty hands?'

'I should have known,' apologized Audrey.

Tubby approved this retraction with a grumpy grunt,
and fed his motor a little more fuel. After another mile,
Audrey ventured to ask, 'Do you think they may attack
us?'

'Shouldn't be surprised.' Tubby drawled this as if it didn't matter much. 'They are reckless,' he went on, mostly to himself, 'demanding a trivial amount of money to be left in a conspicuous place, at an hour when there may be people on the streets. A man who would take a chance like that — for two hundred dollars ——' He broke off suddenly to say, indifferently, 'They'll probably kidnap *you*. Are you afraid?'

'Of course,' admitted Audrey.

'You amaze me!' Tubby's tone was maliciously ironical. 'Just as I had begun to think you a remarkably courageous young woman, you tell me you're scared.... I shouldn't have allowed you to come.'

'It will not be your responsibility, Doctor Forrester, if I am hurt. I insisted on coming, and I am glad I did. But — you asked me if I was frightened. Indeed I am. I feel so unprotected.'

Tubby instantly resented that remark with a surly 'Humph!' Then, after a little sour reflection, he said, 'Unprotected; eh? Perhaps you think I'm a coward.' He turned toward her, momentarily, with a challenging look; and, when her reply was delayed, he jerked his head toward her again as if demanding an answer — the right answer, too!

'My Chinese foster-father,' said Audrey, coolly deliberate, 'taught me that it is always dangerous to face conflict in the company of a person who habitually disregards the rights and wishes of other people.'

Too nonplussed even to be enraged, Tubby considered this shocking audacity with a perplexed stare, and presently remarked, 'I suppose you are trying to tell me, first, that I have no respect for other people's rights; in other words, a bully. In the next place, you assume that the bully will save himself, in a pinch, which implies that he is a coward. So — you do think I am a coward; don't you?'

'I do not know, sir,' replied Audrey, thoughtfully. 'But — I am verree much interested in this adventure.'

'With a coward!' insisted Tubby, bitterly.

'My Chinese foster-father ——'

'*Damn* your Chinese foster-father!' shouted Tubby, thoroughly exasperated. For the next half-mile the dial showed fifty-five; then retreated gradually to forty. 'Well ——' barked Tubby. 'Go on! Say it! What about your precious Chinese foster-father?'

'He frequently remarked,' said Audrey, ignoring Tubby's outburst, 'that many a man never finds out whether he is brave or cowardly — at heart. May-bee nothing ever happens to put him on trial. May-bee he goes for a long, long time, thinking himself very big and strong because he makes others do his will. And then something happens, over which he has no command. He shouts, "Halt!" But the other man keeps coming on as if he had not heard.... My foster-father said it is always dangerous to ——'

'Yes, yes!' cut in Tubby. 'You said that before. It's always dangerous to get in a scrape in the company of a bully. He would undoubtedly run off and let you take the beating. I'm a bully — and a coward — and you're scared. I get your point. It was very delicately stated — but I get it.... But — who told you I am a bully? You don't know me. I haven't bullied you; have I? Did Beaven say that about me? Or was it Cunningham?... Proceed, please: you're so candid. Let's have it all!'

'I should not have said what I did, Doctor Forrester.' Audrey's tone was genuinely contrite. 'It was verree rude, I fear. I beg your pardon.'

'But that does not answer my question! Did Beaven give you the impression that I try to impose my will on other people?'

'Why should he?' countered Audrey. 'Would Jack have some reason for saying that, may-bee?'

'Beaven doesn't understand — at all,' blustered Tubby. 'What I have done for him has been for his own good — and he ought to know it.' He turned toward her accusingly. 'I suppose you think I was assuming control of his affairs in the advice I gave you at dinner.'

'I accepted the advice: is it not so?'

'Well,' said Tubby, doubtfully, 'it appeared to be so, at

the moment. You were giving him up. And that was a definite promise! But here you are — on the way to him.'

'I shall keep my promise,' replied Audrey. 'I told you I would go back to China. You need not fear. I mean to do so. But — I had to go to him in this emergency. It would have been verree cruel to have refused me. Even *you* would know that.'

Tubby winced, and might have replied, but the asphalt had suddenly changed to brick and the street-lights of little Wheaton were rapidly coming to meet them. It wouldn't be long now. The time had passed for accusations and reprisals. Tubby slowed to thirty and began peering out for identifiable landmarks.

'There it is,' he mumbled, angling toward the right curb. 'I hope you know enough to keep yourself out of sight while I go up to the entrance.'

'It is much better that I should go,' said Audrey. 'They will be less suspicious if they see you have a woman with you.'

'Very silly reasoning,' said Tubby. 'Why should we want to create the impression that we are defenseless?'

'What we want,' replied Audrey, firmly, 'is the information that will lead us to Jack. Is it not so? If these people feel sure that we have not come to capture them, they may return with the directions.'

'Well — maybe so,' conceded Tubby. He delved into an inside coat-pocket and brought up a long envelope. 'Here's the money. You know, don't you, that you are taking a grave risk?'

She made no reply to that. When the coupé came to a stop he quickly opened the door and Audrey started toward the high-school steps. Her heart was pounding hard and her throat was dry. The new snow showed recent footprints. The surgeon's satchel was not in sight. The large open vestibule was cavernous and dark. She stood for an instant on the top step, resolutely consolidating her resources; then proceeded with trembling knees into the deep shadows. On the stone doorstep she found the empty leather bag; drew a quick breath of relief, deposited the envelope, and retraced her steps to the street. Tubby was holding the car door ajar for her.

'Find it?' he asked, anxiously, as she stepped in beside him.

'Yes — and now you should drive away quickly, as they said.'

Tubby pulled out toward the middle of the street and proceeded toward the business district of the town.

'I should not do that if I were you,' advised Audrey. 'If they are watching they may think you are going down to notify the police. Why not turn up this side street and wait?'

This sounded sensible enough, so Tubby followed her counsel without comment, somewhat to Audrey's surprise. Slowing the car, they crept along for a couple of blocks, parking in front of a house that showed no lights. For a long time they sat there in silence. Tubby could not remember that he had ever before heard the ticking of the clock on the instrument-board. Doubtless the ticking was always audible if one gave attention, but he had never noticed it. After three minutes had dragged by, Audrey slipped over a little closer to Tubby and drew half the robe across his knees. He accepted it mechanically, muttering a reluctant 'Very well.' The robe warmed him instantly, a strangely comforting warmth that she had invested in it. He was warmed, too, by the gracious act — and her implied confidence. She had professed a fear that he might not protect her: too selfish to take a risk for anyone but himself. Tubby felt now that she didn't think that, at all. It relieved him a little.

'Do you think we can take him back with us in your car?' asked Audrey, barely above a whisper.

'Depends on his condition.' Tubby's tone was respectful. 'If he is conscious; no serious hemorrhage; no fractures — perhaps we might. We will see.'

There was another long silence.

'Thirteen,' murmured Audrey.

Tubby pushed aside the robe.

'May as well go,' he said. 'It will take two minutes. Time may be precious.'

Again they found themselves at the curb in front of the high school. Audrey laid her hand on the door-latch and Tubby made no remonstrance. This time she ran toward the building and up the steps. She was not afraid now, but almost desperate with anxiety. Perhaps the people had not left the directions. Jack's instrument kit was on the doorstep. Audrey's heart stopped while she groped in the open bag. The envelope she had deposited was still there, but had been opened. It was crumpled and the money was gone. Utterly sick with disappointment and anxiety, she returned to the car with the empty satchel in one hand and the empty envelope in the other.

Under the street-light she paused to inspect the envelope. Her heart bounded. There was a brief message written on the back with a lead pencil. It was not very good writing, but plainly decipherable.

'Your man,' said the note, 'is in a house about seven miles from here. Drive west on highway through town and one mile. Turn left at Larsen Dairy Farm. Carry on five miles gravel. South one mile of mud. House far back from road at end of lane. Your lights will show where cars have turned around. The doctor's head is very bad. He is bleeding. You must hurry. We did not mean to hurt him so much. It was an accident. Don't try to follow us or there might be another one.'

Tubby held the door open and Audrey joined him.

'Drive straight on,' she said, 'while I read this to you.' She held the paper close to the dim light on the instrument-board. Tubby made no comment, but pushed up the speed. They went through Wheaton at fifty, but it was a stormy night and no one seemed to care.

* * * * * * * *

There was no one to warn Tubby that the lane was practically impassable. The old wooden gate stood partly open. Leaving the engine running, he stepped out gingerly into the muddy snow and added his footprints to those revealed by his flashlight. Dragging the gate aside, he returned to the car and drove into the worst road he had ever encountered. Feeling his way cautiously in low gear from one enormous mud-hole to the next, he presently sighted a dim light in a window.

Audrey did not wait for him. When the coupé stopped she leaped out and ran through the tangle of unkempt shrubbery to the house, opened the door into a dark cold hall, and followed the faint gleam. And there Tubby found her a moment later, down on her knees, peering into Jack's white face. He handed her the flashlight and knelt beside her, laid the backs of his fingers against Jack's cheek for an instant, unbuttoned his waistcoat, felt his heart.

Deftly spreading the unconscious eyes wide open, Tubby muttered, 'Hold that light closer. No — throw it into his face; not mine. There. That's it. Steady, please.' Then, with one hand supporting Jack's neck, he raised his head slightly and inspected the wound. It was still bleeding, but not dangerously.

'Will you want hot water?' asked Audrey. 'The stove is warm.'

Tubby was rummaging in his bag.

'No,' he decided. 'I shall do nothing but a simple bandage. There's a very serious concussion here.'

Audrey leaned forward, her face working convulsively, and the tears running down her cheeks. She searched Tubby's eyes.

'Is he — is he going to die?' she asked, in a frightened whisper.

Tubby did not reply. For a long moment he seemed indecisive about his procedure; then got out his stethoscope and listened with his eyes closed and his mouth open, Audrey watching the strained expression on his lips, her own heart pounding so hard she could feel it in her throat. Tubby drew a long, painful sigh and shook his head.

'Can we take him with us?' asked Audrey brokenly.

'I'll call the ambulance,' said Tubby. 'I don't suppose there is a telephone. Take that lamp, and look about.'

Audrey obeyed. Tubby heard her moving about from one room to another; noted, through the open door, that she was starting up the stairs.

'You come back here!' he demanded; then added, less gruffly, 'You don't know what you might run into up there.' She put the lamp on a chair and knelt down beside him again. 'It wouldn't be up there, anyhow,' he said, not unkindly. . . . 'I thought you said you were afraid.'

'Not now,' she answered, dully — 'except for him. . . . Oh, I wish I could drive the car. I should go somewhere and telephone.'

'You're not afraid to stay here while I go?'

'No, no!' she declared. 'But — what if something should happen to Jack while you are gone? I should not know what to do.'

'There's only one thing that can happen to him,' said Tubby, 'and you will be able to do as much for him as any-one — when that happens.' He rose and buttoned his coat. 'I'll be back as soon as possible. Don't move him. Don't touch him.'

'It seems awful,' she cried, 'to let him lie here with his poor hurt head on this bare floor.'

'I know,' agreed Tubby, 'but the way he is lying now there is no pressure. There might be, if he had a pillow. This wound is very sensitive. Let him be.'

Audrey's eyes followed Tubby as he moved toward the door.

'If he wakes up, is there not anything I should do for him?' she asked, shaking her head a little as if anticipating a negative reply.

'He will not wake up,' said Tubby, soberly.

'Never?' Audrey asked the question with her lips rather than her voice.

'Not until that pressure is lifted.'

'And then — he will surely wake up!' she entreated. 'Is it not so?'

'I hope so.' Tubby's voice lacked assurance. 'Can't tell anything about it until we get in there.' He retraced his steps to her. 'Here — keep this flashlight. That lamp is fixing to go out. The oil is almost gone.'

'But you will need the light to find your way,' protested Audrey. 'May-bee there is some oil in the house.'

They joined in a hunt through the scantily furnished kitchen and the small pantry, finding the oil-can, empty.

'It is no matter,' said Audrey, in a spent voice. 'I shall be all right. Take the flashlight — and hurry.'

She was down on the floor again beside Jack, sitting upright, cross-legged, this time. Tubby tarried at the door, tugging on his gloves. She glanced up at him over her shoulder. For a long moment he looked steadily into her eyes, and seemed about to say something more; some word of regret, perhaps, that he must leave her there alone; some expression of approval, maybe. Whatever it was, Audrey divined that it carried at least a trace of sympathy for her. She receipted it with a little nod of her head and a fleeting wisp of pensive smile, as if she were thinking, 'Poor Tubbee.' When he had closed the door she heard him climb the stairs. After a moment he came down again. She heard the big motor roar. Tubby was on his way. Studying Jack's impassive face, she felt it was quite too much to expect that they could save him. Her loneliness and loss suddenly swept all of her courage away. Burying her face in her arms, she shook her head hopelessly — and sobbed.

'Oh, Jack!' she whispered. 'I cannot bear it! Oh — my beloved!'

* * * * * * * *

After a while, the racking sobs subsided and she sat there, swollen-eyed, dejected, exhausted, dully waiting. Tubby had said she mustn't touch Jack, but surely it would do no hurt to lay her hand lightly in his open palm. It seemed strange not to feel those strong fingers tighten warmly. He was so very far away. Perhaps he would never be back. Tubby thought that, she knew.

Tubby had commanded her to go back to China, so Jack could do his work undisturbed by all the cares she would have heaped upon him. And she had promised to do that. And now it had turned out that she would not have to go away, for it was Jack who would be going away. Well — she would return to China, in any event. If Jack lived, she would go promptly, as Tubby had insisted. If Jack died, she would need the sustaining sympathy of her father's house.

The reeking lamp had begun to sputter ominously. Audrey weakly rose to her feet, inspected it critically, shook it a little, lowered the wick. Then she carried it to the table by the window where they had found it. Perhaps it should be left there. If it did not go out before Tubby returned it might aid him in locating the house. She glanced at the grimy, cobwebbed window, wondering how she could clean the long-neglected dust, and saw something that froze her to the spot with one grip of paralyzing horror. Her heart stood still and her breathing was suspended.

Transfixed with terror, she found herself staring into a pair of eyes. For a long moment she stood there unable to move. The eyes did not waver. They were weary, haggard, beaten, desperate eyes.

Presently they vanished in the darkness. Audrey turned dizzily and leaned back against the table, fearing for a moment that she was going to faint. The vertigo passed, and there was a long interval in which she waited with every sense alert, tensely expectant. Then the front door latch rattled and there were heavy footsteps in the little hall. Audrey pressed her knuckles hard against her mouth and stared at the closed door. It slowly opened and a man entered, half staggered into the room, and slumped down on a chair. He was somewhat under average height and appeared far from well, though that might have been accounted for by his quite obvious fatigue. He was shabbily dressed, wet with snow, his feet and legs caked with mud. He paid no attention to her; and, after a minute of recovery, Audrey, feeling that she had little to fear from this intruder, walked slowly toward him. She was still weak and shaken, but the terror was gone.

'What are you doing here?' she inquired quietly. 'Is this your house?'

He shook his head without looking up.

'Are you ill?' asked Audrey.

'Tired.' The word was feebly exploded as the tag end of a wheezy breath. Then he drew a long sigh and straightened his shoulders a little. 'I have been running,' he croaked. 'Have you any whisky, lady?'

Audrey was sorree but there was no whisky. The man slumped forward again, head hanging, arms dangling. Within a few feet of him lay Jack's unconscious figure, but he had exhibited no surprise; knew all about it, doubtless; had been in the fight, perhaps. It was clear now that he intended no harm to her, and her heart beat more steadily. She returned to Jack's side, knelt, lightly trailed her fingers across his arm. The stranger coughed painfully, and Audrey glanced up at him.

'Billows did phone, then,' he muttered. 'Where's old Doc Forrester?'

'Telephoning for the ambulance,' said Audrey. 'How much do you know about this?'

'I was brought here by a couple of fellows who wanted to get me out of the way, so I couldn't testify against them.'

'In that water-pipe trouble, I think,' said Audrey. 'You are Mr. Buckley: is it not so?'

Thomas gave a little start. After a moment's hesitation he nodded; and having revealed his identity he proceeded to tell the story.

'They must have had you tied up,' reflected Audrey, 'or you would have helped Doctor Beaven when they attacked him.'

Thomas winced a little and made haste to explain how quickly the fight had begun and ended. He'd hardly realized what was happening until it was over.

'They tried to scare him, but Doc isn't scary. I guess you know that.' Thomas gave Audrey a frankly appraising look.

'Mebby you're his girl. Leastways you don't look like a nurse. You probably know that Doc couldn't be bluffed or ordered around. Well — Billows and Rusty made a lot of big talk about what they'd do to him and before they had a chance to put up their dukes the fight was goin' on. Doc was lettin' 'em have it — hard. Then, when he was finishin' off the work on Rusty, Billows picked up this chair and socked him on the head. He just went down like a beef. Then they were scared. Billows said he would phone to town for a doctor. Rusty and me said we'd wait a while. Then we found that Billows had stolen Doc's medicine-bag. We figured he wasn't intendin' to phone. So — we got out. I felt terrible bad about leavin' him, but Rusty was goin' — and I couldn't stay here — by myself. Down at Angus, about five miles south, we stopped for gas, and I got out and ran.'

'Intending to come all the way back here,' asked Audrey, 'and give yourself up? Something must have happened — to change your mind.'

'Yeah — that's right. It was sumpin' Rusty said, just before we got to Angus.' Thomas was hesitant, but Audrey encouraged him with inquiring eyes and a deeply interested 'Yes?'

'You see — it was like this, lady. We weren't more 'n' started till I was sorry we'd left, and I told Rusty that Doc had been good to me.'

'Treating your little girl, may-bee?'

'Well — more 'n' that. I'd complained a good deal about the docs and the nurses, and one day Doc here took me up to his workshop and give me a talk. I guess you know — if you're his girl — that there ain't much foolishness about him. We got to talkin' about this infantile paralysis, and he questioned me too close, so I thought I'd better blow while he was at the phone. He didn't catch up with me till I was down on the lower floor. Then he collared me and dragged me back up there. I guess you know he could do it, all right. He's pretty hard, you know. You wouldn't think, to look at him, that Doc was interested in anything except takin' people apart and puttin' 'em together again.... Well — after he was done with me, he took me down town and made me eat supper with him. I was hungry, too.'

Audrey's eyes had brightened. She sat there, with parted lips, gently caressing Jack's hand, intent on Buckley's narrative.

'Well — this was on my mind, so I was tellin' Rusty about it, and he said he was ashamed to be in the same car with me —— '

'And then, I think,' commented Audrey, 'you decided to come back.'

'I thought, lady, that if I'd got so low that a bum and jail-bird like Rusty was ashamed o' me, I'd have to do something about it — or else —— '

'I think, Mr. Buckley,' said Audrey, gently, 'you did the right thing. You were afraid to come back — but you came. That is verree brave.'

Thomas squared his shoulders a little and grinned shyly. 'Mebbe I can fix up that' fire,' he said. Crossing to the rusty stove he poked noisily at the embers, went outside, and came back with a few sticks of snowy wood. With this attended to, he resumed his chair. There was a long silence punctuated by the crackling of the reviving fire. After a while, Thomas said, 'Were you scared when you saw me through the window?'

'Horribly!' confessed Audrey with a shudder.

'Then you are brave, too,' said Thomas, willing to share his honors.

'Not like you, Mr. Buckley,' Audrey conceded. 'I did not run, because I had to stay here. There was nothing else to do. But you had escaped danger and came back into it, of your own accord. When Doctor Beaven learns of this, he will be glad to have had such a good friend.'

Thomas, much improved in mind, rose, approached; and, hands on knees, stooped over to inspect Jack's face. The light, which had lately grown dimmer, now sputtered out completely. In a steady voice Audrey said, 'Be careful, now! He must not be touched! Better sit down.'

Suddenly a flash lit the east window. Neither spoke. Presently they heard a motor slowly grinding an approach through the muddy lane.

'Mebbe I'd better open the door for him,' said Thomas.

'Stay where you are!' commanded Audrey. 'That will be much safer.'

Tubby was opening the front door now. Then the flashlight was thrown into the room.

'Are you all right?' called Tubby, anxiously. 'How's Beaven? Who is this man?' He stopped to scowl severely at Thomas. 'Are you the fellow who telephoned?'

'Mr. Buckley escaped from the men who hurt Jack,' explained Audrey. 'He walked back — five miles — to see what he could do.'

'Humph!' grunted Tubby. He gave Thomas another inquiring scowl and knelt down by Audrey. 'The ambulance will be here almost any minute now,' he reported with satisfaction. 'They drive very fast.' He unlimbered his stethoscope. 'Here — hold this,' he commanded, handing her the flashlight. For a long minute he listened to Jack's heart. Then, easing himself into a more comfortable position on the floor, he said, 'Well — he's hanging on.'

'You are — just a little more hopeful?' pleaded Audrey, her face upraised to Tubby's.

'While there's life,' he answered.

She caught at Tubby's words, interpreting them as a faint glimmer of encouragement. Jack was hanging on. A strange feeling of lassitude began to sweep over her. She realized how very tired she was. The long, agonizing strain, the fear of the dark, the paralyzing fright at the window, the anxiety and grief: it had all been too much. The tension had been too tight. Gradually she felt herself drifting. Jack was hanging on — but she was letting go. Slowly her head bent forward and she sagged limply, quite powerless to exert her will.

Tubby, instantly recognizing this slump for what it was, caught her with his arm and drew her back roughly.

'Here! — None of *that*!' he shouted, hoping to shock her

back to consciousness. But she had quite let go. Supporting her with his arm Tubby rummaged in his kit for a restorative. Then he became aware that this muddy Buckley had left his chair and was leaning over him with a menacing look. It occurred to him that Buckley had misunderstood his sharp command to the fainting girl, and thought she was being mistreated. Saturating his handkerchief with ammonia, Tubby held it close to the white face that lay against his breast. Buckley, satisfied that his services were not needed for her defense, shuffled back to his chair.

After a few involuntary breaths of the pungent spirits, Audrey stirred and made a futile effort to sit up. Tubby held her where she was, drawing her close.

'S-s-still,' he whispered, soothingly. 'You will be all right in a minute.' But it was a long minute before she stirred again.

'Sorree,' she murmured, lifting her head and drawing a deep sigh.

'Better now?' rasped Tubby, severely professional.

She rubbed the back of her wrist against her forehead, bewilderedly, and sat up; then turned to Tubby with a penitent little smile.

'You were right,' she said, thickly. 'I am only a bother.'

Tubby cleared his throat noisily.

'Bother?' he barked. 'Nonsense! Who said you were a bother?'

They sat together in silence for a little while, Audrey gently stroking Jack's unresponsive fingers.

'Through with that handkerchief?' growled Tubby. She passed it to him without turning her head from her brooding concentration on Jack's drawn face. 'I wasn't quite satisfied with the man on emergency duty tonight,' said Tubby. 'Fellow named Abbott. Capable fellow, I suppose, but he's Chinese. I'd rather he were a white man.'

'I think Jack would be glad,' replied Audrey, 'if Doctor Abbott came out for him. They are good friends. I do not think his being Chinese would offend Jack.'

'Perhaps not,' remarked Tubby, stiffly. 'Especially when he's unconscious. But — all the same — I told Abbott he'd better bring a regularly qualified surgeon along.'

Audrey nodded her head, as if agreeable to anything that Tubby thought wise. Suddenly she straightened; listened; held up her hand.

Then Tubby heard it, too; the short, sharp, peremptory siren-blast. A burst of light splashed against the window. The ambulance was toiling up the lane. Buckley went out. Tubby followed. Audrey sat still, her heart pounding hard. They had come for him. It wouldn't be very long now until — until she would know whether she would have to go away — or Jack.

Tubby came in first, holding the door open; then a young chap — presumably the driver — carrying the front end of a stretcher; on the other end of the stretcher was Abbott in a white uniform; and, behind Abbott — to Audrey's immeasurable relief and joy — Doctor Cunningham! And how amazed he was to find her there! He made no comment, but his eyes were wide with astonishment.

They put the stretcher down beside Jack, and the driver set a big flashlight on a chair.

'Want to examine him?' asked Tubby.

'No, no,' said Cunningham. 'You've done that. How's he making it? Pulse fairly good? Stand the trip, all right?'

'He is holding his own pretty well,' said Tubby. 'You want to be very careful. It's a bad fracture.'

'Right. Well — let's go.' Cunningham surveyed the little crew. 'I suggest that Miss Hilton and Abbott ride in the ambulance. I shall come along in Doctor Forrester's car, if that's agreeable. Who's this other fellow?' he asked, lowering his voice.

'Needn't bother about him,' said Tubby. 'He's a bum that was held prisoner here by the hoodlums that did this.'

'We'll take him along,' said Cunningham. Thomas was leaning against the wall, waiting to learn what disposition was to be made of him. 'What's your name?' Cunningham moved toward him and stared into his face.

'Buckley, sir.'

'Good! I know about you. Doctor Beaven told me. . . .
There will be room in your car for the three of us, I think,
Doctor Forrester.'

Tubby said he supposed so, though the tone of the invitation was not hearty.

'And then you'll turn me over to the cops,' grumbled
Buckley.

'Maybe not,' said Cunningham. 'Not unless they ask
for you, Thomas. We're your friends. Better stick with
us. If you have to take some nasty medicine, you'll take
it, I think. The fact that you're here, when you might
have run off, shows that you're all right. Now you keep
on playing the game straight. O.K.?'

Audrey had retreated, out of the way. She had expected
that Tubby would be barking orders and arranging the
trip; but, without any effrontery, Doctor Cunningham had
calmly taken charge of everything. And it seemed so
soundly right that he should do so. Tubby was not resent-
ing it; was welcoming it, apparently.

With the caution of experience, they eased Jack onto the
stretcher, and filed out of the room, Tubby and Audrey
bringing up the rear.

'I suppose you're much gratified,' said Tubby, crisply,
'that Doctor Cunningham is here.'

'Oh — yes!' murmured Audrey, thankfully. 'So glad!
He is wonderful! So kind!'

Tubby picked up the big flashlight from the chair. He
was standing directly in her way. And now he detained
her with an outspread hand.

'This is none of your business, at all, Miss Hilton, and we
will decide the matter ourselves; but — I am curious to
know — would you prefer Doctor Cunningham to do this
operation — seeing he is so wonderful — and so kind?'

'Oh — *no!*' Audrey looked up into Tubby's face, wide-
eyed with apprehensiveness, shaking her head. '*You* must
do the operation! Oh — please!' She laid her hand on his
arm entreatingly. 'We must save him!' Hot tears were

racing down her cheeks. 'Oh — I know that Jack would
say there is nobody in the world who could do it so well
— as you! Oh — please!'

'Button your coat!' growled Tubby. 'I suppose your
feet are soaking wet. When we get back to the hospital,
I'm going to put you to bed!'

'Not until we know how Jack comes through the operation,' said Audrey, firmly.

Tubby frowned, and motioned her to precede him. She
tarried for an instant, and said, very seriously, 'Don't
worry, Doctor Forrester. I think your skill can pull him
through. And then — I shall keep my promise. You need
have no fear. *You save him — and I'll go!*'

Had she been a princess, Tubby's bow could not have
been more deferential. He took off his hard hat to accom-
plish it. Then, stalking stiffly behind her, his shoulders
squared, he lighted their way toward the lane.

Chapter XVIII

AT QUARTER after four Warren slipped out quietly into the corridor and started for the kitchen. Abbott was still hovering outside the door but did not detain her with queries. Doctor and Mrs. Cunningham, who were sitting with Doctor Shane in the alcove near the floor supervisor's desk, glanced up as she passed; but Warren merely shook her head as to say there was nothing to report, and the three of them resumed their low-voiced conversation.

In the kitchen she helped herself to a cup of hot bouillon and prepared a tray of it for six. Returning, Warren paused to serve the group in the alcove and poor Abbott who, she thought, should at least find himself a chair if he proposed to wait there the rest of the night. He pushed the door open for her and held it until she had entered.

Audrey Hilton, seated near the foot of the bed, accepted her cup with an appreciative but very weary little smile. Tubby did not bother even to turn his tousled gray head. Warren put down the tray; and, crossing to her seat in the corner by the window, resumed her deliberate appraisal of Tubby's profile.

She had worked with him closely for more than six years, but this was the first time she had ever seen the chief completely off guard and indifferent to his appearance. It was a rare thing, after an operation, for Tubby to show up in a patient's room until ample time had elapsed for the anaesthesia to clear, and when he came he would be coolly dignified and starchily spruce. Warren surveyed this disheveled stranger with unabashed and unobserved curiosity. It was difficult to identify as the smartly self-sufficient Forrester this pouchy-eyed old man who sagged astride the straight-backed chair staring at the flushed face on the pillow.

Still in his surgical togs, minus only the cap, mask, and gloves, the long white gown absurdly drawn up in an untidy bunch across his legs and gaping down the back between the straining tapes, his bare arms folded on the top of the chair, Tubby sat immobile except for the regularly spaced jerk of his shoulders at the beginning of each measured inhalation — a little jerk with a heart-kick in it, as if he had been winded from running up a long hill.

The whole affair, Warren felt, was crowded with drama. Some of it was obvious enough and duly accounted for; most of it needed explanation. Of course everybody knew that Tubby and Beaven were hopelessly at odds and had been so for years. It was such an old story that the hospital no longer had any interest in it. You just took it for granted: and so had they, apparently. It didn't seem odd that Tubby had performed the operation. Perhaps it might have if it had been a mere stomach excision or some other simple thing that almost anyone could have done alone in the dark; but this terrific skull-fracture was directly in Tubby's exclusive alley. It was unthinkable that anybody else on the surgical staff should have attempted it if Tubby was available. But — all the same — it did give you the shivers to watch Tubby boring a hole in Beaven's head when you remembered the way they had always scowled at each other across this very table.

Naturally, Tubby would be keen on insuring the success of this operation. The animosity between him and Beaven, far from making him indifferent toward this job, would furnish an added reason why he should give it the best he had. It would have been a shocking scandal if the report ever breezed about that Tubby hadn't gone to much pains to save Beaven's life. Indeed the chief was taking a pretty heavy risk, no matter how much skill he exercised. If Beaven didn't come through — and nobody believed he was going to — there were plenty of people connected with that hospital who would wag their heads meaningly, even if they didn't express an opinion.

Warren's eyes widened a little at this reflection. Perhaps it explained something that had occurred in the operating-

room. The seven of them had gathered about the table
waiting for the anaesthesia to settle in — and that was a
tricky job, too — and just as Carson nodded that he was
ready, Tubby had cleared his throat and said, very impressively, '*This — must not — go wrong!*'

That was the reason, then, why the operation must not
go wrong. Tubby couldn't afford to have it hinted that he
had done a slack job on a colleague he despised. But —
and Warren's eyes narrowed again as she studied Tubby's
drawn face — that theory wasn't so good, after all. Now
that old Tubby had done his very best — and she had overheard Shane saying to Cunningham that it was the most
brilliant piece of surgery he had ever witnessed, to which
Cunningham had solemnly agreed — there was no reason
why the chief should sit here like a stone statue, tuning his
own breathing to the labored respiration of his patient.

Maybe, speculated Warren, he was smitten with remorse
over the way he had mistreated Beaven. But no — that
didn't quite fill the order: there was something other than
remorse in Tubby's anxious eyes. He was genuinely concerned. Wouldn't it be funny if, underneath all the nagging
and surliness, he had secretly liked Beaven, but had been too
pompous and cantankerous to admit it. Tubby had been
hard hit: anyone could see that. He had the agonized
this-is-the-end-of-the-world look that you saw sometimes
on the face of a young husband or a doting father.

Warren's eyes shifted from Tubby to the beautiful Hilton
girl. She had not seen her since the days when the bright
little nephew had been here, oddly insisting that his auntie
was Chinese — and sometimes she had certainly looked it,
too, though she didn't now. Warren remembered that she
had wondered, at the time, if Beaven wasn't uncommonly
interested in this mysterious, petite, but beautifully formed
brunette, with the straight blue-black bangs and the for-
eignish manner of speaking. There was that night she had
put in a late call for him and found him at the Livingstone
Hotel: this girl had answered the telephone. Warren's lips
curved slightly in an understanding grin. Apparently

Beaven had stolen a march on them; had made love to the girl right under their very noses without stirring a bit of talk — no small feat, that.

Well — he had done a good job of love-making: you could see that at a glance. The Hilton girl hadn't been a bit hysterical; but she, too, had that end-of-my-world look in her long-lashed brooding eyes. Ever since they had brought Beaven down from the operating-room at half-past one, she had sat there hardly moving a muscle, her small white hands folded flatly under her high breasts — just like the quaint pictures you saw of Chinese women. Occasionally her eyes drifted slowly over to Tubby, but she had not spoken to him, nor had he taken the slightest notice of her. This, too, was queer enough; for, according to the story, they had driven out into the country together when the news came of Beaven's injury. If they were thick enough to have been at the same place, that late in the evening, you would think they were friends.

This, Warren felt, deserved a large basketful of explanation; and, having nothing else to do for the moment, she put her imagination to work on it. First off, she reflected, you have to remember that Tubby and Beaven have nothing whatever to do with each other. Then you have to keep in mind that Beaven and the girl are deeply in love. Naturally, the girl feels that Tubby is her enemy. Yet when something happens to Beaven, Tubby and Audrey Hilton set forth to the rescue in the chief's car — which doesn't make sense. And, supposing you cleared that up, why had they sat here for three hours — within a few feet of each other, without exchanging a word or a glance?

Studying the girl's tragic face, Warren noted a sudden change. The weary eyes widened, the lips parted. At the same instant, Tubby's back stiffened. Then Beaven's rhythmic, bellows-like respiration skipped a stroke; and, after a momentary delay, was resumed with a long deep sigh, exhaled in a half-articulate 'Oh-h-h,' as if there were a faint glimmer of consciousness behind it. She stepped to the bedside, Tubby at her elbow. Audrey Hilton had come to her feet and was holding hard to the round foot-rail with tense hands. Tubby had whipped out his stethoscope and was leaning over the bed listening intently. Then the Hilton girl came around beside him, leaning close against him as if she might hear something too. When Tubby straightened, she looked up from fairly under his elbow, and asked, eagerly, 'Does that mean anything — that longer breath?'

'Yes,' replied Tubby, studying her face almost as if he had never seen her before, 'it means that he is recovering consciousness.'

If Warren had found the problem of this relationship interesting and perplexing, now she gave it up completely; for the girl, upon learning the good news, pressed her forehead against Tubby's big bare arm — as if she were his daughter — and murmured thickly, '*Oh — dear God!*'

Occupied for a little while with her patient, moistening his parched lips with ice, Warren had turned away from this baffling scene. She hoped Tubby had been humane enough to put his arm about her, for it was easy to see that the girl had had about all she could take, and needed only this sudden relief, to unbuckle her into utter collapse. But when she glanced at them, they were still standing there as they were. Warren glimpsed Tubby's face and couldn't help staring, though she felt she had no right to. He had made no move to comfort the girl, who clung to his arm with her face pressed hard against it, but his gray head was bent and he was looking down on her with an expression of helpless pity. His face was grotesquely contorted. Warren knew she should turn away, but the strange sight held her hypnotized. Then the girl pulled herself together and walked unsteadily to the window, staring out into the darkness. Tubby mumbled an order to Warren; sat down wearily, drew a long sigh; and, leaning far forward, dug his fingertips hard into his temples. Warren went to the door, then, and told Abbott that Doctor Beaven was coming out. And Abbott, bowing, glided effortlessly down the corridor to tell the others. Trailing him, Warren stopped at the

floor-supervisor's desk and gave her Tubby's message
which she telephoned to the office. Mrs. Cunningham,
overhearing, said, 'That's very thoughtful.'

* * * * * * * *

When they had arrived at the ambulance entrance,
everybody had gone quickly about his business with no
thought for Thomas who, having no business there at all,
was uncertain about his next move.

Something told him the sensible thing was to go home.
It would be safe enough, and he was very tired. But he
couldn't quite bring himself to this prudent decision. His
cold feet and hot lungs entreated him, but it had been the
most eventful night of his life and he disliked the thought
of bringing it to so drab a conclusion. Besides, he was sincerely concerned about Beaven whose immediate operation
would probably determine whether he was to live or die.

Thomas had had a wonderful experience; a whole string
of wonderful experiences packed into the space of a few
hours. Unexpectedly he had been served with generous
helpings of praise; and, unaccustomed to the heady ambrosia on which heroes are nourished, he was more than a
little intoxicated. Ordinarily sullen and sore in the company of his betters, he had blossomed under the warming
commendations he had earned. It wasn't simply that he
had come back, at considerable risk, to make sure that
Beaven was cared for: he had managed to say the right
thing, later, to Doc Cunningham.

For the first few minutes of that swift ride back to town,
tailing the red lights of the fleeing ambulance — and you
certainly had to give it to old Doc Forrester: he knew how
to drive: wasn't afraid to push it right through to the floor-
board — Thomas had been talked to in man-to-man fashion
by this grand fellow, Doc Cunningham, and Doc had added
much to Thomas's self-confidence.

It seemed very strange to be riding in this expensive and
powerful coupé between two such important men; a bit
crowded — for both of the docs were big men and wore

very heavy coats — but he hadn't minded that. And he wasn't much in the way. Once they'd hit the road, old Doc hadn't shifted gears all the trip into town. Cunningham had treated him as if he really was somebody, asking him what he had worked at; and, when Thomas had told him about the airplane factory, Doc had said he knew about that and thought a man good enough to work on such a particular job shouldn't have any trouble finding employment. 'How'd you like to be a mechanic in a good garage?' Doc had asked. And Thomas had said he'd like it. And Doc had said he'd look into it at once. And Thomas had said he hoped that he'd be free to take a job; hoped he wouldn't get into trouble with the cops. And Doc had said that maybe they could get him cleared, unless Beaven died: in that case he'd probably be held; certainly as a state witness. And then Thomas had said, 'I hope to God Doc gets well.' And Cunningham snapped out, 'So you won't be held?' And that had made Thomas mad and he had replied, pretty sharply, too, 'I don't like that, Doc! This fellow's a friend of mine. And if he dies — well — you needn't bother about the job for me.'

But that hadn't peeved Doc a bit. The way they were sitting, all squashed together, Doc had his arm over the back of the seat and he had given him a whack on the shoulder, and said, 'That's the stuff, Thomas! That's what courage does to you! Couple of hours ago you were running off, leaving Beaven bleeding and unconscious. Then something gets to eating you, and you run all the way back through the mud. And now you don't care what happens to you, so long as Doc gets well! Now you'll probably amount to something important. Whenever a man gets reckless about what happens to himself, and frets over what may happen to his friend, then he begins to take on weight! You know the kind of weight I mean, Thomas.'

'Excuse me, Doc, for blowing off,' Thomas had said.

'Quite right you should,' said Doc. 'I beg your pardon for my insinuation. I knew you'd helped yourself to something good tonight — and I was curious to find out how much it was worth to you. You've got some valuable property there, Thomas.'

And all the time this talk was going on, old Doc Forrester was bearing full weight on the accelerator. It was a funny thing, Thomas had reflected. Here he'd always thought of the docs as a lot of soft sissies who swanked around in white coats; nothing but a bunch of stuck-up, lily-fingered Nancys; but he guessed he'd have to give it to these birds on this ride. Halfway in, the old man said they might as well push along and get things ready; damned if he hadn't plowed past that ambulance same as if it was a-settin' there on the road parked; and all the time Cunningham kept a-talkin' along cool as you please. You'd 'a' thought these fellows were at home smokin' their pipes. And when they'd reached the town lights, the old man never slowed down a bit; damned if he hadn't roared right through the business district at 65; and while he was doin' it Cunningham was a-talkin' about the girl that Thomas had scared half out of her wits; talkin' now as if Thomas wasn't there.

'You're going to pull him through, all right, Tubby,' Cunningham was saying. 'He has got to get well, you know. Two or three big reasons. Valuable man. Can't afford to lose him. And then he has to get well so he can find out how you went after him without stopping to think what might happen to you. And he has to get well so he can find out what kind of girl he's going to marry. She'll never tell him. It will be your job, Tubby. I'll say that will be a grand assignment! I suppose he thinks he knows what kind of property he's getting — but you tell him the rest of it — about his great fortune. It will double the value of the gift if *you* tell him. He knows you aren't a bit sentimental.... Tubby — By God — you've got to pull him through — *if you have to work a miracle!*' And Forrester hadn't said a word; just kept feedin' her gas; right through town; right straight down the middle of the street; turning into the hospital grounds on two wheels, and bringing up at the ambulance entrance with a screech of the chains — or what was left of 'em — that tore up the frozen gravel.

Then the big docs had flung the doors open and popped out, leaving Thomas sitting there in the middle of the seat, not quite sure what was expected of him. He was, however, certain of one thing: they had forgotten all about him. For a minute he was a bit crestfallen. Doc Cunningham had made him feel mighty important, and now he wasn't needed at all. They had rushed away to do their job. But — why shouldn't they? They were big men! So was *he!* They knew their place — and so did *he!* Nevertheless Thomas was more than a bit lonesome. He slid across to the right end of the seat and got out. The ambulance was arriving. He moved down to the rear doors. Maybe they would let him help carry Doc in. But they didn't.

First, the girl got out and stood waiting for the driver and the Chinaman to lift the stretcher. Thomas marveled at the ease and speed with which they did it. Gosh — these fellows must have so much of this to do that they know every move to make, he thought. In an instant they had filed through the door and into the big elevator. Thomas stood for a long time, wondering what he should do. He felt he wouldn't be welcome upstairs. It occurred to him that it might be all right to go up to the ward where Martha was and wait in the hall. But that wouldn't do. It was midnight, and, anyway, they didn't like him up there. Maybe they would when they heard what he'd done — but he wouldn't tell 'em — no, sir. Somebody else would have to tell 'em, like old Doc Forrester would do — about the girl — if Beaven got well.

Thomas shivered. Certainly nobody could object if he came inside out of the snow. He opened the heavy door and ambled to and fro in the corridor. Presently he heard the elevator coming down. The Chinaman stepped out.

'Glad you are still here, Mr. Buckley. Doctor Cunningham says he is sorry he forgot to tell you that arrangements have been made for you to stay here tonight. Come, please, and we will go up. An orderly will show you to your room, and if you are hungry he will find you something to eat.'

Thomas tried to say something, but he wasn't going to

let a Chink see that he was a softie, so he made no reply. All the way up to the third floor, Thomas kept saying to himself that Cunningham was a grand guy, grandest guy in the world. Doc Cunningham hadn't forgotten him, after all.

* * * * * * * *

Approaching the trio in the alcove and standing respectfully at attention, Abbott had said with dignity, as if announcing the arrival of the Emperor, 'Doctor Beaven is coming out.'

Cunningham leaped to his feet, clenched his fists, stretched his long arms to the full torsion of an ecstatic hallelujah, and exclaimed, '*Thank God!*'

Shane hustled away after Abbott who was retracing his steps to Beaven's room. Edith Cunningham, dashing the sudden tears out of her eyes, stood waiting for Bill, who had sat down again, with his elbows on his knees and his head in his hands, trying to compose himself. Warren had whispered an order to the floor supervisor, who was now phoning it to the office. Edith, overhearing, said, 'That's very thoughtful.' Then she walked slowly toward Jack's room. Audrey, coming out into the corridor, walked weakly into her arms.

'There, there!' murmured Edith, softly. 'Don't let go, dear. It has been an awful strain and you're quite worn out. But everything is going to be all right now. Come: we've a bed for you.'

'Oh — but I cannot go to sleep,' protested Audrey, shaking her head.

'But you have to,' declared Edith. 'It has been ordered for you by high authority. Tubby's command! It has been a hard night for the old rascal, darling. Do as he says. He doesn't like to be disobeyed.'

'I know,' said Audrey, woodenly. 'I think I must go back to the hotel. We are going home today: is it not so?'

'Home!' Edith's eyes were puzzled. 'When Jack hasn't had a chance to speak to you? No — indeed. We're going to stay until he's quite himself again.'

'Are you sure it was Doctor Forrester said I must spend the night here?' asked Audrey.

'Of course, dear. Miss Warren just told me. Come along, now. Get some rest, and you can see Jack in the morning. He should be wide awake then and inquiring for you.'

With obvious but mysterious misgivings written on her face, Audrey permitted herself to be led down the corridor and put to bed. Edith told the nurse to run along; said she would help Miss Hilton undress.

'Just think, darling!' Edith was hanging up the dinner-gown in the closet. 'We've got him back! Bill says it was a very close thing. I'm afraid he didn't have much hope.'

'I know,' mumbled Audrey. 'You must excuse me, please, if I cannot say anything. I am verree tired.'

Edith drew the covers up over her, kissed her cheek, turned out the light, and softly closed the door behind her. She was much puzzled; just a little hurt, too. It had seemed so unlike Audrey to withhold her confidence. A good deal had happened to Audrey tonight that hadn't been explained. When they had arrived at midnight with Jack, it had taken a half-hour to get him ready for the X-ray pictures and the operation. Edith had taken Audrey tenderly in hand. They had gone to a private sitting-room, and she had done her best tactfully to get the whole story; but Audrey had been strangely uncommunicative.

Yes — she had admitted, as from afar — she had dined with Doctor Forrester. Yes — at the University Club. No — she hadn't known of the engagement until shortly before she went to keep it. Yes — they had received the word there, and had gone to the country at once. That was about all there was to tell, said Audrey.

'But — fancy your dining with Tubby — of all people!' Edith had exclaimed, incredulously. 'Whatever came over Tubby to ask you? That seems very odd!'

'I know,' Audrey had murmured, remotely.

'And you don't want to talk about it,' Edith had said, realizing that this comment was an understatement of a demonstrated fact.

'Not now, please,' Audrey had replied.

And as if that wasn't baffling enough, here was Audrey
— at a moment when you might have supposed she would
be hysterical with happiness — going to bed with all the
weight of the troubled world on her shoulders, after she had
muttered something about going home in the morning.

* * * * * * * *

For quite a little while Audrey had been trying, inter-
mittently and with no success, to orient herself; but it did
not matter much, for something kept saying there was no
good reason for waking up at all. A heavy lethargy
weighted her.

With an effort she raised her arm and rubbed it across
her face. The gown she wore was rough and raspy and
smelled of a disinfecting chemical. Then the scattered
fragments of the picture began to drift together, and it all
slowly came back. She was in the hospital and she had
been dead asleep for hours and hours and hours. She had
had such a dreadful time going to sleep. She had cried,
uncontrollably, until her chest ached and her throat was
afire. And then — after hours and hours — a nurse had
given her an injection of something in her arm. And everything had begun to flatten out, slowly. All the world had
been rolled up so tightly that you could hardly breathe in
it — and now everything had gradually unrolled, and
smoothed itself out — flat, relaxed, serene.

Sunshine was flooding the room; so bright that it hurt
her eyes. Slowly she turned her face away from the glare,
and saw him sitting there by the bed in his white coat,
regarding her soberly. She tried to wink her eyes wider
open, but they were very heavy.

'You have had a good sleep,' said Tubby, quietly.

Audrey nodded slowly, moistened her lips with an
apathetic tongue, and said, 'Yes; did you?'

'Enough,' said Tubby.

It was some time before she could summon the energy to
speak again.

'How is he?' she asked.

'Awake.'

'He — he will be — all right — now?'

Tubby nodded.

'I shall go then,' said Audrey, 'as I promised. And may-bee it is better I should go — now. You can say that I had to go home. Yes — I think that would be better.'

Tubby shook his head and frowned.

'No — that wouldn't do,' he muttered. 'He's not out of the woods yet. Two heavy shocks; the blow, and the surgery. We can't have an emotional disturbance. Needs all his resistance. You stay here until he has gathered a little more strength.'

'That will be verree hard for me,' said Audrey.

'Well — you can do it.' Tubby's tone was business-like. 'Any woman who could carry on as you did, last night, can do it. . . . Hungry?'

'I have not thought about it.'

Tubby rose and stood behind the chair, and laid his hands on the top of it. 'The nurse will bring you some-thing. When you feel strong enough, go to Beaven's room. He has been asking for you, and will be bothered if you don't show up pretty soon. He is very weak, and you are not to stay long.' Tubby paused and drummed a little on the back of the chair with indecisive fingers. 'I don't sup-pose I need say to you that no reference should be made to your — your going away, and I hope you will appear to be cheerful. Mrs. Cunningham has sent your day clothes. You will find them in the closet. I think you should arrange to remain in town for at least a week.'

'Verree well,' agreed Audrey, pensively. 'Thank you.'

'And if there is anything I can do for you, it will be a pleasure — and an honor.' Tubby bowed respectfully.

'There is nothing; thank you,' she said, shaking her head.

Tubby walked to the door where he tarried with some-thing on his mind. Whatever it was to be, he was having difficulty organizing it.

'May I venture to inquire,' he asked, stiffly, 'whether Doc-tor or Mrs. Cunningham have been advised of the request I made, last night at dinner, and your promise to comply?'

'No,' said Audrey. 'Would you like me to tell them?'
'That can wait,' said Tubby.

* * * * * * * *

McFey, who had replaced Warren, came to the door in response to Audrey's light tap, and stepped out into the corridor.

'You're Miss Hilton,' she said, smiling. 'You are expected. If he wants anything, push the bell. You'll not be needing me for a little while,' she added, archly.

Jack was holding up his hands to receive her. Audrey crossed the room softly, laid her hands in his, and tried to speak, but no words would come. Bending over, she pressed her cheek against his and felt his hot tears on her face. He tried to put his arms around her, but lacked the strength.

'Darling,' he whispered. 'So glad — you're here.'

Audrey raised her head and smiled happily.

'You will be well soon,' she murmured, caressing him lightly on his forehead.

'Tubby says' — Jack drew a deep breath and winced — 'Tubby says you were very brave. I am proud of you.'

'Have you two made up — may-bee?'

Jack drew a feeble smile.

'We haven't talked about it,' he drawled. 'I don't know whether he is pleased with me — or the operation. Tubby is always pleased over — success — of — good — operation.'

'May-bee you should not talk, dear.' Audrey slipped her arm under his shoulder and nestled her face against his breast.

'Lan Ying.'

'Yes, Jack.'

'I want you to do something — for me. All the time I was half-conscious — waking up — it was on my mind. I want you to buy a doll — for a child — Collins child. Nurse — Slattery — will know.'

'Of course, dear. I shall do it now — soon as I leave you.' Her tone was indulgent, maternal. 'And you were fretting about it.'

'Well — it was a promise. Got to keep promises.'

There was a rap on the door, and after a discreet interval Cunningham entered.

'I'm called home,' he said, breezily. 'Stopped in to say "Good-bye and good luck." Taking Edith with me. Leaving at four.' He put an arm about Lan Ying's shoulders. 'Tubby says you're staying on for a few days. Quite right. Any message for your sister?'

'Thank you — no. I shall be writing.'

'I'll be running along. Have some packing to do. See you both soon, I hope. . . . By the way, I saw Tubby stomping up and down the hall, out here, as if he wanted to come in. Shall I tell the old rascal you want to see him?'

Jack nodded. Bill waved a hand and left them.

'May-bee I should go now,' said Lan Ying. 'He wants to see you professionally, I think.'

Jack laid a hand on her arm.

'You stay here,' he said, weakly. 'Tubby has not seen us — together. I'd like to get him used to the idea — our belonging — to each other.'

She frowned a little. He noted her perplexity.

'Tubby won't hurt you,' he said, reassuringly. 'Perhaps he even likes you. He spoke of your courage. Tubby admires courage — hardness — toughness.'

'You want me to be hard and tough?' asked Lan Ying, shaking her head, her eyes childishly wide.

'Not — too — tough.'

Lan Ying drew away.

'I am going now, dear. You are wearing yourself out, talking to me. We can see Tubby — together — tomorrow.' She kissed him lightly, moved to the door, smiled, twinkled her fingers, and went out. Tubby was standing by the floor supervisor's desk, scowling at a clinical chart. He glanced up, as she passed, nodded, and resumed his reading.

* * * * * * * *

It was a queer sensation to be shopping for Jack; queerer still to be shopping for a doll. She would get a verree

nice one and let him see it before she gave it to the little
girl.

'A verree nice doll,' she said, to the sales-woman.

'Yes, madam. Will you be seated?'

So — they had brought her several beautiful dolls, expensively and modishly dressed, with real shoes that could
be taken off, and picture hats.

'This child,' said Lan Ying, 'is an invalid — in bed.
I think — instead of the hat and shoes and parasol — the
doll should be a verree young baby that she can hold in
her arms — with many baby dresses to put on.'

'Very well, madam,' said the sales-woman.

So — they found a chubby, cherubic, baby doll, and
Lan Ying painstakingly selected the little gowns; muslin,
silk, dainty dimity, gingham; and an assortment of little
socks. It seemed verree queer to be buying such things —
for Jack to send to his patient.

At first, she was delighted with her discoveries. She had
not known the stores were stocked with so wide a variety
of dolls' garments. After a while she settled to her task
quite seriously, examining the workmanship, fingering the
little hems, gently smoothing out the lace insertions.

So attentive had she been to her novel task, that she
had not spoken for a long time. Then, realizing that she
should come to a decision about her selections, she shook
herself loose from her reverie and glanced up to meet a
curious expression in the sales-woman's eyes — a sort of
compassionate look. And then she knew that the woman
had guessed what she was thinking; though, of course,
she could not know everything that she was thinking.

'Shall we deliver your purchase, madam?' asked the
sales-woman, when Lan Ying had paid her.

'No — I shall take it with me.'

It was a quite bulky parcel, but the Livingstone was
only a block away. Back once more in her room, Lan
Ying locked the door, tossed her coat and hat aside, opened
the big package, and spread everything out on the bed.
Then she lay on the bed, propping herself up on her elbow,

and dreamily toyed with the sweet little garments. After
a while she slipped down onto the pillow, with her face
buried in the crook of her arm, and quietly wept herself
to sleep.

* * * * * * * *

Jack was so much brighter and stronger today; almost
gay, indeed. McFey, as Lan Ying entered, carrying her
large parcel, seemed to have some difficulty performing a
multitude of last-minute errands before she left the room.
Jack was frankly amused.

'McFey,' he confided, when the door had closed, and
Lan Ying was in his arms, 'is devastated with curiosity.'
He drew her down and gave her a lingering kiss. 'And —
so am I,' he added, when he had found his breath.

'Verree well, then,' said Lan Ying, brightly. 'I shall
not keep you waiting.' She set the mysterious package on
the bed and began opening it.

'By Jove! — it *is* a baby!' said Jack, astonished at the
lifelikeness of the doll. 'About three months old, I should
say. Where did you find it, darling? I had no idea ——'

'See his dresses.' She began handing him the little
garments.

'His?'

'I think so.' She slipped a tiny stocking on the chubby
foot.

Jack's eyes grew very tender.

'You — sweetheart!' he murmured.

'This is our best dress,' said Lan Ying, proudly. 'We
wear this one when we have company.'

'And our mother shows off our tricks,' assisted Jack.

'He is verree — verree snuggly,' observed Lan Ying,
cuddling the doll in her arms.

They both glanced up apprehensively. The door was
opening. Tubby had stepped inside the room. For a
moment they just stared at him — and Tubby returned
the stare. Then, without a word, he turned to go.

'Come back, please,' called Jack.

Tubby hesitated; then came slowly toward them. They were all very much flustered and at a complete loss for words.

'It is for a sick child,' explained Lan Ying, unsteadily.

'Him?' asked Tubby, with a grin, nodding toward Jack. They all laughed a little, and felt relieved. Lan Ying was still holding the doll in her arms.

'Precious!' murmured Jack.

'Appears to be a healthy child,' said Tubby, huskily, but trying to be casual. He stooped over to inspect its face.

'Want to hold him?' asked Lan Ying, soberly.

Jack was smiling broadly. This, he felt, was going to be good. Lan Ying certainly had old Tubby on the spot.

Tubby frowned a little and reached out his arms. Lan Ying maternally passed him the doll and stood very close, patting the ribbons into place.

'I shall take him,' she murmured, feeling that poor old Tubby needed rescuing. 'He is not used to strangers.' She gathered up the doll from Tubby's arms.

Tubby made a poor attempt to smile.

'I'll come back — after a while,' he muttered; and, turning abruptly, he left the room.

'I wonder what got into Tubby — just now,' said Jack.

Lan Ying shook her head — and said she did not know.

'I must go now, dear,' she said, 'and give the little girl her doll. Then I shall come back — for a minute — and tell you what she said.'

Jack watched her with brooding eyes as she folded the tiny garments and tied up the parcel.

'So sweet!' he whispered, patting her hand.

Outside the door she was surprised, and a bit confused, to find Tubby. Apparently he had been waiting for her. Without a word, he took the parcel and fell into step beside her. When they came to the open door of the little waiting-room, he paused and motioned her to go in. Mystified, Lan Ying obeyed. He pushed the door shut. He faced her solemnly, and she looked up with inquiring eyes. Tubby's chin was trembling a little.

'My dear,' he said, thickly, 'I have been very much —

stirred. I — I don't know quite what to say to you — but — I feel I must say — something.'

'I know,' agreed Lan Ying, softly. 'It has been verree difficult — for both of us. Do not worry, please. It was unfortunate — but — it was not your fault. . . . And — as I told you — I mean to keep my promise.'

'*Damn your promise!*' muttered Tubby.

Lan Ying's eyes were swimming as she looked up into his contorted face.

'You mean' — her voice broke, and the big tears rolled down her cheeks — 'I am to stay' — she shook her head unbelievingly — 'to stay — with Jack — always?'

'Of course!' growled Tubby. He laid both hands on her shoulders. 'But — I'd like to have you make me another promise.'

'Verree well,' murmured Lan Ying.

'You can guess — perhaps,' said Tubby.

'You mean — may-bee — I must never tell Jack.'

'Yes, my dear. Promise?'

Lan Ying smiled and nodded her head.

Tubby whipped a big handkerchief out of his pocket, blew a mighty trumpet blast, and cleared his throat tremendously. Then he straightened his shoulders, and resumed his accustomed pomposity.

'May I go now?' asked Lan Ying. He opened the door for her and followed her out; handed her the big package and bowed with deep respect.

'Not going with me,' said Lan Ying, 'to deliver the doll?'

'No,' replied Tubby, 'that's your job. . . . And — I want to have a word with Jack.'

Lan Ying drew a long breath, and stood where she was, watching Tubby's confident strides as he stalked down the corridor; watched him push open Jack's door, and disappear. Then she went back into the little waiting-room and sat down — for her knees were trembling.

THE END